THE PENGUIN CLASSICS

[illegible] 64): E. V. RIEU

PIER[illegible] VAUX, playwright and [illegible] son of a provincial offici[illegible] more than a perfunctory [illegible] nwards lived in the world of the [illegible] of his inheritance in 1720, however, he had to [illegible] earnest and the next twenty years were his most fruitful. His election to the Académie française in 1742 seems to have marked the climax of his career, and in later life he produced relatively little.

After some false starts, he found his true gift for writing comedy, principally for the then recently re-established Italian troupe in Paris, who staged nearly all of his thirty-odd plays. His most characteristic creations are comedies of love and courtship, done with great delicacy of feeling and psychological insight, and in which he creates comic effect by basing his plot upon the introduction of obstacles, often imaginary social barriers or false preconceptions. The term *marivaudage* is used to signify the subtle, affected style used by Marivaux to dissect the sentiments of the heart in his comedies. His two masterpieces in this line are *Le Jeu de l'amour et du hasard (The Game of Love and Chance)* and *Les Fausses Confidences*. In addition, he ranges over a variety of other styles of comedy, from the allegory and satirical fantasy to the sentimental moralizing play in the manner of Nivelle de La Chaussée. Marivaux wrote two novels, *La Vie de Marianne* and *Le Paysan parvenu*, both left unfinished, which are notable for their delicate analysis of sentiment and the realistic picture they give of middle-class society. He did some serious writing on ethical and literary subjects as well in his *Spectateur français*. He died in 1763.

LEONARD TANCOCK has spent most of his life in or near London, exceptions being a year as a student in Paris, most of the 1939–45 war in Wales, and three periods in American universities as visiting professor. He is a Fellow of University College, London, and was formerly Reader in French at the university. Since preparing his first Penguin Classic in 1949, he has been intensely interested in problems of translation, about which he has written, lectured and broadcast, and which he believes is an art rather than a science. His numerous translations for the Penguin Classics include Zola's *Germinal*, *Thérèse Raquin*, *The Debacle*, *L'Assommoir* and *La Bête humaine*; Diderot's *The Nun*, *Rameau's Nephew* and *D'Alembert's Dream*; Maupassant's *Pierre and Jean*; Constant's *Adolphe*; La Rochefoucauld's *Maxims*; Voltaire's *Letters on England*; and Prévost's *Manon Lescaut*.

DAVID COHEN studied psychology and philosophy at Oxford, where he translated and then directed *Infidelities* and *The Game of Love and Chance*. After leaving Oxford he began work as a writer and film-maker, his last film being the ATV production *After the Hijack*. He is the author of *Psychologists on Psychology* (1977), a biography of John B. Watson, the psychologist who founded behaviourism, and *All in the Head* (1979), a book on psychology for children.

PIERRE CARLET DE CHAMBLAIN DE MARIVAUX

UP FROM THE COUNTRY

TRANSLATED WITH AN INTRODUCTION BY
LEONARD TANCOCK

INFIDELITIES
and
THE GAME OF LOVE AND CHANCE

TRANSLATED WITH AN INTRODUCTION BY
DAVID COHEN

PENGUIN BOOKS

Penguin Books Ltd, Harmondsworth, Middlesex, England
Penguin Books, 625 Madison Avenue, New York, New York 10022, U.S.A.
Penguin Books Australia Ltd, Ringwood, Victoria, Australia
Penguin Books Canada Ltd, 2801 John Street, Markham, Ontario, Canada L3R 1B4
Penguin Books (N.Z.) Ltd, 182–190 Wairau Road, Auckland 10, New Zealand

—

These translations first published 1980

—

Made and printed in Great Britain by
Hazell Watson & Viney Ltd
Aylesbury, Bucks
Set in Linotype Juliana

CONTENTS

Marivaux 7
Introduction to *Up from the Country* 19
Bibliographical Note 27
UP FROM THE COUNTRY 29
Summary of the Anonymous Sequel 238
Introduction to the Plays 247
INFIDELITIES 253
THE GAME OF LOVE AND CHANCE 315

MARIVAUX

In most people's minds the name Marivaux evokes a vision of Watteau and a Never-Never-Land in which graceful and intelligent ladies and their pretty, pert maids gyrate with their male opposite numbers through elaborate dance-movements, often involving changes of partner, until the ballet ends with the definite pairing-off. They may also recall Voltaire's characteristically venomous gibe that Marivaux spent his life weighing flies' eggs in cobweb scales. Like Racine, Marivaux puts his characters into a setting where physical and economic realism count for little, in order to be free to achieve the utmost psychological realism, for these characters can lead a life in which sentimental and psychological relationships are not complicated, mitigated or disguised by the mundane conditions of daily life. The same could be said for the comedies of Alfred de Musset, and these three are indeed the great masters of the analysis of love in French dramatic literature.

But it is equally true that, as in Racine there are usually some underlying political facts and ambitions, so in Marivaux the countesses, serving maids and their opposite numbers are never unconscious of the facts of social standing and financial position, hopes and fears. Indeed, much of the action as well as the humour comes from the embarrassing conflicts between an increasingly clear and irresistible love and the powerful claims of the things of this world.

It is, however, only students of French literature who know that, besides being a versatile and adventurous dramatic author, Marivaux was also a prolific journalist, or rather practitioner of the periodical essay in the manner of Addison and Steele, and a novelist whose two unfinished novels, *La Vie de Marianne* and *Le Paysan parvenu*, occupy a unique place in eighteenth-century literature.

Fewer facts are known about the life and personality of Marivaux than of almost any other French writer of comparable importance, and therefore speculations about autobiographical elements in his works have little meaning. We know that he was baptized in Paris in February 1688 as Pierre Carlet, son of Nicolas Carlet, who was what we should now call a civil servant. When the boy was about ten his father was appointed to a higher post at Riom in Auvergne, and later he went to Limoges. From 1710 until 1713 Pierre was registered as a law student in Paris, but he never qualified. In those days *faire son droit* was a normal form of higher liberal education for young men, and it has been suggested that he kept his name on the books to placate his father while he threw himself into the literary life. What is certain is that by 1712 he had published a play and his first attempt at a novel and was using the name Marivaux, or Carlet de Marivaux, and there followed plays, burlesques of the classics, novels, essays and miscellaneous writings for over forty years. He married in 1717 and had a daughter soon afterwards, suffered serious loss in the great financial crash of Law in 1720 and lost his wife a year or two later, probably in 1723. He was a regular and cherished figure in the fashionable salon of Mme de Lambert and later those of Mme de Tencin and Mme du Deffand; he was elected to the Académie Française in 1742, in preference to Voltaire, and throughout his life he took his duties as an Academician very seriously. His daughter became a nun in 1746 and he died in 1763. That is about all we have as indisputable fact.

Until the crash of 1720 added a sense of urgency to his natural bent for writing, Marivaux was an elegant, well-to-do young man about town, and his urbane, civilized and, in the best sense of the word, feminine temperament was able to develop in the salons, where he was a popular guest and in which he had ample opportunity of observing the subtleties of psychological adjustment and manoeuvre behind elegant conversation. Moreover this atmosphere encouraged his irreverent mockery of the dignified and pompous hypocrites of this world. In those days in France the almost obligatory way for an ambitious literary beginner to make his name was to write a tragedy in verse and get it produced but, given such conditions and the history of his own travesties and parodies, it is not surprising that his début in tragedy, *Annibal*, produced by the Théâtre Français in December 1720, was a failure. But two months earlier the Italian company in Paris had accepted his little one-act fantastic comedy in prose, *Arlequin poli par l'amour*, which ran to twelve consecutive performances, a considerable success at that time. From then onwards the Italians were Marivaux's favourite interpreters, and they gave the first performances of many of his plays, including the masterpieces *La Surprise de l'amour* (1722), *La Double Inconstance* (1723), *Le Jeu de l'amour et du hasard* (1730), *L'Heureux Stratagème* (1733) and *L'Épreuve* (1740).

Since the seventeenth century a company of Italian players (Les Italiens) had been extremely popular in Paris, and indeed they had been among Molière's most dangerous rivals. Their performances were developed from the repertoire of the wandering troupes of Italian actors who had worked all over Western Europe for generations; this kind of comedy was known as the *commedia dell'arte*, which can be roughly translated as the comedy of improvisation upon a set theme. The plays had no set text, but there was a scenario laying down the main lines of a plot, on which the actors improvised and gagged. It was inevitable that certain conventional types developed, and their characteristics were dictated partly by the physical peculiarities of certain favourite actors (tall, short, skinny, fat) and partly because since ancient times comedy had concerned itself with youth mocking and deceiving pompous and tyrannical old age. So the obvious butt is an elderly man – father, guardian or jealous old lover – usually with infirmities such as deafness, toothlessness, bad feet, and so on; the young girl, his daughter, ward or (he hopes) future wife deceives him with the young man (student as often as not), and all parties are helped or frustrated by a team of serving maids or men, the latter sometimes clumsy oafs and sometimes clever smart-alecks. Hovering in and out of the plot are the low comedians – pedants, doctors (the medical profession was always good for a laugh), ancient female prudes or go-betweens and the bombastic soldier who makes himself scarce at the first sign of danger. The analogies between all this and 'regular' comedy, from Shakespeare and Molière to Beaumarchais and beyond, are obvious.

Given the absence of a written text, the success of these Italian players depended upon their skill and invention in mime and expression, especially as often the Italians in Paris did not speak good French. In the early days of *commedia dell'arte* the clowns, harlequin and the rest, had worn masks, but by the eighteenth century facial expression had become an essential ingredient of their technique.

It is not difficult to see why Marivaux was attracted by these Italian players, imperfect French and all, when it is remembered that he ascribed the failure of his tragedy to the stilted, declamatory delivery and static dignity of the acting at the official French theatre of his day. On the face of it one might suppose that he would not think them ideal for his subtle, understated dialogue, but he was faced by an embarrassing choice between dull pomposity and subtle expressiveness. Moreover the Italian company of Luigi Riccoboni included one or two actors very much to the author's liking, especially the actress known as Silvia, one of the greatest actresses of the century, for whom he wrote his most delicate female rôles. His plays are best served in a small, intimate theatre where ever-changing facial expression can be seen clearly, and they could even profit by the modern film technique of the close-up.

Tradition tells a story about young Marivaux when his father held a position at Limoges. The youth was attracted by a local maiden, whose naïve ways, innocent eyes and demure bearing enchanted him. They used to meet at an appointed time. One day he arrived early and found her in front of a mirror trying out the naïve ways, innocent eyes and demure bearing. That ended the affair. No doubt the story is as true as that of Alfred and the cakes, but its implications are clear. Marivaux had a unique understanding of feminine psychology, and for the first time in comedy subtle analysis of woman is as interesting and important as that of man. Until then in comedy (tragedy is another matter) the male characters were the more important and interesting, and women, even Célimène or Philaminte, were in a slightly secondary position. Furthermore, this trivial anecdote gives us the key to the typical quality of a Marivaux character, male or female, not only in the plays but also in the novels. It is *self-awareness*, complete consciousness of what one is saying or doing and why, with equally clear awareness of other people's motives and mental processes. That is why Marivaux has been called the Racine of comedy.

But the comedies are unique in other ways. For the first time in comedy love, and in particular the birth of love, is the sole subject, instead of being a more or less conventional occasion for dramatic development. In most comedies the love element is a kind of obstacle race, with a starting point and a finishing post, and the interest is in the kind of obstacles and how they are overcome or circumvented. The difference between comedy before Marivaux and that of Marivaux is the difference between the starting and finishing points. In 'regular' comedy the starting point is usually one or more pairs of lovers, and the obstacles to be overcome are external – social conditions, lack of money, hostile families, misunderstandings, a rival – but happily, since it is comedy, all is eventually overcome and the way is clear to the logical end, marriage. But in Marivaux the starting point of the course is zero, that is to say that love does not exist at all, or the parties may even suppose they are destined for different matches. Then a nascent feeling of interest comes up against resistances *from within* that fight to prevent that feeling from being identified and consciously admitted. Love's sole concern is to be recognized for what it is: 'Ah!' says Silvia, and it is the best-known speech in the best-known play, 'je vois clair dans mon cœur.' Or, to put it another way, a Marivaux comedy ends where any other begins, with the parties consciously in love. The whole interest is the hidden, instinctive, often only half-conscious processes which precede love or seek to keep it unrecognized. A man or woman is 'surprised' by love in the sense of being taken unawares – Marivaux uses the word *surprise* in the titles of two of his plays. Not only are the characters not at first consciously in love, but often they think that things are in quite a different state, and their normally lucid self-awareness is puzzled and dismayed by the muddle in which they are floundering. This is where the audience finds the fun and interest. It is like reading a detective story: we pit our wits against the author's and try to see what is coming. As the Marivaux play unfolds we begin to have our suspicions. We all have a match-making instinct and flatter ourselves on our percipience, hoping to be able to say at the end: 'Ah, I told you so!'

What are these 'internal' obstacles on the path of love? They are all different forms of vanity and pride, for in Marivaux vanity can assume as many disguises as La Rochefoucauld found for *amour-propre*. It is particularly dangerous when it pretends to be humility, unselfishness or consideration for others. Our vanity is unwilling to admit that another person can have so much power over us, that our happiness in life has to depend on the goodwill of another human being. So it assumes subtle disguises, such as self-mistrust, self-depreciation, self-sacrifice for the sake of another's happiness, and says something like this: 'I am not worthy of him/her. Look at the difference in our social positions. Everything would be against us, it could never last, I shouldn't remain faithful, I might become tired of him/her. I have no right to inflict such suffering upon him/her,' and so on. What is not said so explicitly but is often nearer the truth is: 'And suppose I declared myself and he/she refused? What a humiliation!' So we say nothing out of pride and fear of being turned down. And of course there is the other almost universal obstacle, and that is the instinct for independence. We are unwilling to give up one jot of our personal freedom and put up a desperate resistance in the name of liberty and independence.

These opposing forces, an inclination towards another person versus vanity in one or more of its disguises, may be equally matched in a tug of war capable of lasting indefinitely. What tips the balance and makes love succeed in pulling the victim over to its side? Here Marivaux shows his knowledge of human nature. Sooner or later another casts eyes upon the person we are trying not to love, or that person shows an interest elsewhere, and at once vanity, outraged at the possibility that another may be preferred, crosses over to the same side as love and their combined weight pulls us over at once. This situation, real or deliberately provoked, decides the outcome of several of the plays and it is exactly what happens to the litigant in part 4 of *Le Paysan parvenu*. All this has been admirably summarized by Professor Niklaus:

No other playwright has been able to stage the love relationship as Marivaux saw it. It is never purely gratuitous, never essentially sensual, although the awakening of sensuality attends its birth. It is not cerebral, nor romantic, nor libertine, the terms in which it was largely understood in the society of the time. For Marivaux, the core of the interest in the *jeu de l'amour* lies in the delicate nuances of feeling liberated, the fine shades of emotional experience, the conveying of inexpressible relationships between two people in love, and in the approach and withdrawal, avowal and retraction, discovery and concealment, misunderstanding and revelation, leading always to the point of truth. In his plays the curtain comes down when the protagonists have recognized and confessed their love, overcome any vicissitudes engendered by it, and met together in their moment of complete sincerity.*

Such uniquely subtle analysis of love has to be conveyed by the dialogue, which must be clear, witty and always entertaining, as well as minutely accurate, or else it will be pedantic and irritating. Each word must reveal what is going on in the mind and heart of the character and contribute to the movement of the drama. Marivaux has been accused of having to this end created a dialogue so precious and studied as to be quite artificial and unreal, a tortuous jargon for which the word *marivaudage* has been invented. Sometimes, if judged by the standard of what people actually say in real life, this is true, but then in real life few people in the embarrassing position of fearing that they are falling in love would express themselves articulately. They would mutter disconnected monosyllables, and the function of art should be (or was then) to make the inexpressible lucid. If standards of 'realism' were the only valid ones the operas of Mozart should be dismissed as tissues of absurdities. If you accept the conventions of Marivaux or Mozart their productions are seen as the highest form of art. Neither should it be forgotten that some of the more extreme forms of *marivaudage* are put into the mouths of domestics or plebeians with humorous intent, to show them aping their betters or giving them away, like Arlequin and Lisette in *Le Jeu de l'amour et du hasard*. It is verbal humour comparable with the language of Mrs Malaprop or that of Eliza Doolittle when half way through the chrysalis stage.

These qualities of Marivaux's comedies of love, unique in world literature, have unfairly been allowed to overshadow those of the rest of his work. Apart from the series of great comedies, he wrote plays of real originality on such themes as social class and true human worth, social utopias and a curious forerunner of the

*Robert Niklaus, *The Eighteenth Century*, Volume 4 of *A Literary History of France* (London: Ernest Benn; New York: Barnes & Noble, 1970), p. 97.

theme of 'Women's Lib' called *La Colonie*, in which the women in a party of French settlers on an island inhabited by savages decide to demand equal rights, to have self-government and do away with marriage and subservience to men. The revolt comes to an end partly because the bloodthirsty savages are threatening and the women are frightened to death, but mainly, as one would expect in Marivaux, because of vanity. One of the more intelligent of the men astutely sows discord among the women by playing on their jealousy of each other, and all re-enter the natural order.

But his non-dramatic writings are much more significant than his experimental plays. Marivaux produced, over a period of nearly twenty years, essays or series of essays linked only by a general title of a person whose reflections they are supposed to be. Although here, as everywhere at this time, the powerful influence of La Bruyère made itself felt, the more immediate model was *The Spectator* of Addison and Steele. Early in his career Marivaux was contributing essays to the *Mercure* under the title of 'Lettres sur les habitants de Paris' (1717–18), and *Pensées sur différents sujets* (1719) contains an essay, 'Sur la clarté du discours', which is a daring attack on one of the most sacred dogmas of the French: that an idea must have its crystal-clear equivalent in words, or it is a nonsense ('ce qui n'est pas clair n'est pas français'). No, he maintains, there are many notions and experiences so subtle and intangible that they can only be adequately expressed in subtle and intangible, if illogical, language. Nobody after this would so openly rebel against the tyranny of French logic until Verlaine and the Symbolist poets. More directly imitating his English model, Marivaux brought out his *Spectateur français*, in twenty-five parts, from 1721 to 1724; *L'Indigent philosophe* (seven parts, 1727) is a wandering series of reflections and adventures round the figure of a philosophical vagrant. Finally, *Le Cabinet du philosophe* (eleven parts) began appearing in January 1734, at the moment when part 2 of *La Vie de Marianne* was published, and ran until May, when part 1 of *Le Paysan parvenu* appeared, quickly followed by its four other parts. And a new play was presented in the summer of that year.

In their discursive way these essays are the very antithesis of the typical Marivaux comedies. Here is an author as firmly rooted in the soil of everyday life, usually Parisian, at home in middle- and working-class circles, as earthy and matter-of-fact as the creator of the comedies is apparently heedless of mere material realism.

It is not altogether surprising that in the midst of all this incessant work Marivaux did not finish either of his two major novels, though a probably more powerful reason was that in each one he had reached the logical solution of the real psychological problems, and he was not interested in writing a mere adventure story. *La Vie de Marianne* took about eleven years to appear: part 1 in 1731, then at irregular intervals until part 8 in 1738, which ends the main narrative of the heroine, then, in 1742, parts 9, 10 and 11, which are a huge digression in the form of the story a nun tells Marianne. Marivaux left it at that, but a spurious part 12 came out in 1745, and later another and better one by Mme Riccoboni in 1761, reproduced in the Garnier edition, edited by F. Deloffre in 1963. But in the middle of all this the five parts of *Le Paysan parvenu* (here translated as *Up from the Country*) came out between parts 2 and 3 of *Marianne*, from May 1734 to April 1735. It is not the function of this introduction to discuss the longer and much better-known novel, but inevitably it will be touched on in connection with *Le Paysan parvenu*. It may, however, be of interest to consider this opinion of Marivaux as a novelist expressed by a recent critic, not himself a Marivaux specialist:

> ... Marivaux, the greatest novelist of the century and the brilliant precursor not only of the mediocre Richardson, but of Balzac and Proust, the first to conceive the novel in the *pure* form that Gide tried to define and once tried to realize.*

LEONARD TANCOCK

*Marcel Ruff, quoted by F. Deloffre in his introduction to the Garnier edition of *La Vie de Marianne*, p. lxxxii (my translation).

UP FROM THE COUNTRY

(Le Paysan Parvenu)

Introduction to *Up from the Country*

ON the face of it *Le Paysan parvenu* is the masculine counterpart of *La Vie de Marianne*. Both Jacob and Marianne find themselves in Paris with no resources but their good looks, character and brains, and both win through to social success, money and a happy marriage (as far as we can guess the author's intentions), and a serene middle age from which they look back upon the vicissitudes of their young days. The narrator in each case is my present self looking at my former self and recounting what I thought and did then, but adding reflections and commentaries in the light of subsequent experience of life. So there is, as it were, a double point of view, 'then' and 'now', or 'then' adjusted by a lot of hindsight. Both young people have to deal with the hypocrisy and double standards of so-called Christian society and the unpleasant price it demands from the recipients of its charity; both are fortunate enough to meet some human beings whose natural goodness transcends class prejudice; both, almost without trying, inspire love or lust in the opposite sex.

But there the resemblance ends. Marianne's virtue and intelligence triumph over the wiles of her would-be seducer, but Jacob is a healthy young animal whose face and body women find irresistible. Marianne, in the 1730s, lived in a society in which a well-educated but impecunious young girl's only prospects were a good marriage, an irregular or promiscuous sexual life (with possibilities up to Versailles itself) or the cloister. Jacob, then as indeed now, lived at a time of extreme social mobility despite the appearance of a rigid class structure, and for a man all doors were open, then as now, to brains, personality and energy, especially when backed by influence. Today you may get on because you wear your old school tie or know a tycoon, but equally because the shop steward is your buddy or you have a pal on the local council. Call it what you like, it is still influence.

At first glance also, this is an unpleasant story about a young fellow of eighteen or so who, realizing that his handsome looks and the body of a well-developed country lad inspire longings in female hearts and particularly in those of women who have reached the difficult time of life, exploits these women – old maids and widows who have money but few awkward attachments. He appeals to tired society women because he seems fresh and natural. It is true that the only physical relationship he has is with an old maid with some money, and that it is she who carries him off and marries him rather than the reverse, and their sexual encounters only occur in the marriage bed. However, his not going to the full length with two others is a matter of chance and lack of opportunity rather than purity of heart. But such a simplistic judgement takes no account of the real concern of the novel or indeed of all Marivaux's major dramatic and fictional writing – analysis of the subtle and often hidden workings and interactions of minds and characters.

Not the least artistic miracle of the picture we have of Jacob is that he is not in any way outstanding. He is neither a hero nor an anti-hero. He is ordinary, he is every one of us, were we honest enough to admit it. To make a thoroughly ordinary person interesting in a work of fiction is a rare achievement which needs the genius of a Lesage, a Marivaux or a Flaubert. Lesage created in his Gil Blas a magnificently ordinary average man, but Gil Blas is ordinary because he never learns from experience; his vanity always convinces him that he knows best. Jacob, however, is the ordinary man who has the discernment and the gift of observation that enable him to see what works and what pays. Moreover he is very young and, unlike Marianne, uneducated. We witness, with amused participation, the painful self-education of a young fellow suffering from the desperate self-consciousness and social embarrassment of youth, and are forced to envy his intuitive flair for seeing danger signals ahead, watching his step and not giving himself away.

However, if this ordinariness of Jacob is accepted, some of the questions that have occupied critics cease to be relevant. Much has been written to suggest that he is wholly sincere because he makes no attempt to hide his own meaner side or take up a heroic pose, that the novel is a cynical display of insincerity and wickedness triumphant, that it is fundamentally moral, that it is deeply immoral. But surely the facts of Jacob's story and his own reflections demonstrate that the ordinary *homme moyen sensuel* is never unmixed in his conduct and motives. Jacob is good, bad, disinterested or calculating, pure or impure, straightforward or devious as circumstances and instincts dictate, and he can always find (we can all find) casuistical arguments to justify himself after the event. There is hardly any act of his that has not its good and bad side, and he knows this perfectly well. At the outset of his career he refuses, like Figaro after him, to fall in with his employer's disgusting suggestion that he marry the maid Geneviève as a cover for Monsieur's amours with her (but he reflects that it is always unwise to marry a girl of easy virtue – and what if she has a brood of another man's children?); later he lives on Mlle Habert and deceives her *mentally* with other women (but he is always grateful, kind and attentive to her); as her husband he passionately fulfils his marital duties and gives her all the satisfaction she has dreamed of during thirty years of pious repression (but admits that he is so good in bed because he is thinking all the time of other women with ampler charms); he nobly refuses to accept the job M. de Fécour is taking away from a sick man (but the man's wife is young and pretty). He never tries to hide the reverse of the medal, yet he has basic dignity and generosity, and cannot be pushed too far.

Nor does fidelity to our ordinary human experience stop there. Which of us does not know that some of the vital turning-points in our lives (choice of a career, first job, marriage, change of job) happened by sheer chance? Few indeed are the planners like Julien Sorel, and even his careful plans went awry in the end. Jacob does not plan to find Mlle Habert in a distressed condition on the Pont-Neuf, for he is only there himself because through death he has lost his job, and she is fainting because early that morning through over-scrupulous piety she has left home without any breakfast. Neither does he plan to come upon a young man being attacked in the street by three thugs, and his fine, unselfish gesture in going to d'Orsan's rescue is undertaken partly because his wife has fitted him out with a splendid sword, and he has never possessed such a thing before and here is a chance to use it – besides, it's safer with a sword. Yet these two fortuitous events change the course of his life, and both are largely instinctive gestures of kindness to somebody in trouble in the street.

Finally, Jacob, like everybody else, wants to get on in the world. Some portentous pronouncements have been made about the 'socialist' implications of Marivaux's work, his championing of the underdog, his satire of the 'upper' classes, the symbolical import of Jacob's (the common people's) rising through the effete and corrupt aristocracy. But with the unhistorical and selective view of all axe-grinders they have omitted to point out that all the wealthy characters through or in spite of whom Jacob makes his way are bourgeois and usually jumped-up like himself, the only nobleman in the novel being the admirable M. d'Orsan, the kind and true friend. Marivaux was of his own time and in 1734 could not see Jean-Jacques Rousseau coming, still less the Revolution. Over and over again in his plays and fiction Marivaux expresses the view and uses as a literary device the fact that, even through disguises, birth and breeding will out. After all, the desire to be socially one up on the Joneses is one of the universal, timeless facts of human nature.

Whatever the 'meaning' of the novel may be, it is certainly a comic masterpiece, with its gallery of grotesques like Catherine, the Haberts' cook, the garrulous and tactless Mme d'Alain (from the same stable as Mme Dutour, Marianne's landlady), Mme de Fécour of the vast bosom, the blunt rough diamond Bono with his toothpick, and its many 'situations', in the theatrical sense, such as the whole scene in the house of the obliging Mme Remy, with its mixture of the Feydeau bedroom farce and the knockabout of a Chaplin film. Not a little of the comedy comes from the burlesque of romantic and tragic love, and when it is remembered that *Manon Lescaut*, first published in 1731 as part 7 of the *Mémoires d'un homme de qualité*, had by 1733 been detached from the main work, in which in any case it is a digression, and issued separately in France, and furthermore that Prévost and Marivaux disliked each other intensely, it is not difficult to see what is being burlesqued and even directly parodied. The fifty-year-old beauty, Mme de Ferval, who has run her eye over this bridegroom of one day and summed up his points, arranges for him to come and see her and receives him reclining on a sofa in a revealing *négligée* and (allowing it to slip sometimes) asks him what his wife was like on the wedding night, then gives him an appointment at Mme Remy's house of assignation which, it seems, she frequently visits for her 'charitable works'. Here Jacob addresses her in the same words, *maîtresse de mon cœur*, with which Des Grieux had described Manon at that moment when he knew his fate was tied to her for ever. The loose, discursive style allows Marivaux to pay off brilliantly another very recent score, the mockery of him that an ambitious and facilely clever youngster, Crébillon *fils*, son of the tragic writer and rival of Voltaire, had indulged in during the summer of 1734 in his *Tanzaï et Néardarné*. Crébillon the younger is the conceited young author in the Versailles coach whom the older, military man puts firmly in his place in a piece of very perceptive criticism, as true today as then, about the self-defeating nature of pornography. The average reader, Marivaux points out, is not a prude and likes his bit of smut, but he does require some art in it, some dilution, some pauses, otherwise he gets bored. Possibly Crébillon took note of the lesson, for by 1736–8 he was publishing in parts *Les Égarements du cœur et de l'esprit*, a brilliant, but also never finished, novel in which love and seduction are an elaborate and amoral game and which is a precursor of *Les Liaisons dangereuses*.

Yet the supreme quality of Marivaux, both as novelist and dramatist, is his mastery of language and dialogue as revelations of character and psychology as well as faithful reproductions of the marks of class, dialect and situation. Marivaux had the playwright's eye for entrances, exits and *coups de théâtre*, but also his ear for dialogue. It has been aptly said that *La Vie de Marianne* is a comedy or series of comedies of Marivaux with an extended running commentary by the author in the form of reflections by the narrator upon the mental processes and calculations going on in the characters' minds between one sentence of dialogue and the next. The comments and reflections in *Up from the Country* are fewer and briefer, as befits, perhaps, the sex and character of the narrator, but that throws still more weight on to the importance of the dialogue. For not only does the dialogue have the function of betraying character and class, but it also has the crucial function of showing Jacob's evolution and adjustment to his rising social status. The dialogue has to show him gradually shedding his peasant parlance, learning to imitate his social superiors and deal with them on equal terms. And of course sometimes there are slips and sometimes he puts on a more ignorant speech than he normally uses because he senses that this will appeal to a particular listener.

All this may help us, not indeed to explain, but to make a guess why the novel was abandoned by Marivaux at the end of part 5. Not only was he in mid-career, with only two parts of *La Vie de Marianne* published and at the same time turning out plays, essays and journalistic work, but, much more significant, *Le Paysan parvenu* had reached a point where the purely psychological interest (all-important for him) had worked itself out. Jacob was now on the ladder to fortune and social success and all the rest was bound to be sheer story-telling against a backcloth of the society of the time, like so much of *Gil Blas*. True, there are the intriguing possibilities of a situation in which Jacob's new friend and benefactor d'Orsan is showing signs of falling in love with Mme d'Orville, clearly soon to be a widow and also an object of great interest to Jacob himself, who, we have been told, is soon to lose his elderly wife. That situation is to be exploited to the ultimate satisfaction of all parties by the unknown finisher of the novel. But in the main the real problems have been solved. Moreover the very object and method of Marivaux involve extreme slowness in time, whole pages being devoted to complicated mental processes and reactions which in reality happen in a flash, perhaps between a question and an answer in a conversation; and so the novel could go on for ever. Not that mere length in itself was a disadvantage in those leisured days, for it was common practice for a work to come out in parts over a long period. *Gil Blas*, after all, took its author twenty years to finish, and the novels of Prévost were interminable. But these long novels were basically adventure stories which could go on indefinitely, like some modern TV series. In Marivaux, on the contrary, relatively little actually happens, because so much of the real subject can only be brought out very gradually by language and comment, and this is bound to mean very great length. As M. Deloffre points out, the supreme modern example of this method and its necessary length is the novel of Proust.

So the work was abandoned at part 5 in April 1735. Over twenty years later, in 1756, there appeared in Holland a sequel to the novel in three parts, the authorship of which has never been established. It takes up the story at the moment when Jacob, alias

M. de la Vallée, is at the theatre with d'Orsan and the young men of fashion, and develops it fairly convincingly to the time when the narrator, a middle-aged man, began his story at the beginning of part 1. It does so by introducing one or two important new characters, including the woman La Vallée marries (d'Orsan gets Mme d'Orville), and it ties up some of the ends left loose by Marivaux. But this sequel lacks Marivaux's incomparable style, and much of it, especially one or two 'portraits', is flat and conventional to a degree, the psychological element is poor except where the writer repeats some of Marivaux's own tricks, some of it is sentimental after the manner of the genre paintings of Greuze, and there is little humour. As it progresses the sequel gets more and more perfunctory, the action is crowded, with jumps such as 'sixteen years passed'. As a matter of interest, and to satisfy the curiosity we all feel about how a story ends, a summary of the three parts of the anonymous sequel has been added to the translation of Marivaux's own work.

LEONARD TANCOCK

BIBLIOGRAPHICAL NOTE

THE text used for this translation of *Le Paysan parvenu* is that in the Classiques Garnier (Paris, 1965), edited by F. Deloffre, who points out that almost all editions in the past 150 years have been derived from the complete edition of Marivaux's works edited by Duviquet in 1825–30, which is very corrupt and even bowdlerized. But as an additional precaution I have collated Deloffre with the text in Vol. VIII of the *Œuvres complètes* (Paris, 1781), from which I have been able to rectify at least one misprint.

English-speaking readers will find the following recent books helpful and interesting:

On Marivaux in general – E. J. H. Greene, *Marivaux* (University of Toronto Press, 1965)

Robert Niklaus, *The Eighteenth Century*, Vol. 4 of A *Literary History of France* (London: Ernest Benn; New York: Barnes & Noble, 1970)

On the novels only – Vivienne Mylne, *The Eighteenth Century French Novel* (Manchester University Press, 1965)

To Robert Niklaus, a lifelong friend who shares my love of Marivaux, I am grateful for permission to quote from his book.

LEONARD TANCOCK

UP FROM THE COUNTRY

PART 1

THE title I am giving to my Memoirs explains my origin. I have never concealed it from anybody who has asked me, and it seems that God has always rewarded my honesty, for I have never noticed that anybody on any occasion has shown me any less friendship and respect on that account.

Yet I have seen many fools who had or knew of no other merit in the world than being of noble birth or distinguished rank. I have heard them pour scorn on many people better than themselves, and this solely because they were not gentry. But that was because the people they despised, however estimable they were for a thousand good qualities, were weak enough to be ashamed of their birth and keep it dark or try to invent an ancestry that would disguise the real one and put them out of reach of the disdain of society.

Now that trick hardly ever succeeds, for however you disguise the truth of the matter, sooner or later it takes its revenge for the lies with which you have tried to conceal it; and you are always let down by a multitude of occurrences you can neither ward off nor allow for, and I have never seen a case of vanity on this score come to any good.

Moreover it is a mistake to suppose that humble birth degrades you, so long as you own up to it and people know it from you yourself. Human malice cannot touch you then; you frustrate its claims; its one object is to humiliate you and by humiliating yourself you do the job for it, and there is nothing left for it to say.

Men have moral standards in spite of themselves and they feel it is a good thing when somebody stands up to their unjust scorn; it brings them back to reason. They recognize in courage of this kind a nobility that silences them. Sensible pride confounds arrogant haughtiness.

But that is enough of that. Those whom these thoughts of mine concern will do well to believe what I say.

It is customary when writing a book to begin with a little preamble, and that was it. Let us come back to myself.

I live in a country house to which I have retired and in which my leisure inspires me to reflect on the events of my life. I will set them down to the best of my ability; each of us has his own way of expressing himself which comes from the way he feels.

Some of the facts I have to narrate will, I think, be curious, and I trust that my style will be excused on that account, for I can venture to guarantee that they are true. This is not a tale just made up for the sake of it, as I believe will clearly be seen.

As for my name, I am not mentioning it. The reader can do without it, and it would embarrass me in my story if I did mention it.

A few people may realize who I am, but I know they are discreet and will not take advantage of it. So let us begin.

I was born in a village in Champagne, and it may be said in passing that I owe the beginning of my good fortune to the wine of my province.

My father farmed for the lord of the manor, an exceedingly rich man (I refer to the lord of the manor), who might have been a gentleman if only he had been noble.

He had made his pile in business and had contracted alliances with illustrious families through the marriages of two of his sons, one of whom had gone into the law and the other into the army.

Father and sons lived on a magnificent scale; they had adopted names of country estates. As to their real name, I don't think they remembered what it was themselves.

Their origins were, so to speak, buried under immense wealth – known, but no longer mentioned. The distinguished marriages they had made had totally dazzled the imagination of other people concerning them, so that they were confused with the best people at court and in town. Human pride is basically pretty lenient over certain prejudices; it seems to realize itself how frivolous they are.

That was their situation when I came into the world. The manorial estates they had acquired and which my father farmed for them were only remarkable for the wine they produced in very considerable quantity.

This wine was the finest in the region, and it used to be taken to our master's house in Paris by my elder brother, for there were three of us in the family, two boys and a girl, and I was the youngest child.

My brother, on one of these trips to Paris, fell in love with an innkeeper's widow who was comfortably off, whose heart was not averse to him, and who married him with all his income, that is to say with nothing.

In later years this brother's children were greatly in need of being recognized as my nephews, for their father, who is still alive and with me at the present time, and who went on with his trade as an innkeeper, saw his establishment ruined by his wife's extravagance within ten years.

Concerning his sons: my help has put them on a respectable footing today, for they are well established, but nevertheless I have only made ungrateful wretches of them because I criticized them for being too stuck-up.

They have dropped their name and broken off relations with their own father, whom they used to come and see occasionally.

May I say another word or two about them.

I noticed the airs they gave themselves the last time they came to see him. In the course of the conversation they called him *Monsieur*. Hearing this term the good man turned round, under the impression that they were speaking to someone coming in whom he could not see.

'No, no,' I said to him, 'there's nobody coming, brother, they're talking to you.' 'Me!' he answered. 'Now why do that? Don't you know me any more, my boys? Aren't I your father?' 'Oh yes, you're their father all right,' said I, 'but it isn't refined to call you that.' 'Isn't it respectable to be the father of one's own children, then?' he went on. 'What sort of a fashion is this?'

'It is,' I explained, 'because the term *Father* is too low-class, too coarse; only common people use it, but among people as distinguished as your sons all these commonplace qualities bestowed by nature are banned from speech, and instead of rustically saying *Father*, like the populace, they say *Monsieur*. It's more dignified.'

My nephews went very red at this criticism I made of their impertinence, their father lost his temper, and not like a gentleman but like a real father, and a father who was an innkeeper into the bargain.

Let us leave my nephews at this point, for they have turned me aside somewhat from my story, which is as well because you must get used to my digressions at the outset. Yet I don't know whether I shall go in for them often – maybe yes, maybe no. I can't answer for anything and I shan't put myself out about it; I shall tell the whole of my life story, and if I mix other things in with it, that will be because they turn up, and not of my seeking.

I have said that it was my elder brother who used to take our masters the wine produced on the land my father farmed.

Now that his marriage kept him in Paris I succeeded him in the job of wine-carter.

I was then eighteen or nineteen and was said to be a good-looking fellow, that is to say, good-looking in the manner of a country lad whose face is at the mercy of the open air and work in the fields. But even so I certainly did have a pretty good appearance, and added to that something frank in my expression, and a keen eye suggesting I had some brains, which was not altogether wrong.

So, this year after my brother's marriage I arrived in Paris with my cart and my rustic good looks.

I was thrilled to find myself in this great city, in which everything I saw was not so much surprising as enjoyable, and what is called high society looked delightful.

I was made very welcome in our landlord's household. The servants took to me at once. I boldly said what I thought about everything I happened to see, and often there was some sound country sense about this opinion which made them enjoy asking me things.

For my first five or six days in the house it was nothing but Jacob this and Jacob that. Even the mistress wanted to see me because of the accounts her maids gave of me.

She was a woman who spent her life in all the frivolities of the world of fashion, went to the theatre, had supper in town, went to bed at four in the morning and rose at one in the afternoon, had lovers whom she received while at her toilet, where she read love letters sent to her and then left them lying about everywhere. Anybody could read them, but nobody was in the least interested, for her maids saw nothing strange in all this and her husband did not mind. You might have thought that all these things were the natural concomitants of marriage for a woman. In her own home Madame was not thought to be coquettish, nor was she in fact, for she didn't give it any thought or know what she was doing. A woman doesn't tell herself she is a flirt when she doesn't realize it herself, but lives in her flirtatiousness as you might live in the most respectable and humdrum state.

Such was our mistress, who led this kind of life as openly as one drinks or eats; in a word it was a life of mild libertinism lived in all good faith.

I say mild libertinism, and that is the right word, and although it was quite open on her part and she never gave it a thought, that was nevertheless what it was.

Apart from that I have never seen a better woman, and her manners were like her face, which was round and open.

She was kind, generous, never stood on ceremony, was on easy terms with her servants, cutting short the respectful speeches of some and the curtseys of others; candour with her took the place of politeness. In fact, a character with no affectations. With her there were no unpardonable crimes, and you did not have to face reprimands, for she would rather something went badly than have the bother of saying it must be done well. Loving virtue with all her heart, but without hostility to vice, she censured nothing, not even the malice of people she heard censuring others. You could not fail to get praise or forgiveness from her: I have never seen her hate anything but wickedness, which she hated possibly more strongly than anybody. In fine, the friend of all the world, and especially of any weaknesses she could detect in you.

'Good morning, my lad,' she said when I went up to her. 'Well, how are you getting on in Paris?' Then, turning to her maids, she added: 'He really is very good-looking for a peasant!'

'Oh, Madame,' I said, 'I am the ugly boy of our village.' 'No, no,' she said, 'I don't think you are either stupid or bad-looking, and my advice to you is to stay in Paris, where you will get on.'

'God grant it, Madame, but I have merit and no money, and they don't go well together.'

'True,' she laughed, 'but time will set that trouble to rights. Stay here, and I will place you with my nephew, who is just coming from the country and being sent to school. You will look after him.'

'May heaven reward you, Madame,' I answered. 'Just tell me if it is a certainty, so that I can write to my father. I shall learn so much myself by watching him studying that one of these days, I promise you, I shall say Holy Mass for you. Who can tell? As everything in this world is a matter of luck you often find you're a bishop or priest without knowing how.'

This speech tickled her very much, and her amusement spurred me on. I wasn't ashamed of the silly things I said so long as they were amusing, for I could see through the dark mists of my ignorance that such things did no harm to a man who wasn't supposed to know any better, and that people often gave him credit for having the courage to answer back whatever it cost.

'That fellow is amusing,' she said. 'I mean to help him. Just you others be careful (she was addressing her maids), his simplicity amuses you today and you are laughing at him for being a country bumpkin, but that bumpkin will become dangerous, I warn you.'

'Oh, Madame,' I chipped in, 'there is no point in waiting for that to happen. I shan't become, I am already. For these young ladies are very pretty, and that brings a man out. At the sight of them no village can keep its hold, one is straight away a Parisian born.'

'Really!' she said. 'You're a man of the world already, and which one would you choose? (There were three of them.) Javotte is a pretty blonde.' 'And Mlle Geneviève is a pretty brunette,' I cried at once.

Geneviève blushed a little on hearing this, but it was a blush of satisfied vanity, and she disguised this little satisfaction my preference gave her with a smile which, however, meant: 'I thank you,' but at the same time: 'I'm only laughing at his comical rusticity.'

What is certain is that my remark went home, and as you will see from what follows, my shot made a hidden wound in her heart and I made it my business to be sure of it; for I suspected that what I had said could not have displeased her, and from then on I watched her to see whether my impression was correct.

We were on the point of continuing the conversation, which was turning to Madame's third maid, who was neither dark nor fair, but of nondescript colouring and had one of those unremarkable faces you see on everybody and don't notice on anybody.

I was already trying to avoid expressing my feelings about her with a clumsy and callow embarrassment which was not at all flattering to the said person, when one of Madame's adorers entered and obliged us to withdraw.

I was very pleased indeed with the bargain I had made to stay in Paris. In the few days I had spent there my heart had been awakened and all of a sudden I found I had an appetite for success.

There was the question of letting my father know about the state of affairs, but I could not write. Then I thought of Mlle Geneviève, and without more ado went and asked her to write my letter for me.

She was alone when I spoke to her, and not only did she write it, but she did so with the best grace in the world.

Everything I dictated struck her as witty and sensible, and she merely corrected my expressions.

'Just you make the best of Madame's kindness,' she then said, 'and I think your adventure will turn out well.' 'Oh, Mademoiselle,' I replied, 'if to that you add your friendship, I won't change with anyone else. For already I am happy, there's no doubt about it, because I love you.'

'What? You love me! Whatever do you mean by that, Jacob?'

'What do I mean? I mean real, genuine affection, like a chap, begging your pardon, can feel for such a charming girl as yourself. I mean, it's a great pity I am such an ordinary little man for, good Lord, if I was king, for example, we'd soon see which of us would be queen, and as it wouldn't be me it would have to be you. There's no gainsaying that.'

'I'm much obliged to you for such sentiments,' she said teasingly, 'and if you were king it might be worth considering.' 'Lord, Mademoiselle,' I said, 'there are so many men in the world that the girls love and who aren't kings. Won't there be a way of being like them some day?'

'Really!' she said. 'You are insistent. Where did you learn to make up to a girl?' 'Well now,' I said, 'ask that of your own good qualities, for I've had no other teachers. As they have taught me so I make return.'

At that moment Madame sent for Geneviève, who took herself off, on the whole highly delighted with me, saying as she went out: 'You know, Jacob, you'll get on in the world, and I hope you do with all my heart.'

'Thank you kindly,' I said, bowing and flourishing my hat with more zeal than grace, 'but I am putting myself in your hands, Mademoiselle, and don't forget me, so that I can at any rate begin getting on and you can finish off the job when you are able.' Upon which I took the letter and went to post it.

This conversation I had just had with Geneviève put me in such a lively frame of mind that I became even more amusing than I had been up to then.

To put the finishing touch to my cheerfulness, on the evening of that same day I was sent for to be measured by the family tailor, and I can't say how much this little event enlivened and brightened my imagination.

The delicate attention was Madame's idea.

Two days later my suit was delivered, together with linen and a hat and all the necessary. I had very nice hair, and one of the footmen who had been very friendly curled it for me. My stay in Paris had taken away some of the redness of my skin and really, when I was dolled up, Jacob didn't look at all bad.

The joy of seeing myself in such a good situation made my face look more alive and cast upon it, so to speak, the light of future good fortune. At any rate that is what everyone predicted, and I had no doubt that the prediction would come true.

I was highly complimented on my appearance, and while waiting to see Madame I went and tried out my new charms on Geneviève, who, as a matter of fact, did appeal to me quite a lot.

I thought she was surprised at how I looked in my brand-new rig-out, and I myself felt more witty than usual, but we had hardly begun talking when I was sent for by Madame.

This order redoubled my gratitude towards her. I did not go, I flew.

'Here I am, Madame,' I said as I went in. 'I wish I had the eloquence to thank you as I would wish, but I will die in your service if you will allow me. It is settled, and I belong to you for the rest of my days.'

'That's very nice of you,' she said. 'You are delicate-minded and grateful, I am glad to see. Your new clothes suit you. You have lost that hobbledehoy look.' 'Madame,' I exclaimed, 'I look like your servant for ever, and that's all I want.'

The lady then made me come forward and she examined my outfit. I had a plain suit with nothing of the uniform about it. She asked who had done my hair, and told me always to look after it well because it was very nice hair and she wanted me to do her honour. 'Just as much as you wish,' I said, 'although you already have honour enough; but there is no harm in abundance.' Note that Madame had just begun dressing and that she was in some disarray, which stimulated my interest.

I was not born unsusceptible, far from it. This lady was fresh and appetizing, and my eyes enjoyed taking everything in.

She noticed, and smiled at having made my attention wander. I saw that she had noticed and began to laugh too, in a way that was partly silly and partly tender, through shame at being caught in the act mingled with enjoyment at what I was seeing. So, looking at her with eyes in which all that was mixed, I held my peace.

Thus there was played out between us a little bit of dumb show that was the most amusing thing in the world. And then, taking her time, she put herself to rights and said: 'What are you thinking about, Jacob?' 'Oh, Madame,' I said, 'I was thinking it's nice to look at you and that Monsieur has a beautiful wife.'

I can't say how that struck her, but it seemed to me that my country manners did not displease her.

Tender glances from a man of the world are nothing new to a pretty woman who is used to their messages; they are part of a code of gallantry that she knows all about, and so her vanity enjoys them as part of the ordinary run of things, which does overdo it a bit sometimes.

But this was different: my glances had nothing gallant about them, they could only express the truth. I was a peasant, I was young and quite personable, and the homage I was paying to her charms came from the genuine pleasure I found in them. This homage was seasoned by a rustic simplicity more interesting and all the more flattering because it did not seek to flatter.

I had an unfamiliar look in my eyes, a different way of considering things, a different sort of expression on my face, and all this combined, apparently, to give me a strange attractiveness which I noticed had some effect upon Madame.

'It's very rude of you to stare at me like that!' she said at last, but still smiling. 'Well,' I said, 'is it my fault? Why are you so beautiful?' 'Get along with you!' she then said, in an abrupt but still friendly manner. 'I think you would start telling me the tale if you dared.' At that she went back to her dressing and I took myself off, still turning back to look at her. But she didn't miss anything I did, and her eyes followed me to the door.

That same evening she introduced her nephew and installed me as his servant. I went on flirting with Geneviève, but from the moment I noticed that I was not unpleasing to Madame herself, my inclination towards the girl lost some of its keenness, her heart no longer seemed such an important conquest and I was not so impressed by the honour of being favoured by her.

Geneviève did not act in the same way, but developed a real taste for me, as much because of what she thought I might become as through the natural inclination she had for me, and as I sought her out rather less she sought me out more. She had not been in the house for long, and Madame's husband had not yet become aware of her.

As the master and mistress each had a private suite, from which they dispatched somebody every morning to inquire how the other was (and that was about all the communication there was between them), one morning, as her husband was slightly indisposed, Madame sent Geneviève to see how he was getting on.

On her way there she met me on the stairs and asked me to wait for her. She was a very long time coming back, and when she did her eyes looked full of sauciness.

'You're looking very lively, Mlle Geneviève,' I said when I saw her. 'Oh, you've no idea!' she said with a gay but sly look. 'If I am willing, my fortune is made.'

'If you are not, you are very difficult to please,' I said. 'Yes, but there is one little thing holding me back – it is on condition that

I let Monsieur make love to me, for he has just made a declaration.'

'There is no good in that,' I said, 'that kind of coin is counterfeit. Don't go in for that kind of dealing but keep your own wares. You see, when a girl has sold herself I wouldn't give the purchaser a farthing to buy her back.'

I talked in this way because at bottom I was still fond of her and I was honourable by nature.

'You are right,' she said, somewhat deflated by the sentiments I was letting her see, so I turned the whole thing into a joke and said I wouldn't take him if he gave me all his money.

'Did you at any rate defend yourself properly?' I said. 'Because you weren't very upset when you came back.' 'That's because I was so amused at everything he said.' 'Another time,' I said, 'there will be no harm in showing a bit of anger, for that will be safer than being amused. In the end he might amuse himself with you. When you gamble you can't win every time, but sometimes you lose and, once you have lost, everything else goes.'

As we were on the staircase we said no more about the matter then; she rejoined her mistress and I my young master, who was doing a composition, or rather was having it done for him by his tutor in order that his pupil's knowledge should do him, the tutor, credit and that this credit should maintain him in the job of tutor, which was very lucrative.

Geneviève had taken more notice of her master's passion than she had told me.

This master was not a generous man, but his wealth, into which he had not been born, had made him vain and his vanity had made him ostentatious. So he spent enormous sums of money, especially where his pleasures were concerned.

He had suggested an advantageous arrangement to Geneviève if she would accept him as a lover, and she even told me two days later that he had begun by offering her a purse of gold, and that is the most dangerous method the devil can use to tempt a rather flirtatious young thing who also has an eye to the main chance.

Now Geneviève leaned towards both those little failings, so it would have been difficult for her genuinely to make light of this particular passion; and indeed from that time on she always looked thoughtful, for the sight of all that money, and the ease with which she could get it, tempted her so strongly. Her virtue was now only defending the territory by making cowardly retreats.

Monsieur (I refer to the master of the house) was not rebuffed the first time she turned down his offers. He had observed how much they had weakened her virtue, and so he returned to the charge still better armed than the first time, using in the attack all sorts of little articles of adornment which he forced her to accept without any strings attached, and things like that once bought and waiting to be put on are every bit as attractive as the wherewithal to buy them.

What with gift after gift always accepted and given without demands, things went on until he undertook to purchase a life annuity for her and in addition to set her up in a little clandestine home of her own if she agreed to leave her mistress's employment.

I learned all the details of this unsavoury bargain from a letter that Geneviève had lost, written to a cousin of hers whose sole means of support, as far as I could make out, was an arrangement of the same kind with a wealthy old man, for he was referred to in the letter.

The spirit of self-interest in Geneviève was reinforced by a strange temptation, and that temptation was me.

I have said that she had really fallen in love with me. She also thought that I was very much in love with her, though she did complain of a certain lack of enthusiasm on my part that often came over me when I might have been seeing her, but I put that to rights by the pleasure I displayed when I did. So, by and large, the upshot was that I did indeed love her, but only in a steady sort of way.

Feeling sure about this and also because she was afraid of losing me (for she hadn't a penny, no more had I), she thought that Monsieur's offers, his money and the benefits he promised to bestow, would provide the means to expedite our marriage. She hoped that her fortune, when she secured it, would tempt me too and make me swallow the early repugnance I had shown.

With this in mind she answered her master's proposals with less severity than usual, and allowed her hand to open and receive the money he was still offering.

In such cases when the first step has been taken the other foot is already raised to take a second, and then you go ahead.

The wretched girl pocketed everything, she was loaded with

presents and had enough to set herself up comfortably. When she found herself in this position she said adroitly to me one day as we were walking in the garden: 'Monsieur is still after me, but in such a gentlemanly way that I cannot take exception to it, and as for me, all I need do is to be careful. If you agree, it would do no harm to me to take advantage of the generous feeling he has for me. He knows his passion is unavailing, and I don't hide the fact that it will get him nowhere. But never mind, he says, I am only too glad that you should have something to remember me by, so take what I give you, you will not be committed to anything. So far I have always refused,' she went on, 'but I think I have been wrong. What do you think? He's my employer, he's very friendly towards me, and whether it is friendship or love it makes no difference to the way I respond. He is rich, and really it's just the same as if my mistress wanted to give me something and I wouldn't take it. Isn't that so? Say what you think.'

'What I think!' I answered, utterly revolted by her obvious intentions and determined to treat her as she deserved. 'If things are as you say, that's fine. You can't refuse to take what a mistress gives you, and assuming that Monsieur is like a mistress and his love is only friendship, that's all right. I wouldn't have guessed it was that kind of friendship myself; I thought he loved you in the way a man normally loves a pretty girl, but since he is such a moderate and discreet person, you go ahead. Only mind you don't come a cropper with him, for men are deceivers ever.'

'Oh,' she said, 'I know what I'm about.' And she was right, there was no further question of advice, and what she was telling me was only intended to break the ice gently.

'I am delighted,' she said as she left me, 'that you are of the same opinion. Good-bye, Jacob.' 'Good-bye, Mademoiselle,' I answered, 'and may I compliment you on the friendship of your lover. He is a very virtuous man to be so much in love with your person without actually wanting it. Good day, and may Heaven guide you!'

I said this in such a light-hearted tone as I turned away that she didn't realize that I was making fun of her.

But Monsieur's passion for Geneviève began to get known in the house. The other maids complained, probably not so much out of virtue as envy.

'It's very nasty, very disgraceful!' said Toinette, the pretty blonde I have already mentioned.* 'Shush!' I said. 'Don't you make a fuss, Mlle Toinette. How do we know what may happen? You have a saucy face just as much as she has. Monsieur has good eyesight. It's Geneviève's turn to be loved today, tomorrow it may well be yours, and then what about all the nasty things you're saying about her? Believe me, show a little charity for your own sake if not for hers.'

Toinette was annoyed at my answer and went off and snivelled to Madame, but that was the wrong address to go to for justice. Madame burst out laughing at her naïve story of her conversation with me, for the twist I had given the matter was quite to her taste, and nothing appealed more to her character.

But she did learn about her husband's infidelity. Not that it worried her very much, it was only a joke to her.

'Are you quite sure my husband is in love with her?' she asked Toinette in the tone of somebody anxious to be quite sure so as to laugh with real justification. 'That would be fun, Toinette, for you are better than she is.' That was all Toinette got out of her, and I could have guessed as much, for I knew what Madame was like.

Geneviève, who had misinterpreted the tone in which I had answered her about Monsieur's presents, and who now had a vast store of them, came and showed me some of them so as to prepare me gradually to see the lot.

At first she kept the money dark and I only saw some articles of apparel and the wherewithal to make all sorts of things – dresses, caps, lengths of material and ribbons of every hue – and ribbon alone is a powerful seducer of nice girls, especially chamber-maids!

'Could anyone be more generous?' she said. 'Fancy giving me all this simply because he likes the look of me!'

'Oh,' I said, 'I'm not surprised, a man's friendship for a pretty girl goes a long way, believe me, and you won't stop at that.' 'Yes, I really think that is so,' she said, 'for he often asks me if I need any money.' 'Well, of course you do,' I said, 'and even if you had money up to your neck you should have it over your head. Just you go on taking it, and if it's no use to you I'll manage to

*He had called her Javotte earlier. See p. 34 supra.

find a use for it.' 'Of course I will,' she said, delighted at the interest I was taking and the favourable possibilities she thought this held out for the success of her plans. 'I assure you I'll accept it for your sake, and you'll have some, perhaps even tomorrow, for a day never passes without his giving me some.'

And the promise was kept; the following day I had six gold louis at my disposal, which, together with the three Madame had given me to pay a teacher of writing, made nine prodigious, immense *pistoles* – I mean they made a treasure for a man who had never had anything but fifteen-denier pieces in his pocket.

Perhaps I did wrong to take the money from Geneviève, and I don't think it was acting in accordance with all the rules of honour, for after all I was letting this girl think I loved her, and was deceiving her. I didn't love her any more, and yet she did appeal to me still, but only to my eyes and not to my heart.

What was more, the money she was offering me wasn't Christian at all, and I was well aware that it amounted to participating in the little misconduct through which it had been acquired, and at least encouraging Geneviève to go on acquiring it by the same means. But I did not yet know how to make such delicate reflections, my code of probity was still very summary, and it looks as though God forgave my profiting in this way, for I put it to very good use and it benefited me considerably. Through it I learned to write and do sums, and thanks partly to that I got on in the world later.

The enthusiasm with which I had pocketed this money only encouraged Geneviève to go on with her plans, for she didn't doubt that I would sacrifice everything else to my desire to have a big share, and being persuaded of this she lost her head and no longer bothered to be careful.

'Come with me,' she said one morning, 'I want to show you something.'

So I did, and she took me to her room, and there she opened a little box crammed to overflowing with the profits from her easy virtue. It was literally full of gold – it must have been a considerable sum; only a financier could have found the means to damn himself so expensively, and many a woman much more grand would have obliged him for less than this wench.

I could scarcely conceal my astonishment at this shameful

wealth, but still keeping the frivolous tone I had maintained about it so far, I said: 'Is that for me as well? My room isn't as well furnished as yours, and that little box will look fine in it.'

'Oh, as for this money,' she said, 'you will kindly allow me not to put it to use except for the benefit of the man I marry. That's for you to look into.'

'Well, now,' I said, 'I don't know where to find you one, I don't know anyone who is looking for a wife.' 'What does that answer mean? Where are your brains? Don't you understand me? You haven't got to find a husband for me, you can be one yourself, aren't you made of the stuff they're made of?' 'Never mind the stuff,' I said, 'that's an unlucky word. As to the rest,' I said, not wanting to be rude, 'if it was only a matter of being your husband I would be that straight away, and only be afraid of dying of joy. Can you doubt it? Isn't there a mirror here? Have a look at yourself and give me your verdict. Do you think it needs a lot of time to look into whether one should say yes to the young lady? You don't believe a word of it yourself, with all your talk of looking into it. That is not the difficulty.'

'Well, what is it then?' she said, looking very willing and pleased. 'Oh, nothing very much,' I said, 'just that Monsieur's friendship might mean a beating for me if I snapped up his fancy girl. I've already seen friendships of that kind, and they don't put up with any funny tricks; and besides, what will you do about such an ill-used husband?'

'Whatever is your imagination going to get up to next?' she said. 'I bet he knows I love you and will be delighted for me to marry you, and will even pay the expenses of our wedding.'

'No need for him to, I would do that myself, but the truth is that I daren't go on with it. Your good friend frightens me – in a word, his affection is probably only put on. I suspect that underneath that cloak of friendship there is a fox only out to gobble up the chicken, and when he sees a little mongrel like me after her I leave you to guess what will happen and whether that artful fox will let me get on with it.'

'Is that all that's holding you back? Do you mean that?' 'Yes, I certainly do.' 'Well, I am going to set about putting your mind at rest over that,' she said, 'and proving that nobody wants to take the chicken away. But I should be sorry if somebody found you here in my room. So we must separate, but I guarantee that our business will be settled.'

So I left her, feeling a bit anxious about the outcome of this adventure, and with some compunction at having accepted her money, for I sensed the trick she would play to get the better of me: I expected that Monsieur would take a hand in it, and I was not mistaken.

The following day a footman came to tell me that the master wanted me to go and see him, and I went, feeling very awkward. 'Well, Master Jacob,' he said, 'how is your young master getting on? Is he working at his studies?' 'Not bad, Sir.' 'And how about yourself, are you liking your stay in Paris?'

'Well, Sir, I eat and drink here quite as well as anywhere else.'

'I know,' he went on, 'that Madame has taken you under her wing, and I am very glad to hear it. But you aren't telling me all the story. I have heard about you already, and you're a bit of a lad, aren't you? You've only been here two or three months and have already made a conquest. You've hardly landed here before you're turning the pretty girls' heads. Geneviève is mad on you, and apparently you return her love?'

'Oh dear, Sir, what could she have done to make me not like her, poor thing?' 'Oh,' said he, 'you needn't be afraid of speaking out, you can speak openly to me. Your father has been working for me a long time and I am very satisfied with him and shall be delighted to do anything for his son as soon as a chance presents itself. It is fortunate for you that Geneviève likes you, and I approve of your choice. You are young and good-looking, steady and energetic, I am told, and Geneviève is a nice girl, her parents are under my patronage, and I gave her a job here simply so as to be in a better position to help her and find her a good situation. (He was lying.) The choice she is making does change my plans a little, for so far you have no money, and I would have worked out a more advantageous marriage for her. But still, as she loves you and won't have anybody else, so be it. It occurs to me that I may be able to give you what you need, which would make up for money of your own. I have already made her a gift of a good sum of money which I shall instruct you how to use, and I will go further and furnish a little home for you and pay the rent so as to tide you over until you are better off. And don't worry about that either, for I can promise you some lucrative deals. Just live happily with the wife I'm giving you, she is docile and virtuous, and moreover don't ever forget that at least half of what I am doing is for you. However well disposed I am towards Geneviève's family, I would not have gone to such lengths had I not felt even more so towards you and yours.

'Don't say anything about this here; your sweetheart's companions would never give me any peace, and would want me to marry them off as well. Without calling undue attention to it, ask to be relieved of your post and say you have been offered a better and more suitable situation. Geneviève, meanwhile, will think up an urgent journey to see her aged mother, and as soon as you are out of here you can get married. Good-bye. No need to thank me – I'm busy – just go and tell Geneviève what I have said to you, and take from my table that little sum of money with which you can go to an inn and wait until Geneviève has left here.'

This speech froze me like a marble statue. On the one hand all the benefits I was being promised were considerable.

I could see that from my very first plunge into Paris I, without any aptitude or progress so far, just a poor peasant all set to toil and moil through life in order to acquire something (and that something, in distant hopes, didn't come anywhere near what I was being offered immediately) – I could see, in a word, an assured position being thrown at my head.

And what kind of position? A furnished house, plenty of ready cash, lucrative jobs which I could ask for immediately, and the patronage of an influential man able to put me in a comfortable position at the outset and make me rich later on.

Wasn't that the apple that had dropped right into my lap?

I savoured the proposition: this windfall set my mind working, my heart beat faster and the colour mounted to my cheeks.

Fancy only having to hold out your hand to get happiness – how delightfully convenient! Wasn't that enough to take the edge off my ideas of honour?

But on the other hand honour was pleading its cause in my perplexed soul while my cupidity was pleading its own. 'To which of them shall I accord the victory?' I said to myself. I didn't know which to agree with.

Honour said: Stand firm, scorn these miserable advantages being held out to you; they will lose all their charm when you are married to Geneviève, the memory of her conduct will make her unbearable to you, and since, although you are only a peasant, you harbour me in your bosom, I shall be your tyrant and persecute you all the days of your life, you will see your infamy common knowledge, your home will fill you with horror and you and your wife will lead a cat-and-dog life and everything will go to the devil, her lover will avenge her for your insults and she will be able to ruin you through the influence he has. You won't be the first to whom this has happened: just bear that in mind, Jacob. The wealth your future wife is bringing you will be a present from the devil, and the devil is a deceiver. One fine day he will take it all back again, so as to condemn you to despair after ensnaring you with his wares.

You may find the arguments of honour a bit on the long side, but honour has to have a long time to make an impression, and it has more difficulty in doing the job than the passions.

So, for example, cupidity replied to all that in just a word or two, but with an eloquence which, though laconic, was powerful:

And who do you think you are, you jumped-up nobody, to hold back because of visionary honour? You miserable clodhopper, it befits you well to be so finicky about it, doesn't it? All right, have it your own way, go and find shelter in the workhouse, you and your honour, you'll look well together there.

'Not so well as all that,' I said to myself. 'Honour is a dead loss in the workhouse. I don't think it shines there at all.

'But does honour always land you there? Yes, pretty often, or if not there, then in the same neighbourhood.

'But is anybody happy when he is ashamed of being so? Is it a pleasure to be comfortably off against one's better feelings? What a predicament!'

All that came into my head in a single instant. To make my embarrassment even more acute I was looking at that sum of money on the table. It looked so nice and fat – what a pity to lose it!

Meanwhile the master, surprised at my silence and my not taking the money he had put there to add weight to his arguments, asked me what was on my mind. 'Why aren't you saying anything?' he went on.

'Well, Sir,' I answered, 'I'm thinking, and there's plenty to think about. Look, let us speak plainly. Suppose I am you and you are me. You are a poor man. But do the poor like being cuckolded? For you certainly will be if I give you Geneviève in marriage. Well, that is what is on my mind.'

'What!' he said. 'Isn't Geneviève a good girl?' 'Very good,' I said, 'when it is a case of a bob or a curtsey, but in the matter of being a wife to a husband I don't think her sort of goodness is the right sort.'

'Well, what have you got against her?' 'Ha! ha! ha!' I laughed. 'You know the ins and outs of this affair better than I do, you were there and I wasn't, but people do know more or less how these things work. Look here, Sir, tell me the truth frankly: does a gentleman really need a lady's maid? When he has one, does she undress him? I think it's the other way round.'

'Oh, this time you are talking plainly, Jacob, and I follow you. Peasant though you be, you aren't without brains. So listen carefully to what I am going to say in my turn.

'All these things you are imagining about Geneviève are false, but suppose they were true: you see the people who come here to visit me, they are all people of standing, rich, with fine carriages and horses.

'Do you know that there are some of their number, who shall be nameless, whose fortune is simply due to their marriage to people like Geneviève?

'Now, do you think you are better than they are? Or is it fear of being laughed at that holds you back? And who will laugh at you? Does anybody know who you are, and do you count in society? Will anyone bother about your honour? Does anybody even dream that a hobbledehoy like you has such a thing? You only run one risk, and that is of having as many people coveting your position as there are people who know you. No, no, my good fellow, for the likes of you honour means having enough to live on and to raise yourself above the lowliness of your condition, don't you see? The man looked down on in this wicked world is the one with no money.'

'All the same, Sir,' I answered, half sadly and half aggressively,

'I would still prefer to be the most looked down on than the most sorry of all. The most looked down on always enjoys food when it is given him, but the most sorry of all never has any appetite for anything, not a scrap of anything is any good to him – even if it were partridge – and, my word, an appetite is worth keeping, and I should lose mine, however good the fare, if I married your chambermaid.'

'So you've made up your mind?'

'Yes, I really have, Sir, and I am very sorry, but how can I help it? In our village the custom is to marry only virgins, and if there were one who had been chambermaid to a gentleman, she would have to make do with a lover. But as for a husband – nothing doing. Even if it rained husbands one wouldn't come down for her. That's our way of doing things, especially in our family. My mother married as a virgin, and her grandmother did the same, and I have come straight from grandmother to grandmother, as you see, with a duty to make no change.'

I had hardly finished stating my case in such a decisive tone before, staring haughtily at me, he said angrily: 'You're a rogue. You have been openly courting Geneviève in my house, and she has told me that all you wanted at the beginning was the joy of marrying her some day. Madame's other maids know this. And here's another thing: you dare to accuse her of not being an honourable girl, you have taken that impertinent notion into your head, and I have no doubt that as a result you will start gossiping about her when anybody mentions her name, and you are not the kind of man to spare her in your tittle-tattle. So I and my pure kindness of heart towards her would be the innocent cause of all the harm you might do her. No, Master Jacob, I'm going to put that to rights, and as I have gone to the length of taking a hand, and as you have already pocketed some of her money on account of being the man about to marry her, I don't intend to let you play about with her. I shall not leave you free to hurt her, and if you don't marry her I declare you will have me to reckon with. So make up your mind. I give you twenty-four hours; choose between her hand or a prison cell. That's all I have to say. Get out, you wretch.'

This order, and the epithet with it, gave me a fright, and I reached the door in one bound.

Geneviève, who had been informed of the time when Monsieur would send for me, happened to be waiting. I ran into her on the stairs.

'Oh!' she exclaimed, as though we had met accidentally. 'Have you just been talking to the master? Whatever did he want you for?'

'Now that'll do, Geneviève my pet,' I said. 'I've twenty-four hours to answer you in, and I shan't say what my decision is until the last minute.'

And I went on my way, looking glum and even a bit fierce, leaving Mlle Geneviève staring thunderstruck and all set to weep; but that had no effect on me. The choice between a prison cell and her hand had radically cured me of the little inclination I still had for her; my heart had made as clean a sweep of hers as if I had never met her. To say nothing of the awful panic that had seized me, and which was quite the opposite of love.

She called after me several times in a plaintive voice: 'Jacob, oh, say something to me, Jacob!' 'In twenty-four hours' time, Mademoiselle.' And then I ran on without knowing where, for I was stampeding like a mad thing.

I ended up by finding myself in the garden, with my heart beating wildly, thinking regretfully of the cabbages in my village, cursing the Parisian girls you were forced to marry at gun point. 'I would just as soon,' said I to myself, 'get a wife from the old clothes dealer. My luck's right out!'

My situation touched my own heart and I began to cry. Uttering howls of grief, I was turning to go into a clump of trees when I saw Madame coming out of it with a book in her hand.

'Who's upset you, poor old Jacob, that your eyes are full of tears?'

'Oh, Madame,' I answered, throwing myself at her feet, 'oh, my kind mistress, Jacob will be locked up in twenty-four hours' time.'

'Locked up!' she said. 'Have you committed some crime?' 'On the contrary,' I replied. 'It's because I refuse to commit one. You ordered me to do you honour, didn't you, Madame? Well, where shall I find honour to do you if I am not allowed to keep any? The master won't let me pretend to have any. What a miserable country, Madame, in which they put people who have some honour into prison and house luxuriously those who haven't! Marry gentlemen's chambermaids and you are rolling in money, take an honest girl and you are shut up between four walls. That's how Monsieur sees it, for he wants me to marry *his* chambermaid, if you will excuse my saying so.'

'Explain yourself more clearly,' said Madame, biting her lips so as not to laugh, 'I don't follow you. What's this about a chambermaid? Has my husband got one?'

'Oh yes, Madame, it's yours. Mlle Geneviève is after me, and I am ordered to take her as a wife.'

'Look here, Jacob,' she said, 'you must consult your own feelings.' 'Well, my heart and I have been reasoning with each other about it for a long time now, and my heart won't hear of it.'

'But of course it is true,' she said, 'that your fortune would be made, for my husband wouldn't let you down, I know him.'

'Yes, Madame,' I answered, 'but for pity's sake think what it is like to have children who call you father and are lying. That is a dreadful thing! And yet if I marry Geneviève I am in danger of having no children except that sort, and I shall be obliged to find foster mothers for them, which will break my heart, and you can see how upset I am, Madame. Naturally I don't like spurious children, and I've only got twenty-four hours to say whether I'll take on half a dozen or so or not. Help me and have pity on me. Prevent their giving me this prison cell they have promised. I think I ought to run away.'

'No, no, I forbid you to. I'll speak to my husband, and I guarantee you have nothing to fear. Go back to your duties without worrying.'

After this she left me and returned to her reading, and I went to my young master, who was not very well.

On the way back I had to pass the door of Geneviève's room, which she had left open. She was on the look-out for me, sitting there and melting into tears.

'Ah, there you are, you ungrateful creature!' she cried as soon as she saw me. 'Not satisfied with refusing my hand, you heap shame and scorn upon me!' As she harangued me in this manner she held me by the sleeve.

'Answer me,' she said, 'why do you say I'm not an honest girl?'

'Well, good Lord, Mlle Geneviève, give me time. It's not that you aren't an honest girl, but there is just this little box full of gold and your various other trinkets and gewgaws that nag at me, and I think that you would be even more honest without them. I should be just as pleased with your honour as it was before, but don't let's go on talking and quarrelling about it. You are wrong,' I went on skilfully. 'Why didn't you speak openly about things? Nothing is as fine as sincerity, but you are deceitful. You only had to admit what you were up to, and I shouldn't have been so inquisitive, for then we know where we stand, and anyway a girl is grateful if we take it all in good part. But to try to lead me up the garden, to come and lull me to sleep with a lot of cock and bull stories when I am the nicest chap in the world, well, that's not the way to carry on. You should have said: "Look here, Jacob, I don't want you to buy a pig in a poke, the master's been running after me, I tried to avoid him, but he threw money, clothes and a furnished house at my head, and that stunned me. So I stopped and picked up the money, the clothes and the house, and do you want your share now?" That's the way to talk. Say that and then you will know my last word.'

Thereupon Geneviève's tears redoubled and a shower of them rained down while she squeezed my hands as hard as she could and did not answer, which was an admission of the truth which couldn't come right out.

At last, however, as I was consoling her and urging her to speak she said: 'If only you could be trusted.' 'Who said I couldn't?' I said. 'Come, my dear young lady, courage!' 'Alas,' she said, 'it's my love for you that is the cause of everything.'

'Well, did you ever hear the like!' I said. 'Were it not for my love,' she went on, 'I would have scorned all the gold and fortunes in the world, but I thought that the situation the master was so good as to find for me would make up your mind for you and that you would be very glad to see me well off. But I made a mistake, and you are angry at what I only did for love of you.'

This speech froze me to the marrow. And yet her words told me nothing new, for I was perfectly clear where I stood over this affair without her having to tell me. And for all that it seemed as though I was hearing all she was saying for the first time, and it struck me as quite new.

I could have sworn that I had lost all interest in Geneviève, and

I think I have said so already, but apparently some little spark of feeling for her had still been alive in my heart until then, since I was upset, but it all died out at that moment.

Yet I hid from her what was going on inside me. 'Dear me!' I said. 'What you are saying is a great pity.'

'Well, Jacob,' she said, with eyes begging for forgiveness and calculated to obtain it if one were not sometimes less moved in such circumstances by a beautiful girl than by one who is not. 'What! Were you deceiving me when you led me to hope that a bit of plain speaking would put everything right between us?'

'No, I could have sworn I was speaking truthfully, but it seems that my own heart wants to change its mind.' 'But why should it change, my dear Jacob?' she cried. 'You will never find anyone who loves you as much as I do! Moreover, from now on you can count on everlasting virtue on my part.' 'No doubt,' I said, 'but unfortunately this virtue is coming over you a bit late in the day – it's like the doctor arriving after the death.'

'What!' she went on. 'Am I to lose you then?' 'Let me think that one over,' I said. 'I must have a little time to come to some arrangement with my heart; he is fighting every inch of the way, and today I'm going to try to wear him down. Let me go and think the matter over.'

'You might as well run a dagger through me as not make up your mind at once.' 'Can't be done. I can't decide what I want so quickly. But patience,' I said, 'there'll soon be an answer, and perhaps good news thrown in – yes, quite soon, don't be impatient. Good-bye, duckie, don't fret, and Lord help both of us!'

So I left her, and she watched me go with an affectionate anxiety which I was really quite ashamed of not allaying, but all I wanted to do was to get out of everything, and I went to my room with an unshakeable resolve to run away from the house unless Madame put my embarrassing position to rights as she had promised to do.

During the day I heard that Geneviève had taken to her bed and was ill with pains in the heart, pains that made people smile as they told me about them, and which they made a special point of telling me about. Six or seven members of the household, especially Madame's maids, came and told me in strict confidence.

I kept quiet and was too worried to fool about chattering to people, so I lurked in my little den until seven o'clock in the evening.

I counted the hours, for I was listening carefully to the clock because I wanted to go and speak to Madame, who had been kept indoors by a slight headache.

So I was getting ready to go and see her when I heard a commotion in the house, people running up and down the stairs in a quite unusual way. 'Oh God!' they were saying. 'What a terrible thing!'

The uproar worried me, and I went out to discover what it was.

The first person I saw was an elderly manservant of the master's who was raising his hands to heaven, sighing and moaning, and crying: 'Oh, how unfortunate I am! What a loss! What a disaster!' 'What's the matter, M. Dulois?' I said, 'what's up?'

'Alas, my lad,' he said, 'Monsieur is dead, and I feel like throwing myself into the river!'

I didn't bother to dissuade him because there was no fear of his doing so. There was no likelihood that he would choose a watery grave, for the old toper was the sworn enemy of water, and he hadn't touched any for maybe thirty years.

Mind you, he had every reason to be afflicted, for death did him out of a good source of income: for fifteen years he had been the procurer of his master's pleasures, and he was well paid for it, and in addition to that it was said that he diddled him.

I left him to his grief, half rational, half alcoholic, for he was full of wine when I was talking to him, and I ran off to find out something more detailed about what he had told me.

Nothing truer than his report. The master had been struck down by apoplexy. He was alone in his study when the attack came. There was nobody to help him and a servant had found him dead in his chair at his desk, on which was a letter with a few ribald lines scribbled to a lady of easy virtue, as far as one could tell, for I think everyone in the house read that letter, which Madame had picked up in her husband's room and then dropped in her horror at the dreadful sight.

For my part I must frankly admit that the death shocked but did not distress me. Perhaps I even found it very convenient. I breathed again, and could excuse my callousness because the dead man had threatened me with imprisonment. That had alarmed me, and his death removed that worry and put the finishing touch to the disgrace into which Geneviève had fallen as far as my love was concerned.

Alas, that was the poor girl's unlucky day. She had heard the commotion in the house just as I had, and from her bed she called to a manservant to ask what the reason was.

The one she spoke to was a great brute of a man, one of those servants in a household who are concerned with nothing but their wages and their perks, and for whom the employer is always a stranger who can die, perish, prosper for all they care. Do what you're paid for and make what you can.

I am describing him here, though quite unnecessarily, but at least from the portrait I am drawing you can avoid taking on servants like him.

Well, it was this sly brute who answered Geneviève's call and who, when she asked what the noise was about, said: 'The master is dead!'

Geneviève, who was already ill, fainted away at this sudden news.

Be assured this servant did not spend his time looking after her. The little box full of money I have mentioned was still on the table, and it caught his attention. So from that moment the box and he disappeared. They have never been seen since, and presumably they left together.

Other misfortunes remain to be told. Monsieur's death was soon noised abroad. Nobody knew anything about his financial situation, and until then Madame had lived in luxury without knowing where it came from and had enjoyed it with complete peace of mind.

She was dragged out of this the next day – a thousand creditors swooped down on her with valuers and all their following. The confusion was appalling.

The servants demanded their wages and stole what they could while waiting to be paid.

The master's reputation was not spared, many people did not refrain from calling him a rogue. One said: he swindled me; another: I entrusted him with some money, what has he done with it?

Then they insulted his widow's luxurious way of life, not mincing their words even in her presence, and she held her peace less out of forbearance than consternation.

This lady had never known what distress was, and in the bitter experience of it she was now having, I think the astonishment into which her condition threw her saved her half the grief.

Imagine somebody suddenly whirled away into a terrible wilderness unlike anything she had ever seen or thought of. That is what she went through.

I, who had not been at all upset by her husband's death, and who really had no reason to be, made up for this excusable callousness by my feeling for his wife. I could not see her without weeping in sympathy, and it seemed to me that had I had millions I would have given it all to her with infinite joy, for she was my benefactress.

But how could my being touched by her misfortune help her? What she needed then was the affectionate compassion of her friends, and not of a poor devil like me, who could do nothing for her.

But in this world all the virtues are in the wrong place, and so are the vices. Even if I hadn't bothered about the lady's situation she would not have been any the worse off and my ungrateful insensitiveness would have done no harm except to myself. Those friends of hers on whom she had lavished so much hospitality left her with no resources, and that hurt her most of all.

At first a few of these unworthy friends did come, but as soon as they saw that everything was going to blazes and their friend's fortune was melting away in ruins they never stopped running, and apparently warned the others, for no more came.

I will pass over the rest of those unhappy events because they would take too long to go into in detail.

I only stayed three more days in the house; all the servants were discharged except one maid whom perhaps Madame had never liked as much as the others, and whom she owed all her wages, but this one refused to leave her.

This particular one was the nondescript-looking one I mentioned earlier, about whom I avoided expressing an opinion, and whose looks were so uninteresting.

Nature often plays tricks like that, burying many a beautiful character under faces of that kind. You don't realize there is anything there, and then, when people like that show what they really are, you see virtues rising out of the ground.

Deeply moved, as I have said, by everything I saw, I went to see Madame and swore I would serve her for ever if that would help.

'Alas, my boy,' she said, 'all I can answer is that I wish I were in a position to reward your loyalty, but you see what has happened to me, and I don't know what may still happen or what I shall have left. So you mustn't tie yourself up with me, but go off somewhere else. When I put you with my nephew I intended to do what I could for you, but since I can do nothing now don't stay here. Your position is not good enough, try and find something better, and don't be disheartened. You have a loyal nature which will not go unrewarded.'

I insisted, but she was determined that I should go, and was really crying when I left her.

From there I went to my room to do my packing, and on the way I met my young master's tutor, already seeing his traps off the premises. His pupil cried as he said good-bye and went on crying alone. I said good-bye to the poor youngster as well, and he exclaimed in a voice that broke my heart: 'What! Is everybody abandoning me?'

I could only return a sigh, it was the only answer I was in a position to make, and I left with my few belongings without uttering a sound to anyone else. Yet it did cross my mind to go and say good-bye to Geneviève, but I had no love left for her, merely pitied her, and perhaps in that situation it was kinder not to show myself to her.

My first idea on leaving my mistress's house was to go home to my village, for I didn't know what I could do or where I could go.

I knew nobody and had no skills except those of a farm-worker – I knew all about sowing, tilling the soil, pruning vines, but that was all.

It is true that my stay in Paris had rubbed off much of the rustic air I had come with; I moved quite gracefully, held up my head well and could flourish my hat like a chap who knew a thing or two.

In fact I already had the rudiments of what you might call

polite behaviour, I mean behaviour at my level of society, and it is society of a kind. But that was the sum of my talents, together with the comely visage nature had given me, which played its part with the rest.

While waiting to leave Paris, for I had not settled the date, I put up in one of those little hostelries that people who despise poverty call lodging houses.

I stayed there two days with van-drivers, who struck me as very coarse, for I was less so now.

They took away my appetite for village life. Why go back, I sometimes asked myself. Here the whole place is full of comfortably-off people who once upon a time had nothing but Providence, same as me. Well, why not stay here a few more days and see what turns up; there are so many ups and downs in life and I might have an up. My expenses are not ruinous and I can keep it up for two or three weeks – judging by what a meal costs me I can go on for a long time. For I was frugal and did not find it difficult. When I struck a good meal I enjoyed it, but when things were scarce I didn't miss it; I could adapt myself to anything.

Those are good qualities in a fellow trying to make his fortune. When he is like that he doesn't usually try in vain, chance usually favours him and his efforts succeed. I have noticed that greedy eaters waste half their time worrying about what they will get to eat; they are automatically so preoccupied with this that it distracts a lot of their attention from everything else.

So I made up my mind to stay in Paris longer than I had first meant to.

The day following this resolve I began by going to find out what had happened to the lady whose household I had left, because she might have been able to recommend me to somebody. But I found that she had retired to a convent with the devoted maid I have mentioned, that her affairs had gone badly and she would hardly have money to live in obscurity for the rest of her days.

This news made me heave a few more sighs, for I remembered her with affection, but there was nothing to be done about it, and the best way I could think of to find somewhere to lay my head was to go and look up a certain M. Jacques who came from our part of the world and to whom my father, when I left home, had told me to pay his respects. I had his address, but until then I had forgotten all about it.

He was chef in a big house, and so off I went to find him.

I was crossing the Pont-Neuf between seven and eight in the morning, walking fast because it was cold, and thinking of nothing but this man.

When I was level with the bronze horse* I saw a woman swathed in a scarf of heavy plain taffeta, leaning against the railings and saying: 'Oh, I'm going to faint!'

Hearing these words I went up to see if she needed help. 'Are you feeling unwell, Madame?' I asked. 'Oh dear, young man,' she answered, 'I can't go on. I have come over giddy and have been obliged to hold on to the railings.'

I looked at her a bit while she was talking and I saw a chubby, well-fed-looking face which obviously was usually florid when not pale through some indisposition.

As to this person's age, the chubbiness of her face, her pallor and her full figure made it difficult to decide.

My own guess was round about forty, but I was wrong because she was quite fifty.

This simple heavy taffeta scarf and her plain mob-cap and dress to match, together with a sort of churchgoing austerity written all over her, emphasized by her prim neatness, made me conclude that she was a woman in the hands of a spiritual director. Women of that kind have the same look almost everywhere; it is their uniform, and it never appealed to me.

I don't know whether one should blame the person or the clothes, but it seems to me that those people have an air of fault-finding severity which is ill disposed towards everybody.

However, as this person was fresh and appetizing and had a plump, round face of the kind I have always liked, I was concerned about her. And helping her to stand up I said: 'Madame, if you will allow me I won't leave you here, but offer you my arm to take you home, for you may have another giddy turn and need help. Where do you live?'

'In the rue de la Monnaie, young man,' she said, 'and I won't

*The famous equestrian statue of Henri IV on the island between the two sections of the bridge. Compare the 'Copper 'oss' statue of George III in Windsor Great Park.

refuse your arm as you so kindly offer it. You seem a nice young fellow.'

'You are right,' I said as we started walking. 'I only left my village three or four months ago, and I've not yet had time to go to the bad.'

'It would be a great pity if you ever did,' she said, casting a kindly and virtuously languishing eye at me. 'You don't look cut out for such a terrible fall.'

'You are right, Madame, God in His mercy made me simple and honest and fond of good people.'

'It is written on your face. But you are very young. How old are you?' 'Not yet twenty,' I answered.

Note that all through this conversation we were going astonishingly slowly, and I was almost lifting her from the ground so as to save her from dragging along.

'Oh dear, how tiring I must be for you, my boy,' she said. 'No, Madame, don't you worry. I am delighted to render you this little service.' 'Yes, so I can see, but tell me, young man, what did you come to Paris for? What is your job?'

This question gave me the happy thought that this meeting might do me some good. When she had said that it would be a pity if I went to the bad, her eyes had accompanied the compliment with so much kindness and such a striking look of sweetness that I thought it a good sign. However, I did not envisage any practical outcome from this chance meeting, but hoped for something without knowing what.

With this in mind I also thought that my story was well worth telling her and very much to the point.

I had refused to marry a pretty girl I loved, who loved me and was offering to make my fortune, and had done so through a proud and modest revulsion which could only have occurred in a man of virtue and honour. Wasn't that a very advantageous story to tell her? And I did so to the best of my ability, in a straightforward manner that rang true.

It worked; my story pleased her very much indeed.

'Heaven will reward you for such a virtuous way of thinking, my boy, I am sure. I see that your sentiments fit in with your looks.' 'Oh, Madame, as for my looks, I don't know about them, but that is what my heart is like.'

'How artlessly he talks!' she said with a kindly smile. 'Listen, my boy, you should be grateful to God for the honest heart He has given you, it is a gift more precious than all the gold in the world, a gift for eternity. But it must be preserved, you are inexperienced, and in Paris there are so many snares for your innocence, especially at your age. Believe me, it is clearly Heaven that has brought about our meeting. I live with a sister whom I love dearly and who loves me just as much; we live in obscurity but are comfortably off thanks to divine goodness, and have an elderly cook who is a virtuous woman. The day before yesterday we got rid of a lad who did not suit us. We had noticed that he was not religious and was given to a dissolute life. So I came out this morning to ask a priest of our acquaintance to send us someone as he had promised. But this manservant has now found a house he doesn't want to leave because there he is with one of his brothers, so it is up to you to take his place, provided you have somebody to recommend you.'

'Then in that case, Madame, I cannot take advantage of your kindness, for I have nobody here who knows me. I have only been in the house I told you about, where I didn't do either well or badly. Madame took a liking for me, but she has now retired to a convent and I don't know which, and that good lady and a chef from my own part of the world, who is here but not qualified to act as sponsor for me to people like yourself, are the only guarantors I possess. If you give me time to find the lady I am sure you will be pleased with her report. As to M. Jacques the chef, what he tells you about me can be thrown in as well.'

'Young man,' she said, 'I can see truthfulness in what you are saying, and that will do instead of a reference.'

As she was saying this we reached her front door. 'Come up with me, come along,' she said, 'and I'll speak to my sister.'

I did so, and we entered a house in which everything looked well-appointed and in which the fittings and the furniture were in the same taste as the clothes of these pious females. Plainness, simplicity, elegance were in evidence.

You would have taken each room for an oratory, for as soon as you went in you felt like saying your prayers, everything was simple and shining with polish, everything invited the soul to enjoy the comforts of pious meditation.

The other sister was sitting in her own room, with her hands on the arms of her chair, recovering from the fatigue of a breakfast she had just had and waiting for it to digest itself in peace.

The remains of the meal were on a little table; it had consisted of a half-bottle of Burgundy almost all gone, two new-laid eggs and a little milk loaf.

I don't think this detail will be thought tedious – it makes part of the portrait of the person concerned.

'Oh good gracious, sister, you have been a long time coming back, I was quite worried about you,' said the one in the armchair to the one entering. 'Is this the manservant who was to be found for you?'

'No, sister, it is a nice young man I met on the Pont-Neuf, and if it hadn't been for him I wouldn't be here now, for I came over very faint. He noticed it as he was passing and offered to help me home.'

'Really, sister,' replied the other, 'you always find scruples that I can't approve of. Why go out in the morning for a long journey without having some food, all because you hadn't been to Mass? Does God demand that we make ourselves ill? Can't one serve Him without killing oneself? Will you serve Him any better when your health has gone and you have made yourself incapable of going to church? Hasn't your religion got to be prudent? Aren't we obliged to look after our life for as long as we can, so as to praise God who gave it to us? You overdo things, sister, and should ask advice about it.'

'Anyhow, my dear sister,' answered the other, 'it is done now. I thought I should be strong enough, and I did indeed want to eat something before I left, but it was very early, and besides, I was afraid it was just weakness on my part, and if one risked nothing there would not be much merit. But it won't happen to me again, for it is true that I should make myself ill. Yet I think God has blessed my little journey, because He has ordained that I should meet the young man you see here. The other one is already in a job and this one has only been in Paris for three months. He has told me his story and I think he is a very good lad, and certainly Providence has sent him to us. He wants to lead a respectable life and our situation here suits him. What do you think of him?' 'He certainly looks promising,' said the sister, 'but we will discuss that when you have had something to eat. Call Catherine, and she can bring what you want. And as for you, young fellow, go to the kitchen and you can have something to eat too.'

I acknowledged this order with a bow, and Catherine, who had been summoned, came up. She was told to see that I had something to eat.

Catherine was tall and gaunt, plainly dressed, and on her face wore an expression of forbidding piety, angry and blazing, which apparently came from the heat her mind acquired from her kitchen fire and ovens, apart from the fact that the brain of a devout female, and a cook into the bargain, is naturally dry and burnt up.

I wouldn't say this about the mind of a genuinely pious woman, for there is a great deal of difference between the truly pious and those who are commonly called religious. The religious upset people and the pious uplift them. In the former it is only their lips that are religious, in the latter their hearts; the religious go to church just for the sake of going and enjoying the pleasure of being there, but the truly pious go to pray to God, and have humility, whereas the religious don't hold with it except in others. The ones are true servants of God, the others only look like it. They go through their devotions so as to be able to say, I am performing them, carry books of devotion to church so as to handle, open and look at them, retire into a corner and lurk there in order to enjoy a posture of meditation ostentatiously, work themselves up into holy transports in order to convince themselves how very distinguished their souls are if they do indeed feel any; in fact they really experience transports, born of their own conceited anxiety to experience something of the kind – for the devil, who spares nothing to deceive them, supplies plenty. Then they return from church inflated with self-satisfaction and lofty pity for ordinary souls. And then they imagine that they have acquired the right to give themselves a little rest after these holy exercises by indulging in a thousand little luxuries meant to protect their delicate health.

Such are what I call the religious, from whose religiosity the wily tempter gets all the benefit, as it is easy to see.

As for genuinely pious people, they are kind even to the wicked, who do much better out of them than out of their own kind, for the worst enemy of the wicked is somebody like them.

That I think should do to put my thoughts on the religious out of the reach of any censorship.

Let us return to Catherine, in connection with whom I have said all this.

Well, Catherine had a bunch of keys hanging from her belt, like sister porter in a convent. 'Bring my sister some new-laid eggs, for she has still had nothing to eat,' said Mlle Habert, the elder sister of the one with whom I had come, 'and take this young fellow to your kitchen and give him a glass of wine.' 'One glass!' Catherine answered in a brusque but good-natured way. 'He'll certainly have two because of his size!' 'And both will be to your good health, Mme Catherine,' I said. 'Good,' she said, 'so long as I am well they won't do me any harm. Come along then and help me do my eggs.'

'Oh no, Catherine, it isn't worth bothering about,' said the younger Mlle Habert, 'just give me the pot of preserves, that'll do.' 'But, sister, there's no nourishment in that,' said the elder. 'Eggs would blow me out,' said the younger. And so it went on – sister this and sister that. Catherine, with a peremptory gesture, decided for the eggs and took herself off, for, she said, a lunch was not a dessert.

I followed her down to the kitchen, where she confronted me with the remains of yesterday's stew and some cold poultry, an almost full bottle of wine and bread ad lib.

Oh, what lovely bread! I have never tasted better, whiter, more appetizing. You have to put much loving care into making bread like that, and only the hand of a religious person could have kneaded it, and of course it was Catherine's work. Oh, what an excellent meal I had! The very look of the kitchen made you want to eat; everything in it made you throw yourself into the meal with relish.

'Eat away,' said Catherine, busying herself with her eggs, 'God bids us keep ourselves alive.' 'Well, here's the necessary for doing His will,' I said, 'and what's more, I'm hungry.' 'All the better,' she said, 'but tell me, have they taken you on? Are you staying with us?' 'I hope so,' I said, 'and I should be very upset if I wasn't, for I think it must be nice to work for you, Mme Catherine, you look so nice and reasonable!' 'Well,' she said, 'I do the best I can, Heaven help us! We all have our faults, and I'm not without mine, and the worst of it is that life goes by and the further on you go the more dirtied you get; for the devil is always after us, the church tells us so, but we fight on. Anyway, I'm very glad that our ladies are taking you on, for you seem a very friendly fellow. Ah well, come to think of it you and the late Baptiste are as like as two peas – he was the one I thought I should marry. He really was the nicest fellow, and a good-looking one like you – not that that was what I was interested in, though good looks are always welcome. God took him from us and He is the master and it is not for us to criticize Him. But you look the very spit of him and you talk like him. Oh Lord, how he loved me! I have changed a lot since then, and no doubt shall go on changing. My name's still Catherine, but it's not the same.'

'Oh, I'm sure,' I said, 'that if Baptiste had not died he would love you still, for I who am like him wouldn't have to be asked twice.' 'Good, good,' she laughed, 'I am still not bad to look at, but eat your food, my lad, eat it up. You'll know better when you've had a closer look at me. I'm no good now for anything except to save my own soul, and that's quite a job. God grant I succeed!'

Saying these words she dished up her eggs, which I offered to take upstairs. 'No, no,' she said, 'have your meal in peace so that it does you good, and I'll see what they think of you up there. I believe you will suit us, and I shall say what I think. Usually our ladies take ten years to know what they want, and I have the job of making up their minds for them. But don't you worry, I'll take care of everything. I enjoy helping my neighbour, and that's what they tell us to do in the sermon.'

'Thank you very much indeed, Mme Catherine, and above all bear in mind that I am a neighbour who looks like Baptiste.' 'But don't stop eating,' she said; 'that's the best way to be like him for a long time in this world; I like a neighbour who lasts.' 'And I assure you that your neighbour likes lasting,' I said, toasting her with a brimming glass.

That was my first experience of dealing with Mme Catherine, from whose speeches I have cut out *God be praised!* and *Heaven help us!* without number, which sometimes acted as a refrain and sometimes as the main body of her discourse.

Apparently that was part and parcel of her verbal piety, but it didn't matter to me, for what is certain is that I was not displeasing to the good lady any more than to her mistresses, especially the younger Mlle Habert, as the sequel will show.

While waiting for the verdict Catherine was to bring I finished my lunch, and she soon came back and said: 'All right, young man, all you need now is your nightcap, for your lodging is here.'

'Nightcap, we'll soon get that,' I said, 'and as for my slippers, I've got them on already.' 'Very well, my boy, go and fetch your things so as to be back for dinner. While you were having your lunch your wages were being fixed, and I have got it settled.' 'Are they running into a large figure?' 'Oh yes,' she smiled, 'I see what you mean, and they are mounting up at a decent pace.' 'I rely on you,' I said, 'and I won't even look at them closely. I bet I'm better off than I deserve, thanks to your kind help.'

'Oh you are laying it on!' she said, delighted at the directness I put into my flatteries. 'It's Baptiste all over again, I think I can hear his voice. But come on, come on, I've got my dinner to do, don't distract me, let me get on with my work while you go and fetch your traps. There and back, quick!' 'It's as good as done,' I said as I went out, 'it won't take a jiffy, I don't need mules to carry my trunks.' Whereupon I went off to my lodging-house.

However, on the way I thought over whether I ought to go into service in that household. But, I reflected, I've nothing to lose, I only have to clear out if I don't like it, and meanwhile that lunch is a good sign, and it looks as if the religion of these people doesn't count the helpings and is not mad on abstemiousness. Anyway, the whole household looks favourably on me and they are not averse to fine lads of my age, I am in favour with the cook and so my four meals a day are safe. My heart tells me that all will go well, so courage!

Reasoning thus I came to the door of my lodgings. I owed nothing except a good-night to my landlady, and all I had to do was clear off with my bundle.

I was back at the house just as they were going to sit down to the meal. Golly, what a succulent little repast! That was what I call a soup, not to mention a nice little roast, so exquisite, done to a turn ... You had to have a soul well fortified against the pleasures of good food not to fall into the sin of gluttony as you ate that roast. And then that stew, for there was one, delicately seasoned as I have never met elsewhere. If they ate in Heaven I wouldn't want to be better served there. Mahomet could have made one of the joys of his paradise out of that meal.

Our ladies didn't touch boiled beef, and it made an appearance on the table only to be taken away again and given to the poor.

Catherine also did without it, out of charity, she said, and I at once agreed to be as charitable as she was. There is nothing like a good example.

I learned later that my predecessor had not taken part in the almsgiving, as I did, because he was too sinful to do so and confine himself to roast and stew.

I don't know, incidentally, how our two sisters managed about eating, but the way they did it certainly was a conjuring-trick.

They never had any appetite, or at any rate you never saw the appetite they had, for it whisked away the portions, which vanished without apparently having been touched.

As far as one could see these ladies used their forks languidly and hardly had the strength to open their mouths as they glanced without interest at the good fare: I don't feel I want anything today. No more do I. It all seems so tasteless. All seems too salt to me.

These remarks threw the dust in my eyes, and I thought I saw the most apathetic creatures in the world, and yet the result of all this was that the dishes were so very depleted by the time they were cleared away that at first I couldn't make it all out.

But eventually I saw how I had been taken in at first. I had been deceived by these airs of distaste on our mistresses' part, which had concealed the stealthy activity of their teeth.

The funniest thing about it was that they themselves imagined that they were very small and frugal eaters, and as it was not becoming for the religious to be greedy, and as one must eat to live and not live to eat, and as in spite of that reasonable and Christian maxim their greedy appetites didn't want to miss anything, they had found the secret of giving those appetites full rein without being tainted by gluttony. It was by having recourse to these outward signs of contempt for food, and by the lack of interest with which they touched it, that they persuaded themselves that they were frugal while keeping the pleasure of not being so. It was through this play-acting that their religion innocently left the door open to self-indulgence.

We must admit that the devil is very artful, but also that we are very stupid!

The dessert was in the same style as the main meal; preserves both dry and in syrup, the whole topped up with nice little liqueurs to aid the digestion and revive their taste that had been so mortified.

After which the elder Mlle Habert said to the younger: 'And now, dear sister, let us give thanks to God.' 'That is right and proper,' answered the other with an abundance of gratitude which at that moment she would have been quite wrong to withhold from God.

So she said: 'That is right and proper,' and then the two sisters, rising from their chairs with a solemnity which they assumed with the best faith in the world, and which they thought as meritorious as it was legitimate, calmly put their hands together to make a common act of prayer, in which they responded to each other verse by verse in tones rendered most touching by their feeling of well-being.

Then the cloth was removed and they drifted into armchairs, the softness and depth of which was conducive to repose, and there they conversed about certain thoughts they had had while reading pious books, or about a sermon of that day or the day before, the subject of which, they thought, applied admirably to M. or Mme So-and-so.

That sermon was absolutely made for them: avarice, love of this world, pride and other shortcomings had been so well discussed!

'But,' said one, 'how can one hear the holy word of God and not come home resolved to correct oneself? Sister dear, can you understand it at all?'

'How on earth does Mme So-and-so, who has come assiduously to the sermons all through Lent, interpret them? For I see no change in her flirtatious airs, and speaking of coquetry, dear God, how outraged I was the other day by the indecent way Mlle — was dressed! Fancy coming to church in that state! I tell you, she made my mind wander in a way I pray God to forgive and which prevented my saying my prayers. Really, it's terrible!'

'You are quite right, sister,' chimed in the other, 'but when I see such sights I lower my eyes, and the anger it causes me makes me refuse to see them and praise God for the grace He has vouchsafed in preserving me at any rate from those particular sins; and I pray with all my heart that He will shed the light of His grace on those who commit them.'

You will ask: How did you know of these conversations in which their neighbours suffered during these ladies' digestive processes?

While clearing the table and tidying up in the room where they were.

After I had cleared away, the younger Mlle Habert called me over, and speaking in an undertone because of a slight drowsiness that was beginning to close her sister's eyes, she said what you will find in the second part of this story.

PART 2

I SAID in the first part of my life-story that the younger Mlle Habert called me over as her sister was dozing off.

'Young man,' she said, 'we are keeping you on. I have made my sister agree and have vouched for your good character, for I don't think your face and your words have deceived me. They have made me feel friendlily disposed, and I hope you will deserve it. You will work with Catherine, who is a good and virtuous woman and seems well disposed towards you too, and she will tell you the terms we have agreed on for you. I think you will have reason to be satisfied, and perhaps later on you will be even more so, I can assure you. So go along and have your dinner, go on being as good a lad as you seem to be; you can be sure I think well of you and won't forget how ungrudgingly you came to my aid this morning when I had my attack of faintness.'

There are some things neither the spirit nor the letter of which can be communicated, and I cannot give you a really adequate idea either of everything Mlle Habert's words meant or the way she said them. What is clear is that her face, eyes and tone of voice said far more than her words, or at least added a great deal to the literal meaning of the terms, and I believed I could see in them a kindness, an affectionate gentleness, a concern for me which need not have been there, and which surprised me and made me curious to know what they meant.

But for the moment I thanked her in almost the same manner, and answered in heartfelt tones that would have deserved a reproof if my remarks had not been true. Apparently they were, for my way of answering did not displease. You will see later where this will lead us.

I was making my bow to Mlle Habert before going downstairs to the kitchen when an ecclesiastical gentleman came into the room.

He was the regular spiritual director of these ladies – I say regular because they were friendly with many other priests who were on visiting terms and with whom they also discussed the state of their consciences.

But this one was director-in-chief, the arbiter of their behaviour.

Once again let nothing I am saying outrage anybody or lead anyone to think I am poking indiscriminate fun at the custom of handing over one's conscience to the control of what we call directors and consulting them about all one's acts.

This custom is no doubt praiseworthy and pious in itself, and it is good to follow it when one follows it properly. That is not what I am laughing at, but there are trifling details that directors should not dabble in as earnestly as they do, and I am laughing at those who carry their spiritual direction to such lengths.

This particular director was quite short, but well built if a little plump. His complexion was fresh but not florid, his eye bright, but with nothing impulsive or passionate about its keenness.

Haven't you ever seen those faces which in those who have them suggest something accommodating, indulgent and consoling for others and which, as it were, vouch for a soul filled with meekness and charity?

That was exactly the face of our director.

For the rest, picture short hair trimmed evenly, which suited him excellently and turned up in little curls round his cheeks in a natural wave owing nothing to the wearer's efforts; add red lips and good teeth, fine and white simply because they also were fortunately made like that, without his having to do anything about them.

Such were the charms, quite innocent let it be said, of this ecclesiastic, who in his attire had not forgotten that religion itself ordains a certain modest pride in one's appearance so as not to offend anybody. He did, however, slightly overdo this professional neatness – but it is difficult to put one's finger on the exact spot – so that our priest, no doubt unintentionally, had become a little dandified.

The elder Mlle Habert, who had dozed off, guessed rather than heard that he had come in, for he made very little noise about it. But in such cases a pious female has a very sharp sense of hearing.

She woke up at once, smiling at the good fortune she was enjoying in her sleep – entirely spiritual good fortune, I mean.

This priest, for whom I was a new face, looked at me attentively.

'Is this a servant of yours, ladies?' 'Yes, Monsieur, he is a young man we have taken on today,' answered the elder, 'and it is because of a service he rendered my sister.'

Thereupon she told him what had happened to me and her younger sister, and I thought it appropriate to depart during the story.

When I was half way down the stairs, thinking about the way the director had looked at me, I was seized with a desire to know what he would say. It was true that Catherine was expecting me down in her kitchen, but never mind, I softly went upstairs again. I had shut the door of the room, and now I put my ear as close to it as I could.

My adventure with the younger Mlle Habert was soon told. From time to time I looked through the keyhole, and the director was placed so that I could see him full-face as well as the younger sister.

I noticed that he was listening to the story with a cold, thoughtful and almost disapproving expression.

Gone was the mild, indulgent look he had worn as he came into the room. He was not yet putting on the appropriate face, but I guessed he soon would, and that my adventure was about to become a case of conscience.

When he had heard the whole story he lowered his eyes like a man about to pronounce a weighty judgement and give the result of profound deliberation.

Then he said: 'You have acted very hastily, ladies,' and looked at them both with eyes which made it a grave and important issue, and prepared my employers to see him treat it almost as a crime.

At these opening words, which did not surprise me, for I didn't expect anything better, the younger sister coloured with embarrassment, through which could be seen annoyance.

'You have acted very hastily,' he said again. 'But what harm can there be in this,' went on the younger in a half-cowed, half-mutinous tone, 'if he is a decent fellow, as there are grounds for believing? He is out of a job, I came across him on the road, he does me a kindness and brings me home, we need a manservant and we take him on – what offence to God can there be in that? On the contrary, I thought I was doing an act of charity and gratitude.'

'We know that quite well, sister,' chimed in the elder, 'but never mind, since Monsieur, who is wiser than we are, does not approve of what we have done we must accept it. To tell you the truth, just now when you talked to me about keeping that young man, I think I did feel some qualms. I had a presentiment that it would not be our director's opinion, and God knows that I have left it all for him to decide.'

The speech did not convince the younger sister, who did not answer except to make faces that went on saying: I see no harm in it.

The director had let the elder sister talk on without interrupting her, and indeed seemed a little vexed at the other one's obstinacy.

However, adopting a quiet and kindly tone he said to the younger: 'Listen, my dear lady, you know with what special affection I give both of you my advice.'

These last words, addressed to both, were shared out so that the younger received at least three-and-a-half quarters for herself, and indeed it was only on a sudden thought that he gave the rest to the elder, for to begin with the holy man had not thought of her at all.

'Yes indeed,' said the elder sister, conscious of this inequality and of having at first been overlooked, 'yes indeed, Sir, we know that you consider each of us quite as much as the other, and that your piety allows no preference, as is only right and proper.'

The tone of this remark was somewhat sour although it was said laughingly, for fear that it might sound like jealousy.

'Alas, sister,' went on the younger with some acerbity, 'I don't disagree with you at all, and even if the gentleman were more attached to you than to me I would have no cause for complaint; he would be doing you justice, he knows the depths of your soul and the grace God sheds upon you, and you are certainly worthier of his attention than I am.'

'My dear sisters,' intervened the priest, seeing that this little debate was all his fault, 'do not distress yourselves. You are equals in my sight before God because you both love Him equally, and if my care had to devote itself more to one than to the other it would be in favour of the one I saw treading more slowly along the path to salvation, her weakness would bind me closer to her because her need for help would be greater. But Heaven be praised, you both walk at the same pace and neither lags behind, and so that is not the question. We are discussing the young man you have taken on (it was youthfulness he was so concerned about). You see no harm in it, I am quite sure, but be so good as to listen to me.'

Thereupon he made a slight pause as though for reflection.

Then he continued: 'God in His goodness sometimes allows those who lead us to see more clearly than we are permitted to do, and this is to show us that we must not have too high an opinion of ourselves, and that we would go astray if we were not docile.

'What does it signify, you may say, to have taken on this young fellow who seems to be well-behaved? It is of very grave significance.

'First, that of having acted contrary to normal prudence, for after all you only know him from having met him in the street. His face looks pleasant to you, very well; everybody has his own point of view about this and mine is not so favourable, but I will grant you that. Well, since when has one entrusted one's money and one's life to strangers simply because of their looks? And in your case when I am saying money and life I am not exaggerating. You are only three women quite alone in a house; what risks do you not run if this face deceives you, if you are in the clutches of an adventurer, as may well be the case? Who can speak for his morals, his religion, his character? Cannot a rogue have the face of an honest man? I don't suspect him of being a rogue – God forbid – charity bids us think the best of him, but charity must not go to the length of imprudence, and it is imprudent to trust him as you do.'

'Oh, sister, what Monsieur is saying is very sensible,' cried the elder at this point. 'Of course that fellow has something about him that predisposes one in his favour, but our director is right, and now I come to think about it, there is something about the way he looks at you which made me hesitate, it really did.'

'And one other thing,' cut in the priest. 'You agree with what I have said, but it is nothing compared with what I still have to say to you.

'This young man is in the first flush of youth, he looks enterprising and a bit of a rake. You are not yet of an age to be free from criticism; aren't you afraid of the evil things that may be thought about it by people seeing him in your home? Don't you know that people are quick to see scandal, and that it is a terrible thing to give our neighbour the slightest cause for scandal? This is not what I am telling you, but what the Gospel says. Moreover, my dear sisters, for we must not shrink from saying everything, are we not all weak? What do we do in life but fight unceasingly against ourselves, falling and rising again? And this in the most trivial things. Is this not bound to make us tremble? Oh, believe me, where our salvation is concerned, let us not seek new difficulties to vanquish, let us not expose ourselves to new occasions for weakness. This man is too young; you would be under the same roof with him, see him almost every minute. The seed of sin is always within us, and already I mistrust (my conscience obliges me to say this), already I mistrust the good opinion you have of him, this stubborn affection you have already conceived for him. It is innocent now, but will it always be so? Once again, I mistrust it. I have noticed that Mlle Habert,' he added, looking at the younger sister, 'is not pleased with the sentiments I have already expressed about it; what is the cause of this obstinacy, this departure from my principles in one whom I have never known to offer a moment's resistance to the advice my conscience has dictated for the safety of hers? I do not like this frame of mind, it makes me suspicious, it looks like a snare set by the devil; and that being the case I am obliged to exhort you to get rid of this young man whose looks, moreover, don't appeal to me as much as to you. I will undertake to send you a manservant of my own choosing; it is a bit awkward for me, but God inspires me to to do so, and I beg you, in His name, to allow yourselves to be led. Do you promise?'

'As for me, Sir,' said the elder, falling in completely with his wishes, 'my answer is that you are the master, and you see how I submit. From now on I undertake to give no job to the young man in question, and I am sure my sister will do the same.'

'Really,' chimed in the younger, and her face was almost aflame with anger, 'I don't know how to interpret all this. Now my sister is already in league with you against me; look at her, delighted with the imaginary offence I am charged with, and it isn't just today that she is like this about me, and I've got to say this, and the way she is talking forces me to. She is sure, she says, that I shall conform to her way of doing things. Well, I have never done anything else since we have been living together, and I have always had to give way to her in order to have a bit of peace. God knows – and without reproaching anybody – how many times I have sacrificed my wishes to hers, and they had nothing wrong about them except they weren't hers. And frankly I am beginning to get tired of this submission which I'm not bound to give her. Yes, sister, you can make what you like out of what I am saying; but you are very high-handed, and that is what the reverend gentleman ought to be worrying about in you, and not the step I have taken in bringing home a poor fellow to whom perhaps I owe my life, and whom you want me to reward by turning him out after we have both given our word that we are keeping him. Our director objects that he has nobody to recommend him, but the young man has told me that he would find somebody if we wished, and so that objection falls to the ground. As for me, to whom he has rendered such a great service, I shall not tell him he has got to go, sister, I couldn't do it.'

'Very well, sister,' answered the elder, 'if you will let me I'll undertake to sack him for you without your being involved, and with a promise from me to atone for my past high-handedness by deferring completely to your wishes, even though you are my junior. If you had had the charity to let me know my shortcomings, I might perhaps have corrected myself with God's help and Monsieur's prayers – though he has never criticized me for this high-handedness you are referring to. But as you are cleverer than anybody else, with more penetration, you couldn't have been wrong, and I am very glad you see in me what has escaped even Monsieur's perspicacity.'

'I have not come here,' said the priest, rising with an irritated air, 'to sow discord between you, Mademoiselle, and since I allow your sister's faults to go unchecked and am not sufficiently perceptive to see them, and since, moreover, my opinions about your behaviour do not strike you as well founded, I conclude that I am no use to you and must therefore withdraw.'

'What, Sir, withdraw!' gasped the elder sister. 'Oh Sir, my salvation is even more precious to me than my sister, and I realize that only through a man as holy as you can I find it. Withdraw! God forbid! No, Sir, it is from my sister that I must withdraw. We can live apart from each other, she has no use for me nor I for her. Let her stay here, I will hand this house over to her and go at once to look for another, where I trust that of your goodness you will be so kind as to continue the visits you paid us here. Oh Lord, what a pass we have come to!'

The priest made no reply to this pious and even tender outburst in his favour. To keep only the elder sister would mean a heavy loss. I thought he looked extremely put out, and as the scene bade fair to become noisy, what with the tears the elder sister was beginning to shed and the shrill cries with which she was filling the room, I left my position and hurried downstairs, where Catherine had been waiting nearly a quarter of an hour for me to come down to dinner.

I don't think there is any need for me to explain why the director was so determined that I should go. He had said in his homily that it was unseemly for me to stay with them, but I think he would have passed over that and not even thought of it had there not been this other motive, namely that he saw that the younger sister was determined to keep me. That might mean that she was fond of me, and that liking for me might have made her disinclined for piety, hence for submissiveness, which meant good-bye to his authority; and people do like dominating other people. It is very pleasant to see other people obedient and dependent on their king, so to speak, and a king is often all the more loved for being inflexible and authoritarian.

In addition, I was a strapping and good-looking young man, and maybe he knew that Mlle Habert was not averse to good-looking fellows, for after all a confessor knows a thing or two! Let us get back to our kitchen.

'You've been a long time coming back,' said Catherine, who while waiting for me was doing her spinning and warming up the soup. 'What were you all shouting so loud about in the parlour? I heard somebody screeching like an eagle. Just listen to the nice racket they're still kicking up! Are our ladies having a fight?'

'I've really no idea, Mme Catherine, but they can't be having a row because that would mean offending God, and they are not capable of that.'

'Oh yes they are,' she replied, 'they are the best women in the world, and live saintly lives, but it is just this holiness that makes them so mulish with each other, for it means that not a day passes when they don't squabble about what's good or evil, because the love of God makes them so pernickety. And sometimes I come in for it too, but it doesn't worry me, I put them firmly in their places, shrug my shoulders and go off and let God have the last word – come on, let's have our dinner, and that'll be one job done.'

What the confessor had said about me didn't put me off my food. Whatever happens, I said to myself, let's save this dinner from the wreck, at any rate.

So I took double portions and was beginning on the thigh of an excellent young rabbit when the noise upstairs redoubled, and turned into bedlam.

'What the devil are they up to?' asked Catherine, with her mouth full. 'It sounds as though they are murdering each other.'

Still the noise went on. 'I must go up,' she said. 'I bet it's some case of conscience sending them off their heads.' 'All right,' I said, 'say it's a case of conscience. Isn't there a casuist up there with them? He can stop the fight. He must know the Bible and the Gospel by heart.' 'Oh yes,' she said as she got to her feet, 'but that Bible and Gospel don't cater for all the queer ideas of some folk, and our good mistresses have got Lord knows how many of those. You just get on with your meal while you're waiting. I'm going to see what's up.' And off she went.

I carried out her orders to the letter and went on eating as I had been told to, particularly as I was very glad, I have already said, to take in a good meal in my uncertainty about what all this shindy might mean for me.

Catherine had still not come back by the time I had finished my dinner. Sometimes I heard her voice dominating all the others – it was recognizable by its fierce and peremptory tone. The noise went on and even increased.

I glanced at my bundle, which I had brought into the house that same day, and which was still in a corner of the kitchen. I look rather like carting you off again, I said to myself, and I'm very much afraid this will cut off the good wages I was promised, which started from this morning.

These thoughts were running through my mind when I thought the racket was giving over.

A moment later the door of the upstairs room opened and somebody came down the stairs. I stood at the kitchen door to see who was going out. It was our priest.

He looked like a man whose soul is sore troubled, and came down with faltering steps.

I purposely shut the kitchen door to save myself from having to show my respect if I was seen, but it didn't help, because he opened it again and came in.

'My son,' he said, summoning all the resources of his art, I mean those sanctimonious and pathetic tones which make you feel that a saintly man is addressing you.

'My son, you are causing a great deal of trouble here.' 'Me, Sir? But I never say a word! I haven't uttered four words upstairs since I've been in the house.'

'Never mind, my son, I don't say that it is you who actually make the trouble, but you are the occasion for it, and it is not God's will that you should be here, since you are depriving the place of its peace, even though you are only doing so by your presence.

'One of these ladies is willing to have you here, but the other does not want you, and thus you are sowing discord between them, and these pious ladies who before you came only vied with each other in meekness, kindness and humility towards each other are now on the point of separating, all because of you. You are the bone of contention between them. You should regard yourself as the instrument of Satan, who is using you to tear them apart and take from them the peace in which they lived in mutual edification. For my part I feel heartbroken, and I declare to you in the name of God that some great disaster will befall you unless you make up your mind. I am very glad to have seen you on my way out, for to judge by your face you are a good and clean-living fellow and will not reject the advice I am giving you for your own good and that of everybody else here.' 'Me, Sir, a clean-living fellow?' I said, having heard him out absent-mindedly and untouched by his exhortations. 'You say that you can tell from my face that I am a respectable man? No, Sir, you are making a mistake, you are not thinking about what you are saying. I maintain that you don't see any of that in my face. On the contrary, you think I look like a rogue whose hands are itching to take away the cash from a house. I can't be trusted. I might well cut people's throats to get their purses. That's what you are thinking.'

'Oh, whoever is saying such a thing, my son?' he answered, colouring up. 'I am expressing the opinion,' I said, 'of a man of the world who has had a good look at me, and God tells him that I am no good. You are trying to look discreet, but I know what you are thinking. This same worthy man has also said that I am too young, and that if these ladies keep me it might put evil thoughts into the neighbours' minds. To say nothing of the devil being an artful dodger who might use me to tempt my mistresses, for I am a handsome villain. Is that not so, your reverence?' 'I don't know what you mean,' he said, lowering his eyes.

'Oh yes, you do. Aren't you thinking that the younger Mlle Habert is already too attached to me because of that service I rendered her? Perhaps there is some sin hidden under this and trying to take root, you know. There is nothing to fear for the elder sister – that one is quite obedient, and I could stay if she were the only one, my face isn't a temptation to her, for she wants me sacked. But the younger one is being difficult, which is a bad sign, she might be too well disposed towards me and she mustn't be friendly with anybody except her director, for the health of her conscience and the satisfaction of yours. But bear this in mind: if we are discussing consciences, if your own had not been so tender the peace of God would still be in this place, and you know it perfectly well, your reverence.'

'What does all this mean?' he said. 'Just this,' I answered, 'that God doesn't mean us to look for trouble where there is none. Think that out. When you were preaching at those ladies I wasn't far from the pulpit. As for me, I can't see anything wrong in it. I can't earn my living by controlling ladies' lives, I am not all that well off, and I earn my keep by doing odd jobs in the house. Let other people stick to their jobs as well as I do. I think your job is even more precarious than mine, and I am not as worried about my position as you are about yours. I shall never get somebody else the sack for fear of getting it myself.'

At this speech our friend turned his back on me and went out without a word.

There are some home truths people are not armed against. His confusion left him no time to work out his answer, and the quickest way was to take himself off.

But still Catherine did not come back, and I waited a full quarter of an hour. At last she came down and entered with her arms raised to heaven and shouting: 'Oh, dear God! What does it all mean?'

'What, Mme Catherine, have they been fighting up there? Is somebody dead?' 'No, it's our home that is dying, young fellow, it is all going to pot.'

'Well, what's killed it?' I said. 'Alas, it has been hounded down by religious scruples, all through some sermonizing by the reverend director. I've been saying for a long time that that man was splitting too many hairs over consciences.'

'But what's this all about?' I asked. 'It's all up, and our ladies can't go to Heaven together. And the upshot of it is that the younger of our two ladies is going to take another house, and she told me to tell you to be ready to go with her, and you might as well both wait for me too, for the older one is an old harridan and I'm a bit short-tempered, and the priests have never managed to cure me of that, for I am from Picardy and it's bred in the soil, and as two heads in one house won't work I shall have to go and take mine with the young one, who hasn't got a head at all.'

Scarcely had Catherine finished this speech before the young one appeared.

'Young man,' she said as she came in, 'my sister doesn't want you to stay here, but I'm keeping you on. She and that priest who has just gone have said things which settle it for me, and you will benefit from the shocking audacity with which they have spoken to me. I brought you here, and in any case I am indebted to you, so you will go with me. I am off at once to look for accommodation. Come along and help me to walk, I am not very strong yet!'

'I am ready, Mademoiselle. You are my only mistress here, and I am sure you will be pleased with the way I serve you.'

'Mademoiselle,' Catherine said, 'we shall not be parted either, shall we? I'll make just as nice fricassees for you somewhere else. Let your elder sister manage as best she can, I was beginning to get very sick of her – with her you've never finished, sometimes too much of this and sometimes too much of that. I can tell you that if it hadn't been for you I should have chucked her kitchen long ago. But you are kind, I am a Christian and try to be patient, and besides, I'm fond of you.'

'I do thank you for those sentiments,' said Mlle Habert, 'and we'll see how we get on when I have taken a house. I've got lots of furniture here and I cannot get out for two or three days, so we shall have time to make arrangements. Come on Jacob, let's be going.' That was the name I had adopted, and the lady remembered it.

Her reply, as far as I could see, put Dame Catherine out a little, and, prompt though she usually was at answering back, she couldn't find anything to say this time and remained silent.

But I could see quite well that Mlle Habert had no intention of having her with us, and to tell the truth it was not much loss, for although she mumbled more prayers in a day than would have done for a month if they had been properly thought out, she must usually have been the most surly and shrewish creature you could ever have to deal with. When she said something pleasant it was in the tone of voice others use for quarrelling.

But let us leave her there to sulk over Mlle Habert's answer.

She and I set off together, she taking my arm, and never in my life have I helped anyone to walk so gladly as I did then. This good lady's action had won my allegiance. Is anything nicer than being sure of somebody's friendship? I was sure of hers, absolutely sure, and yet I cannot say how I interpreted this friendship, sure though I was of it, except that in my own mind I thought it very flattering, and it touched me more deeply than mere kindness ought to have done. I found it more pleasurable than ordinary kindness, and I showed my gratitude on my side in a very special way in which there was something caressing.

When this lady was looking at me I paid attention to my behaviour and arranged the look in my own eyes; all my glances were almost as many compliments, and yet I couldn't have said why myself, for I was acting by pure instinct, and instinct doesn't go into the why and the wherefore of anything.

We had already gone some fifty paces from the house without saying a single word, but we were walking with light hearts. I supported her with joy and my support gave her pleasure – at least that is what it felt like to me, and I was not mistaken.

While we were walking along in silence, owing, I think, to our not knowing how to begin a conversation, I noticed a board advertising the sort of accommodation Mlle Habert needed, and I seized on this pretext for breaking a silence which was clearly embarrassing to us both.

'Mademoiselle,' I said, 'would you like to see what this house is like?' 'No, my boy, I should be too near my sister. Let's get further away and look in another neighbourhood.'

'Good Heavens, Mademoiselle, how comes it that this sister of yours has quarrelled with you, for you are so nice that anybody would love you, even a Turk. Now take me, I've only known you today, but I've never felt so happy.' 'Really, Jacob?' she said. 'Yes, of course, Mademoiselle, you can easily tell, for you've only got to look at me.' 'I'm very glad to hear it,' she said, 'and you are right, for you are more indebted to me than you think.'

'And I'm very glad to hear that too,' I said, 'for nothing gives greater pleasure than being indebted to people who have won your heart.'

'Well then, Jacob, you should know that I'm only leaving my sister because of you. I must say yet again that you helped me this morning so spontaneously that I was most touched.' 'What good fortune for me!' I answered, with a gesture that made me give a little squeeze to the arm I was holding. 'The Lord be praised for guiding my steps to the Pont-Neuf! As for the help I gave you, there's nothing so wonderful about that, Mademoiselle, for who could see a person like yourself come over faint and not be concerned? I was quite frightened myself. You see, Mistress, if you'll excuse my putting it like this, some people have a face that turns all passers-by into friends, and your mother had the goodness to give you one of those faces.'

'You have a funny way of putting things,' she said, 'but it's so artless that it gives me pleasure. Tell me, Jacob, what do your people do in the country?' 'Oh, dear, Mademoiselle, they aren't rich, but for honour they are the cream of our parish, you can't deny it. As to profession, my father is the vine-grower and farmer for the squire of our village. But no, that isn't right, I don't know what he is now because the squire is dead and I have just left his Paris house. As to the rest of my family, they're not small fry either, and they are addressed as Monsieur and Madame. Except for an aunt I've got who is only called Mademoiselle for want of being married to the local surgeon, who couldn't go through with the ceremony because he died. And because she was so vexed about this death my aunt started up as school-mistress of our village, and she is respected, believe me! Apart from that I've got two uncles: one is a parish priest who has always got some good wine, and the other has nearly had a parish two or three times but is still just an assistant priest until something better turns up. The scrivener in our village is our cousin too, or sort of, and they even say round about that one of our grandmothers was the daughter of a gentleman – it is true, for we mustn't tell a lie about it, that it was on the wrong side of the blanket, but that's not far from the right side. You come into the world whichever side you can, and the wrong side is still noble blood. Anyway, they are all respectable people, and that is the exact total of my relations – oh, except for a little baby cousin who so far is doing nothing except wearing nappies.'

'Well now,' said Mlle Habert, 'that can be called a good country family and there are plenty of people cutting a good figure in the world who haven't such respectable origins. Take us, for example. We have origins like yours, and I don't feel at all ashamed of them. Our father was the son of a rich farmer in the

Beauce, who left him enough to start up in a big way of business, and my sister and I were left very comfortably off.'

'That is quite clear,' I said, 'from the way you live, Mademoiselle, and I am so glad for your sake, for you deserve to own all the market-gardens in and around Paris. But that makes me think what a great pity it is that you should not leave behind any descendant of yours; there is so much bad stock in the world that it's a sin not to breed good stock when you can, for the one makes up for the other, and you would not have been short of suitors any more than the river of water.' 'That may well be,' she laughed, 'but it's too late in the day and there would be a shortage of them now, my dear Jacob.'

'A shortage now! Oh, no, Mademoiselle, then you would have to put a cloth over your face! For as long as it can be seen it is honey that will attract the bees. Oh, my heavenly days! Whoever would not want to marry his face to yours, even if it wasn't in front of a lawyer? If I too had been the son of a father who was child of a rich farmer in the Beauce and had got on in business, good Lord, we should see whether that pretty face would have gone by without having me to deal with.'

All Mlle Habert did by way of answer was to roar with laughter, and it was a laugh due not so much to my jokes as to the flatteries they implied. It was clear that her heart was gratified by the way mine was tending.

The more she laughed the further I went. Little by little my words grew bolder; from being kind they had already become flattering, and then something stronger, and then they came nearer to tenderness until, upon my soul, it really was love except for the word itself, which I didn't risk because I felt it was too crude to use, but I certainly gave her the equivalent and some to spare.

She showed no sign of noticing and let everything pass, ostensibly because of the innocent amusement my simplicity gave her.

I took advantage of the hypocritical way she listened to me. I realized the extent of my good fortune and concluded at once that she must be keen on me, as she did not put a stop to words as tender as mine.

Nothing makes us more lovable than thinking we are loved, and as I was naturally lively and my liveliness was carrying me away, as I was ignorant of the art of beating about the bush and put no check on my thoughts beyond a bit of clumsy restraint (which diminished every moment because I was getting away with it), I blurted out astonishing expressions of affection with an enthusiasm, an ardour that at least suggested I was speaking the truth, and that kind of truth is always acceptable, even from people you don't like.

Our conversation absorbed us both so completely that it made her forget the accommodation she wanted to rent.

But finally we were obliged to stop because the street was so crowded, and I noticed that Mlle Habert's eyes were much gayer than usual.

During this hold-up she also saw a notice-board. 'I rather like this district,' she said (it was near Saint-Gervais). 'Here is a house with rooms to let. We'll go and see what it's like.' So we went in and asked to see the vacant flat.

The owner of the house lived on the premises and came out to us.

She was the widow of an attorney who had left her comfortably off, and she lived up to her income. An attractive woman, moreover, about Mlle Habert's age, as well preserved but stouter. A bit of a gossip, but a good-hearted one, who took to you at once and opened her heart to you, told you all her business, asked you yours, then came back to hers, then to yours again. Told you about her daughter, for she had one, told you she was eighteen and all about her childhood troubles and ailments, then went on to the subject of her late husband and the story of the time when he was a bachelor, then came to their courting days, mentioning how long they had lasted, whence to their marriage and the story of their life together. The best man in the world! Tied to his legal practice, which is why he had made money by dint of carefulness and economy; a little jealous by nature and also because he was so devoted to her; subject to the gravel. The Lord knows what he went through! The care she took of him! Anyway, he made a Christian end. This was said while dabbing her eyes, which were genuinely watering, but because the sadness of the tale required it and not because of the thing itself; for from there she went on to a domestic accident which had to be told with a laugh, so she laughed.

All I have had to do to paint that portrait is to remember all the speeches of the good widow who, after we had viewed the apartment in question and pending an agreement on the rent, about which there was some discussion, took us into a room where her daughter was, made us sit down in a friendly way, sat opposite us and there overwhelmed us, so to speak, with the deluge of confidences and stories I here report.

Her chatter got very much on my nerves, but in spite of it I liked her character, because she gave the impression that the only reason why she jabbered so much was that she had the innocent weakness of loving talk and what you might call a loquacious kindness of heart.

She offered us some refreshments and had them sent in although we declined, made us eat although we didn't want anything, and said she wouldn't let us go until we were agreed. I say we, for you will remember that I was wearing a plain suit without any braid that our squire's wife had had made for me, and in this outfit, which suited me very well, and with my kind of looks, I could be taken either for a shop assistant or for some relation of Mlle Habert. And the simple but elegant way she too was dressed entitled people to do me this honour, especially as during the conversation she often turned to me in a friendly and familiar way, and I adjusted my manner to this pattern as though she had instructed me to do so.

She had her reasons for behaving in this way, which I had not yet grasped, but without worrying myself about it I took the hint and was delighted at her way of acting.

The session lasted a good two hours, partly through Mlle Habert's fault, for she was not averse to rambling talk and did not mind wasting time over it. We must come to terms with what we are: every woman is a chatterbox or takes pleasure in the chatter of others, and love of talk is a tribute she pays to her own sex. Of course silent women do exist, but I don't think that is in their character; it is experience or training that have taught them to be so.

At last Mlle Habert remembered that we had some way to go to get back, so she rose.

We went on talking standing up for quite a long time, after which she moved towards the door, where another halt was called, and that really did end the conversation, in the course of which Mlle Habert, made much of and flattered about her mild, modest appearance, about the impression her moral and Christian qualities and nice character had created, concluded the agreement about the apartment.

It was settled that she would move in three days later, and no questions were asked about who with, or about how many people would wait on her: this question was forgotten amidst the number of things said. Which was just as well, for it will be seen later that Mlle Habert would have been very hard put to it had she had to give an immediate answer about that.

So we were on our way home, and I pass over lots of other things Mlle Habert and I said. We discussed the landlady in whose house we were to lodge.

'I like that woman,' she said, 'and I think we shall be comfortable and I wish we were there already. The only thing left is to find a cook, for frankly, Jacob, I don't want any truck with Catherine. She is surly and awkward, and would be in constant communication with my sister who is inquisitive by nature as in any case all religious women are!' They make up for the sins they don't commit with the pleasure they get from knowing all about the sins of others, at least they get that out of it. This reflection is mine and not Mlle Habert's, who went on, still referring to her sister: 'As we are separating, it must be without any going back on it; it is over and done with. But you can't cook, and even if you could I don't intend to employ you for that.'

'You can employ me for whatever you like,' I said, 'but as we are on the subject, are you thinking of any other job for me?'

'This is not the place to tell you what I am thinking, but meanwhile you must have noticed that I said nothing at our landlady's that could have indicated that you were a domestic, neither will she have gathered from your clothes that you are one, and so I suggest that when we go to live at her house you take your cue from me. Don't ask me any more about it today, that is all the information I can give you at present.'

'May Heaven bless whatever intentions you have,' I answered, delighted at this little speech, which I took to be a good omen. 'But if you don't mind, Mademoiselle, we must settle one other thing. People may question me about myself and say: "Who are you?

Who are you *not*?" Now, from your point of view, who do you wish me to be? You are turning me into a gentleman, but who is this gentleman? Monsieur Jacob? Does that sound all right? Jacob is my first name, and that name is well and good, and we can only leave it as it is, and not change it for something else that wouldn't be any better, so I'll stick to that. But I need another. They call my Dad old La Vallée, and I will be Monsieur de la Vallée, if that suits you.'

'You are right,' she laughed, 'you're right, Monsieur de la Vallée, use that name.' 'But still that is not all,' I went on. 'Suppose someone says to me: "Monsieur de la Vallée, what do you do for Mlle Habert?" What answer must I give?'

'Well,' she answered, 'that's not very difficult. I shall not leave things undecided for long, and in the apartment I have just taken there is a room well away from where I shall be, and there you will be on your own at a respectable distance, as a relation living with me and helping me in my business affairs. However, as I say, we shall soon put ourselves on a quite secure footing as far as that matter is concerned. I only need a few days to decide what I am thinking over, and must be quick because circumstances won't let me put it off. Don't say anything at my sister's house, and carry on normally during the short time we shall be there. Go back tomorrow to our landlady, she seems very obliging, and ask her to be so kind as to find me a cook, and if she asks you questions about yourself answer as we have said – take the name of La Vallée and be a relation of mine. You look nice enough for that.'

'Golly, all this wangling pleases me no end!' I said. 'What joy is coursing through my heart, I don't know why. So I am to be your cousin? And yet, cousin, if I were in a position to claim the status I would wish, it's not your relation I should like to be, no, I should have a bigger appetite than that. To be related is nevertheless a very great honour for me, but sometimes honour and pleasure go hand in hand, don't they?'

As I was saying this we were getting near home, and I at once realized that she was slowing down so as to have time to answer and make me explain what I meant.

'I don't quite follow you, Monsieur de la Vallée,' she said good-humouredly, 'I don't know what this status is that you would like.'

'Hang it all, cousin,' I said, 'I can't go any further, and it is not in my nature to be disrespectful towards you, relation though you be, but supposing some day you felt the desire to take a companion to live with you, say one of those chaps who are not sent off to a separate room but make so bold as to sleep side by side with people, what do you call the profession of such people? In my home village they are called husbands, is it the same here? Well, would the chap who has that status, which you will have also, want to exchange it for that of relation, which I have, thanks to you? Answer me honestly. That is my riddle, guess the answer.'

'I'll tell you the answer another time,' she said, turning towards me with a kindly expression, 'but it is a pretty riddle you have there.' 'Oh yes, cousin, something good could be made out of it if we wanted to come to an understanding.' 'That'll do,' she said, 'this is not the moment for teasing like this.' And just as she stopped me, we were at our front door. It was beginning to get dark.

Catherine came out to meet us, still very concerned about what Mlle Habert intended to do about her.

I will not go into the eager way she fussed about us or the distaste she said she felt for working for the elder sister. And that distaste was genuine, because the withdrawal of the younger one would leave her alone with the other. But it was also true that while they had been together Dame Catherine had only ever been obliging to the elder, whose bossy, interfering nature intimidated her more, and who had in any case always run the house.

But the ending of the association between the two sisters altered the case altogether, and it was much more attractive to transfer to the service of the younger one, whom she could have bossed in her turn.

Catherine told us that the elder sister had gone out, and was going to sleep at the home of one of her church-going friends for fear that God might be offended if the two sisters saw each other in the present situation. 'And good riddance,' said Catherine, 'we shall enjoy our supper all the more, shan't we, Mademoiselle?' 'Certainly,' answered Mlle Habert; 'my sister has acted prudently, and she is mistress of her own actions just as I am of mine.'

There then followed several little questions from the ingratiating cook. 'But you have taken a long time to come home. Have you taken a house? Is it in a nice neighbourhood? Far from here? Shall we be near the markets? Is the kitchen convenient? Shall I have a room of my own?'

She had a few laconic answers to begin with and I came in also for some of her cajoleries, which I answered with my usual high spirits, without telling her any more than Mlle Habert, from whom I took my cue.

'We'll discuss all that another time, Catherine,' she said, so as to cut it short. 'I am too tired now, give me supper early so that I can go to bed.'

And she went up to her room, and I went to lay the table so as to get away from the relentless questionings of Catherine, by whom I felt sure I was going to be pestered as soon as we were together.

I took a long time over my job. Mlle Habert had come back into the room where I was laying the table, and I joked with her about Catherine's uneasiness. 'If we took her with us,' I said, 'we should have to give up being related, and there would be no more Monsieur de la Vallée.'

I amused her with this kind of talk while she drew up a little inventory of furniture belonging to her that she would be taking away from her sister's house, for owing to the estrangement the latter showed by staying away from the house, she intended if possible to sleep the following night in her new home.

'Monsieur de la Vallée,' she said (using the name for fun), 'go as early as you can in the morning and find a moving man to strip my sitting room and bedroom, and tell him to have enough vans to take all my things. One day will do for moving everything if they look sharp about it.' 'I am so anxious to drink there with you that I wish it were done already,' I said, 'for when we get there my place will be laid opposite yours, since a relation takes his meals with a lady relation. So rest assured that everything will be gone by seven in the morning.'

What was arranged was carried out. Mlle Habert had her supper. Now that I had become bolder with her I invited her to drink the last wine I poured out to the health of her cousin, at a moment when Catherine, who came up and down to serve, was down in the kitchen.

The cousin's health was drunk and he at once responded, for as soon as she had emptied her cup (and it was a cup) I filled it to the brim with neat wine and said: 'Your health, cousin!' After which I went downstairs to have my own supper.

I ate well, but hardly chewed at all so as to get it over quicker, preferring the risk of indigestion to staying a long time with Catherine, whose restless curiosity got very much on my nerves. So, with the excuse that I had to get up early next morning I retired, leaving her dazed and depressed at all she saw going on as well as at the haste with which I had got my things together, only answering her in monosyllables.

'But Jacob, tell me this, tell me that ...' 'Look here, Dame Catherine, Mlle Habert has taken a house, I gave her my arm along the streets, we went there and we have come back, and that's all I know, good-night.' Oh, how she would have loved to give me a piece of her mind! But she still had hopes, and the spiteful woman dared not kick up a fuss.

I am anxious to get to more important things, so let us pass at once to our new home.

The moving man came in the morning, our furniture went off, we ate something standing up, postponing a better and more comfortable meal until supper-time in our new lodging. Catherine, sure at last that she was not to go with us, gave us treatment on a par with our indifference to her, which we deserved by the total ruin of her life that we were the cause of. She challenged Mlle Habert's ownership of all sorts of clothes and maintained that they belonged to her elder sister, picked all sorts of quarrels with her and tried to hit me – and I'm supposed to look like the late Baptiste she told me she loved so much! Mlle Habert wrote a short note which she left on the table for her sister, in which she gave notice that in seven or eight days' time she would come to make some business arrangements and settle various little affairs they must deal with jointly. A cab came for us, my cousin and I packed ourselves in without ceremony and then – gee-up, driver!

So here we were at the other house, and from this point you will see my adventures getting more illustrious and more grandiose. From this point my real fortune begins: good-bye to the name of Jacob, henceforth it will be only M. de la Vallée, the name I bore for some time, and which really was my father's name. But to that another name was joined later so as to distinguish me from one of his brothers, and this is the name by which I am now known in society, which it is not necessary to mention here and which I only assumed after the death of Mlle Habert. Not that I was dissatisfied with the other, but the people in my own part of the world insisted on only using that one. Let us get on to the new home.

Our hostess welcomed us like her most intimate friends. The room which was to be Mlle Habert's bedroom was already straight, and I had a little camp bed made up in the room set aside for me which I have already mentioned.

It only remained to get something for supper, and the cook-shop next door would have provided what we needed, but our obliging hostess, whom I had warned that we should arrive the same evening, had catered for it and insisted that we should have a meal with her.

She did us proud, and our appetite did honour to the food.

Mlle Habert began by making it clear that I was her cousin, and I took this up by calling her cousin but, as I still had a bit of a country accent and some rustic expressions, that was explained away by saying that I had only recently come up from the country and had only been in Paris two or three months.

Until then I had always had a bit of a brogue, but for over a month I had been correcting myself pretty well so long as I was careful what I was saying, and I had only kept this brogue with Mlle Habert because it went down well with her, and because under the cloak of this rustic speech I had said anything I wanted. But of course I spoke better French when I liked. I had already acquired enough knowledge of the world for that, and I thought I ought to apply myself now to speaking better still.

Our meal was the merriest imaginable, and I was merrier than anybody.

My situation looked very pleasant to me; there was every appearance that Mlle Habert loved me, she was still quite attractive and rich compared with me, enjoying quite four thousand *livres* a year or more, and I saw a smiling future quite near, which was naturally bound to appeal to the heart of a peasant of my age who could leap almost straight from the plough to the honourable rank of a respected citizen of Paris. In a word, I was on the eve of having my own house fronting the street, and an income to live on, cherished by a wife I was not averse to and to whom at any rate my heart paid a debt of gratitude which so closely resembled love that I didn't bother to examine the difference.

I had a natural talent for fun, as can be seen in the stories I have told about my life, and when this naturally fun-loving temperament is reinforced by new reasons for gaiety, Lord knows how one can shine! And I did. Add to that some mental agility, for I was not without that, and season the whole with a good-looking face, and with all those advantages hasn't one got something to give pleasure at table? Doesn't one deserve one's place there?

I obviously did, for our hostess loved gaiety (she was, it is true, better at enjoying it when she found it than at giving rise to it herself, for her conversation was too rambling to be witty, and at table you need wit and not long stories).

Well, then, our hostess didn't know how to compliment me suitably on the pleasure my company gave her, she alleged, and looked at me with quite undisguised affection. I was winning her heart, and she said so straightforwardly and openly.

Her daughter who, as I have said, was sixteen or seventeen, I don't quite remember which, and whose heart was more discreet and cunning, gave me sidelong looks and, putting on an outward appearance which was crafty rather than modest, betrayed only half the interest she felt in what I was saying.

Mlle Habert, on the other hand, seemed overwhelmed at the brilliance I was displaying. I saw from her face that she had thought I was witty, but not to the extent that I actually was.

I noticed at the same time that she grew in respect and fondness for me, but that this was not without some misgivings.

The eulogies from our simple-hearted hostess upset her, and the sly, knowing glances the girl gave me did not escape her notice. When you are in love your eye misses nothing, and her soul was torn between worry at seeing me so much admired and satisfaction at seeing that I was so charming.

I was well aware of this, and this art of reading into people's minds and finding out their secret feelings is a gift I have always had and which has sometimes stood me in good stead.

I was delighted at first to see Mlle Habert in this frame of mind; it was a good omen for my hopes and confirmed in my mind that she was fond of me and would expedite her kindly intentions, especially as the looks cast by the young person and the nice things her mother was saying were, so to speak, putting me up for auction.

So I redoubled my fascination to my full capacity so as to keep Mlle Habert in the state of alarm into which it threw her. But as the vital thing was that she should be afraid of other people's feelings for me and not of any such feeling she might sense in me for either of these two persons, I contrived not to appear guilty of anything. She could see that I had no other object than to amuse myself and not charm others, in fact that if I was attractive I was only anxious to benefit from it in her affections and not in those of either of these two women.

By way of proof I took care to look at her very often with eyes begging for her approval of everything I said, and in this way I brought off the feat of keeping her pleased with me, leaving her with some anxieties that might be useful to me, and at the same time still pleasing our two hostesses, whom I also managed to convince that they attracted me, so as to inspire them to charm me in their turn and keep them in this friendly mood, which I needed in order to impel Mlle Habert to make herself clear. And to be perfectly truthful I may also have wanted to see what the outcome of this adventure would be and turn everything to good account. It is as well, as they say, to have more than one string to your bow.

But there is one thing I was forgetting, and that is the portrait of the girl, and I must give it now.

I have mentioned her age. Agathe, that was her name, having been given a good schooling, was much cleverer than her mother, whose outpourings and simple-minded chattering struck her as silly. I realized this from certain malicious little smiles she gave occasionally, the meaning of which escaped the mother, who was too good-natured and artless to be so intelligent.

Agathe was no beauty, but her features were quite refined, with keen, passionate eyes, but the little hussy kept the passion under control and only let it be seen very cautiously. All of this gave her a face which was striking and intelligent but also mischievous, and which you began mistrusting because of this vague element of slyness which overlaid all the rest and made her untrustworthy.

You could see at a glance that Agathe was not averse to love, and could sense that she was more disposed to be amorous than tender, hypocritical rather than virtuous, more concerned with what people might say about her than with what she really was, which was the most barefaced liar I have ever met. I have never seen her unable to wriggle her way out; you might have thought her timid, but there was never anyone more firm and resolute, no one less likely to lose her head. Nobody cared less at heart about having committed a misdeed of any kind, but at the same time nobody took greater pains to cover it up or excuse it, nobody was less afraid of reprimands if they could not be avoided. You were, in fact, talking to a guilty party who was so unmoved that the offence itself ceased to appear of any importance.

I did not immediately grasp all this character I am developing here, but only realized it as I watched Agathe.

It is certain that she found me just as much to her liking as her mother did, and she liked me very much and was a simple soul whose affection one could trade on quite a lot. So on both sides I could see quite a promising prospect opening out for my gallantries if I wanted to put them to the test.

But Mlle Habert was a much better proposition; she was answerable to nobody for what she did and her intentions, if favourable to me, were subject to nobody's contradiction. And besides, I did owe her some gratitude, and that is a debt I have always made a point of repaying.

So, in spite of the favour I acquired straight away in the household and all the evidence that I should be in a position to make an effect, I resolved to stick to the heart nearest at hand which was also the freest agent.

It was midnight by the time we rose from table. We took Mlle Habert to her room, and more than ten times during the short time it took Agathe seized a chance to make eyes at me in a most flattering and always sly way, to which I couldn't help responding, and all this was done so rapidly on both sides that we were the only ones who could see these flashes of lightning.

On my side, I think, I only played up to Agathe so as not to wound her pride, for it is hard to be cruel to beautiful eyes trying to catch yours.

Her mother had taken my arm and never tired of saying: 'You really are a nice boy, we shan't have a dull moment with you here.'

'I have never seen him so saucy,' said my cousin in a tone meaning: 'You are too much so.'

'Well, ladies,' I said, 'I'm always like that by nature, but with good wine, good food and good company you get more so than usual. Isn't that so, cousin?' I added, squeezing her arm, which I was holding also.

While talking like this we reached Mlle Habert's apartment.

'I think I shall sleep well,' she said when we got there, putting on a weariness which she did not feel in order to persuade our hostess to take her leave.

But our hostess was not expeditious in her politenesses, and in the superabundance of her friendliness towards us she did not fail to point out a single one of the little comforts in those rooms.

Next she proposed taking me to my room, but I saw from my cousin's face that this excessive civility was not to her liking, and I declined as politely as I could.

At last our lady friends departed, put to flight by Mlle Habert's yawns, which in the end were quite genuine, probably as a result of having done so many artificial ones.

And I was taking leave of our hostesses in order to retire respectably to my own quarters when my cousin called me back.

'Oh, Monsieur de la Vallée,' she called, 'just a moment, there is something I want you to do tomorrow.' So I went back, bidding mother and daughter good night and being honoured in my own right by their civilities, especially those of Agathe, who kept hers very distinct from her mother's, and did so aside, so that I could see them clearly and take note of everything she put into them in the way of expressions of esteem for me.

When I was back with Mlle Habert and we were alone, I assumed that there would be some petulant allusion to our adventures at table and to the advantages for myself of seeming so amusing.

But I was wrong, though not about her intentions, for what she said showed that that matter was merely postponed.

'Well, my cheerful cousin,' she said, 'I want to talk to you, but it is too late and an unsuitable time, so let us put our conversation off until tomorrow. I shall get up earlier than usual to put away things still in these bags, and I shall expect you in my room between eight and nine so that we can decide what steps we should take about all kinds of things I have in mind, you understand. Don't be late, for our hostess looks certain to come tomorrow to inquire about my health and probably yours as well, and we shouldn't have time to talk if we didn't forestall the fury of her polite attentions.'

This little speech, as you will observe, was a prelude of a jealous or at least of a worried nature, so I didn't for one moment doubt what the subject of the next day's conversation would be.

I kept the appointment punctually, and was even a little earlier than she had said, in order to show an impatience that could not fail to please her, and indeed I noticed that she was gratified.

'Ah, that's good, you are punctual, Monsieur de la Vallée. You haven't yet seen either of our hostesses since you got up?' 'Good gracious,' I said, 'I didn't even wonder whether they existed; what have we got to do with one another? Good Lord, I had something else to think about!'

'Oh, what was that, then?' 'Our meeting,' I said, 'and that has been on my mind all night.'

'It hasn't been far from mine either,' she said, 'for what I have to say to you is important for me, La Vallée.' 'Oh goodness, my dear cousin, please be quick, you are making me ill with anxiety. As it's something to do with yourself I can't go on without knowing. Is something giving you trouble? Is there a remedy? Or isn't there? I shall go dotty if you don't say something soon.'

'Don't worry, it's nothing upsetting.' 'Good Lord,' I answered, 'you must realize that where you are concerned my heart is as silly as a child's, and it's not my fault. Why have you been so good to me? I couldn't hold out against that.' 'But, my boy,' she said, giving me a searching look which entreated me to be truthful, 'aren't you exaggerating your attachment to me, and are you saying what you really think? Can I believe you?'

'What!' I answered, recoiling a step. 'Do you doubt me,

Mademoiselle? When I would hazard my life, and a hundred others as well if I had them, to secure a long and happy one for you, can you doubt me? Alas, there will be no joy left in me, for all I have is my poor heart, and if you don't understand my heart I might as well have nothing left, it's all over. If, after all the graciousness I have received from a mistress who has freely accepted me as a relation, you then say: Do you love me, cousin? and I say: Yes, of course I do, cousin; and then you reply: Perhaps you don't, cousin; that means that your relative is worse than a bear, and no beast of the forest is as bad or so unnatural. Isn't that a fine jewel you have added to your family? So, God forgive you, Mademoiselle, for that's the end of cousin – I should be too ashamed to use that name after the barbarous thoughts you think I harbour in my soul – Mademoiselle, I would rather I had never seen you or become aware of you than hear myself accused like this by a person who has been the object of the first affection I have ever had in my heart except for my father and mother; and I don't count that because it is a tie of blood, and the feeling you have for them doesn't take away the share of others. But I had one great consolation, which was believing that you knew my innermost thoughts. Heaven help me, and you too. Oh dear, far from being cheerful, look how miserable I am!'

I clearly remember that while I was talking in this way I was not conscious of anything in me that was inconsistent with what I was saying. But I admit that I did try to look and sound touching, to sound like a man in tears, and that I did want to embellish the truth a little, and the singular thing is that I was the first to be won over by my own intentions. I did it so well that I myself was taken in, and only had to let myself go without bothering to add anything to what I felt. The whole thing was taken over by the emotion which possessed me, and which is cleverer than all the art in the world.

And of course I brought the thing off; I convinced and persuaded Mlle Habert so well that she believed me to the point of weeping with pity, consoling me for the grief I was displaying, and even asking forgiveness for doubting me.

I did not recover immediately, but went on being miserable for a little longer. My feelings directed me in that way, and they did well, for when we are once embarked on reproaching people, especially about their affections, the reproaches always have a certain duration, and we go on a bit longer even after forgiving them. It is like a momentum given to something; it doesn't stop all of a sudden, but dies down and then stops.

So my tender reproaches came to an end, and I gave in to all the obliging things she said to appease me.

Nothing touches both sides so much as scenes of that kind, especially in the early stages of a love affair: this helps love on prodigiously, and no discretion in the heart can hold out against it, such scenes say in a quarter of an hour what, said with decorum, could only have been said in a month, and they say it without seeming to go too fast, for everything is blurted out.

Anyhow, that is what happened to Mlle Habert. I am sure that she had not intended to go as far as she did, and would only have told me of my good fortune after many attempts, but she was not in a position to exercise this control; her heart overflowed and I had the benefit of everything it was meditating for me. And perhaps on her side she drew from mine more tenderness than it really had to give her, for I myself was astonished to find I loved her so much, and I lost nothing by it, as you are about to see from the rest of our conversation, which I must report because it is the one in which Mlle Habert makes her intentions clear.

'Dear boy,' she said, after repeating a score of times: Yes, I believe you, that is settled, 'my dear boy, I think that by now you can perceive what the state of things is.' 'Alas, my gracious kinswoman, I think I can descry something, but fear of being mistaken makes my sight dim, and the things I see embarrass me because of my unworthiness. Could it be possible, God forgive me, that my person might not be displeasing to you? Could happiness like that befall a poor fellow just up from his village? For this is what it looks like, and if I were really sure I think I should die of joy.'

'Yes, Jacob, as you understand my meaning and it gives you so much pleasure, rejoice about it in perfect confidence.'

'Gently,' I said, 'or I shall faint with joy!' But I added: 'There is only one consideration nagging at me over all this.' 'Oh, what is that?' 'It is that you will say: You have nothing, neither income nor savings, no rent coming in but everything to buy, nothing to sell, no other home than somebody else's house or the street, not even enough bread to last to the end of the month, and after that, my little gentleman, aren't you rather tired of rejoicing so much in my love? Shan't I also have to thank you for the trouble you're taking to be so delighted! That, dear cousin, is what you are entitled to reply to the happiness I am showing because of your affection. But God knows, cousin, it is not for love of all those worldly goods that my heart is overjoyed.'

'I am sure it isn't,' she said, 'and you wouldn't think about reassuring me about that if it were not true, my dear boy.'

'Believe me, cousin,' I said, 'I am no more thinking about bread, wine or a home than if there were no such things as grain, vines or houses in the world. However, I will take them if they come, but only because they are to hand. As for money, I no more think of that than of the Grand Mogul. My heart is not to be bought and sold, and nobody would get it if I was offered a thousand crowns more than it is worth, yet they can have it for nothing when it feels like it. And that is what it has done in your case without asking for anything in return. Whether this heart appeals to you or the reverse, no matter, it has taken the plunge and it is yours. All the same, I admit that you can do me a great deal of good, since you have the wherewithal. But I wasn't thinking about that sort of calculation when I fell a victim to your good qualities, your pretty face and charming ways. In fact I no more expected your friendship than to see Saturday come on a Sunday. My love was born on the Pont-Neuf, and it grew in strength and stature between there and your house, where it reached its perfection, and two hours after that nothing needed to be added. That is the true story.'

'What!' she said. 'If you had been richer and in a position to say: I love you, Mademoiselle, would you have said so, Jacob?'

'Who, I? Good gracious, I would have told you so before opening my mouth, just as I really did, if you'll excuse my saying so. And if I had been worthy of your looking at me with your eyes wide open, you would certainly have noticed that my eyes were saying words that I dared not pronounce. They never have looked at you without saying the same things I am saying now; always

I love you, and what else? I love you, those were the only words I had in my eyes.' 'Very well, my dear,' she said, fetching a sigh of deep tenderness, 'you have opened your heart to me, I must open mine to you.

'When you met me, my sister's trying temperament had already for a long time discouraged me from waiting to have much to do with her. On the other hand I didn't know what line to take or what sort of life I should aim at if I left her. Sometimes I thought I should like to go somewhere as a paying guest, but that way of life has its unpleasantnesses, and most often you have to defer to what others want to do, and that put me off. I sometimes thought of marriage: I am not yet too old for it, I thought, and I can bring quite a tidy sum to the man who marries me, and if I meet a worthy man with an equable temper and good character my peace is assured for the rest of my days. But where to find this good man? I saw plenty of men who threw out hints so as to attract me. Some were well off, but they didn't appeal to me, others in a profession I didn't like. I found out that others lived disreputable lives; one was fond of his glass, another of gambling and yet another of women, for so few people in this world live in the fear of God, and so few marry in order to fulfil the duties of that state! Of those who hadn't these drawbacks, one was silly, another miserable and moody, and I wanted someone blithe and gay, with a kind, tender heart that would respond to the affection I felt for him. I was not concerned with his being rich or poor, or whether he held some rank or not. I was not fussy, either, about family origins as long as they were respectable, that is to say as long as they were merely obscure and not too low or contemptible. And I had reasons for not thinking too grandly along those lines, for I myself was only born of honourable but quite unknown parents. So I was waiting for Providence, in whose hands I left everything, to lead me to the man I was seeking, and it was at that time that I met you on the Pont-Neuf.'

I broke in at this juncture:

'I mean to buy a notebook and write down the year, day, hour and moment, together with the month and the week and what the weather was like on the day of that blessed meeting.'

'It has been bought already, my dear boy,' she said, 'and I will give it to you. But let me finish.

'I was very weak when we met, and I must say you helped me without a moment's hesitation.

'When, thanks to your help, I came round, I looked at you very carefully and you seemed to have such an attractive face.'

'Thanks be to God for giving it to me,' I cried at those words. 'Yes,' she said, 'you appealed to me at once, and the feeling I had for you seemed so sudden and so natural that I couldn't help wondering about it. What can this mean, I said, I feel as if I were constrained to love this young man. At once I put myself into the hands of God who disposes of all things, and prayed that He would thereafter reveal to me His holy will about a happening that astonished even me.' 'Well, cousin,' I said, 'that day our prayers went up at the same time, for while you were saying yours I was quietly saying my own too. Oh God, I was saying, you have led Jacob on to this Pont-Neuf, oh God, how merciful you would be to me if you put it into the head of this good lady to keep me all her life, or only all mine, in the joy of serving her!'

'Is it possible that this idea came to you, my dearest boy?'

'Yes, it really did,' I said, 'and I didn't feel it coming, I found it there already.'

'How very strange,' she went on. 'Anyway, you helped me back home, and on the way we talked about your circumstances. I asked you a lot of questions, and I can't say how delighted I was at your answers and the good character you displayed. I could see in you a simplicity and openness that charmed me, and always I came back to this liking I couldn't help feeling for you. I never ceased asking God to deign to enlighten me and show me what He wanted to happen. If His will is that I marry this young fellow, I said, something will happen to prove it while he is at our house.

'And I reasoned rightly; God did not leave me in uncertainty for long. That same day our friend the priest came to see us, and I have already told you about the quarrel we had.'

'Oh, cousin, what a fortunate quarrel!' I exclaimed. 'And how well that worthy director acted in being so awkward! How everything works out for the best! A street where we meet, a prayer on one side and a supplication on the other, a priest happening to come and reprimand you, your sister discharging me and your saying don't go! A difference between two sisters over a young man sent by God – how wonderful it all is! And then you ask whether I love you? Oh, but how could it be otherwise? Don't you see that my love has come through divine prophecy and that all was decided before we existed? Nothing is clearer.'

'Yes indeed, you put it admirably,' she said, 'and it seems that God is giving you the means of finally convincing me. So, my dear boy, I am quite sure that God means me to marry. You are the man I was seeking, with whom I am to live, and I will give myself to you.'

'And I feel very humble before this blessed gift,' I said, 'this hallowed marriage for which I am all unworthy, except that it is God who is commanding you, and you are too good a Christian to go against His commandment. All the benefit is mine and all the charity yours.'

I had fallen to my knees to say this, and I kissed her hand, which she piously felt called up to abandon to my transports.

'Rise, La Vallée, yes, yes, I will marry you, and as one cannot be too prompt in entering on a state ordained by Providence, and as, moreover, in spite of our ostensible family relationship it might appear unseemly to be seen living under the same roof, we must hurry on our marriage.'

'It is quite early,' I answered, 'and with some rushing round and coming and going for the rest of the day couldn't we arrange with the notary and priest for us to have the blessing after midnight? I don't quite know how it is done.'

'No, my dear, things can't go as fast as that. You must write first and ask your father's consent.'

'Oh well, my father's not averse at all. He would consent even if he were dead, for he would be so pleased at what has befallen me.'

'I'm sure he would, but begin by writing your letter this morning. We shall need witnesses, and I want them to be discreet, for my plan is to keep our marriage dark at first because of my sister, and I don't know whom to ask.'

'Let's have our hostess,' I said, 'and some friends of hers. She is a kind soul and she won't say a word.'

'Yes, I agree,' she said, 'particularly as that will put an end to all these little familiarities she showed you yesterday, and might go on doing; like her daughter, who is a badly brought up little baggage, it seemed to me, whom I trust you will cold-shoulder.'

We had reached that point when we heard a noise. It was our hostess, escorted by her cook bearing coffee.

'Are you up, neighbour?' she shouted outside the door. 'Yes, I have been for a long time,' said Mlle Habert, opening it, 'come in, Madame.' 'Oh, good morning,' said she. 'How are you? Have you had a good night? M. de la Vallée, how are you?' I pass over all the compliments and conversation while we were having coffee.

When the cook had gone off with the cups: 'Madame,' said Mlle Habert, 'you seem the nicest person in the world, and I want to take you into my confidence about something in which I actually need your help.' 'Oh, of course, my dear lady, what service can I render?' answered our hostess with an outpouring of genuine zeal and kindness. 'Tell me . . . but no, wait while I go and shut the doors. If it's a secret we don't want anybody to overhear us.'

So saying she rose and went out, and then from the top of the stairs called down to the cook. 'Javote!' she shouted. 'If anybody comes for me say I've gone out, and stop anybody from coming up to Mademoiselle's, and especially see that my daughter doesn't come in here because we have something to discuss in secret, you understand.' After which measures so discreetly taken against intruders, back she came, shutting and bolting doors so that, out of respect for the secret we were going to confide in her, she began by announcing to the whole building that one was about to be confided – that was the very best her zeal and kindness could think of, and that is typical of the best people in the world. These overkind souls are apt to be imprudent through their very excess of kindness, whereas prudent souls are seldom kind.

'Oh Madame,' said Mlle Habert, 'there was no need to tell your cook that we had something to discuss in secret. I didn't want people to know that I had anything to confide in you.'

'Oh, never mind,' she said, 'don't be upset. If I hadn't given a warning somebody would have come and interrupted, and even if it were only my daughter it was a necessary precaution. Now, Mademoiselle, tell us what it's all about. I defy you to find anybody more devoted to your interests than me, and besides, I am entrusted with the secrets of everyone who knows me. When somebody tells me a secret my lips are sewn up, you know, I have lost the power of speech. Only yesterday Mme So-and-so, whose husband squanders every penny, brought me a thousand francs and asked me to hide it, for he would spend that as well if he knew. But I am keeping it for her. Well now, tell me.'

All these proofs of our hostess's discretion were no encouragement to Mlle Habert, but once having promised her a secret it was probably still worse to withhold it than to tell her, so she had to speak.

'It will only take a couple of words. M. de la Vallée and I are going to be married.' 'To each other!' cried the hostess, looking surprised. 'Yes,' said Mlle Habert, 'I am marrying him.'

'Oh, oh! Well, well! He's young and he'll last a long time. I wish I could find one like him, and I'd do the same. Have you been in love with each other a long time?' 'No,' said Mlle Habert, with a blush. 'Ah well, that's better still, my dears, you are quite right. For making love there's nothing like being husband and wife. But have you got your dispensation? For you are cousins.'

'We don't need it,' I broke in, 'we were only related out of prudence and for fear of what people might say.'

'Oh, ah, how funny!' she said. 'But honestly, you are telling me things I should never have guessed. So you are inviting me to your wedding?'

'That's not all,' said Mlle Habert. 'We want to keep our marriage secret because of my sister, who might make a fuss.'

'Oh, why should she? Because of your age?' went on our hostess. 'Well really, that's a fine reason! Last week wasn't there a woman of at least seventy who got engaged in our parish to a young fellow of twenty. Age is nothing to do with it except for those who are old, it's their own business!'

'I am not all that old,' said Mlle Habert with the slightly piqued air she had had all along. 'Oh, Lord bless you, no,' said the hostess, 'you are of an age to marry, now or never. After all, you love the one you love, and if it happens that your intended is young, all right, you take him young. If he's only twenty, that's not your fault any more than it's his. All the better that he should be young, my dear, and he will have youth for you both. Ten years more or less, even twenty, even thirty, that leaves another forty on top of that, and one of you doesn't offend God any more than the other. What would you like me to say? That you could be his mother? Well, the consolation for that is that he could be your son. If you had one of your own he might not be as handsome and he would already have cost you much more. Don't you take any notice of tittle-tattle, and finish telling me your story.

'So you want to keep your marriage secret, do you? Well, that will be quite easy because there's no fear of a baby, so you are safe, and that's the only thing that might give you away – so what?'

'If you spin out your reflections as long as that over each point,' said Mlle Habert, now exasperated by this talk, 'I shan't have time to explain things. As regards age, Madame, I am glad to tell you that I have no reason to fear gossip, and that at forty-five . . .'

'Forty-five!' the other cut in. 'Oh, but that's nothing at all, only twenty-five years older than him. Why, bless you, I thought you were fifty at least – it's his face that took me in compared with yours. Only forty-five, my dear! Oh, your son may well be able to give you another one. Just opposite us there is a lady who had a baby last month at forty-four, and isn't giving up at forty-five, and what's more her husband is over seventy-two. Oh, it'll be all right, with you so attractive and him so young there'll be a family. Oh, by the way, is it a notary for the contract you would like me to find for you? I'll take you straight to my own, I'll go and tell Javote to ask him to step round.'

'Oh no, Madame,' said Mlle Habert, 'don't you remember that I want to keep my marriage secret?' 'Oh yes, of course,' was the answer, 'so we'll go and find him in secret. And by the way, what about banns now?' 'It's about all that,' I said, 'that Mlle Habert wanted you to help her, possibly about witnesses or to speak to the parish clergy.'

'Just leave it to me,' she said. 'The day after tomorrow is Sunday and the banns must be published; we'll go out in a minute and arrange everything. I know a priest who will do the job quickly, don't you worry, I'll see him this morning. I'll get dressed. So long, my dear. At forty-five, afraid people will gossip about a marriage? Oh, don't you believe it. Good-bye, good-bye, my dear, at your service, Monsieur de la Vallée. Oh, by the way, you said something yesterday about a cook, you will have one in no time, Javote told me so, she went this morning and told her to come, someone she knows, they both come from the same part of the world, they are from Champagne, and so am I, that's three already, and with you it will make four, you do come from Champagne, don't you?' she laughed. 'No, I do,' I said, 'you have made a mistake, Madame.'

'Oh yes, I knew one of you came from there, never mind which. Good-bye, see you again soon.'

'What a silly woman!' said Mlle Habert after she had gone. 'What with age, and mother, and son, I'm sorry I told her our business. Jacob, if I'm as old in your eyes as I am in hers, I don't advise you to marry me.'

'Oh, but don't you see,' I said, 'that it is a bit out of jealousy? Between you and me, cousin, I think she would pick me up if you dropped me, supposing I were willing, which I wouldn't be; for no woman could mean anything to me after you. But just a minute, I'm going to show you how old you are,' and so saying I ran and took down a little mirror that was hanging on the wall-tapestry. 'Now look at your forty-five years and see if they don't look more like thirty, and I bet that is nearer the truth than you say.'

'No, my dear boy, I am the age I said, but it is true that hardly anybody would say so. It is not as if I made a special point of being well-preserved and pretty, although if I had wanted I could have had lots of attention, but I never have bothered about what people said about my looks.'

We had no time to say anything else, for Agathe appeared.

'Oh dear, Mademoiselle,' she said as she came in, 'do you take me for a gossip, since you didn't want me to know what you said to Mother? She says she is going to see her lawyer for you and then on to the priest. Is it about a marriage?'

At the word marriage Mlle Habert coloured up and was at a loss for a reply. 'It's about a contract,' I broke in, 'and as a matter of fact it is to do with this that I must write an urgent letter at once.' I said this deliberately so that the girl should leave us in peace, for I realized that her presence irked Mlle Habert, who had not yet got over the amazement caused by the crazy behaviour of the mother.

I at once looked for some paper and prepared to write to my father, and Mlle Habert pretended to be dictating softly what I was writing, so Agathe left.

Indiscreet though the mother was, she was a wonderful help. In fact all the steps were taken, and two days later the banns were published. On the afternoon of the same day we went to see the lawyer and the contract was drawn up. In it Mlle Habert gave me everything she possessed to enjoy during my lifetime. My father's consent came four days later, and we were on the eve of our secret wedding when, for some reason or other, I forget what, we were obliged to go and see this priest our hostess knew. He was to marry us the following day – or rather, during the night – and he had undertaken to see about lots of small details out of consideration for our hostess, to whom he was in some way indebted.

It was Mlle Habert who entertained our hostess, her daughter and four witnesses to supper. The arrangement was that we should finish the meal at eleven, when mother and daughter would retire to their own quarters, Agathe would be allowed to go to bed and at two o'clock in the morning we should set off, our hostess, her friends the four witnesses, Mlle Habert and myself, for the church.

So at about six we went to the parish where the priest whom we had to see was supposed to be. He had been told we were coming, but he had not been able to wait for us, and one of his colleagues told us on his behalf that he would come to our hostess's house in an hour or two.

We went home and were ready to sit down at table when the priest in question was announced, whose name we did not know, and who had not been told our names either.

He entered. Imagine our amazement when, instead of a man we thought we did not know, we saw the director who in the Haberts' home had decided that I must go!

On seeing him my bride uttered a scream, a rather unwise scream, but impulses like that come faster than sober thought. I was in the act of bowing politely but stopped half-way, he had his mouth open to speak and stood without uttering a sound. Our hostess was stepping towards him but stopped goggle-eyed on seeing us all motionless; one of the witnesses, a friend of the hostess, who had gone forward to embrace the priest, stayed with arms outstretched. We all made the strangest tableau in the world – a group of statues you could have put into a painting.

Our silence lasted a good two minutes. In the end the director broke it and said to the hostess:

'Madame, are the persons in question not here?' (For he did not imagine we could be the subject of his present mission, that is to say the parties he was to marry five or six hours later.) 'Yes, of course they are,' she answered, 'here they both are, Mlle Habert and M. de la Vallée.'

He could scarcely believe it, and indeed it was very strange that it should be us. It was one of those stories you hear of but would never credit.

'What!' he said, after looking us up and down for a moment in astonishment. 'You call this young man M. de la Vallée, and he is the one who is marrying Mlle Habert tonight?'

'He's the one,' replied the hostess, 'I don't know of any other, and Mademoiselle isn't marrying two, I shouldn't think!'

My wife-to-be and I said nothing. I held my hat in my hand with as much unconcern as I could muster, and even smiled as I watched the director while he was questioning our hostess, but I was only smiling with my face, and not from inside, and I am sure that my unconcerned manner did not prevent my looking pretty silly. You have to have a tremendous nerve to carry off certain situations, and I was only born cheeky, not insolent.

As for my future wife, her attitude was to have downcast eyes with an expression it would be difficult to define. There was everything in it, annoyance, embarrassment, timidity due to the remains of a reverential respect for a spiritual director, and, to complete it all, a puzzled look suggesting somebody wanting to say: 'I don't care,' but who was still too nonplussed to be so resolute.

Having looked at us the priest addressed our hostess. 'Madame, this affair needs a little thinking over; may I have a word with you in private? Let us go into your rooms for a moment, please. Our conversation will only take a minute.'

'Oh my! Yes, Sir,' she said, delighted anyhow to find herself such an important figure in the story. 'Don't you worry, Mademoiselle,' she called back to Mlle Habert, 'the gentleman says we shan't be long.'

Thereupon she took up a candlestick and went out with the priest, leaving us in the room – my intended, those who were to be our witnesses and who at that moment bore witness to nothing, Agathe, from whom everything had been kept dark, and myself.

'Monsieur de la Vallée,' said one of the witnesses, 'what does this mean? Does M. Doucin (meaning the priest) know you?' 'Yes,' I said, 'we met at Mademoiselle's home.' 'Oho! So you're getting married?' chimed in Agathe. 'Oh no, not just yet, as you see,' I said.

So far not a word from Mlle Habert, but during her silence her embarrassment wore off, love took the upper hand again and freed her from all those little instinctive reactions that had upset her at first. 'And it will make no difference one way or the other,' she said, courageously taking a seat.

'Do you know,' said one of the witnesses, a friend of our hostess, 'what M. Doucin is going to say to Mme d'Alain (our hostess's name)?' 'Yes, Sir,' she answered, 'I strongly suspect I do, but I don't really care much.'

'M. Doucin, at all events, is a very good man, a saintly man,' said the spiteful Agathe. 'He is my aunt's confessor.' 'All right, Mademoiselle, I know him better than you do,' said my bride, 'but we are not now concerned with his saintliness; if he is so holy he will be canonized. What has that got to do with us here?'

'Oh,' went on the little hussy, 'what I am saying about him is only to show the esteem in which we hold him. As to anything else, I am saying nothing, it's none of my business. I am sorry he is not behaving as you would wish, but we must suppose it is for your good, for he is such a prudent man!'

At that point her mother came back. 'You haven't got M. Doucin with you?' said our witness. 'I thought he was going to have supper with us.'

'Supper!' replied Mme d'Alain. 'We don't feel much like supper! Well, well, there'll be no wedding tonight either, and if there isn't one at all it will be better still. But let's have supper, as we are here. That M. Doucin is a good soul, and you are very much indebted to him, Mademoiselle. You can't imagine how devoted he is to both of you, you and your good sister. Poor man! He went off almost in tears, and I cried myself as I said good-bye – I've only just dried my eyes. What a piece of news for that sister, dear God! What are we all coming to?'

'Who are you getting at, Madame, with your exclamations?' asked Mlle Habert. 'Oh, nobody,' was the answer, 'but I'm quite flabbergasted. Never mind separating from your sister, people aren't obliged to live together, and you will be quite as well off here, but marrying in secret, and then the Pont-Neuf as a meeting-place – a husband on the Pont-Neuf! You who are so religious, so reasonable, from a good family and well-to-do, oh, surely you can't think of it! But I don't mean to say another word, for I was urged only to speak to you on your own, and this is a matter we don't want everybody to know about.' 'And which you are announcing to the whole world,' answered Mlle Habert tartly.

'No, no,' went on the discreet Mme d'Alain, 'I am only referring to the meeting on the Pont-Neuf, and nobody knows what that means. Just ask my daughter or this gentleman (pointing to our witness) if they understand anything about it? Only you and this young man who was with you understand what I mean.'

'Oh,' said Agathe, 'as for me, I don't know anything about it, except that it was on the Pont-Neuf that you and M. de la Vallée met each other, that's all.'

'And that was only six days ago,' went on her mother, 'but I'm not saying a word about that.' 'Six days?' cried the witness. 'Yes, six days, neighbour. But don't let us go on talking about it, for you will learn nothing from me; no use questioning me, Mlle Habert and I will discuss it, that's all. Let us sit down to the meal, and M. de la Vallée as well, since M. de la Vallée is there. Not that I look down on anyone, and that's a fact; he is a nice young man and good-looking, and I wish him every sort of prosperity. If he's not a gentleman yet, perhaps he will be one some day – servant today, master tomorrow – many another beside him has been in a paid job and then had people in his pay.'

'M. de la Vallée in a paid job!' exclaimed Agathe. 'That'll do, child,' said her mother, 'mind your own business.'

'Was he employed by this lady here?' asked the witness. 'Oh, what does it matter?' she answered. 'Let us drop the subject, whoever the cap fits can wear it. Today he is M. de la Vallée, that's what we've been told he is, accept it and let's have our supper!'

'Just as you say,' he said, 'but one likes being with people of one's own kind. For the rest, I shall do the same as you. We can't go wrong if we imitate you.'

Incidentally this little dialogue was so rapid that Mlle Habert and I scarcely had time to know where we were; every detail was a terrible blow and on such occasions all one's time is spent blushing. Just imagine what it is like to have your whole story retailed, item by item, by this woman who's supposed to discuss it with nobody but Mlle Habert, and who falls over herself saying: I shan't say a word, and says it all – saying all the time that she won't say anything.

I was stunned, struck dumb, not a word would come, and my future wife could only weep, having collapsed in the armchair on which she was sitting.

However, I recovered at the remarks of our witness when he said that one likes being with people of one's own kind.

This worthy guest was not very impressive to look at, in spite of the new suit he had put on, in spite of the spotless white cravat, long, starched and stiff, and a new wig as well, which his head was bearing with visible awe and which embarrassed him more than it covered him, apparently because he hadn't yet got used to it, as the wig had probably been worn on only two or three Sundays.

The good man, the grocer from the corner as I learned afterwards, had got himself up in that finery to honour our marriage and the function of witness he was to fulfil. I say nothing about his cuffs, which had a gravity all of their own – I have never seen such stiff ones.

'But you, Sir, who are talking of people of your own kind,' I said, 'what kind are you, then? My heart tells me that I am quite as good as you, apart from the fact that I have my own hair and you somebody else's.' 'Oh yes,' he said, 'we are quite as good as each other, one to call for drink and the other to serve it. But don't move, I'm not thirsty. Good night, Mme d'Alain, and I wish you a good night, Mademoiselle.' And off went our witness.

PART 3

UNTIL that moment our other witnesses would have said nothing and would gladly have stayed, I think, if only for the sake of a good meal, for certain people are not averse to being guests, and a good meal means quite a lot to them.

But the witness who was leaving was their friend and neighbour, and as his pride would not allow him to eat with me they felt they ought to follow his example and be seen to be as delicate-minded as he was.

'As Monsieur So-and-so (meaning the other one) is going, we can no longer assist you,' said one of the three, a short, stout person, to Mlle Habert, 'and I think it is indicated that we should take our leave of the company.'

This speech was delivered in a voice almost as sad as it was solemn, and he seemed to be saying: 'We are going with great regret, but we can't do anything else.'

And what made their retreat even more difficult was that while their spokesman was having his say, the first dishes of our supper had been brought in. They thought these looked most attractive, as I could tell from the way they eyed them.

'Gentlemen,' said Mlle Habert rather sharply, 'I am sorry to cause you trouble, but it's up to you.'

'Now why need you go away?' said Mme d'Alain, who loved big, noisy parties and saw her hopes vanishing of an evening in which she could have gossipped to her heart's content. 'Oh, surely as supper is all served we've only got to take our places at the table.'

'We are extremely vexed, but it is not possible,' answered the short, stout witness, 'it is not possible, neighbour.'

His colleagues standing next to him only expressed their opinion by looking at the floor, and let themselves be led without finding the strength to utter a word, the viands that had just been served having struck them dumb. He bowed, they bowed, he went out first, they followed.

So that left us with only Mme d'Alain and her daughter.

'And that's what comes,' said the mother, rounding on me, 'that's what comes of answering out of turn. If you had said nothing they would still be here, and wouldn't have gone off in a huff.'

'Then why was their colleague so rude?' I asked. 'What did he mean with his "People of one's own kind?" He treats me with contempt, and I am not supposed to say anything?'

'But between ourselves, M. de la Vallée,' she went on, 'is he so very wrong? You see he is a shopkeeper, a citizen of Paris, a man in a certain position. Honestly, are you his equal – a man who is churchwarden in his parish?'

'Churchwarden in his parish, well, what about it, Madame?' I said. 'Hasn't my father been one in his? Wouldn't I certainly have been one too if I'd stayed on in my village?'

'Ah yes,' she said, 'but there are parishes and parishes, M. de la

Vallée.' 'Granted,' I said, 'but I think our saint is as good as yours, Mme d'Alain, Saint-Jacques is worth as much as Saint-Gervais.'

'Anyway, they've gone now,' she said in quieter tones, for she was not one to keep anything up for long. 'It's not worth arguing about and it wouldn't bring them back. As for me, I don't stand on my dignity and I won't refuse to have supper. With regard to your marriage, that will be as God wills – I only said what I thought out of friendliness, and I don't want to upset anybody.'

'But you have upset me very much,' said Mlle Habert through her tears, 'and were I not afraid of giving offence to God, I would never forgive the way you have gone on over this. Coming in and talking about all my business in front of a lot of people I don't know, insulting a young man you know I think highly of, referring to him as a scoundrel, treating him like a flunkey when he only was one for a moment by sheer chance and then only because he hadn't any money, and then talking about the Pont-Neuf and making me look like a crackpot and an unfeeling, fast woman, repeating all the tales of a priest who has not behaved at all like a man of God in this affair. For what is behind his telling you all these tales? Let him say truthfully: is it because of religion or because he stands to lose through me and my actions? If he has so much regard for me and takes such a Christian interest in what concerns me, why did he always allow me to be bullied by my sister while we were both living together? Was it possible to live with her, and could I have stood up to her? He knows perfectly well it was not so. Therefore I am getting married today – all right, I should have had to tomorrow, and I might not have found such a good man. M. de la Vallée has saved my life, and were it not for him I might be dead now, his family is as good as mine, so what is it all about and who is M. Doucin objecting to? Really, what a marvellous thing self-interest is! Because I am leaving him and he won't get the perquisites from me that I gave him every day, he has to persecute me on the pretext of thinking of my own interests. And a person in whose house I am living and in whom I have trusted has to expose me to the most brutal insult in the world, for can anything be more humiliating than what I am going through?'

Tears, sobs and sighs and all the evidence of bitter grief stifled Mlle Habert's voice and prevented her going on.

I wept myself instead of saying consoling words to her. I returned the tears she was shedding for me, which made her weep even more bitterly to reward me for my crying. And as Mme d'Alain was such a kind soul and anyone who cried was right in her eyes, we won her over at once, and the priest was in the wrong.

'Oh, there, there, my dear,' she said, going over to Mlle Habert, 'oh, how terribly upset I am that I didn't know what you are now telling me! Come along, M. de la Vallée, cheer up, my boy, come and help me to console this poor lady who is torturing herself over a word or two I really dropped without thinking. But don't you see, I never guessed – one hears a priest saying it is not right for somebody to marry you, and, well, I believed him! Fancy his having his own little reasons for being so scandalized! As to his liking people to give him things – oh, I'm quite sure of that – it means candles, coffee, sugar. Yes, yes, I have a friend who is very religious and she sends him all that sort of thing. Now that you mention it, it all comes back to me – and so you gave him things as well, and that's how it is. Just you do what I do, I talk about God as much as you like, but I don't give anything away. There are three or four gentlemen of his cloth who come here and I welcome them: how are you, Monsieur, how are you, Madame; and we take tea and sometimes dine, then take your partners again, a little word of uplift here and there and so good-bye. So if I marry twenty times instead of once I'm not afraid they'll bother about it. Besides, my dear, cheer up, you are of age and it is a good thing to marry M. de la Vallée, and if it's not tonight it will be the next, and there's only one night lost. I'll back you up, you leave it to me. Just fancy, a man but for whom you might have died! Well, it stands to reason! Oh, he'll be your husband all right, and I'd be the first to blame you if he wasn't.'

She had reached that point when we heard coming up the stairs Mlle Habert's cook (Mme d'Alain had found one for us and I had forgotten to mention it).

'Come along, dear,' she said, putting her arm round Mlle Habert, 'sit you down, dry those eyes and stop crying. Bring up your chair, M. de la Vallée, and cheer up. Let's have our supper. Put yourself there, my girl.'

She was speaking to Agathe. The said Agathe had not uttered a word since her mother had come back.

Our predicament had not touched her, and compassion for one's neighbour was not one of her weaknesses. She had remained silent so as to watch us out of curiosity, and to enjoy seeing what we looked like when we were crying. I saw from her expression that this whole little upset amused her, and she was enjoying our grief while putting on an expression of sadness.

There are many people in the world with that sort of character, who prefer their friends to be sad rather than happy; they only congratulate you on something good out of politeness, they console you for a misfortune out of relish.

However, in the end, as she sat down, Agathe did utter a little exclamation in our favour, and it was an exclamation worthy of the hypocritical interest she was taking in our sorrow. You give yourself away in everything you do, and instead of saying: 'Oh, it's nothing to worry about,' the young person exclaimed: 'Oh, how upsetting this is!' That is always the line spiteful souls take in such cases, that is their style.

The cook came in, Mlle Habert dried her tears, Mme d'Alain, her daughter and I were served, and we all ate with quite a good appetite. My own was enormous, but I concealed it to some extent for fear of outraging my intended, who was eating very little, and she might perhaps have accused me of not being very concerned if I had had the courage to eat that much. One should not be hungry when grief-stricken.

So I held myself back out of decorum, or at least I was sharp enough to cause them to say more than once: 'Come along, eat up!' Even Mlle Habert begged me to eat, and after repeated pleas I was obliging enough to have a very respectable meal without giving any cause for criticism.

There was nothing remarkable about our conversation during the meal. Mme d'Alain, as was her wont, ranged over topics pointless to repeat, referring to our adventure in what she thought was a most enigmatic manner, but which was as clear as daylight. Then she noticed that the woman serving us was giving ear to her discourse and told her that servants should not listen to what their masters were saying.

In fact Mme d'Alain continued to behave with her customary discretion, and when the meal was over she kissed Mlle Habert, promising her friendship, help and almost her protection and left us, if not consoled, at any rate easier in our minds than we should have been without her assurances of help. 'Tomorrow,' she said, 'failing M. Doucin, we shall certainly find another priest who will marry you.' We thanked her for her interest and she went off with Agathe, who that evening put nothing special for me into the curtsey she made to us.

While Cathos was clearing the table (that was our cook's name), Mlle Habert whispered to me: 'M. de la Vallée, you must go, it is not seemly that that girl should leave us together. But can't you think of someone to protect you here? I'm afraid my sister will make trouble, for I wager that M. Doucin will have gone and told her. And I know what she is; I don't expect she will leave us in peace.'

'Never mind, cousin,' I said, 'so long as you back me up what can she do? If I have your love what else do I need? I am an honest fellow first and foremost, son of respectable people, my father gives his consent, you consent, and so do I, that's the main thing.'

'Above all,' she said, 'whatever happens don't let yourself be intimidated, that is what I do urge, because my sister has many friends and she may well use threats against you. You are inexperienced and may take fright and leave me, out of sheer lack of firmness.'

'Leave you?' I said. 'Yes, when I am dead, for only that will send me away. But so long as my body and soul are together they will follow you everywhere, the one supporting the other. Is that clear? I am not timid by nature, conscience clear hath nought to fear, so let them all come. I love you and you are worthy to be loved – nobody can deny that. Love is for everybody, you have it and so do I – who hasn't? When you are in love you get married, respectable people do that, we are doing that, and that's all.'

'You are right,' she said, 'and your steadfastness is a comfort; I can see that it comes from God. He is behind all this, and it would be over-scrupulous of me to doubt it. So, my boy, let us put all our trust in Him and thank Him for the care He is manifestly taking of us. Oh Lord, bless a union which is Thy work. Good-bye, La Vallée, the greater the obstacles the more dear you are to me.'

'Good-bye, cousin, the more they harry us the more I love you,' I said in my turn. 'Alas, how I wish it were tomorrow and then this hand I am holding will be mine! Just now I thought it was, together with your whole person. How unfair that priest is to me!' I added. And I pressed her hand while she gazed at me with eyes that said over and over again: 'How unfair he is to us both!' But they said it in the most Christian way possible, considering the passion with which they were filled and the difficulty of reconciling so much passion with modesty.

'Go along now,' she said, still in an undertone and with a sigh after these words. 'Go along, we are not yet allowed to be so affectionate. It is true that we were to have been married tonight, but we shan't be, La Vallée, it's only till tomorrow. So go along.'

Just then Cathos had her back to us, and I took advantage of that moment to kiss her hand – a piece of gallantry I had already seen others do and which is easily learned. It now earned me another sigh, and then I straightened and said goodnight.

She had urged me to pray to God and I did not omit to do so. I even prayed more than usual, for we love God so much when we need Him!

I went to bed very pleased with my piety, and satisfied that it was very meritorious. I did not wake up until eight next morning.

It was nearly nine when I went into Mlle Habert's room. She also had got up later than usual, and I scarcely had time to say good-morning to her before Cathos came and said that somebody wanted to speak to me.

This surprised me because I had no business with anybody. 'Can it be someone in the house?' asked Mlle Habert, even more puzzled than I was.

'No, Mademoiselle,' said Cathos, 'it's a man who has just come.' I was for going to see who it was. 'No, wait,' said Mlle Habert, 'I don't want you to go out, let him come and find you here, that's all.'

Cathos brought him in. He was quite well-dressed, like a man-servant but with a sword at his side.

'Is your name M. de la Vallée?' he asked. 'Yes, Monsieur, what is it, and what can I do for you?'

'I have been sent by M. le Président —' (one of the most important magistrates in Paris), 'and he would like to talk to you.'

'Me! But it can't be. It must be some other M. de la Vallée, for

I don't know this President, whom I've never seen or set eyes on in my life.'

'No, no, you are the one he wants, the one who is to marry a certain Mlle Habert. I have a cab waiting downstairs and you cannot refuse to come, for then you would be made to. So there is no point in refusing. In any case nobody wishes you any harm, they only want to talk to you.'

'I have the great honour of knowing a lady in M. le Président's family, who lives at his house,' said Mlle Habert, 'and as I suspect that this is something concerning me as well, I will come too, gentlemen. Don't worry, M. de la Vallée, we are going together. All this is my elder sister's doing, it is she who is trying to thwart us. We shall find her at the President's house, I'll be bound, and perhaps M. Doucin with her. Come along, let us see what it's all about. I shan't keep you waiting long, Monsieur, I just have to change my dress.'

'No, Mademoiselle,' said the manservant (for that is what he was), 'I have clear orders to bring only M. de la Vallée. They must have foreseen that you would want to come, as they gave me this positive order. So you cannot come with us, begging your pardon for the refusal I have to give you, but I must do what I am told.'

'Well, what elaborate precautions and strange procedures,' she said. 'Never mind, M. de la Vallée, you go on ahead and present yourself without any misgivings; I shall be there almost as soon as you, for I'm going to send for a cab.'

'I don't advise you to, Mademoiselle,' said the man, 'and I am instructed to tell you that if you did you would see nobody.'

'Nobody!' she exclaimed. 'Now what does that mean? The President is reputed to be such an honest man, such a good man: how can he behave like this? What's become of his religion? Is the mere fact of being a President enough to make him send a warrant for a man who is no concern of his? It's like sending to arrest a criminal, I really don't understand it at all. God cannot approve of what is being done, and my opinion is that one shouldn't go. I am interested in M. de la Vallée, I openly declare it. He has no office or employment, I admit, but he is a subject of the King like anyone else, and nobody has a right to maltreat the King's subjects or use force to make them go like this under the pretext of being a magistrate and that they are of no account. My feeling is that he should stay here.'

'No, Mademoiselle,' I broke in, 'I'm not afraid of anything (and that was true). Don't let us look into the rights and wrongs of sending somebody to make me come. Who am I to be proud? Mustn't we keep to our own station in life? When I am a proper citizen of Paris that'll be all very well, but while I am still of such small account I must put up with the disadvantages and keep to my own size – the poor must do the chores, as they say. The President sends for me, all right, I am sent for in a proper manner. The President will see me and his Worship will tell me his reasons and I will tell him mine. We live in a Christian country, I'm going to him with a clear conscience and God is above. Let's go, I am quite ready.'

'Very well, I'll let you,' said Mlle Habert, 'for indeed what can come of it? But before you go, come and let me have a word with you in this little room, M. de la Vallée.'

I followed her in; she opened a cupboard, put her hand into a bag of money, took out some in gold and told me to take it. 'I suspect that you haven't much money, my boy, so put this in your pocket, just in case. Off you go, M. de la Vallée, and God be with you, guide you and bring you back. Don't be long and come back as soon as you can, and remember that I am impatiently waiting for you.'

'Yes, cousin, yes, mistress, yes, my charming future wife and all I hold dearest in the world, yes, I shall be back at once. I shall be fretting until my return, I shan't live until I see you again,' I said, seizing the generous hand that had put the money into my hat. 'Oh, even a heart of stone would soon become one of flesh and blood with you and your endearing ways! What goodness of soul! Oh God, what a charming woman, and how I shall love her when I am her husband! The very thought of it makes me die with pleasure. Let all the Presidents and Clerks in the world come, and this is what I shall tell them, even a thousand of them, each with their lawyer. Farewell, queen of my heart, farewell, beloved being, I am so full of love that I daren't talk about it any more unless we are married, only then can I say the rest.'

Her only answer was to collapse into a chair and weep, and so I set off with the waiting servant, who struck me as a decent man.

'Don't be alarmed,' he said on the way, 'it's no crime to be loved by a woman, and M. le Président is only summoning you in order to be obliging. He has been asked to do so in the hope that he may frighten you, but he is a most reasonable and upright magistrate, so set your mind at rest, defend yourself properly and stand firm.'

'That I will certainly do, Sir, and thank you for the advice. Some day I will repay you if I can, but I assure you that I am going to this as cheerfully as to my wedding.'

While we were talking along these lines we arrived at his master's. It seemed that my story had made a sensation in the house, for all the assembled servants made a hedge up the stairs.

It didn't put me out of countenance at all – each one had his word to say about my appearance, and fortunately there wasn't one of their remarks that could upset me, and some of those from the women were most complimentary. 'He's no fool, by the looks of him,' said one. 'Really, that pious lady knew how to choose, he's a very handsome fellow,' said another.

On the right it was: 'I'm very glad he's done so well for himself,' and on the left: 'I like his face.' I heard one say here: 'If I got one looking like that I should hang on to him,' and: 'You sound far from displeased,' someone said there.

In fact I can say that my path was strewn with compliments, and if that was running the gauntlet the blows were at any rate the softest in the world, and I should have been justified in being very pleased with myself had not an elderly housekeeper I met at the top of the staircase spoiled it all. No doubt she was annoyed at seeing how young I was, whilst she was so old and so far removed from Mlle Habert's good fortune.

Oh dear! the blow I got from that one was not gentle at all. Casting a baleful eye on me and a disdainful look, she said: 'Hum! What's all this? What a fool of a woman to want to marry this country lout at her age! She must be out of her mind.'

'Be careful what you say, Ma, you would certainly lose him at that rate,' I answered back, emboldened by all the flattering things the others had said.

My answer had quite a success, and a general peal of laughter re-echoed all down the stairs. The manservant and I went into the private rooms, leaving behind us a pitched battle between the housekeeper and the rest of the staff, who were booing her in my favour.

I don't know how the old girl got out of it, but as you see, my début had its funny side.

The company was assembled in Madame's room, I was expected, and so my guide took me straight there.

Modesty and courage, with those I made my entry. There I found the elder Mlle Habert – I begin with her because it is against her I have to plead. Then the President, a middle-aged man.

Next, the President's wife, whose face alone would have reassured me had I been afraid: only one woman like her is needed in a gathering to make you take to all the others. Not that she was beautiful, far from it; I won't say that she was ugly either, I wouldn't dare, for if kindness and straightforwardness, indeed all the qualities that make up a lovable soul, were united in one face, they would take on none other than hers.

I heard her whisper to the President: 'Good gracious, Monsieur, I think the poor fellow is trembling, do treat him gently,' and then at once she looked at me in a way that said: 'Don't worry.'

It was one of those impressions that are so clear that they are unmistakable.

But what I am saying is beside the point. I was counting the people present, and three of them have been mentioned so far. Let us come to the others.

There was a priest with sensitive features, dressed with all the elegance that his habit would allow, making decorous but graceful gestures. He was an ecclesiastical fop, and I'll say no more, for I have never seen him since.

There was one more lady, a relation of the President, the one Mlle Habert had said she knew, who lived in part of the house, a widow of about fifty, tall and good-looking, whose portrait I shall draw in a moment. That was all.

It is noteworthy that this lady, whose portrait I am promising, was a religious churchgoer also. What a lot of religious ladies, you will say, but I can't help that, it was the reason why the elder Mlle Habert knew her and had been able to make her take an interest in the affair. They both frequented the same confessional.

And while we are on the subject of religious females, this was an occasion when I could have said:

'Tant de fiel entre-t-il dans l'âme des dévots!'*

I have never seen a face so convulsed with fury as that of the Mlle Habert there present. It changed her so much that I could hardly recognize her.

Truly it is only people like that who have violent impulses, they alone are really impassioned. Perhaps they think they are so well in with God that they can take such liberties with impunity, and imagine that what is a sin for the profane like the rest of us changes its name and is purified when it passes through their souls. Be that as it may, I don't know how they look upon it, but it is certain the rage of the devout is terrible to behold.

Apparently you get a lot of spleen in that occupation – I am only ever referring to the sham religious, and always make an exception of the genuinely devout; their religion purges it away.

The fury with which Mlle Habert looked at me did not have much effect on me. I glanced at her as casually as at the rest of the company, and went forward and bowed to the President.

'So you are the man Mademoiselle's sister wants to marry?' he asked.

'Yes, Sir, at any rate she says so, and certainly I shall not stop her, for it is a great honour and pleasure,' I answered in a simple but firm and quiet way. I was carefully watching what I was saying, be it noted.

'Marry you?' he went on. 'Are you fit to be her husband? Are you forgetting you are only her servant?'

'I could easily forget it,' I said, 'for I only was for a short time and through a chance meeting.'

'The cheek of it! Look how he is answering back, M. le Président,' said Mlle Habert.

'Not at all, Mademoiselle,' broke in the President's wife in a tone of voice perfectly matching the face I have described. 'You are angry, the President is questioning him and he is obliged to answer. There is nothing wrong with that and we must listen.'

*Literally: 'Can so much venom enter pious souls?' (Line from Boileau, *Le Lutrin*.)

This piece of dialogue made the priest smile behind his hand with a knowing and amused look and the President lowered his eyes like somebody determined to be serious and holding in his laughter.

The other lady, the relation of the family, was doing some tatting, I fancy, keeping her eyes lowered and limiting herself to the occasional sly glance up at me. I noticed that she was sizing me up from top to toe.

'Why,' went on the President, 'do you say you were her servant for only a short time, since you are her servant at this very minute?'

'Yes, Sir, her servant as I am yours. I am very much her servant, friend, husband-to-be, and that's all.'

'But, you little wretch,' cried my future sister-in-law on hearing this, for she was not finding the President's remarks to her liking, 'can you at your age lie in such a barefaced manner? Now put your hand on your heart and remember that you are before God who is listening to us. Didn't that silly sister of mine pick you up in the street? Weren't you down-and-out and with no idea where to go when she took you on? What would have happened to you if it hadn't been for her? Wouldn't you have come down to begging from passers-by if she had not brought you home out of charity? Poor girl, it would have been much better for her if she had not taken pity on you – her charity must have been displeasing to God since such a great misfortune has resulted for her. And what a fall from grace, M. le Président, how terrible are God's decrees! One morning she is crossing the Pont-Neuf, she meets this little rake, brings him home to me, I don't like the look of him, she insists on keeping him against my advice and the inspired judgement of a holy man who tries to dissuade her, she quarrels with him, breaks with me, takes a house elsewhere and goes and lives with this vile creature (God forgive me for calling him that!), goes silly over him and wants to be his wife – the wife of a servant at close on fifty!'

'Oh, age has nothing to do with it,' said the religious lady without looking up, for this matter of fifty years of age did not please her because she herself was fiftyish and she was afraid that this discussion might draw attention to her. 'Besides,' she went on, 'is your sister as old as that? You are very put out just now, but I seem to have heard her say that she was my age, and at that rate she would be five years younger.'

I saw the President smile at this arithmetic; apparently it didn't seem quite correct to him.

'Really, Madame,' the elder sister went on in an injured tone, 'I do know my sister's age, I am her senior and I am nearly two years older than she is. Yes, Madame, she is fifty all but two months, and I think that at that age a woman might be considered old. I confess that I think of myself as such. Not everybody wears as well as you, Madame.'

That was another silly remark to let out, whether through carelessness or spite.

'As me, Mlle Habert?' said the lady, colouring up. 'Pray what are you saying? What is all this to do with me? I wear well, you say, and I think I do, but I don't bother about it. Not that there's anything very miraculous about wearing well at my age.'

'It is true,' teased the President, 'that Mlle Habert does cut the prime of life a bit short, and that old age doesn't come quite so early, but shall we leave the discussion of ages at that?'

'Yes, M. le Président,' replied our elder sister, 'it is not the years I am concerned with in this affair, but the position of the husband she is taking, the humble nature of her choice, think what an insult it will be to the family. I know that we are all equal in the sight of God, but in the sight of men it is not the same thing at all, and God wants us to take notice of established custom among them. He forbids us to bring dishonour on ourselves, and people will say that my sister has married a scoundrel, that's what they will call this young fellow, and I want a poor, besotted woman to be prevented from bringing so much shame upon us. In fact it will be working for her own good. We must show pity for her, and I have already commended her to the prayers of one holy community. M. Doucin has promised his, and Madame too,' she added, eyeing the pious dame, who didn't find this direct reference very much to her liking. 'Now Mme la Présidente and M. l'Abbé, whom I haven't the honour of knowing, I am sure that they won't refuse theirs (the prayers of the Abbé were something really priceless on that occasion, enough to make you explode with laughter, and indeed he acknowledged the invitation in a way which assessed his prayers at their real worth), and you will have a share in a work of charity,' she said again to the President, 'if you will be so good as to bring your influence to bear on our behalf.'

'Don't you worry, Mademoiselle,' said the President, 'your sister won't marry him. He wouldn't dare to take things to those lengths, and if he wanted to go any further we should stop him, but he won't give us that trouble, and to make up for what is being taken away from him I mean to look after him myself.'

I had been keeping quiet for a long time because I wanted to set out my case in a proper order, and I hadn't wasted my time during my silence. I had glanced frequently at the religious lady, who had noticed and had even covertly returned a few of my glances. But why had I taken it into my head to look at her? Because I had noticed that she herself had looked at me, and that made me reflect that I was a handsome fellow, and these things connected up in my mind. On countless occasions we act as a result of vague notions that occur somehow and take charge of us, and we don't think them out.

But I had not neglected the President's wife either, though in her case with a humble and supplicating air. With my eyes I had signalled to the one: you are delightful to look at, and she had believed me; and to the other: take me under your protection, and she had promised to. For I think they both understood my message and answered as I am telling you.

Even the priest had a share of my attentions. A few extremely polite looks had also disposed him in my favour, so that in fact I already had two-thirds of my judges on my side by the time I began speaking.

First I asked for silence, by the way I began, which really meant: 'Listen to me.'

'M. le Président,' I said, 'I have let Mademoiselle speak as she wished, and let her insult me to her heart's content, and even if she made another speech an hour long she could not say more than she has. So it is my turn to speak now – a turn for each is not too much to expect.

'You say, Sir, that if I want to marry the younger Mlle Habert I shall be stopped, to which I answer that if I am stopped of course I shall have to give her up – nobody can expect the impossible. But if I am not stopped I shall marry her, that is certain, and anybody would do the same in my place.

'Let us come now to the insulting things being said. I don't know whether the requirements of a devout life permit them, and in any case I leave that to the conscience of the lady who has given vent to them. She says that God is listening to us, and so much the worse for her, for she hasn't let Him hear very pleasant language – in short, I am a wretch and a rogue, her sister is crazy and a poor misguided female. In all this only other people are reviled and He must make what He can of that. Now let us talk of myself. Take for example the elder Mlle Habert. If you were to say to her: "You this," and "you that," "who are you?" and "who aren't you?" she would certainly think it very strange and say: "Sir, you have a funny way of treating me," and you would think to yourself: "She is right, I ought to say Mademoiselle." And so you say: "Mademoiselle this," and "Mademoiselle that," always politely, but I always get just "you". It is not that I am complaining, M. le Président, there is no cause to, and it is the custom with you grand gentlemen. "You" is my portion and that of poor folk, that's how things are done, and why do poor folk exist? It isn't your fault, and what I am saying is only by way of making a comparison. But my point is that Mademoiselle, to whom it would be wrong to say: "What do you want, you?" is really hardly any more Mademoiselle than I am Monsieur. In fact it's about the same.'

'What do you mean? The impertinence! The same thing?' she exclaimed.

'Oh, bless you, yes it is,' I replied, 'but I haven't done yet, let me go on. Was Monsieur Habert, your father, God rest his soul, a rogue, Mademoiselle? He was the son of an honest farmer in the Beauce and I am the son of an honest farmer in Champagne, that's farm for farm for a start, so already Monsieur your father and I are on an equal footing. He went into business, didn't he? Perhaps I shall too, so it will still be shop for shop. Therefore you ladies, his daughters, only beat me by a shop, but if I set up in business my son will say: "My father had it," therefore my son will be equal to you. Today you are going from shop to farm and I shall be going from farm to shop; there isn't much in it. You are one stage ahead of me, and is a person low class for being one stage behind? Do people who serve God as you do and devote themselves to meekness as you do, count stages, especially when there's only one to count?

'As for that thoroughfare in which you say your sister picked me up, well, everybody goes along there; I did and she did, and one might just as well meet there as anywhere else if one is fated to meet somewhere. Had it not been for her I should have had to beg; not on the same day, but a bit later, I'm afraid, I would have had to come to that or go back home to the farm. I frankly admit, for I don't believe in beating about the bush, that it really is a pleasure to be rich, but there is no glory in it except for fools, and so is there anything all that surprising in what I did? A fellow is young, he has a father and mother, he leaves home to make a way for himself, so what wealth do you expect him to have? He has very little, but he looks for something, and I was looking for something when along comes your sister. "Who are you?" she asks. I tell her all about myself. "Would you like to come to our house? We are a couple of God-fearing sisters," she says. "Not half!" say I, so until something better turns up I go with her. We talk as we go along, I tell her my name, surname and financial position and all about my family. She says: "Ours is about the same." I am delighted to hear it and she says she is very glad. I answer this and she answers that, I flatter her and she does the same to me. "You strike me as a nice young man." "You, Mademoiselle, strike me as the nicest lady in Paris. I am so glad," I say. "So am I." And then we reach your home, you pick a quarrel with her over me and say you will leave her, but she leaves you first. She takes me with her, but when she is alone she gets unsettled and her thoughts turn to marriage, we discuss this and there I am all handy, she thinks well of me and I deeply respect her. I am a farmer's son and she a farmer's grand-daughter, and she doesn't quibble about one stage more or less or a business here or there, she has enough money for both and I have enough devotion for four. We summon a notary, I write off to Champagne and get an answer, and everything is in order. I appeal to M. le Président, who knows the law off by heart, Mme la Présidente who is listening, this other lady who is so intelligent and M. l'Abbé who has a conscience. I appeal to all Paris as though it were here present, what is so very insulting to you in all this?' At these words the company said nothing; nobody made any answer. Our elder sister, who expected the President to speak, gazed at him in astonishment when he said nothing. 'What, Sir!' she said. 'Do you abandon me?'

'I would very much like to help you, Mademoiselle,' he said, 'but what do you think I can do in a case like this? I thought this was quite a different matter, and if everything he says is true it would be neither fair nor possible to oppose a marriage which has nothing wrong with it except a ridiculous disparity of ages.'

'To say nothing,' added the lady who was related to him, 'of the fact that every day you see far greater differences, and that this one will only be apparent in some years' time, for your sister is still very young for her age.'

'And besides,' said the President's wife in conciliatory tones, 'this lady is her own mistress and this young man has nothing against him except his age, really.'

'There is nothing wrong in having a young husband,' said the priest in a suggestive tone.

'But isn't she committing a folly,' said Mlle Habert, whose head was awhirl with all these genealogies, 'and isn't it an act of charity to prevent her? You, Madame, who promised so faithfully to get the President to help me,' she said, looking at the religious lady, 'won't you urge him to act? I was counting so much on you.'

'But, dear Mlle Habert,' was the rejoinder, 'we must listen to reason. You referred to this young man as the worst kind of wretch, a real down-and-out, and I was very indignant. But that is not the case at all, he is the son of worthy people of a good Champagne family, and moreover a sensible young fellow, and I confess I would have scruples about spoiling his little bit of good fortune.'

At this speech the sensible young fellow bowed to the scrupulous lady – my bow came instantly.

'Oh Lord, what is the world coming to?' exclaimed my sister-in-law-to-be. 'Just because I said to Madame that she was wearing well at my sister's age, I have lost her good graces. Who would guess that one is still a nymph at fifty? Good-bye, Madame, Monsieur le Président, your servant.'

With that she nodded to the rest of the company, while the

religious lady gave her a sidelong and contemptuous look without deigning to answer.

'Run along, my boy,' she said when the other had gone, 'and get married, you don't need telling.'

'I even advise him to make haste,' added the President's wife, 'for that sister is very ill-intentioned.' 'However she set about it,' the President said coldly, 'her evil intentions would lead nowhere, and I don't see what she could do.'

Just then someone was announced. 'Come along,' said the nymph of fifty, rising, 'I'll give you a little note for Mlle Habert. She is a very nice person, and I have always liked her more than the other one, and I am very happy to let her know how this has passed off. M. le Président, may I go into your study for a moment to write something?' And off she went at once, and me after her, very pleased to be a messenger.

When we were in the study, 'To be honest, my boy,' she said, taking a sheet of paper and trying out one or two quills, 'at first I was against you, for this virago who has just gone had told us so much to your disadvantage that your marriage seemed the most outrageous thing in the world. But I have changed my mind since seeing you, for I have discovered you have a face that gives the lie to all the evil she has said, and indeed your face is handsome, and even radiant. The younger Mlle Habert is right.'

'I am most obliged to you, Madame, for the good opinion you have of me, and I will endeavour to deserve it.'

'Yes,' she said, 'I do think well of you, extremely well, I am delighted at what has happened to you, and if that tiresome sister should be a nuisance again you can rely on me to help you to deal with her.'

She went on trying different pens while talking to me like this, and could not find any good ones.

'What nasty quills these are,' she said, trying to cut, or rather trim one. 'How old are you?' 'Nearly twenty, Madame.' 'That is the right age to make your fortune, and all you need are friends to give you a helping hand and I mean to give you one. I am fond of your Mlle Habert and am very gratified at what she has done for you. She has discernment. But is it true that you only came up from the country four or five months ago? One wouldn't believe it to look at you, your skin is not all that rough and you don't look a bit like a rustic. He really has the loveliest complexion in the world!'

At this compliment the roses in the lovely complexion blossomed: I blushed a little out of modesty, but far more because of a certain feeling of pleasure that came from being praised in such a way by a woman in such a high position.

You feel very confident and at ease when you appeal to people by your looks, for that is a quality it is not hard to maintain and make last – your face doesn't change, it's always there and your advantages come from it, and as that is what interests people you don't fear that they will change their mind about you, and that gives you confidence.

I think my looks please people, I said to myself. And I felt how pleasant and at the same time how useful this way of pleasing people was, and this made me appear to be quite at home.

Meanwhile the pens were still giving trouble, attempts were being made to trim them but without success, and, with a certain show of annoyance at this, the conversation was being kept going.

'I can't write with this,' she said. 'Could you cut one for me?'

'Yes, Madame, I'll try.' So I take one and try cutting.

'Are you getting married this very night?' she went on, while I was bothering with the quill. 'I think so, Madame.'

She smiled. 'Tell me, my boy, Mlle Habert is very much in love with you, I don't doubt, and it doesn't surprise me at all. But, between ourselves, are you fond of her, too, do you feel love for her? You know what is meant by love, and I don't mean friendship, for she deserves a great deal of that from you, and you are under no further obligation. But has she any charms in your eyes, elderly though she is?'

These last words were pronounced in a flippant tone that dictated my reply, and seemed to urge me to say no and make fun of her charms. I sensed that I should please her by not being too impatient to possess them and, well – I couldn't help giving her what she was asking for.

In love affairs, however committed you are already, your vanity at pleasing somebody else makes your heart so unfaithful, and at such times you are so cowardly in order not to displease!

So I was weak enough to be wanting in honour and sincerity at this moment, for I did love Mlle Habert, or at least I believed

I did, and it comes to the same thing as far as the mean trick I did then is concerned. And even had I not loved her, the circumstances in which I was involved with her, my indebtedness to her in the past and in the future – did not all this demand that I should say with no hesitation: 'Yes, I love her, and with all my heart'?

Yet I did nothing of the kind because this lady did not want me to love her and I was flattered because she did not.

But as I was not by character a brazen rogue and was scarcely capable of a disloyal act, except in a case of this nature, I took what I imagined was a middle course, which was to limit myself to smiling without answering and making a face instead of saying the word that was expected of me.

'Yes, yes, I understand,' said the lady. 'You are more grateful than in love. I thought as much. Yet that lady was not unpleasing in her time.'

While she was talking I was trying out the quill I had trimmed; it did not work as I wanted, and I tinkered with it again so as to prolong the conversation I was enjoying very much and the end of which I was curious to see.

'Yes, she is very faded, but I think she has been quite pretty,' the lady went on, 'and as her sister says, she really is fifty, and had it been in my power just now she might have been much younger, for I made out she was my age so as to make her actions more excusable. If I had sided with her elder sister, I should have prejudiced your case with the President, but I took care not to.'

'Yes, I noticed the help you were giving me, Madame.' 'It is true,' she said, 'that I declared my interest quite openly – poor younger sister, I put myself in her place, she would have been too grief-stricken at losing you, old though she is. And besides, I wish you well.'

'Oh dear, Madame,' I went on in a naïve way, 'I would say the same of you were I worthy of saying anything.' 'Well, why not?' she answered, 'I don't scorn anybody's friendship, my dear boy, especially of those who appeal to me as much as you do, for I like you. I don't know why, but you have made a favourable impression upon me, and I don't look at people's position in the world, I don't let my taste be governed by such considerations.'

Although she slipped in those last words like a woman just saying words for the sake of saying something and not having to bother about what she thinks, yet the emphasis with which she said them obliged her to lower her eyes, for you cannot play tricks with your own conscience.

However, I couldn't think of anything else to do about that pen, and it was time I returned it properly done or gave it up.

So I said: 'Do please keep up this good will you are showing me, Madame. I couldn't receive any benefaction from anywhere that I value as much as yours.'

I spoke in this way while handing back the pen, which she took and tried out, and then said: 'It works beautifully. I suppose you can write legibly?' 'Not too bad,' I said.

'That'll be good enough, and I want to give you something to copy out that I should like to be clear.' 'As soon as you like, Madame.'

So she began her letter to Mlle Habert, glancing up at me now and again.

'Is your father a good-looking man? Do you take after him or your mother?' she said after writing two or three lines. 'I take after my mother, Madame.'

Two lines later: 'Your adventure with this elderly spinster who is marrying you is a strange one,' she went on, as though reflecting with amusement. 'For all her cloistered life so far, she must have a good eye, and I think she has nothing to complain of. But above all do behave considerately to your wife, and then afterwards do what you like with your heart, for at your age a man doesn't keep it to himself.'

'Alas, Madame, how would it help me if I did give it away? Who would want anything to do with a yokel like me?' 'Oh,' she said, nodding her head, 'that wouldn't be the difficulty.' 'But excuse me, Madame, it wouldn't be anyone of my own station I should love, I wouldn't care about that, it would be some person higher than me. That is the only thing that would tempt me.'

'Well,' she said, 'that is very well reasoned, and I respect you all the more for it. The sentiment suits you well and you must not lose it, it does you honour and will bring success, I can prophesy. I know about these things, and you must take my word for it, don't be faint-hearted.' And she said this with a persuasive look. 'Now about your heart,' she went on, 'were you born a bit tender-hearted? That is the sign of a good character.'

'Oh well, in that case I have the finest character in the world,' I said. 'Oh, fancy!' she exclaimed. 'Ha! ha! ha! The fellow answers back with the most amusing sharpness. Now tell me honestly, have you by any chance anyone in view already? Do you love somebody now?'

'Yes,' I said, 'I love anybody to whom I am indebted, as I am to you, Madame, whom I love more than all the others.'

'Mind what you are saying,' she said. 'I am talking about love, and you don't feel that for these people any more than for me. If you love us, it is out of gratitude, and not because we are attractive.' 'When people are like you,' I answered, 'it is because of everything, but I shouldn't be saying this.' 'Oh, go on, say it, say it, my boy. I am neither silly nor ridiculous, and so long as you act in good faith I forgive you.'

'Of course I am acting in good faith,' I answered, 'and if I weren't I should be very hard to please.' 'But be careful,' she said, putting her finger on her lips. 'Don't tell anyone but me, whatever you do, for people would laugh, my boy, and besides, you would cause trouble between Mlle Habert and me if she knew.'

'I would take care not to say it if she were here,' I said. 'Really, these old women are jealous, and the world is malicious,' she added, finishing her letter; 'and silence is always essential.'

Then we heard a noise in the adjoining room.

'Could there be some servant in there listening?' she said, folding up the letter. 'I should be very annoyed. Let's go. Take this note to Mlle Habert and give her my love, won't you, and as soon as you are married come and tell me here – this is my home. My name is at the end of the letter I have written, but don't come except in the evening, and then I will give you these papers to copy and we'll talk about how I can help you after that. So go along, my dear boy, and mind how you behave, for I have some good things in mind for you.' She said this in a softer and more affectionate voice, as she held out the letter in a manner which meant: 'I am offering you my hand as well.' At least I took it to mean that and so, as I took the letter, I kissed the hand that seemed to be offering itself, and it did not draw back in spite of the passionate and affectionate gratitude with which I did so. And it was a beautiful hand.

'Now that's something else you mustn't talk about,' she whispered as I was holding her hand and she was making as if to go. 'Oh, you can trust me, Madame,' I said in a very confidential tone, and for this occasion talking like a real country yokel, who frankly recognizes that he is being encouraged and has no patience with the affected modesty of grand ladies.

It was a brutal thing to do, and she coloured a little – for I was not worthy of being blushed at a lot. I didn't realize the enormity I was committing. So she recovered at once, and I noticed that on reflection she was quite pleased by the coarse remark that had escaped me, for it was a sign that I read her feelings aright, and that spared her the devious expedients she would have been obliged to adopt on some later occasion in order to express those feelings.

So we parted, she going back to join the President's wife and I leaving full of pleasant emotions.

'Did you intend to make love to her?' you will ask. I had no fixed intention, but was simply charmed to find I had appealed to a great lady. I was bubbling over in anticipation without knowing where all this would lead or thinking out the course I ought to steer.

To say this lady meant nothing to me – no. To say I loved her – no, I don't think so, either. What I felt for her could scarcely be called love, for I would never have noticed her if she hadn't noticed me, and I would not even have bothered about her attentions had she not been a person of distinction.

In fact it was not her I loved, but her rank, which was very exalted compared with mine.

I saw a society woman who looked distinguished, who apparently had servants and a carriage of her own, who found me attractive, who let me kiss her hand and didn't want anybody to know, in fact a woman who was raising both me and my pride out of the void we were still in; for until then had I thought of myself as anything at all? Had I known what self-respect was?

It is true that I was about to marry Mlle Habert, but she was just a middle-class woman who had begun by saying that I was as good as she was, had given me no time to get proud of having won her and whom, apart from her money, I considered my equal.

Had I not been her cousin? After that how on earth could I see any appreciable distance between her and me?

But in this case the distance was enormous; I could not measure it and my mind boggled at the thought of it. Yet it was across this distance that I was being sought, across this distance that I was being suddenly transported towards a person who shouldn't ever have known I existed in the world. Can't you see that that was enough to turn my head and give me reactions very like those of love?

So I was in love out of respect and amazement at what had befallen me, out of the inebriation of my vanity, anything you like to call it, and also the boundless admiration I had for this lady's charms. For I had never seen anyone as beautiful as she was in my wildest dreams so far. And yet she was fifty, and I had got that clear in the President's room, but I never gave that another thought, I did not wish she had any other quality, for even if she had been twenty years younger she would not have seemed any better to me because of it; she was a goddess, and goddesses have no age.

So I went off home filled with joy, puffed up with pride and full of my wild exaggerations about the merits of the lady.

The thought never occurred to me for a moment that my feelings were irreconcilable with those I owed to Mlle Habert. Nothing in my mind had changed towards her, and I was going to rejoin her as tenderly as ever. I was delighted to marry one and please the other, and it is quite possible to feel two pleasures at the same time.

But before setting out to go back to my intended I ought to have painted the portrait of this goddess I had left. So let us put it here, it won't take long.

You know her age, I have told you she was good-looking, but that is not enough. I have seen few women with such a noble figure and distinguished manner.

She always dressed unpretentiously which, however, detracted in no way from those natural charms she still had.

A woman might have dressed like that so as to look attractive yet not be accused of seeking to do so – I mean a woman basically coquettish, for she would have to be that in order to use such clothes to her advantage. There were little secret devices that could be called into play to make them as becoming as they were seemly, and perhaps more striking than a louder type of costume would have been.

She had beautiful hands and arms beneath the plain sleeves; they are better shown off under such cover and better appreciated.

A slightly old, but still beautiful face, which would have looked really old with expensive headgear but just looked handsome with a simple cap. Such lack of adornment was unnecessarily negligent, you felt like saying.

A well-shaped bosom (we must not forget this item, which in a woman is almost as important as the face), a very white bosom, very much covered, but now and again the covering was disarranged by a movement which showed up its whiteness, and the little you saw then gave you the best idea in the world of the whole.

Large dark eyes which were made to look wise and serious whatever their natural tendency, for they were in reality lively, tender and amorous.

I will not describe them at length; there would be so much to say about those eyes, so many things were put into them by art and so many others by nature that there could be no end to it if you wanted to say it all, and even then perhaps you wouldn't succeed. Can one express all one feels? Those who think so don't feel very much and only seem to see half what can be seen.

Let us come to the face, the sum total of all this.

At first glance you would have said of its owner: this is a very serious and sedate person.

But at the second glance: this is a person who has acquired that look of moderation and solemnity, she has not always had it. Is that person virtuous? The face says yes, but only with an effort; she keeps control of herself better than she is often tempted to, she denies herself pleasure, but she likes it, so watch out in case she gives in. So much for her behaviour.

As for intelligence, she was suspected of having a great deal, and rightly suspected. I did not get to know her well enough to say more on that subject.

As for character, it would be difficult for me to define that too, but what I am about to report will give a fairly extended impression and a rather strange one.

She did not love anyone, yet wished she could do more harm to her neighbour than she actually did.

The prestige of being thought good prevented her showing that she was bad, but she had the gift of exciting malice in others, and that stood her own malice in good stead.

Wherever she found herself the conversation was nothing but backbiting, and she was the one who put the others into that mood, either by praising or defending somebody in the wrong way, in fact by countless remarks full of apparent kindliness towards those she handed over to be torn to pieces, and then, while they were being pulled to bits, there were charitable exclamations which were at the same time encouraging: 'But whatever are you suggesting? Aren't you mistaken? Is it possible?' So that she invariably emerged innocent of the crimes she instigated (for I call any vindictive mockery a crime) and always the defender of people whose reputation she ruined through other people's mouths.

And the funny thing is that this woman, as I am describing her, didn't know that her own soul was so evil, for the depths of her heart eluded her, she was taken in by her own skill and ensnared in it; because she pretended to be good she thought she really was.

Such was the lady whose presence I had just left. I am describing her from what I heard about her later, from the few dealings we had with each other and such reflections about her that I have had since.

She had been a widow for eight or ten years. She was out of favour, it was said, with her husband when he died and he had accused her of some irregularity in her behaviour. To prove him wrong she had thrown herself during her widowhood into a religious life which had cut her off from the world and in which she had remained as much out of pride as habit, and also because it would have looked so unbecoming to reappear on the scene with charms nobody remembered, which were somewhat overripe and which the mere fact of withdrawal from the world had tarnished. For withdrawal does leave that effect on people who emerge from it. Retreat, especially Christian retreat, only suits those who stay therein, and nobody ever brought back a fashionable face – it always turns out ridiculous or disreputable,

Well, then, I was on my way back to Mlle Habert, my future

wife, and was happily quickening my step to get to her the sooner, when I was stopped by a great pack of carriages and carts at the corner of a street. I did not want to get caught up in this for fear of injury, and while waiting for the hold-up to clear itself I went into a passage in which, to pass the time, I began to read the letter Mme de Ferval (this is what I shall call the lady whom I have been describing) had given me for Mlle Habert and which was not sealed.

Scarcely had I read the first words when a man came down the steps at the end of the passage, rushed through it at full speed, banged into me as he passed, dropped a naked sword he was holding and made his escape, slamming the gate to the street in my face.

So there I was, shut in the passage and very disturbed by what I had just seen.

My first concern was to hurry to the gate and open it, but I tried in vain and could not manage it.

I heard some noise at the top of the steps at the far end. The passage was rather dark and this scared me.

As at such times all our instincts tend automatically towards self-preservation, and I had no stick or cudgel, I picked up the sword without realizing what I was doing.

The noise up there increased; I even thought I heard screams coming from the window of a room overlooking the street, and I was not mistaken. I heard someone shouting: 'Stop him! Stop him! And I was still holding the naked sword in one hand, just in case, while still trying with the other to open that wretched gate, which in the end I did, without thinking of dropping the sword.

But that didn't help me, for a whole mob had gathered, and seeing me looking wild-eyed and holding a naked sword, they didn't doubt that I was either a murderer or a thief.

I tried to escape, but it was impossible, and my struggles to that end only strengthened their suspicions.

At the same time police or guards from some nearby barrier came along and forced their way through the crowd, snatched the sword away from me and seized me.

I tried to shout my explanations, but could not be heard above the noise and tumult, and despite my struggles, which were ill-advised, was hauled into the house and up the stairs, and found myself, with the officers holding me and some of the neighbours following on, in a little apartment where we saw a young lady lying on the floor gravely wounded and unconscious, and an elderly woman trying to prop her up against a chair.

Opposite her was a very well-dressed young man, also wounded and lying on a sofa, who, although losing a lot of blood himself, was asking for help for the young lady, while the old woman and some sort of servant girl were screaming.

'Quick, gentlemen, a doctor, quick!' he said to the men holding me. 'Hurry up and help her, she is near to death, but perhaps can be saved' (he was referring to the young lady).

The doctor was not far away, there was one opposite the house, and they called to him through the window and he came up at once. There also came a police officer.

As I was protesting volubly that I had nothing to do with this affair and it was unlawful to hold me, I was dragged off into a little room adjoining, where I waited until the wounds of the lady and young man had been attended to.

The lady recovered consciousness, and when everything had been dealt with I was brought from the other room into theirs.

'Do you know this young man?' asked one of the police. 'Have a good look at him, we found him in the passage with the door shut on him, and he opened it, holding this sword that you see.' 'There is still blood on it,' exclaimed someone else, 'so he must be one of the men who wounded you.'

'No, gentlemen,' answered the young man in a very weak voice, 'we don't know this man, and he is not the one who left us in this condition. We know who our murderer is, he is — (he said a name I can't remember now), but as this man was on the premises and you seized him with this sword still stained with our blood, perhaps the man who attacked us used him as an accomplice in case of need, so you must arrest him all the same.'

'You wretch!' said the young lady without giving me time to answer. 'What has happened to the man whose accomplice you must be? Alas, gentlemen, he has given you the slip.' She was too weak to say any more, for she was mortally wounded and beyond hope of recovery.

I thought I could speak then, but hardly had I begun to explain myself before the officer who had been the principal spokesman cut in:

'This is not the place to justify yourself. Come on.' Thereupon I was dragged down the stairs, where I waited for a cab somebody had gone to fetch, and in it was taken to prison.

The place where I was put was not exactly a cell, but very nearly.

Happily the man who locked me in, though he was a gaoler, didn't look pitiless and didn't frighten me, and as at such times you cling on to anything, and a slightly less ferocious face than the others looks like that of a kindly man, I said: 'Sir' (slipping into his hand one or two of the gold coins Mlle Habert had given me, which he didn't refuse, and therefore had to listen. I had kept the coins even though I had been made to give up everything I had because, in plain English, I had a hole in my pocket and they had fallen somewhere lower down. So all I had left now was my letter, which I had popped into my shirt after holding it crumpled in my hand for a long time).

So then: 'Sir,' I said, 'as you are free to come and go, will you do me a kindness? I am not guilty of anything, as you will see, and this is only a misfortune that has befallen me. I have just left the house of President —, and a lady who is related to him gave me a letter to take to a lady called Mlle Habert, who lives in such and such a street and house, and as I can't deliver it myself I am entrusting it to you. Be so good as to take it or send it to this lady and at the same time let her know where I am. Look,' I said, taking out a few more coins, 'here's something to pay for the message if necessary, and this is nothing to the reward you will get when I am set free from here.'

'Just a minute,' he said, taking out a little pencil, 'did you say Mlle Habert, in such and such street?' 'Yes, Sir, and write down as well that it is in the house of a Mme d'Alain, widow.'

'Right you are,' he said, 'you can sleep in peace, I've got to go out, and in an hour at the outside your affair will be settled.'

He went straight out after these words, and I stayed there between my four walls weeping, but more out of shock than out of fear, or if it was fear it was due to the emotional upset of the mishap, for I never dreamed of fearing for my life.

On such occasions we are first overcome by the reactions that come naturally – our souls, so to speak, do themselves justice. The innocent man merely sighs whereas the guilty trembles, the one is upset, the other disquieted.

So I was merely upset, which was all I deserved. What a disaster, I thought. Curse that street, with its traffic! What was I in that beastly passage for? It must have been the devil shoving me in there.

And then my tears flowed. 'Oh Lord, what have I come to? Oh Lord, get me out of here!' I went on. 'What wicked people the elder Mlle Habert and M. Doucin are! What a dance they have led me with having to go to this President!' And then sighs and tears, then silence, then talk: 'My poor father little dreams that I am in prison on my wedding day! And dear Mlle Habert is waiting for me – but aren't we on the way to seeing each other again?'

All these considerations were breaking my heart, but finally some other thoughts came to my rescue: 'Don't let us despair, God won't forsake me. If that gaoler delivers my letter to Mlle Habert and tells her the trouble I'm in, she will not fail to work for my deliverance.'

And my hopes were justified, as will be seen. The gaoler did not let me down. Mme de Ferval's letter was delivered in an hour or so to my future wife. He carried it himself and told her where I was, then came and told me about it on his return, bringing some food which didn't appeal to me.

'Cheer up,' he said, 'I gave your letter to the lady and told her you were in prison, and when she heard it she passed right out – ta-ta!' Real gaoler's language, as you see.

'Oh, one minute,' I interrupted, 'there was somebody there to help her, surely?'

'Oh yes, of course, it won't be nothing much, there were two people with her.' 'Then didn't she say anything?' I went on. 'Course not, because she was struck speechless! Anyway, have something to eat while you're waiting for better news.'

'I simply couldn't,' I said. 'I'm only thirsty, and would like a drop of wine. Could you get me some?' 'Oh yes, give me some money and I'll get some to you.'

After all the money he had had from me, and in any other place than the one I was in, the word 'give' would have been ungrateful and unwarranted, but in prison I was the one in the wrong and who didn't know how things were done.

'Oh dear,' I said, 'excuse me, I forgot the money.' And I took out yet another gold coin, for I had nothing smaller.

As he went off he said: 'Would you like me to go on supplying wine while the money lasts, instead of giving you the change? You'll have plenty of time to drink it.'

'Just as you please,' I said humbly, depressed at having to deal with this new kind of person – a man you have to thank for the good you are doing him.

The wine was very welcome, for I was almost fainting by the time it was brought, but it set me up again, and the only unpleasant thing I felt was extreme impatience to see what the news I had had delivered to the ever helpful Mlle Habert would produce.

At times the story of her fainting worried me somewhat, for I was afraid it might have made her incapable of acting herself, and I had much more faith in her than in all the friends she might have been able to employ on my behalf.

Yet on the other hand this fainting fit was a proof of her love and the speed with which she would come to my aid.

Three hours had already gone by since the wine had been brought, when I was told that two people wanted to see me downstairs. They would not come up, but I could go down.

My heart leaped with joy. I followed the gaoler who took me to a room in which I was embraced by Mlle Habert, who burst into tears.

With her was a man in black whom I did not know.

'Oh, M. de la Vallée, my dear boy, whatever has brought you here?' she exclaimed. 'Sir, don't be surprised that I am kissing him, we were to be married today,' she said to the man with her. Then turning to me again:

'What has happened to you? What's it all about?'

I did not reply at once, for I was so moved by Mlle Habert's greeting that I had to have time to weep as well.

'Oh dear,' I finally said, 'it's a most absurd story. Just imagine, I am here all because of a passage – while I was in it they shut the gate – there were two murders committed upstairs, they thought I had something to do with them, and consequently here I am.'

'What! Something to do with two murders because you went up a passage? My dear boy, what on earth does this mean? Do explain yourself, who did the killing?' 'I've no idea,' I said, 'I only saw the sword, which I inadvertently picked up in the passage.'

'This looks serious,' said the man in black. 'What you have told us doesn't help to make it clear. Let's sit down and you tell us the story as it really is. What is all this about a passage that we can't make head or tail of?'

'It all happened like this,' I said, and then I began my tale from the time of leaving the President's house, thence to the traffic mix-up which had stopped me at that passage, then the unknown man who had shut me in as he escaped, the sword he had dropped and I had picked up, and then the rest of it.

'I don't know the killer or his victims, who were not yet dead when I was taken up to them and they admitted that they did not know me either, and that's all I know myself about the reason why I am in prison.'

'It makes me shudder all over,' said Mlle Habert. 'What, wouldn't anyone listen to reason? Since the wounded people don't know you, what can they say?' 'That I may be the accomplice of the criminal who attacked them, and whose back is all I have seen of him,' I replied.

'The bloodstained sword with which you were taken,' said the man in black, 'is an awkward matter, and it worries me. But your story puts an idea into my head.

'We heard them saying along there that three or four hours ago they brought in a prisoner who, it is alleged, stabbed two people in the street you mention. It might well be the man who ran along the passage where you were. You both wait here, and I'll try and find out in more detail what it is all about. They may tell me.'

Off he went. 'My poor boy,' said Mlle Habert when he had gone, 'what a plight I find you in! It gave me a turn which is still affecting me, and I can't get my breath. I thought today would be the last day of my life. Oh my darling, when you saw that hold-up why didn't you go some other way?'

'Oh cousin dear,' I said, 'it was for the sake of seeing you sooner that I wanted to go by the most direct route. Who would think that one particular street would be so fatal? You are on foot, you are in a hurry, you love the person you are on your way to see, and you take the shortest cut. It's natural.'

As I was making this speech I bathed her hands with my tears, and she, too, was weeping most bitterly.

'Who is that man you brought with you, and where have you come from, cousin?' I asked. 'Oh dear, I have done nothing but rush about ever since getting the letter you sent. In that, Mme de Ferval was so obliging and so anxious to help that my first thought was to go to her and ask for her assistance. She is a kind lady, and could not have done more had it been for her own son. I could see she was almost as upset as I was. "Don't fret," she said, "it won't be anything, we have friends, and I will get him out of there. You stay here and I'll go and talk to the President."

'And with no more ado she left me, and came back in a moment with a note from the President for M. de — (one of the leading magistrates for cases like mine). I took the note and at once went with it to this magistrate, who read it and then summoned one of his secretaries, had a word with him in private and then told him to accompany me to the prison and get me permission to see you. And so we have come together to find out what this affair of yours is all about. Mme de Ferval also promised to go anywhere with me if I wanted her to.'

The secretary returned just as Mlle Habert was finishing this story.

'I thought as much,' he said. 'The man they brought in this morning is certainly the killer of the two people in question. I have just been talking to one of the officers who arrested him as he was running away, hatless and without his sword, pursued by a mob that saw him rush like a madman out of a house said to be in the very street where you found the way blocked. There was a considerable lapse of time before they could catch him because he had run a long way; and then he was taken back to the house he had come out of which, they said, another man had just left, having been caught there and already taken to prison under suspicion of being his accomplice. Now according to what you have told us this other man, thought to be an accomplice, looks very much like being you.'

'He is none other,' I answered. 'I am the man in that passage, and that is exactly how I come to be here, without anybody knowing that I was going about my business when I was unlucky enough to run into all that.'

'This prisoner will soon be interrogated,' said the secretary, 'and if he doesn't know you and his answers fit in with what you are telling us, as I am sure will be the case, you will soon be out of here, and your release will be expedited. You go back home, Mademoiselle, and don't worry. Let us go. And you,' he said to me, 'you will stay in this room where you will be more comfortable than where you were, and I will see that some dinner is brought to you.'

'It's no use,' I said. 'They have already brought me a miserable ration to my hole up there, and it might be mouldy by now and I've no stomach for it.'

They urged me to eat something, and left. Mlle Habert and I embraced and did a little weep all over again. 'Don't let him want for anything,' said that kind lady to the man who locked me up again; and the rattle of keys continued for quite two or three minutes after they had gone. Nothing grates on you so much as the locks in that particular place, and I think they are more unpleasant to the innocent than to the guilty, for they have other things than that on their minds.

My dinner came a few minutes later, and I was somewhat cheered by the comparison I made between it and what I had been given before; the change was a good omen. After all, we only want to live, everything urges us that way, so I cast a few unenthusiastic glances at a rather nice-looking chicken and, also unenthusiastically, took up the two wings, which somehow got eaten; then I idly gnawed some of the rest. Without knowing what I was doing, I had one or two drinks of a wine which seemed passable, and finished my repast with some fruit which I sampled because it happened to be there.

I felt less depressed after eating. Food is a wonderful thing when you are bowed down with sorrow. It certainly is balm to the spirit, and you can't be really sad while your stomach is busy digesting.

I am not saying that I thought no more of my plight. I still had it in mind, but in a calm way. However, eventually my sadness came back. I pass over the account of everything that happened after Mlle Habert's visit and come to the moment when I appeared before a magistrate, with whom was another lawyer who seemed to be taking notes and whose name and functions I didn't know. Opposite them was a man looking deathly pale and quite overwhelmed, and other people from whom I thought they were taking statements.

I was interrogated. Do not expect exact details about this interrogation. I don't remember the order in which things were taken, and I will only report the essential item, which was that this desperate-looking man was the very man in the passage, and he said he didn't know me and I said the same about him. I told my story, and told it, referring to my misfortune, in such artless words that some of the people present were obliged to put their hands over their faces to hide their smiles.

When I had finished, the prisoner declared with tears in his eyes: 'I repeat once again that I had no confidant or accomplice. I don't know whether I could plead for my life, but it is a burden to me and I deserve to lose it. I killed my mistress, I even saw her die (and indeed she died when he was taken back there). She died of horror at seeing me again and called me her murderer. I killed my friend, whose rival I had become (and it was true that he was dying too), I killed them both in a fit of madness. I am in despair, I look upon myself with loathing as a monster. I would have stabbed myself as well had I not been arrested. I am not worthy to be given the time to come to my senses and repent of my madness, let me be condemned and let them be avenged. I ask for death as a favour, spare me the long delays that make me die a thousand deaths instead of one, and free this young man whom it is pointless to keep here, whom I have never seen except in that passage – where I would have killed him as well for fear he might identify me, but in my frantic state the sword flew out of my hand. Set him free, Sir, let him go, I blame myself for the distress that has been inflicted upon him and beg him to forgive me for the state of alarm I see he is in and of which I am the cause. He has nothing in common with a foul creature like me.'

I shuddered when he said he had meant to kill me – it would have been decidedly worse than being in prison! And yet, in spite of that admission, I was sorry for the unfortunate criminal, his speech touched my heart, and in reply to his plea for pardon for my misadventure I said: 'And I, Sir, pray God to have mercy on you and on your soul.'

That is all I am going to say about this affair. Mlle Habert came back to see me after all the ordeals I had been through, the secretary was still with her, but he left us alone for a little while, and you can imagine how lovingly our hearts overflowed! You are so happy and your soul feels such bliss when you have come through a great peril, and both of us were emerging from one in our own way. For after all my life had been in danger and Mlle Habert had run the risk of losing me, which she on her side thought of as the greatest possible disaster, especially if she had lost me just at that juncture.

She told me all she had done, the new steps Mme de Ferval had taken with both the President and the magistrate who had interrogated me.

We called down a thousand blessings upon this lady for the kind services she had rendered, and my future wife went off into ecstasies about her charity and piety. 'What a fine Christian!' she exclaimed. 'What a fine Christian!' And I said: 'What a good-hearted woman!' For I dared not repeat Mlle Habert's terms or use the same eulogies. I deliberately used others; and as a matter of fact it would not have been very becoming in the presence of my betrothed to praise the piety of a person who had cast eyes on her husband, and was only being so helpful to me because of the very fact that she was not so Christian. But remember I was still in prison, and that made me careful, and I was afraid God might punish me if I attributed to piety attentions for which there was every likelihood that the devil and man had all the credit.

I even blushed more than once while Mlle Habert was singing these praises of Mme de Ferval, in connection with whom I wasn't above reproach myself, and I felt ashamed to see this good woman, who so little deserved it, taken in in this way.

From praises of Mme de Ferval we moved on to what had happened in my prison – joy is very talkative, and we went on and on – I told her everything the real culprit had said, how honourably he had exonerated me and how terrible it was that he had unfortunately given way to such violence, for he must have been a good man at bottom. Then we came to ourselves, our love, our marriage, but you will perhaps ask me about that guilty man. Here in a word is the explanation of his conduct.

For nearly a year his best friend had been in love with a girl but, as he was not as well off as she was, her father had refused to let him marry her and had even forbidden his daughter to see any more of him. In their predicament they used the man who killed them as a go-between for exchanging letters.

This young man, one of the friends of the family but not, however, a frequent visitor, fell passionately in love with the girl himself through seeing her and hearing her grieving for the other. He had more money than his friend. He talked of love, the girl poked fun at it for a time as though it were a joke, took offence when she realized it was serious, and informed her lover, who rounded angrily on his disloyal friend. At first this friend was ashamed and seemed to be sorry, promised to leave them in peace, but then went on with it and eventually quarrelled with the dead man, who broke with him. Finally he carried his treachery to the length of asking for the girl's hand. The father accepted him and tried in vain to force his daughter to marry him.

In desperation the lovers had recourse to other means, both for writing and speaking to each other. An elderly widow who had been a maid to the girl's mother made them welcome in her home, where they would sometimes meet and talk over what steps could be taken. The other man got to know of this and became insanely jealous. He was a violent man with apparently no strength of character, the sort of man whom a strong passion can render evil and capable of anything. One day he had them followed when they went to the widow's house, slipped in after them and surprised them just as his friend was kissing the girl's hand, and in his rage first wounded him with his sword and was about to deal him a second blow when the girl, trying to throw herself in front of him, was herself stabbed and fell. The man ran off and you know the rest of the story. Let us come back to mine.

The secretary came back and said I would be released the next day, so let us get to the next day, for all this prison detail is depressing.

Mlle Habert called for me at eleven. She did not come up, but sent word and I went down. A carriage was waiting at the door, and what carriage? Mme de Ferval's, and Mme de Ferval herself was in it, so as to attract more notice to my release and make my innocence more widely known.

Nor did the lady's helpfulness stop there. 'Before we take him home with you,' she said to Mlle Habert, 'I think we should drive him through the whole district and right in front of the place where he was arrested; it is a good thing that people who saw him taken off and might recognize him somewhere else should know that he is innocent. This seems to me a necessary precaution, and perhaps,' she went on, turning to me, 'you yourself will recognize some of the people who were round you when you were arrested.'

'Oh yes, I would,' I said, 'and if it were only the doctor who was opposite the house and whom they called in to attend to the victims, I should be very glad to see him and show him I'm a better fellow than he imagines.'

'Oh dear Lord, how wonderful Madame is!' cried Mlle Habert. 'For you must be assured, M. de la Vallée, that she has done it all and yet her only concern in the matter is God's will.' At this mention of God, whom Mme de Ferval knew to have nothing to do with the case, she cut in: 'Never mind that; when do you propose to get married?' 'This very night, if nothing prevents,' said Mlle Habert.

Just then we reached the street that had been so fateful for me and to which the coachman had been told to drive. We stopped outside the doctor's house, he was standing at his door and I noticed that he was looking hard at me. 'Sir,' I said, 'do you remember me? Do you recognize me?'

'Oh yes, I think so,' he answered, politely raising his hat to a man he saw in a grand carriage with two ladies, one of whom looked like a very important person. 'Yes, Sir, I do remember you, I think you are the man who was in that house the day before yesterday (pointing to the one where I had been arrested), and to whom ...' He hesitated to say the rest. 'Go on,' I said, 'yes, Sir, I am the one they arrested and took away to prison.' 'I didn't dare say so,' he went on, 'but I looked at you so carefully then that I recognized you at once. Well then, Sir, you had nothing to do with the matter in question?'

'No more than yourself,' I said, and then explained how I had got mixed up in it. 'Well, I'm very glad indeed,' he went on, 'and so are all of us here, the neighbours, my wife and my children, me and my apprentices, we all said who the devil can you trust now after that chap, for he has the nicest face in the world. In fact I want them to see you. Come here, Babet (one of his daughters), and come here, wife, come here, you others (his apprentices), look, have a good look at this gentleman, do you know who he is?'

'Oh, Father,' exclaimed Babet, 'he looks like that prisoner the other day.' 'Yes indeed he does,' chimed in the wife, 'he is so like him that it *is* him.' 'Yes,' I said, 'the very same.' 'Well, well,' said Babet, 'isn't that funny, so you didn't have anything to do with killing anybody, Monsieur?' 'No, certainly not,' I said, 'and I should be very sorry indeed to have a part in anyone's death – in his life, well, perhaps.' 'Honestly,' said the wife, 'we couldn't understand it at all.' 'Oh, as to that,' said Babet, 'if ever anyone looked like an innocent man it was certainly you.'

People were beginning to gather round, and several of them recognized me. Mme de Ferval was kind enough to let this scene go on long enough to re-establish my good name all over the neighbourhood; I said good-bye to the doctor and all his family, and had the consolation of being waved at in a very friendly way by the crowd and cleared all along the street of the crimes I had been suspected of – to say nothing of the pleasure I took in hearing on all sides praises of my good looks, which made Mlle Habert extremely happy and led her to look upon me with a desire she had never felt before.

I saw how she was filled with pleasure at contemplating me and was telling herself how right she had been to find me so attractive.

It even served me well in Mme de Ferval's opinion, and she also cast at me some more attentive glances than usual, and I am sure she was thinking: 'So my taste isn't so bad, since everybody thinks the same as I do.'

All that, incidentally, happened as we were talking, and I felt very gratified; but it was not all.

We were approaching Mlle Habert's house, which was as far as Mme de Ferval was to take us, when we saw outside a church my future wife's elder sister and M. Doucin in earnest consultation together. A coach which made ours slow down gave them plenty of time to see us.

Whenever I think of it I still laugh at the prodigious amazement that transfixed them at the sight of us.

We petrified them; they were so taken aback and so flabbergasted that they hadn't even enough presence of mind left to scowl at us, as they would certainly have done had they not been so thunderstruck, but there are things that knock you flat, and to add to their discomfiture, we could not have burst upon their gaze at any moment more humiliating and painful for them. Chance added accidental happenings expressly calculated to infuriate them, so that we triumphed over them in an arrogant manner which would have been insolent if we had thought it out. For, if you please, just at the moment when they caught sight of us Mme de Ferval, Mlle Habert and I were bursting with laughter at something funny I had said, and that, together with the triumphal pomp with which Mme de Ferval seemed to be conducting us, must certainly have pierced them to the heart.

We politely bowed to them and they returned our greeting in a daze, not knowing what they were doing, bowled over by the shattering blow which struck them down.

You should also know that they had just come from the younger Mlle Habert's lodgings (we found out when we got home), and that there they had been told that I was in prison. For Mme d'Alain, who had been present when the gaoler I had sent from the prison had told his tale, had not been able to keep her mouth shut, and even while upbraiding them because of us she had delighted them with this good news.

Imagine the grounds for hope this had given them against me. A man in prison – what for? It can't be anything to do with us, nor the President either, who refused to help us, so it must be for something quite unconnected with our business. How do I know whether they didn't go to the length of suspecting me of some crime; they both hated me enough to have that charitable opinion of me. Religious bigots take their own hatred of you as proof that you are a bad lot. Oh what a disappointment to run into us suddenly in such a brilliant and prosperous situation!

But let us leave them to their confusion and come to dear Mlle Habert's home.

'I won't come up,' said Mme de Ferval, 'because I have an appointment. Good-bye, see to it that you are married as soon as possible, don't waste time, and please let M. de la Vallée come and tell me when it is an accomplished fact, for until then I shall be worried.'

'We'll both come and tell you,' answered Mlle Habert, 'it's the least we can do, Madame.' 'No, no,' she said, casting at me a look of complicity, which she saw I understood, 'it will do if he comes alone, Mademoiselle, but just as you like.' And she departed.

'Well, well, Lord forgive me!' cried Mme d'Alain when she saw me again, 'I do believe it's M. de la Vallée you're bringing back to us, my dear.' 'Just as you say, Mme d'Alain, you're quite right,' I said, 'and God certainly will forgive you for believing it, for you are making no mistake. Good morning, Mlle Agathe' (the daughter was there as well). 'Welcome,' she said, 'Mother and I thought you were lost.'

'Lost!' exclaimed the widow. 'If you hadn't come this morning I was going to send all my friends to scour the highways and byways this afternoon. Your sister and M. Doucin have just gone,' she added to my future wife, 'they came to see you and, I tell you, I gave them a few home truths. "That poor fellow is in prison," I said, "and you know it, you are responsible and it is very wicked of you." "In prison? Oh, since when?" "Since when? I like that, since your intrigues, since you have been running about everywhere to get him put there." And then they went off, and I didn't so much as ask them to take a seat.'

This speech of Mme d'Alain as I report it shows that she didn't know why I had been sent to prison, and as a matter of fact Mlle Habert had taken care not to tell her, and had let her believe that I had been put there through her sister's intrigues. If Mme d'Alain had been told all about it what a windfall such a tale would have been to her! The whole neighbourhood would have re-echoed with my adventure, she would have gone and told it from door to door to give herself the luxury of displaying her sorrow on my behalf, and we were spared that amount of scandalmongering.

Oh, do tell us this, do tell us that! She wanted all the details of my prison life. I invented a few for her, but didn't tell her the true ones. 'And then I have found you a priest who will marry you whenever you like,' she said, 'straight away if it isn't too late, but it can be after midnight if that is your plan.'

'Oh yes, Madame,' said Mlle Habert, 'and we shall be much obliged if you will let him know.' 'I'll go and see him myself later,' she said, 'but now we must have something to eat. Come along and have some of my soup, and you will have me to supper this evening. And I will find you some witnesses who won't be as stuck-up as the first ones we had.'

But all these fiddling details are boring even to me, so let us skip them and suppose that night has come, that we have dined with our witnesses and that it is two o'clock in the morning and we are setting off for church.

So this time we really are here, Mass is said and we are married in spite of our elder sister and her priestly accomplice, who won't get any more coffee or sugar from Mme de la Vallée.

I have seen many kinds of love in my life, many ways of saying and proving that one is in love, but I have never seen any love to equal my wife's.

The most passionate, tender women of the world, old or young, do not love in that way, and I would even defy them to imitate it. No, to resemble Mlle Habert, whom I should no longer call by that name, it is quite unavailing to have the most responsive heart in the world. Add to that passion, and it still doesn't come up to it – in fact put everything you like into a woman's heart, and you will make her a very lively, passionate creature, but you won't make her into a Mlle Habert, and all the love such a woman is capable of will still not give you an adequate conception of my wife's.

In order to love like her you need to have lived for thirty years in religious bigotry, and you need to have had courage all through thirty years to do so. For thirty years you must have resisted the temptation to think about love, and for thirty years considered it a sin even to listen to men or look at them, although liking them very much.

Oh, get married after thirty years of that intensity, find yourself from nightfall until morning wife of a man: that is already a great deal; but I add to that a man you are really in love with, which is still more, and you will be another Mlle Habert, and I warrant that whoever marries you will see I am right when I say that her love was not the same kind as anyone else's.

Describe this love to us, I shall be asked. Just a moment, I can't. All I can say is that she looked upon me as though I were a graven image, not more nor less, and it was her long habit of praying and rolling her eyes adoringly while praying that made her look at me in that way.

When a woman loves you she tells you so in terms of love. She, however, told me so with religious worship, but such delicious worship! You would have thought her heart was engaged with me in a passionate affair of conscience, and that it meant: God be praised, for He commands me to love you, and His holy will be done. And all her passionate transports were in that tone, and fleshly love lost only a little of its airs and graces but none of its intensity, so try to imagine what it could be like.

It was ten by the time we got up; we had gone to bed at three and we had had reason to want some rest.

'M. de la Vallée,' she said a quarter of an hour before we got up, 'we certainly have four or five thousand livres a year on which we can live tolerably well, but you are young and must have something to do. What do you think of doing?' 'Whatever you like, cousin,' I said, 'but I am rather keen on this tax-collecting racket, it brings in such a lot, and is the foster-mother of all the have-nots. I don't need a foster-mother with you, cousin, and you won't let me go short of food, but an abundance of supplies does no harm, so let's become financiers with the help of a profession which doesn't cost us much and brings a lot in, as is customary in that trade. The squire of our village, who died as rich as a cash-box, had got on in that way, so let us get on in the same way.'

'Yes, that's fine,' she said, 'but you don't know anything about it, and it is my opinion that you should study a bit first. I know someone who is Learned Counsel with whom you could work. Would you like me to speak to him?'

'Wouldn't I just! Oh Lord, yes, cousin, can there be two wills here, isn't your will mine?' 'Alas, my darling,' she went on, 'I shall never wish for anything but your good. But by the way, dear husband, all these bothers of ours have driven one thing out of my head. You need a suit and some linen, and I will go out this afternoon and buy all that.'

'And while we are on men's outfitting, little wife,' I said, 'there is one small item I have always longed for. Could your wishes perhaps run to that? In this life there is no harm in being well turned out.'

'Oh, what is it, my dear?' she asked. 'Only a sword and belt so as to be M. de la Vallée good and proper. There's nothing like it for cutting a good figure, and then you are on a level with all the best people.'

'Yes indeed, my handsome husband, you are right, we'll make that one of this morning's purchases. There is a swordsmith quite near here, and we only have to send for him. Now just think a bit, what else would you like?' she went on, for on this first day of her married life this piously inflamed soul only breathed for her young husband, and if I had told her I wanted to be king I think she would have promised to get me a crown.

Just then it struck ten and our coffee was ready. Mme d'Alain, who was having it brought, was shouting outside our door and asking to come in with a din she thought was the last word in tact, seeing that we were newly-weds.

I wanted to get out of bed. 'No, my boy, no, it would take you too long to dress – which reminds me that you need a dressing-gown.' 'All right, so I do,' I laughed. 'Get along with you, you don't understand, my dear; I needed you, cousin, then I'd have everything!'

So she got out of bed, put on a gown and opened the door to our noisy hostess, who came in shouting: 'Come here and let me kiss you, with your lovely tired eyes. What's this hefty young man like, will he do? You are laughing – that means yes! Well, that's all to the good, I thought he would be all right, the young scamp, I expect it's nice living with him, isn't it? Come on, up you get, young man,' she said, coming over to me, 'out of that bed, your wife isn't in it now, and it will be dark again tonight!'

'I can't,' I said, 'I'm too well-mannered to get up in front of you – tomorrow by all means, for then I shall have a gown to put on.' 'Good Lord,' she said, 'what a lot of fuss! If that's all you need I can go and get one for you. It's as good as new, my poor late husband didn't wear it ten times. When you have it on I shall think I'm seeing him in the flesh.'

Thereupon she went to her own room and brought back the dressing-gown and threw it on the bed. 'There you are,' she said. 'It's good and in perfect condition, you keep it, I'll let you have it cheap.'

'Would you like it, love?' asked Mme de la Vallée. 'Not half!' I said. 'How much is it? I'm no good at haggling.'

And then: 'I'll let you have it for so much, that's settled.' 'No, that's too much.' 'It's not enough.' In short, they came to an agreement and the dressing-gown was mine. I paid for it with what money I had left from prison.

We had our coffee. Mme de la Vallée detailed our needs in clothes and linen to our hostess and asked for her help to do her shopping in the afternoon. But as for the suit itself, chance ordained otherwise.

A tailor to whom Mme d'Alain let some rooms at the back of the house came a quarter of an hour later and paid some rent he owed her. 'Oh fancy, M. Simon, you come just at the right moment', she said, pointing to me. 'Here's a customer for you, and we'll get you to cut the cloth for a suit for the gentleman straight away.'

M. Simon bowed and had a good look at me. 'Well I never!' he said. 'It wouldn't be worth the trouble to cut a length of cloth. I've got a brand-new suit down there that I put the finishing touches to yesterday, and the man it was for left it with me as a surety because he couldn't pay off the credit I gave him. Then yesterday morning, if you please, he decamped from his inn without so much as a good-bye to anybody. I think it will be just right for the gentleman, and it's a chance for him to fit himself out right away and cheaper than at a shop; there is the coat, vest and breeches, in a really fine cloth with no pattern, lined with red silk, all complete.'

This red silk appealed to my vanity – a silk lining, what a joy and what magnificence for a country lad! 'What do you say, my love?' I asked Mme de la Vallée. 'Oh my dear, if it's a good fit it's settled.' 'It will fit you like a glove,' said the tailor, and went off to fetch it. He brought it, I tried it on, it fitted me better than my own suit and my heart beat fast beneath the silk. We came to the price.

It took longer to conclude the haggling than for the dressing-gown, not because of my wife, for Mme d'Alain said to her: 'Don't you worry about this, leave it to me. Now look here, Monsieur Simon, perhaps you won't find such a suitable customer for these togs in a whole year. For they fit one particular size, and here he is. It's as though God sent him to you, and there may not be another quite like him in Paris. So just you give over – by wanting too much you get nothing at all!' And with offers and counter-offers our officious haggler concluded the deal.

When the suit was bought my wife was overcome with a loving desire to see me all fitted out. 'My dear boy,' she said, 'let's send out at once for a sword-belt, stockings, a hat (I'd like it to be braided), a new ready-made shirt and the whole outfit, shall we?'

'Just as you like,' I said, with joy in the depths of my being, and no sooner said than done. All the tradespeople were sent for, Mme d'Alain being always present, always bargaining and haggling. Before dinner-time I had the joy of seeing Jacob turned into a fine gentleman, with his silk lining, the smart silver braid on his hat, and the adornment of a wig that came down to my waist and on which the hairdresser had lavished all his art.

I have told you already that I was a handsome young man, but until then you had to have your eyes open to notice it. What is a good-looking fellow in shabby clothes? He is buried under them, and our eyes are so easily deceived in such matters! Do people so much as notice his good looks? What is the use of them? People would be more likely to say: what's he doing here, what's this to do with him? Only once in a while a few women not so frivolous or shallow as the others have a taste for the more essential things and are not taken in. I had already met one or two of these, as you have seen, but Good Heavens, in my new outfit you only needed eyes to see how attractive I was, and it didn't matter about their being very good eyes either. I was a fine man, I had a good figure and was naturally graceful, and all that could be taken in at a glance.

'Just look at him, the dear boy!' exclaimed Mme de la Vallée when I emerged from the little room where I had gone to change. 'Well, well,' said Mme d'Alain, 'don't you think he is charming?' And it wasn't just chatter on her part this time – I realized that she was speaking as a woman who really thought so, and for a few moments it even stopped her babble. To judge by the astonishment with which she looked at me I think she coveted my wife's husband. I already appealed to her, in any case.

'There's a fine fellow for you!' she said. 'If ever I marry I shall go for a man who looks like that!' 'Oh yes, Mother,' said Agathe, who had just come in, 'but that isn't all. You must have the right look about you as well.'

Thereupon we had dinner. Mme d'Alain launched into endearments of all kinds, Agathe spoke with her eyes only, and they said more than her mother, my wife saw nothing but me, thought only of me, and I in return seemed to pay no attention to anyone but her.

Our witnesses, whom Mme de la Vallée had invited to supper when she saw the last of them at three in the morning of the same day, arrived towards five.

'M. de la Vallée,' said my cousin, 'I think it would be a good idea if you went and called on Mme de Ferval; we shan't have our meal before eight and you will have time to see her. Give her my compliments and tell her that tomorrow we shall both have the honour of seeing her together.'

'Oh yes, of course,' I said, 'she did ask us to keep her informed, and that is only right. Good-bye ladies, good-bye gentlemen; if you will excuse me, I'll be back quite soon.'

My wife thought she was reminding me about Mme de Ferval, but I should have reminded her myself if she had forgotten. I was dying for her to see me as I now was. Oh, how delighted she will be with me, I told myself, it will be very different indeed from these past few days. You will see in the sequel how things turned out.

PART 4

So I went to Mme de Ferval's, and the only person I met in the courtyard was a manservant who took me up to her rooms by a little staircase I didn't know.

One of her maids, who appeared first, said she would go and tell her mistress, and she came back a moment later and took me into the lady's room. I found her lying on a sofa reading, with her head supported by one hand, in a very elegant if rather carelessly arranged négligée.

Picture a skirt not quite pulled down to the feet and even disclosing a little of the loveliest leg in the world (and a lovely leg is a great attraction in a woman).

Of these two dainty feet one had lost its slipper, and in something like semi-nudity it looked most alluring.

None of this appealing posture was lost on me; it was the first time in my life that I really appreciated the value of a woman's foot and leg, which until then I had not considered of any importance, having seen only women's faces and figures. But now I found out that they were women all over. Yet I was still only a peasant, for what is a stay of four or five months in Paris? But you need neither delicate perceptions nor knowledge of the world to be suddenly aware of certain things, especially when they are seen in their true perspective. All you need is senses, and I had those.

In fact that beautiful leg and pretty little slipperless foot were a great pleasure to contemplate.

Of course I have seen such things since and always with pleasure, but never with so much pleasure as then; what's more, as I have said already, it was the first time I was aware of them. Enough said: there is no pleasure that doesn't lose a little through familiarity.

As I went in I bowed once or twice to Mme de Ferval, but I don't think she noticed whether I did so properly or not, for she was not looking for acquired graces in me, but was only interested in my natural ones, which she could observe better than she had before because I was better turned out.

From the way she looked me over I realized that she had not expected to see that I had such a good figure and was so handsome.

'Well fancy!' she exclaimed in surprise, rising a little from her sofa. 'It's you, La Vallée! I don't recognize you, you really look very nice, very nice indeed. Come here, dear boy, come here, get a chair and sit there. But what a well set-up figure! And that head and hair are really too beautiful for a man, and a perfect leg, too. You'll have to learn dancing, La Vallée, you really must. Sit down. You couldn't look better,' she concluded, taking my hand to make me sit down.

As I was hesitating out of respect, she said yet again: 'Do sit down,' in a tone suggesting: forget who I am and don't let us stand on ceremony.

'Well, young man,' she said, 'I have been thinking about you, for you know I like you.' She said this with eyes explaining what she meant by *liking*. 'Yes, I do like you, and want you to be a friend of mine and like me too, do you understand?'

'Alas, charming lady,' I answered, in a transport of vanity and gratitude, 'I may well like you too much if you don't take care.'

Hardly had I said this before I threw myself upon the hand she yielded to me and kissed it with ecstasy.

For a moment or two she said nothing, and enjoyed watching me in action, but she was breathing audibly like someone sighing gently. 'Tell me, my dear, do you like me so very much?' she asked, while my head was bowed over this hand. 'Now why should you be afraid of being too fond of me, La Vallée? Explain yourself, what do you mean?'

'I mean that you are so attractive and so beautiful, and because I am conscious of those things, you see, I am afraid of liking you more than I should.'

'Really, it sounds as though you were talking about love, La Vallée.' 'And it sounds right,' I answered, 'for I can't help it.'

'Speak softly,' she said, 'my maid might be in there (pointing to the anteroom). Oh my dear boy, what have you just said? So you love me?' 'Alas, being such an unimportant little fellow, dare I say yes?' 'That's up to you,' she sighed, 'but you are very young, and I too am afraid of trusting you. But come nearer so that we can be closer for talking.' I forgot to mention that during the conversation she had resumed the posture in which I had first found her, still with one slipper off, still with legs partly uncovered – sometimes more, sometimes less, according to the attitude she took up on the sofa.

My glances in that direction did not escape her. 'What a dainty little foot you have, Madame,' I said, bringing my chair closer, for I was imperceptibly slipping into a more familiar tone.

'That's enough about my foot,' she said, 'and put my slipper on again for me. But we must talk about what you have just told me and see what we shall do about this love you have for me!'

'Would that love be unfortunate enough to annoy you?' I asked. 'Oh no, La Vallée, it doesn't annoy me. On the contrary, I am touched, you appeal to me too much, you are as beautiful as the statue of Love himself.'

'Oh,' I said, 'but what is my beauty beside yours? One of your little fingers is more precious than everything in me, everything in you is admirable. Look at that arm, that beautiful form, eyes the like of which I have never seen in anyone else.' And at that my own eyes ran over her whole person. 'Didn't you notice how I looked at you the first time I saw you? I guessed that your body was enchanting, whiter than a swan. Oh, if you only knew the joy I have felt in coming here, Madame, and how I still thought I was holding your dear hand that I kissed the other day when you gave me that letter.' 'Oh stop!' she said, putting this hand over my mouth to close it. 'Stop, La Vallée, I can't listen to you and keep calm.' Then she fell back on the sofa and her face betrayed an emotion which filled me with great emotion too.

I looked at her, she looked at me, she blushed. My heart beat faster and I think hers did too, and we were both beginning to lose our heads when she said: 'Listen, La Vallée, you can see that someone may come in at any moment, and since you love me we mustn't see each other any more, for you can't be sufficiently trusted.' This speech was cut off by a sigh.

'You are married now?' she went on. 'Yes, last night!' 'Well, tell me all about your love-making – did you have plenty? What do you think of your wife? Would you love me as much as her? Oh, how much I would love you in her place!' 'Oh,' I answered, 'and how I would return it!' 'Really?' she said, 'but don't let us go on talking about it, La Vallée. We are too close to each other. Get a bit further back, I am always afraid of being taken by surprise. There was something else I wanted to see you about, and your marriage drove it out of my head. We should have been safer in my own room, where I usually am, but I didn't foresee that you would be here this afternoon. Come to think of it, I would still rather like us to go there so that I can give you the documents I mentioned the other day. Would you like to come?'

Thereupon she stood right up. 'Would I like to!' I said. She pondered a moment, then said: 'No, don't let us go there. If that maid came in and we were not here, whatever would she think? Let's stay here.'

'But I would like those documents,' I persisted. 'It is not possible,' she said, 'you can't have them today.' Then she sank on to the sofa again, but only in a sitting position. 'And those dainty feet?' I said. 'If you stay like that I suppose I shan't see them any more?'

She smiled at this, stroked my face tenderly and said: 'Let us change the subject. You say you love me, and I am not objecting to that; but, my dear, suppose I went and loved you back, as I foresee could well happen, how could I resist such a nice young man as you? Tell me, La Vallée, can I rely on you to keep it secret?'

'My dear lady,' I said, 'who do you think I should run and tell our business to? I would have to be wicked indeed. As if I didn't know that such a thing isn't done, especially about a great lady like yourself, a widow who is honouring me a hundred times more than I deserve by returning my feelings. And besides, don't I know that you profess to be a devout woman, and that doesn't allow such things to be noised abroad?' 'No,' she replied, colouring slightly, 'I am not so much religious as living in retirement.'

'Well then,' I went on, 'religious or not, I love you just as much one way as the other, and does that prevent a man from giving you his heart or you from taking what has been given you? We are what we are, and other people have nothing to do with it. After all, what do we do in this life? A bit of good, a bit of bad, sometimes the one and sometimes the other, we do what we can and we aren't saints, either male or female, and we don't go to confession over nothing, and then back to confession again. Only the dead have given up going, but as for the living, I've yet to find any who have.'

'What you say is all too true, we all have our weaknesses,' she said. 'Yes we have indeed, dear lady, so there's no need to be surprised if you happen to feel drawn towards your young servant. It's true I am married, but it wouldn't make any difference one way or the other if I were not, and in any case I was single when you first saw me. If I have taken a wife since, that's not your fault and you didn't make me take her; and then again it would be worse still if both of us were married, whereas you aren't. That's something to the good, anyway; you take people as you find them or else it's better to leave them alone, and I haven't the courage to do that now that I have held your lovely hands so long in mine and you have said such sweet things to me.'

'And I would say more if I didn't watch out,' she said, 'for you enchant me, La Vallée, and you are the most dangerous little fellow I know. But back to business.

'I told you we must be cautious, and I see you realize how important it is. The circles I move in and what people think of my behaviour, your gratitude for the things I have done for you and those I plan to do, all this makes caution essential. If you let drop the slightest word I should be ruined, bear that well in mind and don't ever forget it, I beg of you. Now let us think how you will set about seeing me sometimes. If you went on coming here people might talk. What excuse would you have for coming? I have a certain position in society, and you are not the kind of person who should be paying me frequent visits. People would not fail to suspect me of being fond of you – your youth and good looks would soon convince them, and that's what we must avoid. So this is what I have thought of.

'In a certain district in the outskirts (I forget which now), there is an elderly party whose husband, dead six or seven months ago, was under an obligation to me. This is where she lives and her name is Mme Remy. Look, write down her name and address straight away, there's the wherewithal on the table.'

So I wrote down the name, and when I had done that Mme de Ferval went on with her plan: 'She is a woman I can make use of. Tomorrow I will send word for her to come and see me during the morning. We shall meet at her house, the district is a long way away and I shall be completely unknown there. Her little home is very convenient, she lives alone and there is even a little garden you can go through, with a back gate on to a very quiet road. I shall stop my carriage in that road and always go in by that gate, and you always by the front door. As for what my servants will think, I'm not at all worried because they are used to taking me to all sorts of places for various charitable visits that two or three ladies and I often make, and sometimes it has happened that I have gone on my own as well as with others, either visiting the sick or families in need. My servants know this and will think I am doing the same thing when I go to Mme Remy's. Can you be there tomorrow afternoon at five, La Vallée? I shall have seen Mme Remy and all steps will have been taken.'

'Bless you, I shan't fail! I'm only sorry that it isn't straight away. Oh tell me, dear lady, there won't be some maid to overhear us as there is here, and to prevent my having the documents?'

'Oh certainly not!' she laughed. 'And we can talk as loud as we like there. But something occurs to me. It's a long way from where you live to that district, and you'll have to get there and back by carriage and the expense would be awkward for you.'

'Never mind that,' I said, 'it'll only be my legs that will bear the expense, don't worry.' 'No, my boy,' she said, rising. 'It's too far and it would make you tired.' So saying she opened a little box and took out a purse, a quite plain one but nice and full.

'Here you are, my dear, this will pay for your carriage journeys, and when it has run out I will give you some more.'

'Oh really, dear mistress,' I said, blown out with conceit and dazzled with my own worth, 'don't. Your purse makes me feel ashamed.'

And the funny thing about it was that I was speaking the truth. Yes, for all my vanity there was a twinge of embarrassment in the conceited self-esteem with which I regarded myself. I was delighted to be offered money but blushed to take it; the former seemed flattering, the latter degrading.

However, in my bedazzled state I did eventually give in to her pleadings, and after saying two or three times: but Madame, but mistress, I should run you into too much expense, there is no need to buy my heart, it is already paid for since I have given it to you for nothing, so what is this money for . . ., after all that, I repeat, I took it.

'Anyhow,' she said as she shut the little box, 'we shall only be going to the address I'm giving you to prevent people from talking. You will have more freedom to see me there, my dear, but with at least as much circumspection as here, you do realize, La Vallée? I beg you not to take advantage of what I am doing for you, I don't mean anything more than I am saying.'

'Alas,' I said, 'I don't mean anything more, either. I'm going there quite simply for the pleasure of being with you and loving you in peace, that's all. And besides, I don't want to hurt you in any way, I assure you, and my aim is to please you. I love you here, I shall love you there, I shall love you everywhere.' 'There is nothing wrong in that,' she said, 'and I don't forbid your loving me, La Vallée, but I wouldn't like to have anything to reproach myself with, that's what I mean.

'By the way, there is one thing I do want to talk to you about, and that is a letter I have written on your behalf and am sending to Mme de Fécour; you are to take it. Her brother-in-law, M. de Fécour, is a very influential man in the finance department, he never turns down anything his sister-in-law asks for, and I am asking her either to introduce you to him or write on your behalf so that he can find you a situation in Paris and put you in the way of promotion. There is no more certain way for you to make your fortune.'

She then took the letter from a table and gave it to me. I scarcely had it in my hand before a footman announced a caller, and it was Mme de Fécour herself.

Then there entered a stoutish woman, not very tall, and carrying before her one of the most staggering bosoms I have ever set eyes on. She looked, incidentally, a straightforward sort of woman, clearly fond of pleasure and fun, and her portrait I will give you now, as I have reached this point.

Mme de Fécour might have been three or four years younger than Mme de Ferval. I think that in her youth she had been pretty, but the most noticeable thing in her face at that time was an open, friendly expression which made her quite pleasant-looking.

Her movements had none of the heaviness of fat women, neither her plumpness nor her bosom got in her way, and her bulk darted about with an energy that passed for agility. Add to that an appearance of rude health and a kind of fresh colour that was pleasing, the fresh colour which comes from an amorous disposition but which is, however, somewhat weary.

Hardly any woman exists who is without some kind of affectation or who does not try to suggest this, which in itself is another sort of coquetry, and in this respect Mme de Fécour had nothing of the woman about her. Indeed it was one of her graces that she never sought to have any.

She had beautiful hands without knowing it, but if they had been ugly she still wouldn't have known; she never thought about giving love but was not averse to taking it. She was never the one who tried to appeal, but others always appealed to her. Other women, when they look at you, subtly convey: love me so as to satisfy my vanity; but this woman said straight out: I want you, do you want me? And she would have forgotten to ask: Do you love me? so long as you had acted as though you did.

From all this the conclusion is that she could sometimes be shameless, but never coquettish.

When you appealed to her, for example, she seemed to be offering you that bosom I have mentioned, but it was not so much to arouse your passions as to tell you that you were arousing hers; it was a kind of declaration of love.

Mme de Fécour was excellent company, more jolly than witty at a dinner, more outspoken than daring, and yet more licentious than tender. She loved everybody but felt friendship for none, behaved herself in the same way with all, rich and poor alike, lord or bourgeois, neither looking up to the rank of the former nor down on the humble estate of the latter. Her domestics were not her servants, but men and women living in her house; they happened to serve her and she was served by them. That is all she saw in it.

She would say to you: 'Monsieur, what shall we do?' Or if Bourguignon came in: 'Bourguignon, what should I do?' Jasmin was her counsellor if he was about, you were if you happened to be at hand; his name was Jasmin and yours Monsieur, that was the only difference she noticed, for she had no pride, nor modesty either.

One more trait of her character and I am done. It is a very peculiar one.

Were you to say to her: 'I am unhappy or happy, I have certain hopes or certain troubles,' she would only enter into your situation because of the word you used, and not the thing itself, she would only weep with you because you yourself were weeping and not because you had reason to weep, and she would laugh in the same way. She would go to endless trouble for you without being interested in your concerns and without realizing that she was not interested, but merely because you had said: 'Do so and so for me.' In a word, it was the terms you used and the way you said them which affected her. If somebody had said: 'Your friend or your relation is dead,' and had said it in an unconcerned manner she would have answered in the same tone: 'Oh really?' But had you then replied dolefully that it was all too true, she would have gone on in a heartbroken voice: 'It is most sad.'

In fact she was a woman with senses and no sentiments, and yet she was considered the nicest woman in the world because on countless occasions her senses were exact substitutes for sentiments and did her equal honour.

This kind of character, however peculiar it may seem, is not as unusual as people think, and it can be seen in countless persons commonly called kind people in society. Kind people, one might add, who live only for pleasure and joy, who need only hate what others want them to hate, are only what others want them to be and have only opinions that others give them.

Of course it was not at that moment that I knew Mme de Fécour as I am depicting her here, for at that time I did not have much to do with her, but I met her again some years later and saw enough of her to understand her. Let us come back to the subject.

'Oh dear,' she said to Mme de Ferval, 'I am so glad to find you at home, Madame, I was afraid you wouldn't be in. It is such a long time since we have seen each other. How are you keeping?'

Then she bowed to me – in that context I looked like a gentleman – and as she bowed she had a good look which lasted a long time.

When the opening greetings were over, Mme de Ferval complimented her on how very well she looked. 'Yes,' she said, 'I am very well indeed, and I have a very healthy constitution. I wish my sister-in-law were the same. I'm going straight from here to see her. The poor woman sent word the day before yesterday that she was ill.'

'I didn't know,' said Mme de Ferval, 'but perhaps as usual it will be more a case of indisposition than illness. She is extremely delicate.'

'Oh, quite likely,' answered the jovial party. 'I think, like you, that it's nothing serious.'

While they were talking I felt rather awkward, yet less so than some others might have felt in my place, for I was beginning to find my feet a bit, and I wouldn't have been as embarrassed as I was if I hadn't been afraid of being so.

Now I had inadvertently kept Mme de la Vallée's snuffbox, which I could feel in my pocket, and so as to have something to do with my hands I set about opening it to take some snuff.

But I had hardly opened it before Mme de Fécour, who was casting her eyes frequently in my direction, and the sort of eyes one casts on people one likes the look of, before Mme de Fécour, I repeat, exclaimed: 'Oh, Monsieur, you have some snuff, please give me some, I have forgotten my own box and for the past half-hour I haven't known what to do with myself.'

So I rose and offered her some, and as I bent forward for her to take some, and in that posture my head was near hers, she took advantage of my proximity to examine me more easily, and while taking some snuff she looked brazenly up at me, and looked so hard that I coloured a little.

'You are very young to be getting the snuff habit,' she said, 'and some day you will be sorry, Monsieur, for there is nothing so tiresome. It's what I tell everybody, especially young gentlemen of your age I see taking it, for you certainly must be under twenty, Monsieur?'

'I shall soon be twenty, Madame,' I said as I went back to my chair. 'Oh, that's the right age!' she said. 'Yes,' said Mme de Ferval, 'but he mustn't waste his time, for he has no money of his own. He only came up from the country five or six months ago, and we should like to find some situation for him.'

'Rather!' was the answer. 'A very good idea too. This gentleman will appeal to everyone who sees him, and I foretell a good marriage for him.' 'Unfortunately, Madame, he has just married a Mlle Habert who comes from his part of the world and has a good four or five thousand livres a year,' said Mme de Ferval.

'Aha, Mlle Habert!' said the other. 'I heard about that in a house I have just been to.'

This made both Mme de Ferval and me blush, though why she blushed too I couldn't say, unless it was because Mme de Fécour, having no doubt heard that I was very much a nobody, had just come upon her talking to me on equal terms. What was more she was in love with this nobody, she was very religious, or at least passed for such, and all this together might be a little awkward for her conscience.

As for me, it was natural that I should be embarrassed: my story, which Mme de Fécour said she had been told, was that of a mere bumpkin, in plain English a servant, some whipper-snapper picked up on the Pont-Neuf. And it was from this little fellow's snuffbox that she had politely taken some snuff and to whom she had said: 'You are only twenty, Monsieur.' Now ask yourself whether it was worth while adopting such a tone with this person, and whether Mme de Fécour must not have laughed at being taken in by my play-acting.

But I had nothing to fear, for we were dealing with a woman whom all these things slid off like water off a duck's back, and who only ever saw the present and not the past. I was well turned out, she found me with Mme de Ferval, and that was enough for her, to say nothing of my good looks, for which I thought she had a singular admiration. And so, continuing her speech as bluntly as she had begun it, she went on: 'Oh, so it's this gentleman who has married Mlle Habert – an extremely pious lady, they said she was – well, that's very amusing. But, Monsieur, you have only been married two days at the most? For the conversation was quite recent.'

'Yes, Madame,' I said, somewhat recovered from my confusion when I saw that for her this was neither here nor there. 'I married her yesterday.'

'That's all to the good, and I am delighted,' she went on. 'She is rather elderly, I'm told, but the wait was well worth her while. Indeed,' she said, turning to Mme de Ferval, 'people had told me that he was a very handsome fellow, and they were right, and if I knew the lady I should congratulate her on a very good marriage. By the way, may I ask what her name is now?'

'Madame de la Vallée,' Mme de Ferval answered for me, 'and her husband's father is a very worthy man, a big farmer with several children, who had sent this one to Paris to try to make a career there. In a word, highly respectable people.'

'Yes of course,' went on Mme de Fécour. 'Why yes, people who live in the country, farmers, I know what they are, yes, very respectable people, very worthy certainly, there is no denying that'.

'And it was I,' said Mme de Ferval, 'who saw his marriage through.' 'Oh, really? Well, this pious soul is indebted to you. I have a high opinion of the gentleman simply from the look of him (just another pinch of your snuff, M. de la Vallée). You are very young to be married, my fine lad, you couldn't have failed to make an advantageous marriage some day with your looks, but you will be better off in Paris and less of a liability to your family. Madame,' she said, turning to Mme de Ferval, 'you have friends, he is attractive, he must be helped on.'

'We very much want to do so, and I can even say that when you came in I had just given him a letter of recommendation to you. M. de Fécour, your brother-in-law, is in a very good position to help him, and I was begging you to ask him.'

'Lord bless you, with all my heart,' said Mme de Fécour. 'Yes, Monsieur, M. de Fécour must find you a situation – I had not thought of it, but he is in Versailles for a few days, so would you like me to write to him pending the time when I see him? Look, it's no distance from here to my home, and all we have to do is spend a moment there. I'll write, and M. de la Vallée will take him my letter tomorrow. Monsieur,' she said as she rose, 'I am indeed delighted that Madame has thought of me in this connection. Let's be off, as I have one or two more calls to pay, so don't let us waste time. Good-bye, Madame, this is a short visit, but you see why I am going.'

With that she kisses Mme de Ferval, who thanks her and is thanked back, leans familiarly on my arm, takes me away, makes me climb into her carriage, sometimes calling me Monsieur, sometimes her dear boy, talks as though we have known each other for ten years, always with that massive bosom well to the fore, and we reach her house.

In we go, she takes me to her boudoir. 'Sit down,' she says, 'just a couple of words to write to M. de Fécour, and they will be pressing.'

Her letter was indeed finished in a moment. 'Here you are, you will be well received on my recommendation. I have said he must find you a job in Paris, for you must stay here to cultivate your friends. It would be a shame to send you into the country where you would be buried alive, and we so enjoy seeing you. In any case I don't want our acquaintance to stop at this point. What do you think about it, M. de la Vallée, does it appeal to you a little?'

'And does me a great deal of honour, too,' I said. 'Oh, honour,' she said, 'that's got nothing to do with it. I'm not a woman to stand on ceremony, especially with people I like and who are likeable, M. de la Vallée, and you are – very, oh, very much so indeed! The first man I was fond of was just like you. I think I can see him now and still love him. I called him darling – that's my way –

and already I've nearly done the same with you, and it'll happen. Will you mind? Wouldn't you like me to treat you the same as him?' she added with her bust, on which by sheer chance my eyes were then glued, and this made my mind wander and prevented my answering. She noticed this and watched me for a time.

'Well,' she said with a laugh, 'whatever are you thinking about?' 'You, Madame,' I murmured, with my eyes still fixed on what I mentioned just now. 'Me? Are you speaking the truth, M. de la Vallée? Have you noticed that I am well disposed towards you? Not that that is hard to see, and if you have any doubts it's no fault of mine. You see, I am a plain speaker and I like people to be the same with me; do you follow, you beautiful young man? What eyes he has, and yet is afraid to speak! Look here, M. de la Vallée, I've a piece of advice for you. You have come up from the country and you have brought with you a shy manner that doesn't go with your age. When a man is made like you he can be a bit more self-confident, especially in this part of the world, for what do you lack to give you confidence? And who can be if you can't, my dear? You are so attractive!' And she said this in such a candid, affectionate manner that I was beginning to take to her caressing ways, when we heard a coach driving into the courtyard.

'There's somebody coming, put the letter safely away, dear boy, and will you come back and see me soon?' 'As soon as I have delivered the letter, Madame,' I said.

'Well, good-bye,' she said, giving me her hand, which I kissed enthusiastically. 'Oh, and another time be sure you believe I love you. I am sorry that I didn't give instructions that I was not at home, I might not have gone out again and we could have spent the rest of the day together, but we shall see each other again. And I shall be expecting you. Don't let me down.'

'And what is your best time, Madame, will you tell me?' 'Any time you like, morning or evening, any time is the right time, except that you can be more sure of finding me in the morning. Good-bye, my tall, dark man (she chucked me under the chin as she said this), I suggest you be completely frank with me in future.'

She had hardly finished speaking when word was brought that

there were three people in her drawing room, and I withdrew as she went through.

Things, you see, were going pretty well for me. Everything happened very quickly, and I was in a whirl myself.

Just imagine a young rustic like me who in a mere two days has become the husband of a rich spinster and the admirer of two society ladies. And on top of that the change in style of my clothes, for it all counts, the title of Monsieur with which I had been honoured, having been called Jacob ten or twelve days earlier, the flirtatious provocations of the two ladies, and above all the charming, if impure, art Mme de Ferval had employed to seduce me, the elegantly clad and provocative leg I had stared at so hard, the lovely white hands that had been so tenderly left in mine, the eyes so languishing, in a word the very air you breathe amidst all this – how many things calculated to make me understand my own mind and heart, what a school of softness, pleasure and corruption, hence of sentiment, for the soul gains in refinement as it is corrupted. Thus I was in a whirl of vanity so flattering, I found something so rare in myself, I had never before tasted so exquisitely the pleasure of living, that from that day onwards I became quite a different person because I had acquired so much training and experience.

So I went back home, blown out with vanity, as I have said, but it was a vanity that made me gay, and not stuck up or ridiculous. Self-satisfaction in me had always been a sociable thing: I have never been so amiable and easy to get on with as when I have had reason to think well of myself and be conceited. Everyone reacts to this in his own way, and that was mine. Mme de la Vallée had never seen me more caressing and attentive than I was with her when I reached home.

It was late and they were waiting for me so as to sit down to the meal, for you will recall that we had invited to supper our hostess, her daughter and the people who had acted as witnesses on our wedding day.

I cannot say how many kind things I said to the company or how graciously I urged them to enjoy themselves. Our two witnesses were a bit stodgy, and they found me so debonair in comparison with themselves, I might even say so much the perfect gentleman in my manners, that I quite took them in, and, for all the high spirits I was urging them to share, they were chary of being too familiar.

I even amazed Mme d'Alain, and, chatterbox though she was, she minded what she was saying rather more than usual. The theme of the conversation constantly turned to praise of me, and they even tried to express these praises in as polished a way as they could, so that I felt that manners had improved out of consideration for me.

It must have been my conversation with the two ladies that was responsible for this, and I must have caught from them an air that was more distinguished than my normal behaviour.

What is certainly true is that I myself felt I was quite a different person, and as I looked at the people round the table I said to myself: these are a lot of worthy folk who are not up to my standard, but whom I must put up with for the time being.

I will pass over everything that was said during our conversation. Agathe eyed me a great deal. I was the comedian of the party, but almost the respected one, and I was so attractive to Mme de la Vallée that in her impatience to have me to herself, she looked at her watch several times and mentioned the time, so as to suggest tactfully to the company that it was time to retire.

At last we rose from table, embraced, all the visitors left, the table was cleared and Mme de la Vallée and I were left alone.

Thereupon, without more ado, alleging that she was rather tired, my pious spouse went to bed saying: 'Let's go to bed, my dear, it's late,' which meant: 'Come to bed because I want you.' I put the same interpretation upon it and jumped quickly into bed because I wanted her too, for she was still desirable and had a pretty face, as I have already said at the beginning of this story. In addition, my mind was full of so many memories of love, and my passions had been stimulated in so many ways, I had been exposed to so much love that day that I was in a mood for being a good lover myself. Add to all this the advantage of having with me a person only too delighted to listen to me, as Mme de la Vallée was, and that is another encouragement.

While I was undressing I wanted to tell her all about my day; I mentioned the helpful plans Mme de Ferval had for me, Mme de

Fécour's arrival at her home, the letter she had given me, the journey to Versailles I was to make the next day to deliver the letter. However interested Mme de la Vallée might be in my affairs I chose my time ill, and nothing of what I was saying was worth her attention; I could get nothing out of her but monosyllables: 'Oh yes, good, fine,' and then: 'Come on, come on, we'll discuss that in bed!'

So I went, and good-bye stories, I forgot to go on with them and my dear wife didn't remind me.

How many burning but chaste words of love did she not use! You have already seen how her impulses worked, and the only thing I shall add is that no deeply religious woman was ever so passionate as she was in exercising the privilege of expressing her chaste love. I could see her wanting to cry out: 'What joy to refuse the devil his due and to be able without sin to be as thrilled as the sinful!'

At last we both went to sleep, and my stories of the day before were only taken up again in the morning at about eight.

She was full of praise for Mme de Ferval's kind intentions and prayed that God would reward her and Mme de Fécour. After that we rose and went out together, and while I went off to Versailles she went to hear Mass for the success of my journey.

I went to the place where there are carriages for hire, and found one with four seats, three of which were already occupied, and I took the fourth.

My travelling companions were an elderly officer, a sensible man of impressive appearance but whose manner was very simple and straightforward.

A tall, lean, cadaverous man, with a haunted expression and small, dark, blazing eyes; we soon learned that he was a habitual litigant, and this occupation, in view of the gentleman's appearance, was extremely suitable.

After these gentlemen was a good-looking young man. The officer and he looked at each other as though they had met somewhere else but could not place each other. Eventually they did remember that they had dined together.

As I was not with any Mme d'Alains or any ladies who were in love with me, I watched my language very carefully, trying not to say anything smacking of the country farmer's boy. So I spoke guardedly and limited myself to paying a great deal of attention to what was being said.

A man who never says anything but listens attentively passes almost unnoticed, or at least people always think he is on the point of speaking, and to listen well is almost to answer.

Now and again I said: yes, no doubt, oh certainly not, you are quite right – and always in agreement with the sentiment I could see was the most general.

The officer, who was a Knight of Saint-Louis, began the conversation. His air of the blunt warrior, his age and open, easy manner, gradually thawed the litigant, who was decidedly taciturn and more of a dreamer than a talker.

I don't know what chance made our officer mention to the young man a woman who was suing her husband for a separation.

This item interested the litigant who, having looked the officer up and down once or twice and, it seemed, taken to him, joined in the conversation and joined in so enthusiastically that, in the course of speech after speech and invective after invective against women, he gradually admitted that he was in a similar case to the man they were talking about, and was suing his wife too.

This admission made them shelve the story in question and come to his, and rightly, for it was much more interesting than the first. It was, so to speak, to be preferred as an original to a mere copy.

'Ah, ah! Sir, you are in a lawsuit against your wife,' said the young man. 'Very upsetting, an unfortunate position for a gentleman. Now why have you fallen out?'

'Well, why not?' was the answer. 'Is it so difficult to fall out with your wife? Doesn't being a husband already mean having a permanent case going on against her? Every husband is a plaintiff, Monsieur, and either defends himself or attacks. Sometimes the case does not go outside the house, sometimes it bursts forth, and mine has burst forth!'

'I never wanted to get married,' said the officer. 'I don't know whether I have done right or wrong, but so far I don't regret it.'

'How fortunate you are,' said the other, 'I wish I were in your shoes. And yet I had meant to stay single, and had even resisted quite a few temptations with more in them to carry me away than the one I succumbed to. I don't understand it at all, and you never know how it happens! I was in love, but very mildly, and only half as much as I had been with others, and yet I got married.'

'Perhaps the lady had money?' said the young man. 'No, she was no richer than any other and not even all that young. A lanky spinster of thirty-two or thirty-three, and I was forty. I was suing a certain nephew of mine, a very tricky person with whom I have not yet finished, and I shall ruin him for the rascal that he is even if it costs me my last sou – but that is quite another story which I'll tell you if we have time.

'My demon (I refer to my wife) was related to one of my judges; I knew her and went to ask her to put a word in for me; and as one visit leads to another I paid such frequent visits that finally I was seeing her every day, without quite knowing why, by force of habit. Our families got on well with each other, she had money which I needed, rumour spread that I was to marry her, and that made us both laugh. "But we shall have to see less of each other to stop that talk," she laughed, "or else they will say something worse." "But why?" I said, "I should like to love you; what do you say? Would you like me to?" She said neither yea nor nay.

'I went back the next day, still joking about this love I said I wanted to feel and which, I think, I felt already or which was coming on without my noticing. I didn't feel it myself and never said to her: "I love you." It is a most extraordinary thing, this wretched love that is a matter of habit, that gives no warning and still infuriates me every time I think about it, and I can't get over my own adventure. Just think, a couple of weeks later a widower, very well-to-do and older than me, took it into his head to woo my fair – I laughingly call her fair because there are a thousand faces just like hers that nobody ever notices, and apart from her large innocent eyes, which are not as beautiful as they first appear to be, it is a quite commonplace face with nothing remarkable except the pale complexion.

'I disliked this man I have mentioned; he was always about the place and that made me ill-tempered. I never agreed with him and was always picking quarrels. There are some people whom you can't abide, and I thought that was why he repelled me. That was all I saw in it, and I was mistaken once again, for I was jealous. This man, it seemed, was tired of widowhood, he talked of love and then of marriage. I got to know this and hated him all the more, still with the utmost good faith.

'"Do you mean to marry that man?" I asked the lady. "My parents and friends advise me to," she said, "and he on his side is urging me and I don't know what to do and haven't yet made up my mind about anything. What do you advise yourself?" "Oh, nothing," I sulked, "you are your own mistress. Marry him, Mademoiselle, marry him since you wish to." "Oh really, Monsieur, how you talk! If you don't care about people, at least don't say so." "Good Lord, Mademoiselle, you're the one who doesn't care about people." A funny kind of declaration of love, as you see, and yet it is the strongest I ever made her, and even then it slipped out and I didn't think anything about it, and then I went off home with my mind on other things. One of my friends came to see me that evening. "Do you know," he said, "that tomorrow they are going to draw up a marriage contract between Mlle — and M. de —? I have just been there and all the family is already gathered together. She herself doesn't look very enthusiastic, and I even thought she looked sad. Would it by any chance have anything to do with you?"

'"What!" I said, without answering the question. "They are talking about a contract? Oh my friend, but I think I love her, and would as soon have married her as anybody else. I would desperately like to prevent that contract being signed."

'"Well," he said, "there's no time to lose, hurry along to her home and see what she says." "Perhaps things have gone too far," I said, sick at heart, "and if you would be kind enough to go yourself and talk to her for me I should be so pleased," I added in a silly and shamefaced way.

'"By all means," he said. "Wait for me here, I'll go at once and come straight back with her answer."

'So he went, told her I loved her and wanted to be given preference over the other man. "Does he really?" she said. "Isn't that funny, he kept it hidden from me. Tell him to come and we'll see."

'On hearing this answer from my friend I rushed to her home. She went into a room away from the others, where I spoke to her.

'"What's this your friend tells me?" she said, gazing with her big affectionate eyes. "Do you want me?" "Yes, of course," I said, somewhat taken aback. "Well, why didn't you say so? What is to be done now? You are making it very awkward for me."

'I took her hand. "You are a funny man!" she said. "Well, that's as may be, aren't I as good as the other one?" "Fortunately he has just gone," she went on. "In any case there is a bit of trouble over the contract, and we must see whether we can take advantage of that. There's nobody in there now but my parents, let's go in."

'I followed her in and spoke to her parents and got them on my side; the young lady was willing, and one of them suggested sending for the notary straight away so as to settle the matter.

'I couldn't say no, and hey presto! off goes somebody and the notary arrives. My head was swimming with the speed with which it was being done. They treated me just as they liked, I was caught, I signed, they signed and banns were dispensed with. Never the slightest whisper about love in all this, and so I married her and the day after I was surprised to find I was married. To whom? Well, anyway, to a very sensible person, I said to myself.

'Sensible! Good Lord, it shows how well I knew her. Do you know what this woman I thought was so sensible turned into in three months? A sour-tempered bigot, solemn and yet talkative, for she never stopped criticizing my words and deeds. In fine, a solemn maniac who now never displayed anything but a long, austere face, indulged her gloomy vanity and lived as a recluse, but not for the benefit of her household, which she let slide. She would have considered it beneath her to look after her home, and didn't go in for such common or garden piety as that – oh no, she only stayed in her own home so as to spend her days in idle contemplation, to be free for edifying reading in a room which she never left except with a devotional and self-satisfied glumness on her face, as though a face like that was meritorious in the eyes of God.

'Then Madame took up arguing about religion, she had opinions about it and talked about doctrine, in fact was quite the theologian.

'Yet I would have let her get on with it had that been all there was to it, but this theologian was tiresome and awkward.

'If I asked a friend to stay to dinner, Madame refused to eat with this impious man, and was indisposed and ate alone in her room, where she besought God's forgiveness for the godlessness of my behaviour.

'To be a guest in my home you had to be a monk or a bigot like her, there was always some cowl or cassock at my table. I don't say they weren't worthy people, but such worthy people are not designed to be friends of ordinary people like ourselves, and my home was neither a monastery nor a church, nor was my dining-room a refectory.

'And what irritated me was that nothing was too good for these high and mighty servants of God, whilst I only had ordinary fare with my worldly, sinful friends. You can see that there was neither common sense nor virtue in that.

'Well, gentlemen, I am telling you a long story, but I got used to it; I am a peace-loving man, and if it hadn't been for that clerk who worked for me . . .'

'A clerk!' broke in the young man. 'Ah, now we're coming to something.'

'Yes, I became jealous, and God grant that I was wrong. My wife's friends treated my jealousy as malice and calumny, and regarded me as vindictive for having suspected such a virtuous woman of carrying on with a man, a woman whose only outings were to churches, who loved nothing but sermons, services and benedictions. That's all very fine and large, and people can say what they like.

'All I know is that this clerk, whom I needed in my office, who was the son of her dead mother's maid, a great brainless noodle whom I kept on out of kindness, and incidentally a very good-looking young man with a face like one of God's elect, according to her . . .

'This fellow, then, usually ran errands for her, went to find out for her how Father So-and-so, Mother So-and-so, Monsieur This and Monsieur That, some rector, parish priest, chaplain or just plain priest, were getting on. Then he brought back the answers, went into her private room, talked away with her, arranged a picture, an Agnus Dei or reliquary, fetched and carried books and occasionally read them to her.

'This upset me and made me swear from time to time. What sort of weird piety is this, I asked, what sort of saint is it that takes my clerk away? So the union between her and me was not uplifting enough?

'Madame called me her cross, her tribulation; I called her the first thing that came into my head, and I was not choosy. The clerk annoyed me and I couldn't get used to it. If I sent him for any distance I tired him. "Really," she said, with a charity that I don't think will benefit her soul, "really, he'll kill the poor lad!"

'The creature took ill, and the next day I had a temperature, too.

'I had a very severe attack. The servants looked after me and Madame tended this lout.

' "Monsieur is master," was her comment, "and he has only to give orders for everything he wants, but who will look after this boy if I abandon him?" Thus it was also out of charity that she left me in the lurch.

'Her disgraceful behaviour probably saved my life – I was so indignant that I got better out of sheer rage, and as soon as I was on my feet again the first sign of convalescence I showed was to throw the object of her charity out of the house – I sent him to find a cure elsewhere. My blessed saint shook with rage and rushed in like a Fury to know the reason why.

' "I can see what your motives are," she said. "This is an insult to me, Sir. The baseness of your suspicions is clear, and God will avenge me, Sir, God will avenge!"

'Her prophecies were not well received; she made them like one possessed and I answered almost brutally. "Damn it," I said, "it won't be the departure of that scoundrel that will turn God away from me. Now be off with you and your dubious piety. Don't make me lose my temper, leave me alone."

'What did she do? We have a young maid in the house, a nice, pleasant little thing who didn't please Madame, I suppose because she was younger and prettier and I liked her. If it hadn't been for her I might have succumbed to my illness.

'The poor little thing sometimes sympathized with me for my wife's strange goings-on and calmed me when I was angry, and that meant that I took her side and was kindly disposed towards her. In fact I have kept her on because she has been capable and very useful to me.

'Very well, after dinner my wife made her come to her room, picked some sort of quarrel with her, boxed her ears for answering back, blamed her for my being kind to her and gave her the sack.

'Nanette (that's the girl's name) came to say good-bye to me in tears and told me what had happened, including the box on the ears.

'As I could see that all this was simply due to my wife's vindictiveness, I said: "Now, now, you let her do what she likes and just you stay here, Nanette, and leave the rest to me."

'My wife exploded with rage and refused to see her, but I stuck to my guns – one must be master in one's own house, especially if one is in the right.

'My resistance didn't sweeten the sourness of our life together; sometimes we did speak to each other, but only to bicker.

'Please note that I had taken on a new clerk who was my wife's pet aversion; she could not abide him. So she nagged him over nothing at all, and simply to annoy me, but it didn't bother him much because I had told him to take no notice, and he carried out my intentions precisely, and just didn't listen.

'A few days later I realized that my wife wanted to drive me to desperation.

' "Perhaps God will grant that that bully will hit me," she said, meaning me. I got to hear of this. "Certainly not," I told her, "don't you count on that, be assured that I won't give you that satisfaction. Mortifications you will certainly have – and there won't be any lack of them, I'll see to that – but that's all!"

'My vow brought me ill-luck, you should never take your oath on anything. For all my laudable intentions, she so exasperated me one day with the most piously worded barbed shafts, and the devil tempted me so successfully that, remembering her impertinence and the box on the ears she had given Nanette because of me, I was sufficiently off my guard to hit her in the presence of several of her friends.

'It happened as quick as lightning, and off she went at once to have the law on me, and since that time we have been involved in a lawsuit, much to my regret. For in spite of the clerk I have called as a witness, whom they were obliged to call too, this holy person might well win her suit unless I find some influential friends, and I am off to Versailles to find some.'

'That fact of hitting her makes me anxious for you,' said the young man when he had finished, 'and I'm afraid it will do your cause no good. It is true that the clerk is a factor in the case, and I have no higher opinion of him than you have. I certainly think you have been very badly treated in that direction, but that is a matter of conscience you have no proof about, whereas the unfortunate blow was before witnesses.'

'That'll do, Sir,' replied the other irritably, 'let's drop the theories about the clerk if you don't mind. I'll make them myself without other people making them. Don't you worry, the blow will have to take its chance, and I'm sorry now I only dealt her one, but for the rest, let's skip the commentary. There may not be as much harm in the business of the clerk as you think; I have my own reasons for making a fuss. That clerk was a fool, my wife may well have been in love with him without realizing it herself, and thus committed an offence against God in principle while I lost nothing in form. In a word, whether there is misconduct or not, when I say there is, the best thing is to let me say so.'

'Oh, no doubt,' said the officer to calm him down. 'Can one trust an angry husband? He is so liable to make a mistake. The only thing I see myself in the story you have told is an unsociable and misanthropic wife, that's all.

'So let's change the subject and find out what our two young friends are going to Versailles for,' he went on, turning to the young man and me. 'You Monsieur,' he said to me, 'who have only just about left school, are apparently just going for pleasure or out of curiosity.'

'Neither,' I answered, 'I am going to ask an official for a job.'

'If men turn you down, try the women,' he laughed.

'And you, Monsieur (to the young man), have you personal business where we are going?'

'I am going to see a noble lord to whom I recently gave a newly published book of which I am the author,' he said. 'Oh yes,' said the officer, 'the book we were talking about the other day when we had dinner together.' 'That's it,' said the young man. 'Have you read it, Monsieur?'

'Yes, I returned it yesterday to one of my friends who had lent it to me.' 'Well, Monsieur, do please tell me what you think about it.' 'What do you want my opinion for?' asked the officer. 'It wouldn't make any difference.' 'All the same,' insisted the other, 'what do you think of it?'

'To tell you the truth,' went on the soldier, 'I don't know what to say. I am hardly a fit person to judge, it isn't the sort of book for me, I am too old.'

'Too old! How do you mean?' replied the young man. 'Yes, I think that if you are quite young you can enjoy reading it: everything is fine at that age, when all you want to do is laugh and are so greedy for fun that you take it wherever you find it, but old greybeards like me are a bit harder to please; in this respect we are like those sated epicures who are not tempted by coarse dishes and are only stimulated to eat by fine, choice food. And then I did not grasp the plan of your book, I don't know what its general line is or what it is aiming at. It looks as if you hadn't bothered to think out ideas, but have simply used anything that came into your head, which is not the same thing. In the first case you work, reject, select; in the second you take whatever presents itself, however incongruous it may be; and something always does present itself, for the mind is always working for good or ill.

'Moreover, if purely sensational things can be interesting, and if they are amusing because they are daring, your book is bound to appeal to the passions if not to the mind. But even there I think you have made a mistake through lack of experience, for leaving aside that there is not much merit in appealing to the senses – and you have seemed to me intelligent enough to succeed in other ways – in general you don't understand readers very well if you hope to make much impression on them in that way. It is true, Monsieur, that we are by nature sensual, or rather vicious, but in the matter of works of literature you must not take that too literally or rush us straight into that sort of thing. A reader wants to be led gently. As an author, do you want to utilize his natural viciousness? If so, gently does it, win his vicious side over, don't press things too hard.

'The reader likes a bit of smut, of course, but not extreme, overdone licentiousness; that is only bearable in real life, which softens its crudeness, it is only in its place there and we make allowances because we are then more men of flesh and blood than at other times. But not in a book, where it becomes bald, dirty and repulsive because it has so little to do with the calm state of mind of a reader.

'It is true that this reader is also a man, but then he is a man in a state of repose and with taste and delicacy, and he expects to be amused through his mind. Of course he wants to be titillated, but intelligently and with a certain amount of form and decency.

'All this doesn't mean that there are not some fine things in your book, and I have certainly noticed several.

'With regard to your style, I don't think it is bad, though there are sometimes some long-drawn-out sentences, loosely constructed and therefore unclear and muddled, which seems to come from your not having sorted out your ideas sufficiently or not having arranged them in some kind of order. But you are only a beginner, Monsieur, and this is a minor flaw which you will cure yourself of with practice in writing, as also of criticizing others, especially in the light, flippant tone you have striven to adopt, and with that over-confidence you will laugh at, or be sorry for, when you have a more balanced view and have acquired a maturer way of thinking more worthy of you. For you will produce better writing than you are doing at present – at any rate I have seen some things of yours that show promise of it – and you will not even think much of what you have done so far, and you will hardly have achieved a fraction of all that can be achieved. At all events that applies to those who have written most, to judge by what they say themselves.

'I mention criticism simply because of what I have seen of it in your book concerning one of the guests (he named him) who was with us that day when we dined together, and I confess I was surprised to find fifty or sixty pages of your work heavily weighted against him. I really do wish, for your own sake, that they weren't there.

'But here we are. You have asked for my sentiments and I have told you what I think as one who admires your talents and hopes that one day he will see you the object of as many criticisms as are directed against the man we are discussing. Perhaps that won't make you a cleverer man than he is, but at any rate you will then appear to be a man worth some consideration.'

That was the end of the officer's remarks which I am reporting more or less as I understood them then.

At that moment our coach stopped, we got down and went our various ways.

It was not yet midday, and I hurried with my letter to M. de Fécour, whose house was easy to find, for he was a man in a very big way of business and very much hand in glove with the government.

I had to cross various courtyards before reaching him and at length I was taken into a spacious office where I found him with a large number of people.

M. de Fécour looked fifty-five or sixty, he was fairly tall and lean, with a very swarthy complexion and a serious manner, not the kind that freezes you, for that kind is natural and part of a man's character. But his kind did not so much freeze you as humiliate you, it was a proud, haughty air born of a sense of one's own importance which one means people to respect.

People who have to deal with us sense these differences vaguely; we all know so much about our own pride that others cannot conceal theirs from us. Sometimes it is the first thing we unconsciously look for when we meet a stranger.

Anyhow, that was my first impression of M. de Fécour. I approached him very humbly. He was writing a letter, I think, while people around him were talking.

I paid him my respects with the emotion you feel when you are very small fry and coming to beg a favour from an important person who neither helps nor encourages nor even looks at you; for M. de Fécour heard everything I said without looking up at me.

I had my letter in my hand and proffered it, but he didn't take it, and his lack of interest left me in a ridiculous posture that I didn't know how to get out of.

Moreover there were all these people I have mentioned, who were staring at me; three or four gentlemen, none of whom wore an expression calculated to comfort me.

They were not magnificent figures, but opulent ones, in front of whom the figure I cut was so plebeian in spite of my silk lining! And they were all people of a certain age while I was but eighteen, and this was not such an unimportant factor as you might think. For if you had seen the way they looked at me you would have realized that my youth was an additional reason for my embarrassment.

'What's this kid up to with his letter?' they seemed to be saying with their insolent, brazen stares, full of undisguised curiosity.

So I was a sort of trivial amusement, simply supplying a moment's distraction which they looked down on in passing, just for fun.

One looked sideways at me, haughtily. Another walked up and down this vast room with his hands behind his back, stopping now and again beside M. de Fécour, who was still writing, and from there he proceeded to have a nice, leisurely look at me.

Imagine the sort of figure I was cutting.

Another, looking thoughtful and preoccupied, stared at me as if I were a piece of furniture or a wall, like a man not taking in what he sees.

And this man, to whom I was nothing at all, embarrassed me quite as much as the man to whom I meant so little. I well realized that the one way promised no more for me than the other.

In fact I was full of an inner sense of shame. I have never forgotten that scene. I have become rich too, at least as much so as any of those gentlemen I am writing about now, and I still fail to understand that there can be men whose souls can be so supercilious towards any other man.

In the end, however, M. de Fécour did finish his letter, and then, holding out his hand for the one I was presenting, he said to me: 'Let me see,' and then at once: 'What's the time, gentlemen?' 'Nearly twelve o'clock,' nonchalantly answered the one who was walking up and down, while M. de Fécour opened the letter and quickly ran his eye down it.

'Right,' he said when he had read it, 'that's the fifth man in eighteen months for whom my sister-in-law has written or spoken and for whom I have found a job. I don't know where she digs out all the people she sends, but she goes on and on, and here is one even more strongly recommended than the others. Strange woman – look, you can tell what she is by what she writes,' he added, showing the letter to one of the gentlemen.

Then: 'All right, I'll fix you up. I'm returning to Paris tomorrow, come and see me the day after.'

I was about to take my leave when he stopped me.

'You're very young,' he said, 'what can you do? Nothing, I'll be bound.'

'I have not been in any position so far, Sir,' I said. 'Oh, I thought as much. The ones from her are all like that, and it will be a great mercy if you can write.'

'Yes I can, Sir,' I said, colouring, 'and I even know a little arithmetic.' 'Oh I say!' he said. 'You really are too kind. All right, see you the day after tomorrow.'

Upon which I was making my way out with the pleasure of leaving these gentlemen in fits of laughter about my arithmetic and writing, when a footman came in and told M. de Fécour that a person called Mme You-know-who (that is how he put it) wanted to speak to him.

'Oh yes, I know who she is, she comes at the right moment, let her in; and stay here, you.' (This meant me.)

So I stayed, and at once two ladies came in, plainly dressed, one a young woman of twenty and with her a woman of about fifty.

They both looked very sad, but even more they looked like humble supplicants. I have never in my life seen anything so dignified and touching as the younger one's face. Not that she could have been called a beautiful woman, she would have needed different features for that.

Picture a face with nothing sufficiently brilliant or regular in it to be striking-looking, but everything in it to appeal to the heart, inspire respect, affection, even love, for the feelings this young woman inspired were a mixture of all these things.

Hers was, so to speak, a soul you could see in her face, but a noble, virtuous, loving soul, and therefore charming to see.

I say nothing about the older woman with her, who was only remarkable for her unassuming sadness.

When he dismissed me M. de Fécour had risen and was now standing in the middle of the room talking to the gentlemen. He nodded perfunctorily to the young woman as she came up.

'I know what brings you here, Madame. I have dismissed your husband, but it isn't my fault that he is always ill and cannot do his job. What do you suppose we can do for him? He is always absent.'

'What, Sir,' she said, in a tone that could obtain any request, 'is there no hope left? It is true that my husband's health is very delicate, and so far you have been kind enough to make allowances for his condition. Do us the same favour again, Sir, and don't treat us with such harshness (and the word harshness, as she said it, pierced the heart), for you would bring upon us troubles that would touch your heart if you knew them all. Don't leave me in my present affliction, to which I should go back if you were inflexible! (Inflexible – it didn't seem as though anybody could be that any more.) My husband will get better; you know who we are and the desperate need we have for your help, Sir.'

Do not imagine she wept as she said this. I think that had she wept her grief would have lost some of its dignity and would have seemed less serious and genuine.

But the woman with her, who was standing a little further back – her eyes were filled with tears.

It never occurred to me that M. de Fécour would not yield; I did not see how he could possibly resist. Oh how inexperienced I was! He was not even touched.

M. de Fécour was a man of substance: for thirty years he had lived in luxury. People might talk to him about embarrassment, need, even poverty or something akin, and he didn't know what it was all about.

But his heart must have been hard by nature, for I don't think prosperity can harden any other kind of heart.

'It is no longer possible, Madame,' he said. 'I am afraid I cannot now go back on my word, and I have filled his post. This is the young man I have given it to, and he will confirm it.'

Being addressed like this made me blush. She looked at me, but her look conveyed such a gentle reproach. 'What, you too?' it seemed to be saying. 'You are a party to the wrong being done me?'

'Oh no, Madame,' I answered in the same language – if she understood it. Then I said aloud to M. de Fécour: 'So it is the position of this lady's husband that you wish me to have, Sir?'

'Yes,' he said, 'that's it. Good day, Madame.'

'Please don't trouble, Sir,' I said, stopping him. 'I prefer to wait for you to give me another when you can. I am not in so much of a hurry; let me leave this one for this good man. If I were in his place and sick like him, I should be extremely glad for somebody to treat me as I am treating him.'

The young lady did not add anything in support of this, which was far the best way, but waited in silence with lowered eyes for M. de Fécour to come to a decision, and did not take advantage with any further plea of the generosity which I was showing and which might be an example to our employer.

But as for him, I could see that the example amazed him but did not please him, and he did not like my giving myself airs for being more sensitive than he was.

'So you prefer to wait? Well, that's something new! Very well, Madame, go back home and we'll see in Paris what can be done. I shall be there the day after tomorrow,' and to me: 'Off you go, I'll speak to Mme de Fécour.'

The young lady bowed low but said nothing, the other woman followed suit and so did I, and all three of us went out. But the tone with which the gentleman dismissed us gave me no hope of my action helping the young woman's husband in any way, and I could see from her expression that she did not think it augured any improvement.

But here is something that will surprise you: one of the gentlemen with M. de Fécour came out immediately after us.

The young lady and I had stopped on the staircase and she was thanking me for what I had done for her and expressing the gratitude with which I could see she was really overcome.

The other lady, whom she called mother, was adding her thanks and I was giving the daughter my hand to help her down (I had already learned that little politeness, and one shows off what one knows), when we saw the gentleman I have mentioned coming towards us and making for the young lady, whom he addressed in a bumbling and somewhat abrupt manner: 'Are you having dinner at Versailles before going home, Madame?'

'Yes, Monsieur,' she said. 'Well, after your meal come and see me at the inn where I am going now. I should be very glad to talk to you, so don't fail. And you too,' he said, turning to me, 'come at the same time and you won't regret it, if you see what I mean. Good-bye, good morning!' And he went his way.

Now this fat little man, for he was both, as well as being a bumbling speaker, was the one who had annoyed me least at M. de Fécour's, and whose attitude had seemed the least hostile. It is as well to note that in passing.

'Have you any idea what he wants us for?' asked the young

lady. 'No, Madame, I don't even know who he is. This is the first time in my life I have set eyes on him.'

Talking like this we reached the bottom of the stairs and I was regretfully going to take my leave, but when I showed the first sign the mother said: 'As you and my daughter have to go to the same address soon, don't go away, Monsieur, but do us the honour of having a meal with us, and in any case after the service you have tried to render us we should be very sorry indeed to have only a moment's acquaintance with such a good man as you.'

To invite me to a meal was to interpret my wishes. This young lady had an indefinable charm which kept me at her side, but I thought it was only respect, pity and interest in her affairs.

Also I had done her a kindness, and we enjoy being with people on whose gratitude we have a claim. That is honestly all I saw in the pleasure I found in seeing her, for as to love, or any sentiment anywhere near that, there was no such idea in my mind. It never occurred to me.

I was even proud of the affection I felt for her, as though it were a praiseworthy emotion, a virtue, and it is pleasant to feel virtuous, so I accompanied these ladies with admirably innocent intentions, telling myself: you really are a decent chap!

I noticed that the mother took the hostess aside for a word or two, presumably to order something to be prepared; I dared not show that I suspected what she was doing or raise any objection. I was afraid it might not be quite the right thing.

A quarter of an hour later the meal was served and we sat down at table.

'The more I look at you, Monsieur,' said the mother, 'the more I think your looks are worthy of what you did at M. de Fécour's.'

'Oh really, Madame, who would not have done the same as I did, seeing the lady in that grief-stricken state? Who would not want to help her out of her difficulties? It is very sad to be powerless when you see people in affliction, and especially people as worthy of admiration as she is. I have never in my life been as touched as I was this morning, and if I had not controlled myself I would have cried my heart out.'

This speech, quite simple though it was, had little of the peasant left in it, as you see. It no longer sounded like the village lad but just a simple, kind young man.

'What you are saying adds yet another debt to what we owe you, Monsieur,' said the young lady, blushing perhaps without knowing why, unless my expression had become tender and she was afraid of being too emotional herself. It is true that her eyes were softer than her words; she said only what she meant to say and stopped at the point she wished. But when she looked at me I didn't think it seemed quite the same thing. These are observations anybody can make, especially in a mood such as I was in.

On my side I lacked my usual gaiety and high spirits, and yet was delighted to be there. But I was concerned with being polite and respectful, which was all her charming face allowed me to be. With certain facial expressions you can't behave just anyhow: they inspire respect.

If I tried to report all the kind and flattering things these ladies said there would be no end to it.

I asked them where they lived in Paris, and they told me, and their name as well, with a friendliness that showed how sincerely they wanted to see me.

The mother was always the first to answer, and then the daughter followed and modestly supported what she had said, and always at the end there was a glance in which I saw more than she said.

When the meal was over we discussed the appointment we had, which seemed very strange.

It struck two and we went. We were told that the gentleman was finishing his dinner, but as he had warned his servants that we should be coming we were shown into a small room where we waited, and to which he came a few minutes later holding a toothpick in his hand. I mention the toothpick because it conveys an idea of the sort of reception he gave us.

I must draw you his portrait. As I have said already, a portly man shorter than average, with a rather clumsy gait and cantankerous face, and he spoke so fast that of every four words he said he stumbled over half.

We welcomed him with much bowing and scraping, which he let us go on with as long as we liked, without feeling obliged himself to acknowledge it by the tiniest nod; and I don't think it was arrogance on his part so much as sheer forgetfulness of all ceremony, for he found it easier like that and had gradually got into the habit through dealing with underlings in his profession every day.

He advanced towards the young lady with the toothpick which, as you see, went well with the crudeness of his greeting.

'Oh good,' he said, 'here you are, and you too,' he added, looking at me. 'Well, what's it all about? So you're very upset, poor young lady? (You can see who that was for.) Who is the lady with you? Your mother or some other relation?'

'I am her daughter, Monsieur.' 'Ah, you are her daughter, good. She looks like a respectable woman, and so do you. I like respectable people. And this husband of yours, what sort of a chap is he? Why is he ill so often? Is he old? Might there be a bit of over-indulgence behind it?'

All of which questions were a bit harsh, and yet he asked them with the best intentions in the world, as you will see in due course, but there was nothing gentle about them. They were almost like little blows to one's pride.

Some people are said to be heavy-handed, and this good man's hand was not light.

But to return: he asked about the husband. 'He is neither old nor dissipated,' answered the young lady. 'He is a very clean-living man and he is only thirty-five, but his misfortunes have weighed him down. It is heartbreak that has ruined his health.'

'Oh ye. I can well believe it, poor fellow. All very upsetting. You aroused my sympathy just now, and your mother – I noticed she was crying. I say, you must be finding it very hard to manage. How old are you?'

'Twenty, Monsieur,' she said, colouring. 'Twenty! Why marry so young? You see what happens: children come along, then troubles, not much money, then life becomes unpleasant, and so much for married bliss! Oh well, all the same, she is nice, your daughter, very nice,' he added, addressing the mother. 'I quite like her face, but that's not why I wanted to see her. On the contrary, I wanted to help her and do something for her because she is good. I set great store by a young woman who lives virtuously when she is pretty and down on her luck, and I haven't seen many like her. The other kind attract men but you don't respect them. Keep it up, Madame, keep it up, go on being the same. And I'm very pleased with this young man too, very impressed, he must be a decent fellow to judge by the way he spoke this morning, yes, you have a good heart and I took to you and I feel very well disposed towards you. What you did at M. de Fécour's was very fine and it astonished me. What's more, if he doesn't give you another job (he was talking to me about M. de Fécour) I will look after you, I promise. Come and see me in Paris, and you too (these words to the young lady). We must see what M. de Fécour decides about your husband. If he reinstates him, well and good, but regardless of the outcome of that, I will do what I can for you. I have some ideas that will appeal to you and be advantageous. But let us sit down, you're not in a hurry, are you? It's only half past two, so tell me something about yourself, I shall be very glad to be in the picture. How comes it that your husband has fallen on evil days? Was he rich? What part do you come from?'

'From Orleans, Monsieur.' 'Oh, Orleans, a very nice town. Have you any relations there? What's your story? I've still got a quarter of an hour I can give you, and as I'm taking an interest in you it is only right that I should know who you are, and it will give me pleasure, you know.'

'Monsieur,' she said, 'my story will not be a long one.

'My family is from Orleans, but I was not brought up there. I am the daughter of a gentleman of limited means who with my mother lived a couple of leagues from that city, on an estate remaining from the family property, and died there.'

'Ah! Ah!' said M. Bono (that was our benefactor's name). 'A gentleman's daughter. That's all very fine, but what's the use of it when you are poor? Well, what then?'

'It is three years since my husband fell in love with me. He was another gentleman from our locality.' 'All right, a lot of good his nobility has done him. What then?'

'As I was considered fairly attractive . . .' 'Oh yes,' he said, 'and they were right. You're not wanting in that direction. Ah, you were bonny and one of the prettiest girls in the district, I'll be bound. And then?'

'At the same time I was being wooed by a rich bourgeois in Orleans.'

'Ah, he was the one, he had some hard cash, it was that bourgeois you should have chosen.'

'You are about to see, Monsieur, why I didn't. He was handsome, and I found him quite pleasant without actually loving him. But he seemed more agreeable than the gentleman who, however, was quite as worthy a person. As my mother, who was the only person on whom I depended, for my father was dead – as my mother, I say, left the choice between them to me, I have no doubt that the slight feeling of preference I had for the bourgeois would eventually have swung me in his favour had it not been for an accident that suddenly made me incline towards his rival.

'It was the beginning of winter, and my mother and I were walking by the edge of a forest with both these gentlemen. I had gone a little way off on my own to look at something or other in that country spot, when a fierce wolf rushed at me out of the forest.

'Imagine my terror. I ran towards my friends, screaming. My mother tried to flee in terror also, but tripped and fell. The bourgeois ran away, though he had a sword at his side.

'Only the gentleman remained, and he drew his sword, ran towards me, faced the wolf and attacked it just as it was about to fling itself on me and tear me to pieces.

'He killed it at the risk of his own life, for he was wounded in several places and even thrown to the ground by the wolf, with which he rolled over and over. But he did not let go of his sword, with which at last he finished off the savage beast.

'Some peasants who lived nearby and had heard our cries, managed to reach us only after the wolf was killed. They carried the gentleman away, for he had not got to his feet again and was losing a lot of blood and needed immediate help.

'I was half a dozen steps away and had fallen in a faint, as had my mother close by, so that they had to carry all three of us back to our house, from which our walk had taken us some distance.

'The wounds which the wolf's fangs had inflicted could be easily treated, but the rabid state of the beast gave rise to fears that they might have the most terrible consequences, so that in spite of his wounds he left us the next day for the sea.*

'I confess, Sir, that I was left deeply impressed by the little value he had set on his own life for my sake (he could easily have saved himself as his rival did), and even more impressed that he took no pride in this act of his and did not use it to his own

*It was believed that sea baths were a cure for rabies.

advantage or to press his suit any more boldly. "I know you don't love me, Mademoiselle," he said, but only on the point of leaving. "I have not the good fortune to please you, but I am not too unhappy because I have been fortunate enough to show you that I hold nothing so dear as you." "And now nobody can be so dear to me," I answered unequivocally and in front of my mother, who approved of my answer.'

'Yes, yes,' M. Bono said, 'that is wonderful, and nothing could be so beautiful as those sentiments – in a novel. I can foresee that you will marry him because he has been bitten, but, you know, I would like it even better if that wolf hadn't come. You could well have done without him, for he did you a bad turn. Oh, and by the way, is that bourgeois still running away? Didn't he ever come back?'

'He had the impudence to reappear that very evening. He came back to our home and for a whole hour faced the presence of his wounded rival, which made him even more despicable to me than his cowardice at the moment of peril when he had abandoned me.'

'Oh,' said M. Bono, 'I really don't know what to say. In a case like this love has nothing to do with it. As for his coming to see you, agreed, I blame him for that, but as for his flight, that's another thing altogether. I don't think he did too badly – anyway it was a very nasty animal and your husband was a hothead in actual fact. To end the story, the gentleman came back and you married him, I suppose?'

'Yes, Monsieur, I believed it was my duty.'

'Oh have it as you will, but I am sorry about the man who ran away. He was better for you because he was rich. Your husband was excellent as a wolf-killer, but wolves don't always come our way, and we always need something to live on.'

'When I married him my husband had some money, he enjoyed an adequate competence.' 'Adequate! All right, but what's the good of that? Anything that is just sufficient never suffices. Well, how did he lose this competence?'

'In a lawsuit against a neighbouring squire over certain dues, a lawsuit of hardly any account at first but which became much more important than we imagined it could, and it was decided against us thanks to a great deal of influence. The loss totally ruined us. My husband had to come to Paris to find employment; he was recommended to M. de Fécour, who gave him a job. It is this same job that he has recently taken away from him, and you heard me asking him to give it back. I don't know whether he will do so, he has made no promise, but I am going away much cheered, Monsieur, since I have had the good fortune to meet somebody as kind as you, and you have been good enough to take an interest in our situation.'

'Yes, yes, don't you worry, you can rely on me. We must help those who are in trouble – I wish nobody was in trouble, that's what I wish, but that cannot be. And you, my boy, where do you come from?' 'Champagne, Sir,' I replied.

'Ah, where the good wine comes from? I'm very glad to hear it. Is your father there?' 'Yes, Sir.' 'That's fine, he can send me some, for so often you are let down over it. And who are you?'

'Son of a respectable man who lives in the country,' I replied. I was telling the truth, yet dodging the word peasant, which sounded a harsh term to me. We aren't forbidden to use synonyms, and in this particular regard whenever I have found them I have used them, but my vanity has never gone beyond those limits, and I would have said outright: I am a peasant's son, if the term son of a man who lives in the country hadn't come to mind.

It struck three, M. Bono took out his watch and rose. 'Well, I must leave you, we'll see each other in Paris. I shall expect you there and I will keep my word. Good afternoon, glad to have met you. Oh, but are you going back to Paris straight away? I am sending my carriage on to Paris in a moment or two; you go in it. Carriages are expensive, and it will be that much saved.'

He called a footman. 'Is Picard getting ready to go?' 'Yes, Sir, he is putting the horses into the shafts.' 'Well, tell him to take these ladies and this young man. Good-bye.'

We wanted to thank him but he was already far away. We went down, the carriage was soon ready and off we drove, very pleased with our man and his brusque ways.

I will say nothing about our conversation during the journey, so let us come to Paris, where we arrived in plenty of time for my appointment. You will remember I had one with Mme de Ferval at the house of a Mme Remy on the outskirts.

M. Bono's coachman took the two ladies home, where I left them after many compliments and renewed invitations to go and see them.

Then I dismissed the coachman, took a cab and set off for my meeting.

PART 5

I SAID in the previous part that I hurried off to Mme Remy's where Mme de Ferval was waiting for me.

It was about half past five in the afternoon when I reached there. I found the place at once. I also saw Mme de Ferval's carriage in the little back street she had mentioned, where there was a back gate through which she said she would enter, and following my instructions I used the other entrance, after making sure that Mme Remy lived there. First there was a narrow pathway, which led to a small courtyard at the end of which you went into a hall, and it was from this hall that you could get into the garden Mme de Ferval had mentioned.

Before I had crossed the courtyard the door of the hall was opened (apparently my arrival had been heard). There came out a tall, elderly woman, thin and pale, dressed in working clothes, but very neat, and she had a self-possessed and cunning look about her. It was Mme Remy herself.

'Who are you looking for, Monsieur?' she said when I reached her. 'I have come to see a lady who should have been here for a few minutes, or who will soon come.'

'And her name, Monsieur?' 'Mme de Ferval,' I said, and at once she replied: 'Come in, Monsieur.'

I went in but there was nobody in the hall. 'So she hasn't come yet?' I asked. 'You'll see her in a moment,' she said, taking a key from her pocket, with which she opened a door hidden from sight – that of a room in which I found Mme de Ferval sitting by a little bed, reading.

'You are very late, M. de la Vallée,' she said, rising, 'I have been here for at least a quarter of an hour.'

'I'm sorry, Madame, but don't blame me, it is through no fault of mine. I have come this very minute from Versailles, where I was obliged to go, and I was most impatient to get here.'

While we were talking our complaisant hostess, without appearing to listen and in an absent-minded way, was tidying up the room, and then she withdrew without a word. 'So you are going, Madame Remy?' exclaimed Mme de Ferval, crossing to the open door on to the garden.

'Yes, Madame, I have something to attend to upstairs for a little while, and perhaps you have something to discuss with this gentleman. Will you be needing me?'

'No,' said Mme de Ferval, 'you can stay if you like, but please don't put yourself out.' Thereupon Mme Remy nodded, left us, locked the door and took away the key, which we heard her take out, though she did it very carefully.

'That woman must be mad. I do believe she's locking us in!' said Mme de Ferval with a smile that opened the way and set the tone for an amorous conversation and meant: 'So we are here alone together!'

'Who cares?' I said (we were on the step of the garden door). 'We don't need the Remy woman to help us talk to each other, it would be even worse than the maid at your home. Didn't we agree to be free?'

While talking like this I took her hand and gazed at its grace and whiteness, kissing it now and again. 'Is this the way you tell me your story?' she said. 'Oh, I'll still be able to tell you that, the story isn't in such a hurry as I am.' 'As you are!' she said, putting her other hand on my shoulder. 'What are you in such a hurry about?' 'To tell you that you have charms that have kept me dreaming of them all day long.' 'I have been dreaming quite a lot about you, too,' she said, 'such a lot that I almost didn't come.'

'Oh why not, mistress of my heart?' I countered.* 'Why not indeed? Because you are so young and so impatient. I remember how high-spirited you were yesterday, for all your embarrassment, and now that has gone will you be any better? I find it hard to believe.' 'Me too,' I said, 'for I am even more in love than I was yesterday, because it seems to me that you are even more beautiful.'

*It is tempting to think that this absurd language is a direct parody of *Manon Lescaut*. Prévost's masterpiece, published only a year or two before, was already a best-seller. (Des Grieux: 'je m'avançai vers la maîtresse de mon cœur ...' etc.)

'That's all very well,' she said with a smile; 'those are very fine sentiments which are very reassuring. Fancy being alone with a wild young man like you and unable to get away, for where has she gone, the silly woman, leaving us here? I'll wager there's nobody here but us now. Oh, just let her come back and I'll give her a piece of my mind. For I ask you, just think of the risks she is exposing me to!'

'Good Lord,' I said, 'it is easy enough for you to talk. You don't know what it is to be in love with you. As if you only had to say to people: keep quiet! I'd like you to be in my shoes and see what you would do.' 'Now, now, stop it,' she teased, 'I've quite enough to deal with in my own shoes.' 'Still, tell me all the same,' I insisted in the same tone of voice. 'Well, then, in your shoes I suppose I should try to be reasonable.' 'And suppose it was no use trying, what would happen then?' I countered. 'Oh then, I don't know at all, you're asking too much and I can't follow you. But what does it matter whether you love me? Can't you do as I do? I am being reasonable although I love you too, and I ought not to tell you so because it will only make you do still more silly things, and that will be my fault, for you are such a disobedient youngster. Just look how he's eyeing me! I can't hold out against him. Let's talk about Versailles.'

'Oh no,' I answered, 'let's talk about your saying you love me. It's such a pleasant topic, it's like a charm to hear it and it delights me and carries me away. What joy! Oh, how enchanting your lovely form is!'

While holding forth in this manner I looked up at her with greedy eyes. She was wearing rather less than usual. 'Nothing could be more delicious than this pretty bodice,' I exclaimed. 'Now, now, you naughty boy, no more of that, I won't have it!'

But she rearranged her clothing rather perfunctorily. 'Oh, gracious lady,' I said, 'it's so nicely arranged, don't touch it.' I took both her hands; her eyes were full of love, she sighed and murmured: 'What do you want me to do, La Vallée? It was wrong of me not to make that Remy woman stay – I shall another time – you won't listen to reason. Get a little further away, there are some windows over there people can see us from.'

And indeed there were some windows opposite which overlooked us. 'We only need to get further back into the room,' I said. 'Yes, we must,' she said, 'but control yourself, my dearest boy, do control yourself. I came here in all good faith, and you are frightening me with this passion of yours.'

'Yet I only have the passion you have inspired. But we are standing, and that's tiring. Let's sit down. Look, go back to where you were when I came in.' 'What, there!' she said. 'Oh I wouldn't dare, I should be too shut in, unless you call Mme Remy. Please call her,' she said in a tone quite lacking in conviction, and we were gradually approaching the spot where I had first found her. 'Wherever are you taking me?' she said with tenderness and without concern. But just as she was sitting down and I was throwing myself on my knees before her we heard voices in the hall.

The noise grew louder, like an argument.

'Oh, La Vallée, whatever is it? Get up!' cried Mme de Ferval. The noise grew louder still.

We could make out the voice of a man in a rage, against whom Mme Remy, whom we could also hear, seemed to be on the defensive. Eventually the key was put into the lock, the door opened and in came a man of thirty to thirty-five, with a very fine figure and handsome face, looking extremely angry. I had my hand to my sword and strode to the middle of the room, very nervous about it all but determined to stand up to this insult, if that was what he intended it to be.

'What's this all about, Sir?' I asked. But without answering me he took one look at Mme de Ferval, immediately changed his manner, respectfully doffed his hat, not without showing utter amazement, and said to her: 'Oh, Madame, I apologize a thousand times, I am horrified at what I have done. I expected to find another lady in whom I am interested, and I was certain that she would be the one I should find here.'

'Oh yes, no doubt,' said Mme Remy. 'It's a nice time now to ask to be excused! Look at the fine mess you've made here! Madame has come here on family business with her nephew, whom she can only see in secret, and she could do without your apologies, and so could I.'

'You are more in the wrong than I am,' he said. 'You never warned me that you let anybody else come here except the lady I came to see and myself. I was on my way back from dining in the country, and as I was passing I noticed a carriage in the back street and thought it belonged to the lady I know. But as I hadn't fixed a meeting I was surprised. I even saw from a distance a manservant and mistook his livery. So I stopped my carriage to find out what this lady was doing here, you said she was not here, I could see you were embarrassed, and would anyone in my place not have suspected something mysterious? However, to dispel any anxiety this may have given the lady, it is as though nothing had happened, and once again I beg her to forgive me.' As he was saying this he drew even nearer to Mme de Ferval in the most gallant way, which had even a touch of the affectionate about it.

Mme de Ferval coloured and tried to withdraw her hand, which he had seized and was kissing with fervour.

At that I strode forward, thinking I shouldn't remain silent. 'Madame doesn't look annoyed to me,' I said to this young squire. 'Even the wisest can make a mistake: you took her for somebody else, no great harm is done, she excuses you and it only remains for you to go away. That is the quickest course now you see how things are, Monsieur.'

That made him look round, and he studied me somewhat attentively. 'I seem to know your face,' he said. 'Haven't I seen you at Mme So-and-so's?'

He was referring, if you please, to none other than the wife of the late squire of our village. 'You might have,' I said, blushing in spite of myself. And indeed I was beginning to recall him too. 'Oh, it's Jacob!' he exclaimed. 'I recognize him, it's the very man! Well I never, I'm delighted, my lad, to see you here in such a grand setting. Your fortune must have changed very much to make it possible for you to have any connection with Madame. I, as a man of some standing, would be glad to have the same honour as you; for four months I have been longing to become one of her friends, and she may have noticed it although so far I have only met her three or four times. From the way I have looked at her she will know how captivating she is. I was born with the most tender feelings for her, and I am quite sure, dear Jacob, that my love goes back further than yours.'

Mme Remy was not present at this speech, having gone into the hall to leave us to sort ourselves out of the mess.

As for me, I lost my head altogether, and like a fool I acknowledged every word this man addressed to me, sometimes by clicking my heels, sometimes by bowing my head, not knowing what I was doing and all at sixes and sevens. The appalling circumstances of our earlier acquaintance, the contemptuous way he had addressed me, the sudden change from the state of prosperous gentleman, in which he had found me, to that of Jacob, into which he had plunged me again, had quite unmanned me.

But as for Mme de Ferval, it would be hard to say how she looked.

Bear in mind that the Remy woman had referred to me as the lady's nephew; note that she was a pious person and I was young, that her dress that day was more fashionable than usual, her bodice more daring and less tightly laced and consequently her bosom more exposed; remember that we had been discovered together locked in a room in Mme Remy's house and that she was an accommodating woman willing to make her house available, as we were now discovering; don't forget that the Chevalier who burst in upon us knew Mme de Ferval already and was a friend of her friends; on top of all these points I have mentioned, note the curious revelation they furnished about the morals of Mme de Ferval. What nice inner recesses of a conscience to display, what goings-on exposed to the light of day – and such goings-on! The kind that most dishonour a churchgoing woman, that make it clear she is a hypocrite and a thoroughly bad lot! For such a woman can be nasty, vindictive, haughty and a scandalmonger, and she is only fulfilling her office and has no less right to hold her head high, for none of that clashes with the imperious austerity of her calling. But to be convicted of amorousness, to be surprised in a naughy assignation – oh, all is lost! The pious female is hissed off the stage and there is no way of talking herself out of it.

Yet Mme de Ferval did try to, and said something in her defence, but with such obvious embarrassment that she clearly thought her case was hopeless.

Nor had she the courage to plead it for long.

'You are mistaken, Monsieur, I assure you that you are mistaken. I am here for quite innocent reasons. I am only here to talk to him about a way in which I wanted to help him.' After this brief speech her voice failed her, there were tears in her eyes and her words were lost in a sigh.

For my part, I didn't know what to say. The name Jacob that he had reminded me of kept me deferential, for I was afraid he would begin addressing me again in the same way, and my one concern was to slip away as best I could. For what was to be done about a rival for whom one's own name was only Jacob, and this in the presence of a woman to whom such excessive familiarity was as humiliating as it was to me? To have a lover was already shameful, but to have one with a name like that was doubly so, and a really delicate affair of the heart between her and a Jacob was quite out of the question.

In fact, on top of my own personal embarrassment I was blushing because I was the reason for her disgrace, and so I was bound to be very ill at ease and was already looking for a reasonable pretext for withdrawing, when Mme de Ferval said that she was only there to help me.

So at once, without giving the gentleman time to answer, I cut in: 'It will do another time, Madame, please remain kindly disposed towards me and I will wait for you to let me know what you have in mind. As you know this gentleman and he knows you, I will take my leave. As for this love he refers to, I don't understand.'

Mme de Ferval made no answer, but kept her eyes lowered and her face looked humbled and mortified, with a tear or two running down it. This gentleman, our spoil-sport, had taken her hand again and she had abandoned it to him, no doubt because she dared not pull it away, for the villain was as it were the arbiter of her fate and he could mete out sentence or acquittal. In a word, he was in a position to be enterprising and she had no grounds for objecting.

'Well, good-bye, Master Jacob, until we meet again,' he called out as I was leaving. Well, at that point I jibbed and lost my patience, and being braver because I was on the way out: 'All right, all right!' I shouted, tossing my head. 'Good-bye Master Jacob then, farewell to Master Pierre and my respects to Master Nicholas – what a lot of fuss over a Christian name!' He burst out laughing at my rejoinder, and I went out in a temper, banging the door on them.

I found Mme Remy at the front door.

'So you are off?' she said. 'Well, of course,' I answered, 'what do you expect me to do now that man's there, and why have you been letting him come here regularly? It is most unfortunate, Madame Remy. A man comes from Versailles for a perfectly honourable discussion here and takes your room, hoping to be undisturbed, but not at all, one might just as well be out in the street. A lot of good badgering me like that! I'm not concerned about myself in all this, it is Madame de Ferval. What is this great God-knows-who going to think of her? A locked door, no key in the lock, a society woman with a young fellow – looks nice, doesn't it?'

'Oh Lord, my boy,' she said, 'I am terribly sorry. When he arrived I had the key of your room in my hand, and do you realize he snatched it away? But in any case there's nothing to fear, he is a great friend of mine and a very respectable man who sometimes comes here to see a lady I know. Between you and me I think he's a bit sweet on her, and being a hasty man he was jealous and determined to go in. But what difference does it make? You stay here, I am sure he is going.' 'No doubt,' I said, 'and after him somebody else. You have too many friends by half, Madame Remy.'

'Well, what do you expect? I have a big house, I am a widow all on my own and respectable people tell me they have something to discuss together in private and will I lend them a room? Am I to say no, especially to people I like and who are good to me? A fine shanty mine is, to be finicky about! And after all, what's wrong with Mme de Ferval being seen with you in my house? I wish now I had opened that door straight away, for what can anybody say about it? Look here, first comes a lady, then a young fellow, I let them both come in and so they are together unless I keep them apart. The man is young, well, has he got to be old? It is true the door was shut; all right, next time it will be open. Sometimes it is and sometimes it isn't, what's so mysterious about that? You open it when you go in and shut it when you're inside. And as for me, if I wasn't with you, well, I was somewhere else. You can't be everywhere at once, I come and go and do odd jobs about the house while my visitors talk. Besides, wouldn't I have come back? What is Mme de Ferval so upset about? Didn't I even say she was your aunt?'

'Well, that only makes it worse,' I said, 'because he knows it's not true.' 'Well then,' she said, 'a lot of good that does him. Aren't you afraid he'll have the law on you?'

While she was talking, my mind was on those two people I had left in the room, and although I was very glad to be out of it because of that name Jacob, yet I was very annoyed at having my conversation with Mme de Ferval disturbed and wished I had had what might have followed. Not that I felt any affection for her, and never had, although I had thought so; I have already gone into that. Even on that day I hadn't felt very eager about coming to the neighbourhood, for meeting that young person at Versailles had cooled a great deal of my ardour for this meeting.

But Mme de Ferval was a woman of some standing and still very well preserved, with snow-white skin and lovely hands, and I had seen her lying in an unguarded posture on a sofa and casting me amorous looks. And at my age, keeping your mind on little considerations like that, you can manage without affection in making love to people, and consequently are annoyed when a rendezvous you have been granted is upset.

There are many love affairs in which the heart plays no part – more of them even than of the others – and, in the main, nature depends upon these for achieving her ends, and not on our sentimental delicacies, which are useless to her. Most often it is we ourselves who indulge in tenderness so as to embellish our passions, but it is nature who makes us passionate, and it is from her that we derive the reality that we doll up with the respectabilities, for that is my name for sentiments which nowadays we have almost ceased dolling up; it is going out of fashion at the time I am writing this.

However that might be, I merely had a very natural passion, and as that kind of love is subject to mishaps I was very annoyed at having been interrupted.

I said to myself: that gentleman has taken her hand and kissed it as bold as brass, and the fellow will get quite impudent because he surprised us together. For I realized perfectly the capital he might make out of that. Mme de Ferval, formerly piety itself and now revealed as a most irreligious woman quite lacking in scruples, could no longer give herself airs as unapproachable. The fellow had looked attractive to me, tall and handsome, and for four months, he said, he had been in love with the lady. He had come upon the secret of her morality and he might perhaps take his revenge if he were resisted but hold his tongue if kindly treated. Mme de Ferval was by nature voluptuous, and this time there were reasons for being so. Would she or wouldn't she? So I was in an indescribable ferment of emotion, motivated by a strange curiosity, anxious, jealous, a bit prurient if you like, in fact very difficult to explain. You don't fret about a woman's heart but about her person, you don't think about her sentiments but about her actions, you don't say: will she be unfaithful? but: will she be circumspect?

While I was in this state of mind it occurred to me that I had plenty of money on me, that Mother Remy loved making some, and that a woman who didn't boggle at letting out her room for two or three hours would be willing to let me hire an anteroom or other place adjacent to that room, if she had such a thing.

'I don't think I am leaving here,' I said, 'but waiting until that man has left Mme de Ferval. Would you by any chance have some place near where they are, in which I could stay? I am not asking you for this pleasure for nothing, I will pay.' As I was saying this I took some money out of my pocket.

'By all means!' she said, eyeing a gold half-louis I was holding. 'There happens to be a little cubby-hole that is only separated from that room by a partition, where I put old clothes, but you'd better go up to the loft, you'd be more comfortable there.'

'No, no,' I said, 'the cubby-hole will do. I shall be nearer to Mme de Ferval and shall know at once when that other man goes. Look, this is for you, do you want it?' I asked, giving her my half-louis, not without some qualms about spending it in this way, for think what a perfidious way of using Mme de la Vallée's money! I felt ashamed; but I tried not to think about it so as to be less in the wrong.

'Oh dear, I didn't want nothing for that,' said the Remy, pocketing what I gave her. 'It's a kind thought of yours, and I am much obliged. Come along, I'll take you to this little place, but mind you don't make a sound, and walk softly. There's no need for our friends to hear anybody, they'd think there was something fishy going on.'

'Oh, never fear,' I said, 'I shan't move.' As we were talking we went back into the hall. Then she opened a door, covered only by a bit of shabby tapestry, which led into the little slip-room, where I took up my position.

In there it was almost as good as being in the room itself. Only the thinnest possible matchboarding separated me from it, so that they could not breathe without my hearing. Yet it took me a good two minutes before I could make sense of what this man was saying to Mme de Ferval – for he was the one who was talking – because at first I was so agitated and my heart was beating so loud that I could not take anything in. I did not quite trust Mme de Ferval, and the funny thing about it was that my mistrust came from her fancy for me. The passion she had conceived for me, far from reassuring me, led me to suspect her.

Well, then, I cocked my ear, and you are about to witness a kind of conversation only possible with a woman for whom a man has no respect but whom, by dint of suggestive talk, he conditions to listen to outrageous remarks which she well deserves. At first I thought Mme de Ferval was sighing.

'Madame, I beg of you, do sit down a moment,' he said. 'I won't leave you in this state. Tell me why you are crying. What is it? What are you afraid I shall do, and why do you dislike me, Madame?' 'I don't, Monsieur,' she said, with a little sob, 'and if I am crying it is not because I have anything to reproach myself with. But this is a most unfortunate occurrence for me, and all the more so because there are circumstances for which I am not responsible at all. This woman who had locked us in – I had no idea. She told you that that young man was my nephew. She was making it up, and in my astonishment I had no time to contradict her. I don't know what she thought she was up to, but it has all rebounded on me. And there is no end to what you could imagine or say about it all. That's why I am crying!'

'Yes, Madame, I agree that if you were dealing with a man devoid of decency and probity you would have reason to weep, and that this adventure could put you very much in the wrong – you especially, because you lead a more retired life than some. But, Madame, do believe first of all that an act which none but you had witnessed could not be more secret than this will be with a witness like myself. So set your mind at rest on this score, be as untroubled as you were before I came. As I am the only person to have seen you it is as though nobody had seen you. Only an evil man could say anything, and I am not one and would not be tempted to act like that even to my worst enemy. You are dealing with a gentleman, a man incapable of a base action, and it would be a vile, horrible baseness to betray you in this affair.'

'That settles it, Monsieur, and you have quite reassured me. You say you are a gentleman, and you certainly seem to be one, and although I don't know you at all well, I have always thought so, as people at whose houses we have met would tell you. If you were deceiving me, there could be no relying on anybody's appearance. Moreover, Monsieur, by remaining silent not only will you satisfy probity which demands it, but you will do even more justice to my innocence. Only appearances are against me in this matter, I beg you to believe.'

'Ah, Madame, you still mistrust me, since you are thinking of self-justification. Do please have a little more confidence. It is in my interest to inspire your confidence, for it would win me that much advantage in your heart, and you would be less unlikely to return a little of my affection.'

'Return your affection!' she exclaimed in heartbroken tones. 'That is a terrible thing to say, and it is cruel that I should be exposed to such a thing. You would have spared me this at any other time, but you think you are free to say anything in the situation in which I now find myself. You are taking advantage of the reasons I have for humouring you, that is quite clear.'

In parenthesis, don't forget that I was there, and that as I heard Mme de Ferval talking in this way I felt a gradual change coming over my feeling for her, and my love for her grew nobler, so to speak, and became worthy of the virtue she was showing.

'No, Madame, don't humour me,' he exclaimed. 'You are in no way called upon to do so. My discretion in this affair is something apart, and concerns me even more than you, for if I were to say anything I should dishonour myself. What! Can you believe that you have to buy my silence? You do me wrong, you do indeed. No, Madame, I repeat, however you treat me it has no bearing on the private nature of what has happened to you, and if at this moment you wish me to leave, if I displease you, I will go.'

'No, Monsieur, that is not what I mean, and my reproaching you does not mean I dislike you, and it is not even your love that distresses me. We are free to love whom we like, and a woman can't prevent a man loving her, and the love of a man like you is more bearable than that of some others. Only I might have preferred yours to show itself at some other time, because then I would not have had any reason for supposing that you are taking a kind of advantage of what is happening to me, however unjustifiable it might be to do so; for nothing, I assure you, could be more unjustifiable. You don't want to believe it, but I am telling you the truth.'

'Oh how sorry I should be if you were telling the truth, Madame,' he said urgently. 'What is the trouble? To have felt some affection for that young man? Oh, but how charming of you, with all your qualities, to have the additional one of being a bit tender-hearted!'

'Oh no, Monsieur, don't you believe it, there's nothing like that about it, I swear!'

As far as I could make out he then fell on his knees and broke in: 'Give up trying to explain to me. To whom are you trying to justify yourself? Am I by age or character a man to make a crime out of your assignation? Do you believe I think any the less of you because you are capable of what is called a frailty? No, no, on the contrary, all I conclude from that is that you are more kind-hearted than some others. The more easily we are touched, the more noble our souls, and consequently the more admirable, and this makes you all the more charming in every way. To be liable to such frailties as these adds a new grace to your sex.' (A nice little sermon to preach in Mme Remy's establishment, but he had to sugar the pill.) 'You touched my heart the very first time I saw you,' he went on, 'and you know it. I looked upon you with the utmost pleasure, and you noticed it. I have read more than once in your eyes that you understood me. Admit it, Madame.'*

*This belief that emotional sensibility automatically makes a person nobler and better will be one of the great tenets of Romanticism, from *Manon Lescaut* to *René* and beyond. It is the opposite of the Classical

'It is true,' she said in a calmer voice, 'that I did suspect something.' (And those few words made me suspect that I would go back to where I was with her.) 'Yes, I loved you,' he added, 'melancholy, solitary and averse to relationships with men though I thought you were. But you are not, and I was wrong. Mme de Ferval was born tender and affectionate, she herself is capable of being drawn towards a man who loves her as she has been towards this young man, and it might not therefore be out of the question for her to be drawn towards me, for I want her and am meeting her half way. Perhaps she did feel so before this happened? If that is the case, why should you hide it from me and why shouldn't you still feel it? What have I done to deserve punishment? What have you done to make you obliged to dissimulate? What could you be ashamed of? What is your crime? Do you depend on anyone? Have you a husband? Aren't you a widow and your own mistress? Can any criticism be levelled at your conduct? Haven't you taken the wisest possible precautions? Must you despair and imagine that all is lost because chance brings me here? For you can treat me as you wish. I am a man of honour and a reasonable man and I adore you; and perhaps you would not altogether dislike me were you not afraid of something that does not exist, simply does not exist, and which is really just a laughing matter if you like me even a little.'

'Ah,' said Mme de Ferval, with a sigh that promised an understanding. 'How you embarrass me, Chevalier! I don't know how to answer, for there seems no way of getting this idea out of your head, and you are a strange man to imagine that I cast eyes on this young fellow.' (Note that at this point my heart withdrew and took no further interest in her.)

'Very well, there's nothing in it,' he said. 'Why am I talking about it, then? Simply to facilitate our conversation and save time. The only way this adventure can be a profitable one for me is that, if you allow, it is putting us straight away in a position to

---

ideal of intelligence and self-control. The character of the speaker, the setting and the comment in parenthesis show that Marivaux did not subscribe to such nonsense, and was here having another sly dig at his rival and arch-enemy, the Abbé Prévost.

speak frankly. Had this not happened I would have had to suffer for a long time before you could have felt justified in listening to me or in saying the least little word of encouragement, whereas at present here we are all in the mood, and only your wishes can decide. And as it is possible to please you, and as I love you, what am I to expect? What are you going to do with me? Give the verdict.'

'Why not say this somewhere else?' she answered. 'Circumstances here are discouraging, and I keep on thinking that you are taking advantage of them. I wish that the only hold you had on me were my feelings for you.'

'Your feelings!' he exclaimed, while I was boiling with rage in my niche. 'Oh Madame, let them guide you, don't fight against them, you will fill me with joy. Let them guide you, and if after all I have said you are still afraid of me, if my word of honour has not completely reassured you, well, what of it? Yes, by all means be afraid of me and doubt my discretion. All right, I overlook the injustice, provided it acts as a spur to those feelings you speak of, which thrill me. Yes, Madame, you must indeed humour me, and you will be right to do so. I feel like telling you so myself, because I feel that through love I may be wanting in delicacy – I love you so much that I haven't the strength to resist using this little weapon I have against you. I should not need it if you really knew me, and then I should owe all to love. So forget that we are here and remember that you would have loved me sooner or later, since you were inclined that way and I would have left no stone unturned to that end.'

'I don't deny it,' she said. 'I was struck by you and more than once had asked about you.'

'Well, then,' he said ardently, 'let us congratulate ourselves on how things have come about, there is no point in hesitating, Madame.' 'When I reflect,' she said, 'that it is a matter of an undertaking, an undertaking, Chevalier, it frightens me! Think what you like about me, whatever your aims are I have given up fighting against them, but it still remains true that the life I live is very far removed from what you are asking of me. And if we are to put our cards on the table, do you realize that I have been avoiding you, and more than once have deliberately not gone to the houses of people where I met you? Even so, however, I went too often.'

'What, you avoided me when I was looking for you! You admit it and I am supposed not to take advantage of this chance that gives me an opportunity for revenge and to leave you free to go on avoiding me! No, Madame, I am not leaving you until I am sure of your love and am safeguarded against that cruel treatment. No, you won't escape me again, I worship you and you must love me and tell me so; I must know it without any possibility of doubt.' 'What vehemence!' she exclaimed. 'And how he persecutes me! Oh, Chevalier, what a tyrant you are, and how unwise I am to have said so much!'

'Ah,' he went on in a coaxing tone, 'what is there to stop you? What is so terrible for you in this undertaking you dread so much? I ought to be the one to be afraid: you run no risk of seeing my love wane, you are too attractive for that, and I am a thousand times less so, and thus liable to have the pain of seeing the end of *yours*. That would be through no fault of yours, nor should I have any right to complain. But no matter, should those lovely dark eyes which enrapture me give me but one tender glance I should still consider myself too happy.'

As for me, listening in fury, you can't imagine the sort of loveliness I was finding in those beautiful dark eyes he was extolling.

'Well, really, you are a nice one to talk about faithfulness!' she said. 'Would you be making love to me today if you were not inconstant? Weren't you coming here to see a different woman? I shall not ask who she is, and you are too much of a gentleman to tell me, but I am sure she is attractive, and yet you are giving her up. Does that bode well for me?'

'How unfair you are to yourself, and what a comparison you are making! Did I take six months before I fell in love with you? What a difference there is between a person you love because you cannot help it, because you had a natural and invincible affinity with her from birth (I refer to you), and a woman you only bother with because you must do something and she is a flirtatious creature who takes it into her head to make for you because she can't do without lovers; one of those women you talk love to without loving and who imagine they love you because they say so, who take up with you for something to do, as a whim, out of vanity, flightiness or some passing lust that I wouldn't dare explain to you and isn't worth talking about – in fact, for any reason you like. Once again, what a difference there is between such a meaningless, dull, unworthy affair and the genuineness of the feeling I had for you as soon as I set eyes on you, which I could well have done without but which I have clung to with no appearance of success! Please let us make a distinction and not confuse a simple amusement with a serious attachment, and let us drop this hair-splitting.'

I am getting tired of saying that Mme de Ferval heaved a sigh, but nevertheless she fetched one at this point and it is true that, when you are dealing with women, situations like this abound with false or genuine ones.

'How pressing you are, Chevalier!' she said after the sigh. 'I confess that you are charming, and too much so. Isn't that enough? Must I say yet again that I may love you some day? And what will that sound like? Won't you yourself suspect that you only owe my kind words to my present plight? If only I had been warned about this passion I could answer you today with a better grace and you would be more grateful too. But to hear a declaration of love, and admit at once that one is willing, all in the space of half an hour, really it is unheard of! I think a little interval is called for, and you would lose nothing by it, Chevalier.'

'Oh, Madame, you can't be serious! Remember I have been in love with you for four months, my eyes have told you so, and you have noticed and been struck by me, as you yourself put it. Four months! Isn't that long enough for the proprieties? Oh please, no more scruples. You lower your eyes and blush' (he probably only invented the last in order to flatter her), 'do you love me just a little? Will you let me think so? Will you? It's yes, isn't it? One more word, to make sure!'

'What a spell-binder you are! This is astonishing, and it makes me feel ashamed. No, nothing is impossible after what has happened. I think I am going to love you.'

'Oh, then why put it off? Why not love me at once?' 'But, Chevalier, aren't you deceiving me even as you speak? Do you yourself love me as much as you are saying? Aren't you a deceiver? You are being so nice that I am afraid and hesitate.'

'Ah, this is it!' I exclaimed involuntarily, not realizing I was speaking aloud and carried away by the tone in which she pronounced those last words, for it was a tone that granted what the actual words she used were still partly refusing.

The noise I made was a surprise even to me, and I at once rushed out of my cubby-hole to make my escape, and as I went I heard Mme de Ferval exclaim in her turn: 'Oh, Monsieur, he has been listening to us!'

He came out of the room, but took a long time to open the door. Then he called: 'Who's there?' But I was moving so fast that by the time he saw me I had already reached the garden path. The Remy rushed, I think, to the front gate, and seeing me moving off at full speed shouted: 'What's up? What have you been doing?' 'Your two clients will tell you,' I shouted back without looking at her. Then I walked down the road at a normal pace.

Actually I was running away not because I was afraid of the Chevalier, but only so as to avoid the sort of scene that would certainly have happened with Jacob, for had this man not known me and had I passed for Monsieur de la Vallée I would certainly have stayed and would not even have gone into the cubby-hole at all.

But he had seen Jacob only four or five months previously, and how could I have stood up to a man with that advantage over me? My metamorphosis was too recent; there are certain bits of effrontery that a man of good breeding cannot perpetrate, and although they may not be downright insolence, I think you would have to be born insolent to be capable of them.

Anyhow, it was not through lack of pride that I gave in on this occasion, but my pride had its sense of modesty, and that is why it did not hold out.

So there I was out of Mme Remy's establishment, with considerable contempt for Mme de Ferval but much admiration for her looks, and there is nothing surprising about that, for it often happens that a guilty mistress thereby becomes more alluring. You now think that I go on my way back home. Not a bit of it. I am seized by a new preoccupation: 'Let's find out what they do now I have interrupted them,' I said to myself. 'When I left them they were well on the way. What line will that woman take? Will she have the courage to stay there?'

Thereupon I went up the passage of a house some fifty paces

away and facing on to the back street in which Mme de Ferval had left her carriage. There I hid and from there kept a watch both on that little back street and on the door I had come out of, and still in my agitated state; but more painfully agitated than in Mme Remy's house, where at least I could hear what was going on, and hear so well that it was as good as seeing. And that meant that I knew where I stood. But I was not on tenterhooks for very long, for I hadn't been waiting more than four minutes when I saw Mme de Ferval come out of the garden gate and get into her carriage. After which the man came out the other way and got into his, which I saw go past. That at once reassured me.

The only feeling I had left for Mme de Ferval was what is usually called a taste, but quite a calm one which had ceased to disturb me; that is to say that if at that moment I had been given a choice of women I would have given her the preference.

You realize of course that all this put an end to our affair, and she herself could not be wanting to see me again now that I was fully aware of her character, and so I did not dream of going back to her house. It was still early, Mme de Fécour had urged me to let her know as soon as I could the outcome of my journey to Versailles, and so I went round by her house before returning to my own. And there I was.

None of her servants were in the courtyard, having apparently gone off duty. I didn't even see the doorkeeper or any maid upstairs, and walked right through her apartment without meeting a soul until I came to a room in which I could hear somebody either talking or reading, for the monotonous tone of voice was more like that of reading than of conversation. The door was ajar and I did not think there was any point in knocking on a half-open door, so to save trouble I went straight in.

I had guessed right. Mme de Fécour was in bed and being read to. At the foot of the bed was sitting an elderly chambermaid, a manservant was standing near the window and a tall, ugly, scraggy lady with a wizened face, austere and censorious, was reading.

When I was inside the lady broke off and exclaimed in shrewish tones: 'Oh bless my soul, didn't either of you shut the door? Isn't there anyone downstairs to stop people coming up? Is my sister in a fit state to have visitors?'

The compliment was hardly fulsome, but it was perfectly in keeping with the appearance of the person expressing it; her face and mode of welcome were a good match.

Yet this one didn't look like a pious female, and as I got to know her later I want to say just in passing what she was like.

Picture one of those plain women who have realized that they are destined to be neglected in society and have the mortification of seeing other women succeed but themselves never; who, to avoid that humiliation and prevent people from seeing the real reason for the isolation in which they will always stay, say to themselves, without any reference to God and His saints: 'Let us stand out by our austere conduct, let us adopt an unapproachable expression, let us assume a haughty correctness in our behaviour so that people may be certain that it is our virtue and not our appearance that explains why nobody speaks to us.'

And indeed that does sometimes succeed, and the lady in question was thought to be hedged about with that kind of virtue.

As I had taken a dislike to her from the first glance, her words did not upset me, but seemed to fit in, and so, ignoring her, I bowed to Mme de Fécour, who said: 'Ah, it's you, M. de la Vallée, come in, come in. Don't make difficulties, sister, there's nothing wrong and I'm very glad to see him.'

'Oh Lord, Madame,' I said, 'what a state you're in! You were so well when I left you yesterday.' 'Yes, that's true, my boy,' she murmured softly. 'I couldn't have felt better, and even dined out, ate well and enjoyed it. And yet last night I thought I was going to die, with such a violent colic that they thought it would carry me off, and it has left me with a temperature and very dangerous complications, it seems. Sometimes I can't get my breath, and they think I should make my confession this evening. It must be serious, and this is my sister who, fortunately for me, arrived yesterday from the country and who just now was being kind enough to read me a chapter of the *Imitation*, which is very beautiful. Well, M. de la Vallée, tell me about your journey. Are you satisfied with M. de Fécour? This upset comes at a most awkward time for you, for I would have hurried him up. What did he say to you? I am having so much trouble with my breathing that I can't talk any more. Will you get a job? I asked for it to be in Paris.'

'Oh my dear sister,' said the other woman, 'do keep quiet. And as for you, Monsieur, please go away. You can see that we have other things to worry about besides your affairs, and you shouldn't have come in without knowing whether you had permission.'

'That'll do,' said the sick woman between her gasps, as I was bowing myself off, 'that'll do. He didn't know the condition I was in, poor fellow. Well, good-bye, M. de la Vallée. Oh dear, now there's someone who looks well! How fresh-looking! But he's only twenty. Good-bye, good-bye, we'll meet again, this won't be anything, I hope.' 'And so do I with all my heart, Madame,' said I, withdrawing and bowing only at her, for obviously the other one would have received my bow with a bad grace, and then I left for home.

Note, as we go along, the precariousness of the things of this world. The day before I had two mistresses or, if you prefer, women in love with me, for the word mistress means too much here. It usually means a woman who has given you all her heart and who wants all yours. And I don't think the two persons I am talking about had either given me theirs or cared much about having mine, which wasn't bothered about them either.

I say the two persons, for I think I can count Mme de Fécour as well as Mme de Ferval, and within twenty-four hours, lo and behold, I am done out of one, who is snatched out of my grasp, and the other is dying. For Mme de Fécour seemed so to me; and supposing she recovered, it would be some time before we saw each other. Her love was only a whim, and whims pass, and besides, was I the only lusty young fellow in Paris who was good-looking and only twenty?

So that was it in that direction, to all appearances, and it didn't upset me unduly. The Fécour, with her enormous bosom, didn't mean much to me. Only the hypocritical Ferval might have excited me a bit.

She had natural graces. And on top of that she gave herself out to be pious, and in matters of love that type of woman is more spicy than others; there is in their way of doing things a strange, indefinable mixture of mystery, trickery and clandestine lecherousness, but at the same time there is an outward modesty that is extremely appetizing. You feel that they would like to enjoy furtively the pleasure of making love to you and being loved without your noticing it, or at least that they would like to persuade you that in this kind of commerce they are your dupes and not your accomplices.

Well anyhow, at last I was on my way back home and about to rejoin Mme de la Vallée, who loved me so dearly and whom all my straying did not prevent me from loving, both for her charms (for she really had some) and on account of that religious devotion she had for me.

And yet I think I would have loved her more still had I only been her lover (and I mean lover in the full sense), but when you are as indebted to a woman as I was the truth is that a decent man does not repay with that kind of love, but is filled with deeper emotions, is conscious of friendship and gratitude. And indeed I was full of these, and I think that love suffered a little in consequence.

Even if I had returned from the longest voyage Mme de la Vallée could not have welcomed me home with greater joy than she displayed. I found her praying to God for my safe return, and it was scarcely an hour, she told me, since she had come back from church, where she had spent part of the afternoon, all the time for my intention, for all she now prayed about was me, and, truth to tell, it was always praying for herself in a different sense.

Now I come to think about it the burden of her prayers must have been extremely diverting. I am sure that there was not one in which she did not say: 'Preserve my husband for me,' or else: 'I thank Thee for giving him to me;' which, properly rendered, meant nothing but: 'Oh God, continue giving me the pleasures Thou hast vouchsafed me through holy matrimony,' or again: 'I thank Thee for these pleasures I am enjoying in perfect virtue and honour through Thy holy will in the state to which Thou hast called me.'

And think how fervent such prayers were, for the pious never love God so much as when they have obtained from Him their little temporal satisfactions, and people never pray better than when spirit and flesh are content and pray together. It is only when the flesh languishes, suffers and does not get its fill and the spirit has to be pious on its own that people find things irksome.

But Mme de la Vallée was not in that situation: she had nothing left to wish for and her pleasures were legitimate; she could enjoy them with a clear conscience. So her piety had increased by half without apparently being any the more meritorious, since it was the pleasure of possessing this dear husband, this dear dark boy, as she sometimes called me, and not the love of God that was the soul of her piety.

We had supper with our landlady who, from the way she behaved, seemed wholeheartedly in love with me without perhaps realizing it herself. The good woman found me to her liking and so showed it as she felt it.

'Oh yes, for sure, Mme de la Vallée, you've got a nice-looking husband there, and no mistake, a nice piece of flesh everyone will love. Now he means nothing to me, yet I love him with all my heart.' And a minute later: 'You oughtn't to be sorry you got married so late in life, you wouldn't have made a better choice quite twenty years ago.' And a thousand other silly remarks of the same kind which Mme de la Vallée did not find all that funny, especially when they turned upon that late marriage and twitted her about her age.

'No I certainly wouldn't, Madame!' she replied in bitter-sweet tones. 'I agree that I chose well and I am very satisfied with my choice and most delighted he pleases you. Moreover, I didn't get married so late that it was not at a quite suitable time, it seems to me. A person is perfectly suitable for marriage at my age, isn't she, my love?' she added, slipping her hand into mine and gazing at me with eyes that said confidently: 'You seemed satisfied, my dear.'

'What's this, my darling wife, whether you are suitable?' I answered. 'And at what age is one more suitable and more attractive, I ask you?' That made her smile and squeeze my hand, and finally she asked, almost with a sigh: 'What's the time?' so as to find whether it was time to rise from table. That was her refrain.

As for the other young person, Mme d'Alain's daughter, I noticed out of the corner of my eye that she was contemplating our chaste love and not finding it, I believed, quite as innocent as it really was. Agathe's arms and hands were not at all bad, and I noticed that the little hussy was deploying her skill to show them off as much as she could, as if to say: 'Look, has your wife got anything as good as this?'

This is the last time I go into details of this kind, and as regards Agathe I may have more to say later; but I am not going to add anything about the way I lived with Mme de la Vallée. You have been told enough about her character and her ways of expressing her love for me. Here we were, married, I was conscious of all I owed her, I should always go out of my way to please her, I was in the flower of my age and she was still desirable in spite of hers, and even if she had not been, gratitude in a young man of feeling can make up for a great deal and is very resourceful. And besides, Mme de la Vallée loved me with a passion so unusual that it would have made up for charms had they been lacking, and her heart yielded to me with a holy alacrity that revitalized mine. Yet, affectionate though she was, Mme de la Vallée was not in the least jealous, and I didn't have to render irritating accounts of my actions, which up to that point, as you see, had been all too unfaithful and gave no promise of improving in the near future. When I was away Mme de la Vallée longed for my return but waited patiently. When I returned no questions were asked; she was delighted so long as I loved her and love her I would.

So you must imagine my paying every possible attention to her and picture our married life as most pleasant and peaceful, for such it will be, and I shall make no further mention of her except in matters in which she will happen to be involved. Alas, soon she will play no further part in my affairs; the moment when she will be taken from me is not far distant, and it will not be long before I come back to her in order to tell the tale of her death and the grief it caused me.

You will not have forgotten that M. Bono had that day told the young lady of Versailles and me that we should go and see him, and we had taken care to get his address from his coachman who had brought us back.

All next morning I stayed indoors and was not bored at all. I revelled in the joys of suddenly finding myself in my own home, I savoured my good fortune and relished my comforts, regarded myself in my own apartment, walked about, sat down, smiled at my furniture, thought about my cook, whom I could send for whenever I liked, and I think I did summon her once just to see her. I contemplated my dressing-gown and slippers, and I can assure you that they were not the two things I liked least. How many little luxuries a man of the world is surrounded by that he doesn't notice because he was born with them!

Just fancy, slippers and a dressing-gown for Jacob! For it was by looking at myself as Jacob that I was so deliciously surprised to see myself in this get-up. All Monsieur de la Vallée's joy was because of Jacob. That moment was only so sweet because of the country lad.

Moreover I can say that, for all my excitement about this pleasant metamorphosis, it only gave rise to pleasure and not vanity. I concluded that I was happier because of it, and didn't go beyond that.

But wait, I must put things exactly as they were. It is true that I did not feel any more conceited, and was free from that vanity that makes a man give himself airs, but I did have another sort, and here it is.

I thought to myself that I must not seem to others to be so delighted and surprised at my good fortune, and that it was as well that people should not notice how conscious I was of it and that if I couldn't contain myself they would say: 'Ah, poor young fellow, how overjoyed he is! He wants to tell everybody.'

I would have been ashamed if people had had such an idea; I would not even have liked it in my own wife. I wanted her to know that I was thrilled, and told her so a thousand times a day, but I wanted to tell her so myself and not have her notice it on her own. To my mind there was a great difference, though I only had a vague idea why, and the truth is that if she had gathered for herself the full extent of my joy she would have realized that it was the humble servant, peasant and pauper who was so glad to have changed his condition, and it would have been unpleasant for me to be seen by her in such guises – it was sufficient that she should believe that I was happy, without dwelling on my former lowliness. That knowledge was only acceptable within myself, and I derived from it the inner source of my joy, but it was not necessary for others to penetrate so far into the secret places of my pleasure and know where I got it from.

At about three in the afternoon the bells rang for vespers and my wife went to church while I read some serious book that I didn't understand much of or want to understand, and which I amused myself with merely to imitate the behaviour of a gentleman in his home.

When my spouse had gone I took off my gown (let me talk about it while I am enjoying it – it won't last long, for I shall soon get used to it), dressed and sallied forth to go to see the young lady of Versailles, for whom I had conceived a rather tender respect, as you may have gathered from what I have said already.

I might be Monsieur de la Vallée – I, who had never had any carriage except shanks's pony or my cart when I brought the village squire's wine up to Paris – but I really didn't need a coach to get to this lady's, nor was I dreaming of taking one. But a cabby who stopped me as I was crossing a square tempted me. 'Will the gentleman be wanting me?' said he.

Well, 'the gentleman' settled it, and I said: 'All right.'

What a lot of showing off, you will say. Not at all, I took that cab for a lark and so as to enjoy that particular pleasure once again, and sample as I went along another little comfort that I had only enjoyed once before, when I went to Mme Remy's.

There was some hold-up in the street where the young lady in question lived. I will tell you her name to simplify my story – Mme d'Orville. My cabby was obliged to set me down a little short of her house.

Scarcely had I got out before I heard a great commotion some twenty yards behind me. I turned and saw a young man with a very handsome face, very well dressed, about my own age, say twenty or twenty-one, who was defending himself sword in hand as best he could against three men cowardly enough to attack him together.

In such cases the crowd yells and kicks up a din but doesn't help. Round the fight there was a ring of louts ever increasing in number, and they were following the battle, sometimes pushing forward and sometimes falling back as the brave young man was forced to fall back either more or less.

The danger I could see he was in and the baseness of their behaviour so affected me that, without a moment's hesitation or thought, feeling a sword at my side I drew it, ran round my cab into the middle of the street and then charged like a lion to the aid of the young man, shouting: 'Hold on, Monsieur, hold on!'

It was high time, for while the young man was struggling with the other two, one was calmly preparing to slash through his body with the blade of his sword. 'Stop! Stop! Take me on!' I yelled, and ran at him, which forced him to jump round and face me. The movement he made took him back with his comrades and gave me a chance to join the young man, who took new heart from this, and seeing the fierceness of my attack he in his turn went for the wretches at whom I was lashing out with thrusts that they could only parry by falling back. I say lashing out, for that is the fighting method of a man of spirit who has never handled the sword. The fact that he knows very little about it and goes in for little ceremony makes him no less dangerous a foe.

At all events, the three men fell back in spite of the numerical superiority they still had, but of course they were not very heroic – their mode of fighting is proof of that. Add to this that my action influenced the mob in our favour. No sooner had they seen these three fellows giving way than one with a big stick, another with a broom-handle and another with a similar weapon charged at them and finally put them to flight.

We let the shouting mob run after them and remained on the battlefield, which somehow by then was right on Mme d'Orville's doorstep, and the unknown man I had defended went into her house to shake off the tiresome crowd round us.

His coat and the hand with which he held his sword were all covered in blood. I asked someone to send for a doctor. These gentry are to be found in any neighbourhood, and one came almost at once.

Some of the people had followed us into the courtyard of Mme d'Orville's building, which caused a stir and brought down the tenants from all the floors. Mme d'Orville lodged on the first floor at the back, and came down like the rest to find out what was going on. Imagine her amazement when she saw me there, still clutching my drawn sword, for at such times you don't quite know what you are doing and in any case I had not had enough elbow room to put it back in its scabbard because we were so hemmed in by the crowd.

Oh, this is where I felt a bit pleased with myself, a bit superior, and my heart swelled at the courage I had just displayed and the noble figure I was cutting. Distracted though my attention was bound to be by what was still going on, I didn't fail to have a few moments of meditation in which to contemplate myself sword in hand and hat rammed down like a real tough. For I could imagine what I looked like, it is a thing you can feel, and you can, so to speak, see yourself in your own self-esteem. And I admit that in the condition I fancied myself to be in I thought I was worthy of a certain consideration, and even looked upon myself with less familiarity and more respect than usual. No more of the young scamp amazed at his own luck and finding his good fortune out of all proportion to his real worth. Oh no, I was a man of merit, to whom fortune was beginning to do justice.

But to return to the courtyard of that building in which we all were, the unknown young man, myself, the doctor and all these people. All of a sudden Mme d'Orville saw me.

'Oh, it's you, Monsieur!' she exclaimed, stopping in alarm at the top of her staircase. 'Oh, whatever has happened to you? Are you hurt?' 'All I have, Madame,' I answered, bowing like an unruffled hero, 'is a little scratch. They weren't after me. But this gentleman is wounded,' I added, pointing out the young stranger, to whom the doctor was speaking and who, I think, had not heard what she said to me or noticed her yet.

This doctor knew Mme d'Orville; he had bled her husband the day before, we learned later. Seeing how pale the young man was getting, probably through loss of blood – he was still bleeding – he said:

'Madame, I am afraid this gentleman is very unwell. I can't examine him here; would you lend us a room for a few moments where I can examine his wounds?'

At these words the young man looked at the person being addressed, and I thought he seemed astonished to see such a charming woman who, in spite of the simple apparel of one who has just interrupted her housework, had a noble bearing which inspired respect.

'Your request is certainly not a favour, and cannot be refused,' she answered, and the way the patient doffed his hat and greeted her showed great regard. 'Come in, gentlemen, as there is no time to waste.'

'I am only so sorry about this accident,' said the young man, 'because I am going to put you out, Madame.' Then he stepped forward and climbed the stairs with my support, having already said more than once many kind things to me, and continually calling me his dear friend. 'Do you feel weak?' I asked. 'Not very. I think I have only been wounded in the arm and a bit on the hand, it won't be anything much, I'll only have lost a little blood, but shall have found a friend who has saved my life.'

'Oh that's all right,' I said, 'there's no need to thank me for what I have done. I was only too glad, and I took to you at once just from your looks.' 'And I hope you will like me always,' he said, by which time we were already in Mme d'Orville's apartment. She had gone on ahead of us to open a small, very pleasantly furnished room into which she showed us and the doctor, and in which there was a small bed, the one in which her mother slept.

We were hardly in the room before a nice young maid came in, sent by M. d'Orville, with his compliments, to tell us that his wife had informed him I was the person to whom he was so indebted, and that he could not get up because he was ill, but hoped I would do him the honour of seeing him before I left.

While the maid was speaking to me Mme d'Orville was taking out of a cupboard any linen that might be needed for the wounded man.

'Tell M. d'Orville,' I said, 'that the honour of paying my respects will be all mine and that I will come to his room in a moment, and am only waiting until this gentleman's wounds have been looked at.' I indicated the young man, whose coat was already off and who was in a big armchair.

Then Mme d'Orville left the room, the doctor did his work and examined the young man and found that he had only a wound in the arm, but it was bleeding profusely. This was seen to, and as Mme d'Orville had provided everything, he changed his underclothes, and while the doctor was helping him to dress again I went to see the lady and her husband who, though ill in bed, struck me as a gentleman, I mean by birth. You could tell by his behaviour and the way he spoke that he should have been in a better place than he was, and that the obscurity in which he was existing was due to some reverse of fortune. Something must have happened to that man, one felt on seeing him; he isn't in the right place.

The truth is that such things can be sensed. In this respect it is like putting a peasant's apparel on a man of a certain position. Do you by that turn him into a peasant? No, you see that he is only wearing the clothes; he is clothed but not dressed, as it were. There are attitudes, movements, gestures in such a person which show that he is a stranger to the dress covering him.

This was somewhat the case with M. d'Orville. Although he had a dwelling and furniture you felt he was neither lodged nor furnished. That is all I shall say about him in this connection, and it is enough about a man I scarcely met and whose wife was soon to be a widow.

He spared no thanks for what had happened at Versailles with Mme d'Orville, and there were no praises he did not sing of my character, but I cut that short. I did not see the mother, who was apparently out. We spoke of M. Bono, who had urged us to go and see him, and it was decided that we should go the next day, and that to avoid the one going earlier or later than the other I should come for Mme d'Orville at half-past two.

We had reached that point when the wounded man came in with the doctor. Further thanks on his part for all the help he had been given in their home, many glances at Mme d'Orville, but modest and respectful, and managed with great discretion. All reinforced by a kind of tender politeness in his words, but an almost imperceptible tenderness of a kind not usually seen in a husband who, although he loves his wife, loves her with the quiet confidence of a man who has won her love, and in such a case this deprives him of a certain emotional acuteness and greatly blunts his intelligence.

But I had noticed this little shade of tenderness immediately because, without yet realizing it, I myself was very disposed to fall in love with Mme d'Orville, and I am sure that the lady noticed it too. At any rate I had for corroboration the way she listened to the young man, with a certain lowering of the eyes and short, infrequent answers.

And besides, Mme d'Orville was so attractive! Is anything else necessary to make a woman perceptive, however sensible she may be? Does it not reveal to her the meaning of everything people say? Can anything of that kind escape her, and isn't she always expecting such things?

'But, Monsieur, why did those three men attack you?' asked

the husband, who most of the time was answering for his wife and who in all good faith vied with the wounded man in compliments, because the latter's seemed to him just expressions of gratitude pure and simple. 'Do you know these three men?'

'No, Monsieur,' answered the young man who, as you will see later, hid the real explanation of his fight at that moment, 'all I did was meet them. They were coming along that street towards me, I was thinking of something else and stared at them as I passed. They objected, one of them said something offensive, I answered and then all three answered back. At that I couldn't help showing a little of what I thought of them. One of them swore at me, and my only reply was to strike him. They joined him and I had all three to deal with, and would no doubt have been killed if this gentleman (meaning me) had not generously come to my aid.'

I said that it was not such a great generosity, and that any gentleman would have done the same in that situation. Then M. d'Orville said: 'But ought you not to rest a little longer, and aren't you going out too soon? Don't you feel weak?' 'Not in the least, Monsieur, there is no danger whatever,' chimed in the doctor. 'This gentleman is quite fit to go home, and all we need is a carriage, which can be found in the square nearby.'

The maid ran off at once for one. It came and the wounded man begged me not to leave him. I would have preferred to stay for the pleasure of being with Mme d'Orville, but it was impossible to refuse after what I had done for him.

So I went with him. The husband had a little fit of coughing which cut short all the renewed compliments and the inevitable bowing out. So we were downstairs again, and the doctor, who came with us as far as the courtyard, seemed very obsequious, apparently because he was well paid. We left him and climbed into our cab.

I did not expect anything out of this adventure, and did not suppose it would bring me any benefit except the honour of having done a noble deed. Yet that was the starting-point of my fortune, and my career could hardly have had a more lucky start.

Do you know who this man was whose life I had probably saved? None other than one of the nephews of the man who then governed France, in short the Chief Minister. You can see that the matter becomes important, especially when you have to deal with one of the most perfect gentlemen in the world, a nephew who was worthy to be a king's son. I have never known such a noble soul.

Whatever chance, you may well ask, brought him into the peril from which you rescued him? You are about to see.

'Where to?' asked the cabby. My friend mentioned a place, but he did not give the name of a street, simply that of a lady: 'The Marquise of So-and-So's,' and the cabby asked no more, which showed that it must be a very well-known house, and at the same time led me to suppose that my friend was a man of some standing. He certainly had that appearance, and my suppositions were correct.

'Now my dear friend,' he said during the journey, 'to you I am going to tell the true story about myself.

'In this district we are just leaving there lives a woman I met a few days ago at the Opera. I noticed her from a box where I was with some other men. I thought her extremely pretty, which indeed she is. I inquired who she was, but nobody knew her. At the end of the opera I left my box to go and see her leave hers and have a good look at her. So I stood where she had to pass and she lost nothing by being seen close up. She was with another quite good-looking woman. She noticed how attentively I was looking at her, and from the way she did so I thought she was saying to me: "Is that as far as you're going?" And then something in her eyes encouraged me and assured me she would not be unapproachable.

'There are certain ways in which a woman can tell you where you might hope to stand with her; you can gather when she looks at you if there is nothing in it beyond flirtation or whether she would like to know you properly. When it is only the first all she wants is to look attractive, nothing else, and her face expresses no more than that. But when it is the second her expression says more and beckons you on, and I thought that this time it was the second.

'But one is afraid of making a mistake, and I followed her as far as the staircase without daring to do anything beyond keeping my eyes always on her and touching her with my arm as we walked along.

'She settled my dilemma and cured my modest discretion by

means of a little artifice she thought of, and that was to drop her fan.

'I saw what she meant and took advantage of the chance it offered to do a courteous act and say a word or two as I returned the fan, which I picked up with alacrity.

'But she was the one to speak first, for fear of not bringing it off: "Monsieur, you are most kind," she said graciously as she took it. "I am too happy, Madame, to have rendered you this little service," I answered as gallantly as I could, and as at that moment she seemed to be trying to put her foot safely on the first step down the stairs, I took advantage of that to say: "There is a great crush and we are being pushed. May I have the honour of giving you my hand for extra safety, Madame?"

' "If you please," she said quite unaffectedly, "for I am a bit unsteady." So I escorted her, keeping up a conversation about how pleasant it had been to see her and how I had contrived to see her more closely.

' "And wasn't it you, too, Monsieur, whom I saw in a certain box?" she said, as though to hint that she also had noticed me particularly.

'And so on from one thing to another until we were at the bottom, where a tall footman (who didn't really look as though he were hers, judging by the kindly way he came forward, which is a liberty these gentry don't usually take with their mistresses) stepped up and said it would be difficult to bring round the carriage, but that it was only a few steps away. "Very well, let's run along as far as there, shall we?" she said to her companion. "Just as you like," was the answer, and I took them along by skirting close to the wall.

'My own, I mean my carriage, was only half way along, our little talk had made me bold, and without more ceremony I suggested that they should get into it and I would take them straight home, which would save time; but they refused.

'But I did notice that the one whose arm I was holding glanced appraisingly at my equipage, and then we reached theirs which, incidentally, didn't belong to either of them but was only a hired one that had been lent to them.

'I forgot to mention that on the way to this carriage I had begged her to agree to my seeing her again at her home. She granted this without any fuss, as a woman of the world quite naturally returns politeness for politeness. "Delighted, Monsieur, you will be honouring me," she had answered, and had added the necessary information for finding her. And so on leaving her I threatened a very early visit.

'In fact I went the next day. Her home looked very comfortable; I saw some servants and there was company, and very good class company as far as I could judge. There were card-tables and I was courteously welcomed. We had a few moments of private talk; I spoke of love and she was not discouraging, which made me like her all the more. We were still talking in a corner when one of the men who recently attacked me came in. He is a middle-aged man who spends a lot of money and comes from the country, I think. He seemed put out at seeing us together, and I thought she took note of his displeasure, for she hastened to rejoin the general company.

'A few minutes later I left, and the following day went back earlier than the previous time. She was alone, and I told her the tale all over again.

'At first she spoke teasingly about my love, but in a tone that meant: "I wish it were true." I persisted and tried to convince her. "But is it serious? You put me in an awkward position. I could listen to you, of course. That is not the difficulty," she said, "but the situation I am in hardly allows of it. I am a widow, I am involved in a lawsuit and probably I shall have little money left. You saw here a fairly tall man with a face nothing like as handsome as yours. He is just a bourgeois, but a very rich one, whom I could have as a husband whenever I please, and he is very pressing. I find it so difficult to bring myself to it that so far I have done nothing about it, and for the past day or two," she added with a smile, "I think I have been even less inclined to make up my mind. There are some people one could love more easily than one could marry others, but I have too little money to follow my inclinations. I could not even stay much longer in Paris, as I should like to, and unless I get married I shall have to go back to a country place I loathe and which is so depressing that it gives me the creeps. So what do you suppose I can do? I don't know why I am telling you all this, incidentally. I must be out of my mind, and I won't see you any more."

'From this speech I realized perfectly that I was with one of those impecunious beauties whose best source of income is a pretty face, I understood the sort of liaison she had with the man she described as a future husband, and I realized also that she was saying: "If I get rid of him will you replace him, or will you only want a passing affair?"

'This was a petty way of treating love and it put me off somewhat. I had only taken her for an easy conquest, but not for a professional, so that while she was speaking I was at odds with myself as to how to answer her.

'But I had no time to make up my mind because the bourgeois in question came on the scene and surprised us. He frowned, but in an insolent way, like a man in a position to put what he finds to rights, and it is true that when he came in I was holding the lady's hand.

'She put on a carefree air with him, and even said: "I was expecting you," but in vain. It did not make him look any more reassured and his face remained sombre and hard. "Fortunately you were not bored," was all she could get out of him.

'As for me, I didn't deign to look at him, but went on addressing all sorts of compliments to the woman so as to punish him for his rude behaviour. Then I went out.'

The young man's story had reached that point when the driver stopped a few steps away from the house to which he was taking us, because two or three carriages prevented his going any nearer. We got out and I saw the young man speak to an impressive footman, who then opened the door of one of these carriages. 'Get in, my dear friend,' said my companion. 'In where?' I asked. 'In this carriage,' he said. 'It is mine, but I could not use it to go to see the lady in question.'

I would have you note that the carriage could not have been more sumptuously appointed.

'Oho!' I said to myself, 'this is going further than I thought. This is grand. What if my friend were a noble lord? Mind how you go, Monsieur de la Vallée, and try to talk good French. You are dressed like a gentleman's son, uphold the honour of your coat, and let your talk correspond to your appearance, which isn't too bad.'

That is roughly what flashed through my mind at that moment, and then I got into the carriage, not sure whether I ought to get in first, but at the same time not daring to stand on ceremony about it. 'Does good form require that I go on or draw back?' I asked myself in mid-air, that is to say as I was climbing in. For this was a new situation for me, and my slender experience had taught me nothing on this point except that you go in for ceremony when there are two of you at a door, and I was inclined to think that this might be the same thing.

To settle it I did get in and was already in my seat while I was still wondering what line to take. So there I was, cheek by jowl with my aristocratic friend, and on equal terms with a man for whom five months before I might have chanced to hold open the door of the carriage I was now sharing with him. But I didn't make that reflection just then; I am only doing so at the time of writing. It did occur to me in a way, but I absolutely refused to pay any attention to it. I needed self-confidence, and that would have taken it away.

'Are you doing anything just now?' said Count d'Orsan (that was his name). 'I am perfectly fit and don't want to go home yet, it is still quite early, so let's go to the theatre. I shall be as comfortable there as in my own room.'

Until then I had been fairly self-possessed and had not quite lost sight of who I was, but this finished me off, and the prospect of being taken like this as large as life to the theatre turned my head altogether. The loftiness of my condition made me giddy, and I felt bemused in a cloud of joy, glory, fortune and a sense of the vanity of worldly pomp, if I may be allowed to put it like that. (For I realize that there are some pernickety, though estimable, readers with whom it is better to leave one's feelings unexplained than to describe them, when they can only be expressed in a way that might seem peculiar – a thing which does, however, sometimes occur, especially when it is a matter of describing what goes on in the soul. For the soul twists and turns in many more ways than we have ways of describing, and we should at least give it, in its need, freedom to use expressions as best it can, so long as people understand clearly what the soul means and that it could not use any other terms without weakening or changing its argument.) It is the frequent disputes about this which have prompted my parenthesis, and I would not have embarked upon it if I had thought it would turn out so long. But to return.

'If you would like to,' I answered, and the carriage moved off.

'I haven't finished telling you my story,' he said, 'and here is the rest. I dined today at the Marquise of —'s, and alleging business I left there at three to go and see this woman.

'My carriage had not yet come back for me, and I saw none of my servants downstairs. There are carriages for hire nearby and I asked somebody to go for one, in which I was taken to her door.

'I had scarcely begun climbing the stairs before I saw this brutish man coming down with two others, and although I saluted him politely out of force of habit he kept his hat on and roughly jostled me as he passed.

' "You're very rude!" I said, shrugging my shoulders in contempt. "Who are you talking to?" chimed in one of the others, who hadn't taken any notice of me either. "All of you," I said.

'At this point he put his hand to the hilt of his sword. I thought it right to draw mine, leaping backwards because two of the men were higher up than me and had two more steps to come down; only the other one had reached the bottom. At once I saw three swords drawn against me, the wretches pursued me right out into the street, and we were still fighting when you came to my aid, and came at the very moment when one of the murderers was about to deal a fatal blow.'

'Yes,' I said, 'I was very afraid he would, and that is why I shouted at him so, in order to foil his plan. But that's enough of that, they are a lot of blackguards, and the woman as well.'

'You can imagine what I think of her, but let's talk about you. After what you have done for me there is no limit to what I feel bound to do in your interests. I want to know to whom I owe so much, and I want you to know me too.

'My name is Count d'Orsan, I have only my mother living, I am very well off. My guardians have a certain influence, and I venture to say that I will do everything I can to be of service to you, and will be only too happy to be given a chance, so do act on that and tell me your name and what you are.'

I began by thanking him, naturally, but very briefly because that is how he wanted it. And moreover I was nervous of getting involved in some form of compliment that was not in quite the right taste. When you lack breeding that lack never shows so much as when you want to display it.

So I thanked him in the simplest terms and then said: 'My name is La Vallée. You are a nobleman, but I am no fine gentleman. My father lives in the country where all his property is, and I am almost fresh from there, and my object is to get on and become something, like all young provincials of my kind (and in what I said note that I was merely being careful, but not a liar).

'But,' I went on in a tone of perfect candour, 'even if I never made anything of my life in Paris, and my journey produced nothing but the pleasure of doing something for such a fine man as you, I should not grumble, but go back home well content.' At these words he held out his hand and said: 'My dear La Vallée, your fortune is no longer your own concern, it is mine, your friend's; for I am your friend and I want you to be mine.'

The carriage stopped, we had reached the theatre, and I only had time to answer such affectionate words with a smile.

'Follow me,' he said, after giving a footman money to buy some tickets, and we went in. So there I was at the Comédie Française, at first in the foyer, if you please, where Count d'Orsan greeted some of his friends.

At this moment all those puffed-up feelings I mentioned, all those fumes of vanity that had gone to my head vanished into thin air.

The airs and graces of this world filled me with confusion and panic. Alas, my bearing showed that I was such a nobody, I realized I looked so clumsy and lost in the midst of this society that had something so easy and elegant about it. 'What are you going to do about yourself?' I wondered.

So I shall say nothing about my demeanour because I hadn't one at all, unless you say that not having one at all is to have a kind of one. However, it simply was not in my power to give myself any other, and I don't think I could ever manage it or achieve any expression that did not look unsuitable or shamefaced. If it had been merely a case of being astonished I should not have minded my face simply showing that – it would only have been a proof that I had never been to the Comédie Française, and there would not have been much harm in that. But there was an inner embarrassment at finding myself there at all, a certain feeling of unworthiness that prevented my putting up a bold front, and this I would very much have preferred not to be seen on my face, and of course it showed all the more because I was endeavouring to conceal it.

My eyes were the trouble, for I didn't know who to look at. I dared not take the liberty of looking at the others for fear that they might read into my nervousness that I had no right to the honour of being with such grand people and was being smuggled in. I can't think of anything that expresses my meaning more clearly than that term, which is not very high class.

It is also true that I had not passed through enough stages of education or advances in fortune to be able to comport myself in the midst of this society with the requisite self-assurance. I had jumped into it too fast; I had just been made a gentleman, and what was more I had not gone through the preliminary training of people of my kind, and trembled lest my appearance should show that the gentleman had been just Jacob. Some in my shoes might have been brazen enough to carry it off, I mean they might have cheeked their way through, but what is to be gained by that? Nothing. Doesn't that make it clear that a man is brazen only because he has reason to be ashamed?

'You don't look too well,' said one of the gentlemen to Count d'Orsan. 'I certainly don't,' he answered, 'but I might have been worse.' Thereupon he told them about his adventure and consequently mine, and in the most flattering way to me. 'So you see,' he concluded, 'I owe to this gentleman the honour of seeing you again.'

A fresh trial for La Vallée, to whom this speech drew their attention. They looked up and down my weird figure, and I think nothing could have been as silly as I was or so funny-looking. The more Count d'Orsan sang my praises the more he embarrassed me.

But I had to make some reply, in my modest silk jacket and my reach-me-down finery that I had given up being proud of since seeing many magnificent outfits all round me. But what could I say? 'Oh, not at all, Sir, you can't be serious,' or again: 'It's only a very small thing, don't mention it; it was the only thing to do; I am your servant.'

Such were my replies, accompanied by frequent jerky bobbings, which apparently appealed to these gentlemen, for not one of them failed to compliment me in order to get one for himself.

One of them whom I saw turn round to laugh put me wise to the joke and finished me off. No more bowings and scrapings, my face behaved as best it could and so did my answers. Count d'Orsan, who was a well-bred man with an honest and straightforward type of mind, went on talking without noticing what was happening to me. 'Let's go to our seats,' he said, and I followed him. He led me on to the stage, where the number of people made me immune from such indignities, and where I sat with him like a man finding sanctuary.*

They were playing a tragedy, *Mithridate*, if I remember. Oh, what a fine actress interpreted Monime! I will describe her in my sixth part, together with the actors and actresses who shone in my time.

*It was still the custom in Marivaux's time to have rows of seats on the stage itself. As these places were expensive, they were patronized by wealthy, fashionable young men, who went there to ogle the ladies and show off generally. This practice, which Molière had found such a nuisance, was finally abolished owing to the influence of Voltaire.

SUMMARY OF THE ANONYMOUS SEQUEL

[THE chronology of the sequel is difficult to establish. The narrator, who henceforth will be called La Vallée, explains that twenty years have elapsed since he wrote part 5, as indeed they had, for the sequel was not published until 1756 and Marivaux had abandoned his novel in 1735. The three parts bring us roughly to the time of the opening of part 1, but at the very end of part 8 the narrator adds that he has passed his administrative position and Paris house to his elder son and for the past twenty years has been living with his wife in peaceful retirement in the country. Assuming that at the end of part 5 Jacob was about twenty, this would make him about sixty when he was finishing his memoirs.]

PART 6

He is in his seat on the stage of the theatre, surrounded by silly fashionable young men talking and ogling the ladies in the boxes. But the music of the overture makes him reflect that his heart, which has never been involved in his relationships with Mlle Habert, Mme de Ferval or Mme de Fécour, is now awakening through the power of music. At the end of Act I he asks Dorsan* why everybody talks all the time, and is told that it is considered very provincial to show any interest in the play. This is La Vallée's excuse for not fulfilling his promise in part 5 to discuss the play and the actors (no doubt Marivaux, had he continued the novel, would have indulged in a long digression about this). Furthermore La Vallée explains that as he could not follow the play because of the chatter he allowed his attention to wander to two lovely ladies in a box, whom Dorsan salutes. One of the ladies gazes at La Vallée with eyes full of meaning.

At the end of the play they join the two ladies (La Vallée quickly represses a twinge of conscience about his wife at home).

*The spelling of some proper names in the sequel differs from that in parts 1–5.

All four go off in a carriage to a party. One of the ladies, Mme de Damville, Dorsan's acquaintance, is fashionable and domineering, but the other, Mme de Vambures, whose gaze La Vallée had returned in the theatre, is sweet and demure. Dorsan tells them of his adventure and how La Vallée rescued him, but hides the real origin of the fight. The ladies gush over La Vallée's bravery. At the party Dorsan tactfully anticipates La Vallée's embarrassment through ignorance of the rules of card games by taking him aside into a quiet room for a chat, at which point La Vallée remembers to send word to his wife that he will be late home, and tells her about Dorsan. In the quiet room La Vallée tells his noble friend about his marriage and about Ferval, Fécour, her brother-in-law, the Versailles adventure and Mme Dorville. Dorsan is touched by the plight of the Dorvilles and says he must help. Dorsan, La Vallée and Mme de Vambures set off in Mme de Vambures's carriage, leave her at her home and go on foot to Mme d'Alain's. At home he tells his wife all his adventures but makes no reference to Mme de Vambures. At this point the author of the sequel repeats Marivaux's trick of making La Vallée praise the fervour of a pious woman as a sexual partner and admit that he himself was a very competent performer because his thoughts were on another woman, in this case Mme de Vambures.

Next morning a note is delivered from Mme de Fécour requesting La Vallée to call on her. As he leaves, his wife complains of feeling unwell (the author is following up Marivaux's prophecy and preparing us for her early death). Mme de Fécour is still in bed when La Vallée arrives, but her brother-in-law Fécour is present. He agrees to keep on Dorville, but suggests that La Vallée send Mme Dorville to him as a reward for reinstating her husband. This provokes a noble and indignant refusal from La Vallée, who, however, privately comforts himself with the thought that in any case he now has hopes of making his fortune thanks to Dorsan's friendship. On his way home he calls at the Dorvilles' home; she is out but he is told that the husband is now seriously ill.

At home he finds that his brother Alexandre (referred to in part 1) has called, looking shabby and miserable. He has found out what has become of his brother Jacob through one of Dorsan's servants, who is a 'regular' at his hostelry. Alexandre tells his story: his wife the hotel-keeper has become lazy and extravagant and they are ruined. La Vallée and his wife offer to be responsible for rearing and educating Alexandre's two boys. Enter Dorsan, who takes La Vallée off to pay their respects to the Dorvilles.

PART 7

EN ROUTE for the Dorvilles' house Dorsan confesses that he is very interested in Mme Dorville (which La Vallée had noticed in part 5), but he fears that even if she were free his family might object on grounds of difference of rank. On arrival they find the house in mourning; M. Dorville is dead. Dorsan is sympathetic, but feels inner hope and joy. After their return to La Vallée's home a letter is delivered from Mme Dorville, in which she says that one of them must have left a purse of money, and asks to which of them it should be returned. Dorsan writes an answer saying neither is responsible, but signs it La Vallée. Alone with La Vallée he admits that he left the money, but urges his friend to call on the lady and test her reactions. He then goes off to see M. Bono about a position for him. La Vallée sets off ostensibly to see his brother, but first calls on Mme Dorville, whom he persuades not to try to find out who left the purse, then on Dorsan to report. The latter says he intends to use his influence to have the Dorville lawsuit reopened.

There follows a long scene at his brother's inn, now in a state of uproar. The wife, wholly under the influence of a priest, talks of leaving the husband she has ruined. La Vallée takes the two boys home, and the next day they are boarded out. Mme de la Vallée is now chronically ill, and La Vallée stays at home to nurse her. Dorsan, mysteriously absent for some time, returns with La Vallée's appointment to a 'farm', that is, a high position in the taxation administration in his province. All this is due, he explains, to the help of Mme de Vambures. She does not yet know that La Vallée is married, and Dorsan advises him to keep this fact dark for the time being. La Vallée confesses to him that he is in love with Mme de Vambures, and together they go to thank her for her help, and then on to thank M. de Fécour (who did not realize whom he was helping when he obliged Mme de Vambures), and finally pay a courtesy call on the kindly rough diamond M. Bono. The latter invites everybody to dinner, and we have a description of the lavish hospitality of M. and Mme Bono. During the entertainment a foppish young man about town reads his own compositions in honour of their host. Then he reads a satirical epithalamium on the marriage of Mme de Ferval to her Chevalier, who has got all her money, and the general drift of the poem is that she richly deserves to be plucked and then thrown away by him after her years of self-indulgence cloaked by appearances of piety and charity.

Back home, La Vallée arranges to leave for Rheims, where he has to learn the technicalities of his new position in the tax-farming business. His wife has become visibly weaker. He learns that Mme de Vambures has gone off to the country but has left with Dorsan some money to help him with his initial expenses. A month later he receives at Rheims a letter from Dorsan to the effect that his wife is now very ill, but there is no need for him to return to Paris yet for he, Dorsan, will see to everything. La Vallée suspects, rightly, that this is his friend's way of telling him that his wife is dead. He sheds, he tells us, sincere tears.

Re-enter M. Doucin, the spiritual director of the Habert sisters, to inform him that Mlle Habert the elder has had seals put on everything and is claiming to be sole heir. La Vallée sends him packing and puts the matter into the hands of Dorsan's lawyer, then spends a month in Paris settling his wife's affairs, during which he is subjected to an intensive campaign by Mme d'Alain, who wants to capture him for her Agathe.

Mme de Vambures returns from the country, and the following little scene is enacted: Mme de Vambures: 'But why are you in mourning?' La Vallée: 'For my wife.' Mme de Vambures: 'What! Your wife?' La Vallée (falls on his knees): 'M. Dorsan told me not to tell you . . . he knows that I worship you . . .' Mme de Vambures: 'Isn't this a bit sudden, with your wife scarcely buried?' So La Vallée tells all – his marriage was not a love match, she is his first and only true love. (Enter Dorsan.) Dorsan: 'Don't worry about Mlle Habert and Doucin, they have been dealt with.' Touching farewells, and encouragement from Mme de Vambures.

Having installed his brother, whose wife has now left him, in a country home near their native village and settled with Mme d'Alain, La Vallée returns for eighteen months to Champagne and carries on a regular correspondence with Mme de Vambures. Then she invites him to go to a country house belonging to Dorsan, where he finds preparations being made for the latter's marriage to Mme Dorville, Dorsan's mother having now enthusiastically approved.

All then go back to Paris, where La Vallée has now been given a permanent appointment. Hiding his own part in the affair, Dorsan tells La Vallée that this is all due to Mme de Vambures's influence. He rushes to thank her and sees on her table his own letters, which she has not been quick enough to put away. This brings a partial avowal from her, but she asks for time. Yet when La Vallée has been installed for some time in Paris and is now rich and influential in his own right, Mme de Vambures still does not consent to marry him.

One day Dorsan comes to ask La Vallée's help for a young man whose uncle's death has left him penniless. The young man enters, and he is none other than Jacob's former 'young master', the nephew of his first employer (see part 1). There is a burst of affection on both sides. In a man-to-man conversation Dorsan advises La Vallée to ask Mme de Vambures again, saying that she wanted him for himself and not because he was under any obligation to her. She set his foot on the bottom of the ladder, but he is now rich and established by his own merits and efforts. La Vallée does so, which leads to transports of joy and marriage. On their way to take up residence on a country estate belonging to Mme de Vambures they meet Dorsan and his wife. It is a triumphal progress. They have with them La Vallée's brother, for whose sons the La Vallées are going to continue to be responsible, for the brother's one ambition is to retire into the obscurity of his little house near his birthplace.

PART 8

THE story could well have been left at that point, with the surviving principals happily married and the secondary characters accounted for. But presumably the anonymous author felt obliged to bring the tale down to the time indicated by Marivaux at the opening of the novel, that is when the narrator is middle-aged and his nephews rather unpleasant young men. For this there were plenty of precedents such as *Gil Blas* and the sagas of Prévost.

The triumphal progress of La Vallée and Mme de Vambures after their marriage brings them back to La Vallée's own home territory, where it so happens that she has recently acquired ownership of La Vallée's village and the grand house. The villagers and old father La Vallée are overjoyed. At the grand house there are festivities, and in an atmosphere of Rousseau-like rustic joy La Vallée's sister, in her Sunday best, is the prettiest of all, and rather improbably becomes a close friend of her new sister-in-law. The only cloud in the sky is the resentment of a haughty local worthy named Vainsac (one might translate this as Windbag?) at having to treat the former village lad as a social superior, but it is quickly disposed of when old father La Vallée reminds him, in a flood of local dialect, that his grandfather and himself were peasants together. It is then disclosed that Vainsac and La Vallée's sister are in love, and their marriage coincides more or less with the news of the death of his brother's horrible wife in Paris.

For the sake of passing on a name and title to estates to any children they may have, La Vallée lets himself be persuaded by his wife to acquire a title by acquisition of some land.

Some sixteen years elapse and the La Vallées have two sons and a daughter. Beausson, the former 'young master', is now in a senior position and almost a member of the family. La Vallée's elder nephew gets a position in Beausson's office and the younger wants to be an officer. La Vallée's own sons differ markedly in character, the elder being bright, keen and a hard worker, the younger equally intelligent but quiet, thoughtful and given to melancholy. The daughter discourages many admirers and languishes. One day Beausson reports to La Vallée that the nephew who works for him has gone melancholy too, and that he has seen on his desk the portrait of a woman, but he dare not say of whom. Forced to say whose portrait it is, he says: 'Your daughter's!'

Forgetting all his own experience, La Vallée is horrified at the thought of such a misalliance and upbraids his nephew for his presumption. But meanwhile his wife has interviewed their daughter and established two facts: the daughter does not love her cousin, and is in love with somebody else whose name she will not disclose as she does not know whether her love is returned. Some days later La Vallée, having noticed that Beausson and his daughter tend to absent themselves for a walk in the garden at the same time, follows them and overhears their mutual declarations of love (less uncomfortable eavesdropping than his earlier listening through keyholes and partitions, but equally illuminating). After some delays all is agreed in principle. Meanwhile his own elder son is showing signs of being very interested in somebody in Paris, and his younger nephew, the officer, whose army career has been helped by the ever-useful Dorsan, makes a good marriage. The elder nephew, Beausson's assistant, summoned by his uncle to explain himself, says that he never loved La Vallée's daughter, but had had her portrait copied out of a simple feeling of cousinly affection. In reality he loves elsewhere, and the one he loves belongs to the same family in Paris as the girl who has captivated La Vallée's elder son. In a word, the two cousins are in love with sisters who are none other than the Mesdemoiselles de Fécour, nieces of La Vallée's former admirer, whose death has left them immensely rich. Minor difficulties are sorted out, such as transferring some of La Vallée's business interests to the nephew in order to give him an established position, and the double marriage is celebrated. Unfortunately thereafter both nephews, ashamed of their own father's humble circumstances and manner, change their names and cut themselves off from him (cf. part 1). In due course, in spite of further delay because of his illness, Beausson and La Vallée's daughter are happily married.

This leaves only La Vallée's younger son unaccounted for, the thoughtful, melancholy one. We now learn that at the surprising age of sixeeen the boy has decided that the celibate life of a religious order is all that matters for him, and the boy's mother endorses his decision.

The final episode of this crowded sequel is not the least surprising. The step his son has taken and some conversations with monks in the religious house where the boy serves his novitiate, give La Vallée serious doubts about the morality of some of the events of his own youth, and after making over his Paris house and affairs to his elder son he retires with his wife to the country and to the edifying life of a tranquil, God-fearing old age.

INFIDELITIES

and

THE GAME OF LOVE AND CHANCE

INTRODUCTION TO THE PLAYS

IN a short space it is, of course, impossible properly to discuss Marivaux's whole dramatic output. He was a prolific professional playwright. Generally, he had one new play produced each year between 1718 and 1757. He usually needed the money; unlike his contemporary, Voltaire, Marivaux always made appalling financial investments.

Marivaux in English suffers because his language is peculiarly exquisite. There is no English equivalent for *marivaudage*, that very clever romantic banter which has often been criticized for being a jargon of love. Many critics have argued that, exquisite though it might be, Marivaux's language is so clever and so refined that it is arcane. In tragedies you can get away with rhapsodies of rhetoric, but comedy should be simpler. Both these plays suggest that critics who see nothing but the *marivaudage* in Marivaux are missing much that is interesting. The plays have more to them than that.

Of the two plays translated here, *Le Jeu de l'amour et du hasard* (*The Game of Love and Chance*) is often considered the great classic. Marivaux never thought of it as such. He always said that *La Double Inconstance* (*Infidelities*) was his favourite of all his plays. This is not that surprising. In *La Double Inconstance* Marivaux dissected not just love but also contemporary French society. This was a subject dear to his heart, for he also produced a number of fascinating, if flawed, 'political' plays like the *Ile des Esclaves* (*Island of Slaves*) in which he offered a biting critique of the hierarchies, snobberies and injustices of his day. (Unlike Voltaire, however, Marivaux never went too far and stayed out of political trouble.)

La Double Inconstance was first produced in 1723 by the Theâtre des Italiens under Luigi Riccoboni. The play was a success and ran for more than eighteen performances. It was even played at court despite the unflattering picture of court life it gave. It was often revived during Marivaux's life and is still often staged in France.

On the face of it, the plot of *La Double Inconstance* is predictable and naïve. Arlequin and Silvia are ordinary country folk, a boy and girl who love each other and are to be wed. Their destiny should be to live out an ordinary country life. But the Prince of their land has seen Silvia and fallen desperately in love with her. He wants to marry her. But since he rules a progressive country by the standards of 1720, he cannot marry Silvia unless she agrees, and she will not agree because she has given Arlequin her word. How is the Prince (who just happens to be charming, handsome, good-natured and sensitive) to win Silvia away from Arlequin? His less than charming first move is to have Silvia kidnapped and brought to court. She is furious: in his passion, the Prince has behaved like a bandit. It is at this crisis that the play begins. One of the Prince's court ladies, Flaminia, takes charge of the romantic plot and promises the Prince that she will win Silvia for him. From the second scene, she orchestrates everyone's affections. All their passions are putty in her knowing hands.

Flaminia has Arlequin brought to court. Silvia has to be realistic about Arlequin. He is no Prince Charming. He is greedy, he is gross, he is frequently drunk; though he is funny, he is far too crude, says Flaminia, for someone with Silvia's refined qualities. Silvia basks in all this flattery. Flaminia makes the court ladies mock Silvia for her country manners while encouraging her to humble them by marrying the Prince. Flaminia plays on Silvia's prodigious vanity. It is a frightening spectacle and it is a mark of Marivaux's skill that he makes Flaminia likeable. She, paradoxically, is attracted to the boorish Arlequin.

Arlequin, for his part, is so flattered, touched and moved by Flaminia that he falls in love with her. So Marivaux shows how the course of true love can be made to run quite false. At times, the play may seem rather predictable to us now, but it is rich in its knowledge of human nature. It is about both the birth of love and, more poignantly, its destruction.

But I suspect that Marivaux particularly valued the play because he also used it to level some trenchant and funny criticisms at the state of contemporary French society. The criticisms, based largely on common sense, are made through Arlequin. The moment he arrives at court, he is greeted by Trivelin, an adviser to the Prince. Trivelin is not noble but a kind of elevated lackey. His attitudes are those of a grovelling civil servant. In a wonderful scene when Arlequin arrives, Trivelin informs him that it is inevitable that Silvia will marry the Prince. But in his generosity the Prince will heap honours on Arlequin. For example, he will be given servants and both a town house and a country house. Who, inquires Arlequin, will live in his town house while he is in the country? Why, his servants. So, Arlequin jeers, he is to give up his love to lodge his servants in luxury. But Arlequin could travel between his town and his country house. So he is to give up love for the pleasure of frequent trips. Arlequin deflates each of the advantages Trivelin advertises: servants, two houses, a carriage, ornate furniture. Decent, sensible men don't need such trimmings to live. Subsequently Marivaux returns to this theme. When a Lord comes to confer letters of nobility on him, Arlequin is extremely suspicious, particularly when it emerges that a noble man must die rather than accept an insult. Their exchange illustrates the corruption of the court, where everyone bows and scrapes in a desperate attempt to gain influence with the Prince. Later still, Arlequin finds himself followed by an ingratiating troop of lackeys. Trivelin explains that this, too, is a mark of honour. But, asks Arlequin, why don't the bowing and scraping fellows have other fellows bowing and scraping behind them? Because they are not honourable, explains Trivelin. Arlequin is furious. It is no compliment to be honoured by a bunch of dishonourable men. And he chases them off. Trivelin asks him to calm himself. The fact is that the lackeys are not dishonourable, but not everyone can have servants. It is the way of the world. An odd way of an odd world, is what Marivaux is saying through Arlequin.

Probably the reason why the court play was not banned was that for all that it exposed of the stupid corruptions of the court, the Prince emerges as a true and noble man. He honours Arlequin even though Arlequin denies him Silvia. He is a good advertisement for a just royalty.

The actor who played Arlequin, Thomassin, was one of the greatest actors of his time. He was a superb acrobat, a master of comic timing who could also move audiences to tears. He had a wonderful part. Flaminia, who is so coldly knowing about human nature and yet has enough charm and vulnerability to fall for Arlequin was played by Héléna Baletti. It is one of the most interesting parts Marivaux ever wrote for a woman precisely because she has to be so much in control of her emotions, so aware of everything. And yet in the end she plumps for the simple country life as against the refinements of the court. As she tells the Prince near the end of the play, she has developed an inexplicable taste for those country crudities which Arlequin represents.

La Double Inconstance is, then, a very rich play, for it does not merely trace a mutual set of infidelities but sets them in such a context that they raise a host of social and political questions. The ending was also controversial, for Flaminia, a woman of the court, does actually marry Arlequin, who is irredeemably a low character. In *Le Jeu* much of the comedy depends on the audience seeing from the first how impossible any such match would be. There only Lisette, the pert maid, has any time for Arlequin. In *Le Jeu* Arlequin is a buffoon: in *La Double Inconstance*, the same character is a sharp social critic.

It is traditional to look on *Le Jeu de l'amour et du hasard* as the masterpiece of Marivaux, although, as has been said, Marivaux never thought of it as such. It is certainly a very elegant play and Silvia is a marvellously complex, vain, vulnerable character, but it seems to me to lack some of the rich variety of *La Double Inconstance*.

Le Jeu was first performed in 1730 by the Theâtre des Italiens. The great actress, Silvia, played the part of Silvia. The plot is simple enough. M. Orgon, a rich merchant, has arranged for his daughter, Silvia, to marry Dorante, the son of a friend of his. Silvia asks permission to disguise herself as her maid, Lisette, so that she will be better able to get to know her husband-to-be. Dorante, with the same idea in mind, has disguised himself as his valet, Arlequin. Both Dorante and Silvia are completely baffled and disturbed because he finds he is attracted to what he takes to be a maid and she finds that a valet is captivating her. In a society of strict hierarchy, that was disconcerting. Meanwhile Lisette and Arlequin are buffooning their way into love with lots of high-flown phrases. Here Arlequin is a mere comic caricature, a valet who suddenly has the chance to put on airs; Lisette is only marginally more interesting. The heart of the play is the way that Silvia and Dorante, despite their disguises, fall in uncomfortable love with each other.

It has been argued that the play is about Silvia fighting for her identity as a person. When she chooses Dorante, she has established herself as her own woman, not her father's daughter. This is a seductive argument but, in the end, not a very convincing one. For Silvia is spared having to make that crucial choice when she discovers that her beloved is, indeed, the wealthy Dorante rather than his servant. Dorante does take the crucial step of proposing marriage to Silvia while he believes her to be a servant. But he is a far less interesting character than Silvia and Marivaux does not lead too well to Dorante's proposal. There is almost no indication of how Dorante comes to feel that he *has* to ask her to marry him. Once he is ready to ask, the play is really at an end. But by then we are only at the end of Act II and Marivaux had to have a third act even though it is largely superfluous. It only serves to show off Silvia's vanity further.

Le Jeu, writes the critic V. Greene, 'appears a classic in the sense also that it is the culmination of a particular theatrical tradition, the work that realizes the possibilities of a cluster of ideas and devices which earlier dramatists had been unable to fully develop'. Molière in 1650 was already drawing on a tradition of lovers who disguise themselves from each other. The birth of love even among characters who start by hating each other and are often at loggerheads is the theme both of *Much Ado about Nothing* and *The Taming of the Shrew*. Shakespeare put more interesting obstacles in the path of his characters, for they had to overcome themselves rathers than just social conventions, however strong. Dorante and Silvia would have been gasping for a priest the moment they met but for the fact that each thought the other a social inferior. It was socially shocking to love a servant but, in the end, that is perhaps not quite sufficient a conflict on which to base three acts. If it were not for the fascinating portrait that Marivaux draws of Silvia, the play would merely appear clever. It seems to me a pity that Marivaux did not push Silvia to the brink and force her to confront her love for Dorante while she still thought he was so far beneath her.

Le Jeu is, then, a much more predictable comedy than *La*

Double Inconstance. Its strength lies in the character of Silvia and, to some extent, in the parody of romantic love that Lisette and Arlequin act out. Its weakness is that Dorante remains very much a stock character even when he decides to marry the girl he still thinks a servant. It remains, however, an elegant, witty and knowing play.

These translations were originally made for the stage. I directed *La Double Inconstance* in Keble College, Oxford, and *Le Jeu de l'amour et du hasard* at the Oxford Playhouse. Both plays 'act' very well. I should like to thank a number of those who took part in the productions for their help, especially Gerry McCarthy, Joanna Symonds, Araminta Wordsworth, Cecelia Brereton and Ann-Margaret Willis. Dr Dennis Potts of Keble gave me some very useful advice on the translations.

DAVID COHEN

INFIDELITIES

(*La Double Inconstance*)

The Prince
Trivelin, *his servant*
Flaminia
Lisette, Flaminia's *sister*
Arlequin, *in love with* Silvia
Silvia, *in love with* Arlequin
A Lord of the Court
Footmen and Servants
Ladies in Waiting

A court in 1720

ACT I

SCENE 1

[*Enter* SILVIA, TRIVELIN, LADIES IN WAITING *following* SILVIA. SILVIA *comes on stage as if angry*.]

TRIVELIN: But, madam listen to me . . .
SILVIA: You're getting on my nerves.
TRIVELIN: Should one not be reasonable?
SILVIA [*Impatiently*]: No, one should not be reasonable and I won't be.
TRIVELIN: Nevertheless –
SILVIA: Nevertheless, I don't want to behave reasonably and you could repeat your 'neverthelesses' fifty times and I still wouldn't want to have anything to do with reason. What will you do then?
TRIVELIN: But, madam, you had so little supper last night that you'll be ill if you don't eat something this morning.
SILVIA: Well, I hate being healthy and I look forward to being ill. So you can just send back all this food they have brought because today I will have neither breakfast nor dinner nor supper. And it'll be just the same tomorrow. I just want to be angry and to hate you all, the lot of you, as long as I can't see Arlequin. You separated us. My mind, for what it's worth, is made up, and if you want me to go mad all you need to do is to preach to me to be more reasonable. I'll soon be raving then.
TRIVELIN: Oh, I wouldn't risk it. I'm afraid that you might well be as good as as your word. If I might, nevertheless –
SILVIA [*more angrily*]: There you go. Another 'nevertheless'.
TRIVELIN: Oh, I apologize, madam. That one escaped me. But I shan't say any more. I'll be careful to improve myself. I would beg you only to consider –
SILVIA: You're not improving at all. These considerations don't suit me either.

TRIVELIN [*going on*] : – that it is your Prince who loves you.

SILVIA: I'm not preventing him. He's master. But do I have to love him back? No, I don't, because I can't. That's obvious. A child would see it but you don't.

TRIVELIN: He must choose one of his subjects to be his wife, and his choice has fallen on you. Think of that.

SILVIA: Who told him to choose me? Did he ask my advice? If he'd asked me: 'Do you want me, Silvia?' I would have answered: 'No, my lord, a good woman must love her husband and I couldn't love you.' Now, that is true reason for you! But, instead, he loves me and, hey presto, he has me kidnapped – without asking me if I happen to like it.

TRIVELIN: He has only kidnapped you to offer you his hand.

SILVIA: And what does he want me to do with his hand if I don't want to stretch mine out to take it? Do you force presents on people against their will?

TRIVELIN: But, madam, consider how you have been treated during the two days you have been here. Are you not waited upon already as if you were his wife? Consider how many honours have been heaped upon you. And consider how many ladies wait upon you. And consider how many concerts and ballets the Prince has arranged for you to enjoy! What is Arlequin compared to a prince so considerate that he will not visit you till you want to see him? Where will you find such a young, tender, handsome, loving prince? Madam, open your eyes, see how fortunate you are.

SILVIA: Tell me, have you, and all these other people who have been left with me, have you been paid to annoy me, to lecture me with so little sense that I have to pity you?

TRIVELIN: Well, I know no better. That's all the wit I have.

SILVIA: If that's the case you'd be better off to have none at all.

TRIVELIN: But then, please, have the grace to point out where I am wrong.

SILVIA [*turning on him*] : Oh, yes, I'll show you where you go wrong.

TRIVELIN: Gently, please, I don't mean to annoy you.

SILVIA: Well, you're very clumsy then, aren't you!

TRIVELIN: I am your servant.

SILVIA: Well, my servant, you listen to me now. How many

honours are heaped upon me! What am I to do with the four or five good-for-nothing women who always spy on me? You take away my lover and give me women instead. Isn't that fine compensation? And you expect me to be happy with that! As for all these concerts and ballets which are supposed to delight me, Arlequin sang better and I would rather dance than watch others dancing. Do you see? I was happy in my small village and I would rather be a happy country girl in my village than a princess who floods her palace with tears. Am I to blame if the Prince is susceptible? If he's young and handsome, good for him. I'm happy to hear it. Let him keep his youth and his beauty for women of his own rank. All I ask him is to leave me my Arlequin who isn't nobler than I am, who isn't richer than I am, who isn't more glorious than I am, who loves me simply and whom I love simply. And if I don't see him soon, I'll die of despair. Alas, poor boy, what have you done with him? What's happened to him? He'll be so unhappy, so worried ... he has such a good heart. Maybe you've kidnapped him as well ... [*she moves.*] Tell me, would you like to please me?

[TRIVELIN *nods.*]

Then go away. I can't stand you any more. Just go away. I want to be alone.

TRIVELIN: The compliment is brief but clear. Nevertheless, madam, calm yourself, please.

SILVIA: I would prefer you to go in silence.

TRIVELIN: Calm yourself. You wanted to see Arlequin. He will be here soon. He is being fetched.

SILVIA [*sighing*]: I'll see him then?

TRIVELIN: Even speak to him.

SILVIA: Oh, I'll go and wait for him. But if you're lying to me I don't want to see, or speak, to any of you again.

[*As she exits, the* PRINCE *and* FLAMINIA *enter from another side and watch her go.*]

SCENE 2

TRIVELIN, PRINCE, FLAMINIA

PRINCE [*To* TRIVELIN]: Well, have you any hope to offer me? What does she say?

TRIVELIN: What she says, good my lord, isn't worth repeating. She says nothing yet that deserves your interest.

PRINCE: Never mind that. What does she say?

TRIVELIN: Oh no, my lord, such trifles would bore you. Love for Arlequin, desire to see him again, no wish to know you, hatred for all of us. That is a resumé of her emotions at present. You see that it's hardly encouraging. And, to be frank, my lord, it might well be best to send her back from whence she came.

[*The* PRINCE *looks sad.*]

FLAMINIA: I've already suggested that to the Prince. But it seems that he's determined. So, let's persevere, and concentrate on one thing only: destroying Silvia's love for Arlequin.

TRIVELIN: I feel there is something quite extraordinary about that girl. To refuse what she's refusing is unnatural. A woman would not refuse, you see. She is, my lord, a creature of some species unknown to us. We would have our way with a woman. That tells us she is a prodigy and, my lord, I think it unwise to go too far with prodigies.

PRINCE: She is a prodigy to refuse, and that only makes me love her more.

FLAMINIA [*laughing*]: My lord, don't listen to his talk of prodigies. You find prodigies in fairy tales. I know my sex; they have nothing prodigious in them but their vanity. Silvia may not have ambition but she has a heart and, consequently, she is vain. Have no fear, I'll make her see her duty as a woman. Has Arlequin been sent for?

TRIVELIN: Yes, I'm expecting him.

PRINCE: I confess, Flaminia, that I think we're taking a great risk in letting her meet him again. Her love for him will only increase.

TRIVELIN: Yes, but she gave me her word she'd go mad if she didn't see him.

FLAMINIA: I told you Arlequin is necessary, my lord.

PRINCE: You can promise him a shower of honours and gifts, if he'll agree to marry someone else.

TRIVELIN: And if he doesn't agree, we can have him dealt with.

PRINCE: No, the law that compels me to marry one of my subjects forbids me to use violence against anyone.

FLAMINIA: You're quite right, my lord. Besides, I hope everything will be settled amicably. Am I right in saying Silvia knows you already without suspecting you're the Prince?

PRINCE: Yes. I told you, I met her one day near her house when I was hunting and had lost track of the dogs. I was thirsty and she fetched me some water. I was captivated by her beauty, by her simplicity . . . and I told her so. I saw her five or six times when I was dressed only as an officer of the palace. She was very kind to me but I could never get her to renounce Arlequin, who surprised us together twice.

FLAMINIA: We must use the fact that she does not know who you really are. She has been told you won't see her at once. Yes, my lord, I'll see to the rest provided you do as I say.

PRINCE: Yes. If you win me Silvia's heart, you can expect every gratitude from me. [*Exit.*]

FLAMINIA: Trivelin, go and tell my sister to hurry.

TRIVELIN: No need to, for here she is. I'll go and wait for Arlequin. [*Exit.*]

SCENE 3

FLAMINIA

[*Enter* LISETTE.]

LISETTE: I am yours to command. Your orders?

FLAMINIA: Come closer . . . let me look at you.

LISETTE: Gaze your fill.

FLAMINIA [*after looking at her closely*]: Umm, you're pretty today.

LISETTE [*laughing*]: Yes, I know. But why should you care?

FLAMINIA: Take your beauty patch off.

LISETTE [*drawing back*]: I couldn't. My mirror recommended it.

FLAMINIA: You must. I tell you.

LISETTE [*taking it off*]: Why persecute my beauty patch. It wants to live.

FLAMINIA: I'll tell you why in a second. Otherwise, you're quite pretty.

LISETTE: It's the opinion of many.

FLAMINIA: You like being attractive?

LISETTE: It's my weakness.

FLAMINIA: Do you think you could simply and modestly make someone fall in love with you, pretending to love him, of course, and all for a good cause?

LISETTE: I think I need my beauty patch for such an enterprise.

FLAMINA: Can you never forget it? You don't need it at all. The man in question is a simple countryman, an inexperienced fellow, who probably thinks that women here have to be as modest as women in his village. But their kind of modesty is not at all like ours. Our habits would shock him. So don't mourn your beauty patch! You must rely on your manner, your demeanour ... I wonder if you'll be able to do it. What will you say to him?

LISETTE: What will I say to him ... eh ... what would you say to him?

FLAMINIA: Now, pay attention ... not the least coquettish air. One can see in your face you want to look attractive. You must lose that. There's something scatty, lively and abandoned in the way you move, in your gestures. Sometimes it's casual, sometimes tender, sometimes cute. Your eyes want to be noticed, to strike, to flirt. You carry your head lightly and your chin scornfully. You try to look gay, young and a little dissipated. When you speak to people, you assume certain intonations, you use certain phrases, you pepper your conversation with wit. These pert affectations are pretty in a woman of the world. By common consent, they are thought graceful. Men fall in love with you because of them. But you must now suppress all these charms. The little fellow in question wouldn't like them! His taste isn't that refined. Imagine a man who has drunk nothing but pure water. He wouldn't like wine or spirits.

LISETTE [*surprised*]: Now you've dissected my attractions, I feel quite plain.

FLAMINIA [*naïvely*]: Don't worry. Men are too struck by them to dissect them. It's only because I do that they start to seem ridiculous.

LISETTE: But what will I replace them with?

FLAMINIA: Nothing. You'll let your eyes wander where they will, where they would if your vanity didn't guide them. You'll hold your head up or down as you like. No refined glances. And let your face assume the look it has when no one looks at you. Come on ... give me a sample of how versatile you are ... let's have an ingenuous look.

LISETTE [*turning to her*]: Will this do?

FLAMINIA: It could still improve.

LISETTE: Look, let me tell you. You're a woman – and my sister. You're not exactly inspiring. I needn't give my best performance for you. It is for Arlequin, isn't it?

FLAMINIA: Yes, for him.

LISETTE: But, poor Arlequin, if I don't fall in love with him I'll be deceiving him. I'm an honest girl, I have scruples.

FLAMINIA: If he falls in love with you, you'll marry him and make your fortune. Have you still got scruples? After all, like me, you're just the daughter of a palace official. If Arlequin loves you, you'll become a great lady.

LISETTE: You've set my conscience at rest. In that case I don't have to love him to marry him. Tell me when he comes.

FLAMINIA: I'll withdraw as well, for here they come with Arlequin.

SCENE 4

ARLEQUIN, TRIVELIN

[ARLEQUIN *stares at* TRIVELIN *and all around, astonished.*]

TRIVELIN: Well, Sir Arlequin, how do you find it here?

[ARLEQUIN *is silent.*]

Isn't this a fine house?

ARLEQUIN: What have I and that house in common? For God's sake! And who are you? What do you want from me? Where are we going?

TRIVELIN: I'm an honest man, your servant at present. I only want to wait on you. And we're going no further.

ARLEQUIN: I don't know if you're honest or not, but I do know that I've nothing for you to do. I dismiss you from my service.

TRIVELIN [*stopping him*] : Now, now, sir . . .

ARLEQUIN: Explain yourself, you've some cheek stopping your master!

TRIVELIN: A greater master than you, Sir, made you master over me.

ARLEQUIN: What loony's been giving me servants in spite of me?

TRIVELIN: When you find out who it is, you'll speak better of him. Now, we have some matters to discuss.

ARLEQUIN: Do we?

TRIVELIN: Yes, about Silvia.

ARLEQUIN [*charmed*] : Silvia! Oh, I beg your pardon, Sir. I didn't know I had something to speak to you about.

TRIVELIN: You lost her two days ago.

ARLEQUIN: Yes. Robbers took her away.

TRIVELIN: They were not robbers.

ARLEQUIN: If they weren't robbers, they were still thieves.

TRIVELIN: I know where Silvia is.

ARLEQUIN [*charmed, stroking him*] : You know where she is, my friend, my servant, my master, my everything you want to be . . . Oh, how sad I am not rich! I could give you all my money as a reward! Tell me, my friend, which way must I turn? Where is she – to the left, to the right? In front of me?

TRIVELIN: You will see her here.

ARLEQUIN [*sweetly*] : Oh, you must be an honest man, a good man, to bring me to her. Oh, Silvia! My dear, my love, my soul, I weep for joy.

TRIVELIN [*aside*] : Not an encouraging prelude. [*To him*] : My dear Sir, I have something else to say to you.

ARLEQUIN [*impatient*] : Let's go and see Silvia first. I'm so impatient to see her.

TRIVELIN: I promise you you will see her. But there are some matters I must inform you of before. You remember an officer who visited Silvia five or six times and whom you saw with her.

ARLEQUIN [*sadly*] : Yes; he looked like a hypocrite.

TRIVELIN: He found her very attractive.

ARLEQUIN: He found nothing new, by God.

TRIVELIN: He told the Prince of her beauty, and the Prince was enchanted.

ARLEQUIN: What a gossip!

TRIVELIN: The Prince desired to see her and had her brought here.

ARLEQUIN: But he'll give her back to me, as is just.

TRIVELIN: Unfortunately, there is a small difficulty. You see, the Prince fell in love with her too, and wishes to be loved in his turn.

ARLEQUIN: Well, his turn can't come. She loves me.

TRIVELIN: That's not the point. Pay attention till the end, please.

ARLEQUIN [*raising his voice*]: But that is the point and the end as well. Do you want to deprive me of my right?

TRIVELIN: Please ... you know that the Prince has to choose a wife from among his subjects.

ARLEQUIN: No, I don't know. It doesn't concern me.

TRIVELIN: I'm telling you.

ARLEQUIN [*brusquely*]: The news doesn't worry me.

TRIVELIN: The Prince loves Silvia. He would like her to love him before he marries her. Her love for you is an impediment to his love.

ARLEQUIN: Let him make love somewhere else. If he married her, he might have her body but I'd still have her heart. Both of us would be missing something and all three of us would be unhappy.

TRIVELIN: True. But don't you see that, if you marry Silvia, the Prince will be unhappy.

ARLEQUIN [*after musing*]: Yes, for a little while he might be sad. But he will have acted honourably, and that's a consolation. But if he marries her, he'll make her cry, and make me cry. Only he'll be laughing and there's no pleasure in laughing alone.

TRIVELIN: My dear Sir, believe me, do your Prince a favour. He cannot live without Silvia. I may as well tell you that this turn of events was predicted. She must be his wife. It is written. Up there. [*He points to the sky.*]

ARLEQUIN: Up there? They don't write such rubbish up there. Tell me, if it was written up there that I should assault you from behind and murder you, would you like it if I fulfilled the prediction?

TRIVELIN: No, no. One must never do anyone harm.

ARLEQUIN: Well, it's my death you've forecast. And to forecast that is to forecast nothing. If it's written in the stars, all you need do is hang the astrologer.

TRIVELIN: Good heavens. No one means to harm you. We have attractive girls here. Marry one of them. It will be well worth your while.

ARLEQUIN: Oh yes, if I marry one of them, Silvia will be furious and fall in love with someone else. Oh, my friend, how much have you been paid to trap me? You can keep your girls, you rogue. We won't make that bargain – it costs too much.

TRIVELIN: Do you realize that your marriage to one of them would win you the Prince's friendship?

ARLEQUIN: What would he want with a friend like me?

TRIVELIN: Ah, but think of the riches that his friendship would confer upon you.

ARLEQUIN: I don't need riches. I'm healthy. I have a good appetite and enough to live on. I'm quite happy.

TRIVELIN: You don't know the value of what you're refusing.

ARLEQUIN [*casually*]: So I lose nothing.

TRIVELIN: A town house, a country house...

ARLEQUIN: Wonderful! Just one thing bothers me though. Who lives in my town house while I'm in the country?

TRIVELIN: Why, your servants!

ARLEQUIN: My servants. If I grow rich, they get the benefit. Ha, I can't live in both houses at once, then?

TRIVELIN [*laughing*]: I don't think so. One cannot be in two places at once.

ARLEQUIN: Quite so, my simple friend. If I can't do that trick, what use are two houses to me?

TRIVELIN: You could go from one to the other when you felt like it.

ARLEQUIN: Good, I'm to give up my love for the delight of frequent removals.

TRIVELIN: Nothing tempts you ... it's not natural. Everyone is delighted to have fine houses and many servants and –

ARLEQUIN: I need just one room. I don't want to have to feed lazy good-for-nothing servants and I don't know a more faithful and devoted servant to me than my own self.

TRIVELIN: You'd find him hard to dismiss, that's true ... but wouldn't it give you pleasure to have a fine carriage, a team of superb horses, not to speak of exquisite furniture ...

ARLEQUIN: You are a giant booby, to compare Silvia with horses, houses and furniture! What is a house for, except sleeping, sitting and eating! If I have a bed, a table and a dozen straw chairs, am I not furnished? Haven't I got all I need? Ah, but I don't have a carriage. It won't turn over then. [*Showing his legs.*] Aren't these legs my mother gave me good enough? You're mad. If you left a few of your many horses and carriages to poor people you would be doing something sensible and you wouldn't have so much gout either. Walking's good for you.

TRIVELIN: Great God, you are ... touchy. If you had your way, men wouldn't own any shoes.

ARLEQUIN [*brusquely*]: They would wear clogs. Your stories are beginning to bore me. Anyway, you promised that I'd see Silvia. An honest man sticks to his word.

TRIVELIN: Just one moment. You say you don't care for honours or riches or magnificence or money or houses or carriages ...

ARLEQUIN: None of them are worth a good meal.

TRIVELIN: Would good food tempt you, a cellarful of choice wines? Would you care for a skilful cook who would prepare such fine meals for you and so many of them ... Think of the most delicious meats and fish. You can have all of them for the rest of your life.

[ARLEQUIN *is silent.*]

Hmm, you don't reply ...

ARLEQUIN: What you offer me now is much more to my taste. I confess I am greedy. But I have more love than greed.

TRIVELIN: Well then, my dear sir, make yourself happy. All you need do is leave one woman for another.

ARLEQUIN: No, no, I'll restrain myself. Boiled beef and rough wine will do me.

TRIVELIN: What exquisite wines you could drink! What fine sauces and meats you will miss!

ARLEQUIN: Yes, I'm disappointed, but one can't have everything. Silvia's heart is a daintier morsel than all that. Well, will you let me see Silvia or won't you?

TRIVELIN: You will see her. But it's early yet.

SCENE 5

LISETTE, ARLEQUIN, TRIVELIN

LISETTE [*to* TRIVELIN]: I have looked everywhere for you, Trivelin. The Prince wants you.

TRIVELIN: The Prince wants me? At once. But will you look after Sir Arlequin while I'm gone?

ARLEQUIN: Oh, it's not worth it. I'm quite happy to look after myself.

TRIVELIN: No, no, you might get bored . . . I'll come back soon. [*Exit.*]

SCENE 6

ARLEQUIN

[*Enter* LISETTE.]

ARLEQUIN [*withdrawing to a corner*]: A coquette to tempt me, I suppose.

LISETTE [*sweetly*]: Then it's you, Sir, who are Silvia's lover?

ARLEQUIN [*coldly*]: Yes.

LISETTE: She's a very pretty girl.

ARLEQUIN [*same tone*]: I know.

LISETTE: Everyone adores her.

ARLEQUIN [*colder still*]: Everyone is wrong.

LISETTE: Why? Doesn't she deserve it?

ARLEQUIN [*brusquely*]: Because she'll love only me.

LISETTE: I don't doubt it and I forgive her her passion for you.

ARLEQUIN: What use is your forgiveness?

LISETTE: I mean, now that I've met you I'm not surprised that she is being so obstinate in loving you.

ARLEQUIN: Why were you surprised to begin with?

LISETTE: Well, she is turning down a charming prince.

ARLEQUIN: And if he's charming, aren't I as well?

LISETTE [*sweetly*]: Ah, but he is a prince, after all.

ARLEQUIN: So what? That doesn't make him any better for a girl.

LISETTE [*sweetly*]: I only meant that he has subjects and estates and, charming as you are, you have none.

ARLEQUIN: Oh, subjects and estates! Very magnificent! If I have no subjects, I'm responsible for no one. If things go well, it's good; if things go badly, it's not my fault. And whether or not one has estates, one isn't better or more handsome or any uglier as a result. So you had nothing to be surprised at.

LISETTE [*aside*]: Nasty little man! I flatter him and he's rude to me.

ARLEQUIN: What?

LISETTE: I confess that, when I saw you, I expected a more charming conversation . . .

ARLEQUIN: Well, miss, nothing's more deceptive than people's looks.

LISETTE: Yours did deceive me, I admit. And it just shows how wrong one is to like someone at first sight.

ARLEQUIN: Quite, very wrong. What do you want? I didn't choose my face.

LISETTE [*looking at him, surprised*]: No, I find it surprising when I look at you.

ARLEQUIN: Well, there you are. There's no cure, I'll always look like that.

LISETTE [*as if a little cross*]: I'm quite sure you will.

ARLEQUIN: It doesn't worry you, for heaven's sake?

LISETTE: Why do you ask me that?

ARLEQUIN: Well, to know.

LISETTE [*with a natural air*]: I'd be very silly to tell you the truth. A girl should keep quiet.

ARLEQUIN [*aside*]: There she goes. [*To her.*] Listen, frankly, it's a pity you're such a coquette.

LISETTE: Me?

ARLEQUIN: You.

LISETTE: Do you know that you don't say such things to women? You've insulted me.

ARLEQUIN [*innocently*] : Not at all. There's no harm in seeing what people show you. I'm not wrong to find you a coquette; you're wrong to be one, miss.

LISETTE [*hotly*] : But what makes you think that I am?

ARLEQUIN: Because you've been saying nice things to me for about an hour. You're about to confess that you love me, no doubt. Listen, if you do love me, go away and it'll pass. I'm already engaged to someone, and even if I weren't I wouldn't want a girl to make advances to me. I want to make them to a girl, thank you. It's much better that way. And if you don't love me, well, shame on you!

LISETTE: You're imagining things. Do you have these visions often?

ARLEQUIN: How do the men at court put up with such manners? The moment a woman becomes a coquette, she becomes ugly.

LISETTE: You really do have an imagination ... you say such odd things, poor man.

ARLEQUIN: You were speaking of Silvia. Oh, if I told you the story of our love, how you'd admire her modesty. The first few days she would back away when I came near her. Then, she would back away less and then, little by little, she didn't back away any more. She looked at me, stealthily, and when I saw her she would blush with shame. And I felt like a king when I saw how ashamed she was of looking at me. Then I caught her hand and she let me take it, still all abashed. Then I spoke to her. At first, she didn't answer. Not that she didn't think answers. Then she answered me with her eyes, and then, finally, she let herself go and words streamed out because her heart was pounding quicker than her mind. It was delightful. I was mad with joy, with excitement. There, that is a woman. But you're not at all like her.

LISETTE: Oh, a very amusing story. You make me laugh, you know.

ARLEQUIN: And I'm sorry to make you laugh at your own expense. Good-bye. If all men were like me, you'd find a flying pig sooner than a lover.

SCENE 7

LISETTE, ARLEQUIN

[*Enter* TRIVELIN.]

TRIVELIN [*to* ARLEQUIN]: You're going?

ARLEQUIN: Yes, this lady wants me to love her, but it's not possible.

TRIVELIN: Let's go for a walk . . . it'll put you in a better mood. [*Exeunt.*]

SCENE 8

PRINCE, FLAMINIA, LISETTE

FLAMINIA [*to* LISETTE]: Well, how did you do? How's Arlequin's heart?

LISETTE [*curtly*]: There's no place there for me.

FLAMINIA: He was unpleasant to you?

LISETTE: 'I'm afraid you're a coquette, miss' . . . that's his style.

PRINCE: I am sorry, Lisette. But you mustn't take it to heart you know. What he thinks is of no importance.

LISETTE: I confess to you, my lord, that if I were vain, I would be very hurt. He has proved that not everyone finds me adorable. A woman can well do without such proof.

FLAMINIA: Never mind! So, it's my turn to try my luck next.

PRINCE: Arlequin is faithful . . . and so I'll never have Silvia's love.

FLAMINIA: I tell you, my lord, I've seen Arlequin. I find him quite pleasant, and quite attractive even. Now I've resolved to make you happy, my lord, and I promised you Silvia and I'll keep my promise. I don't take back one word. Oh, you don't know me! What, do you think Silvia and Arlequin could resist me, when I'm determined, when I'm persistent, when I'm a woman? If they did, I'd go into hiding. My own sex would deny me. My lord, you can quite safely order all the preparation for your marriage to begin. I guarantee you loved and wed. Silvia will love you, then she'll agree to marry you. I can hear her say to you . . . 'I love you', and I can picture your wedding day. Now, that's over. Arlequin marries me and you will deluge us with favours . . . there, that's over too.

LISETTE [*incredulous*] : Everything's over . . . nothing's started yet!

FLAMINIA: Keep quiet, silly fool.

PRINCE: You encourage me to hope . . . but I don't really see any reason to do so.

FLAMINIA: I'll give you grounds for hope soon enough. Now, I shall start by getting Silvia. It's time she saw Arlequin.

LISETTE: Once they have met, I doubt your subtleties will achieve much.

PRINCE: I agree.

FLAMINIA [*casually*] : Either I'm right, yes, or I'm wrong, no. But they must see each other. I must have a free hand to corrupt their love.

PRINCE: Do as you wish.

FLAMINIA: Let's withdraw. Here comes Arlequin.

[*Exeunt.*]

SCENE 9

ARLEQUIN, TRIVELIN, *followed by a train of valets*

ARLEQUIN: By the way, just while we're at it, one thing . . . why the hell do these great loons trot after us everywhere? They're very odd.

TRIVELIN: The Prince, who loves you, is anxious to show you his esteem for you. He wants them to follow you in order to honour you.

ARLEQUIN: Oh I see, it's a mark of honour?

TRIVELIN: Undoubtedly.

ARLEQUIN: And who follows my followers?

TRIVELIN: No one.

ARLEQUIN: And no one follows you, either.

TRIVELIN: No.

ARLEQUIN: So, you're not honoured?

TRIVELIN: We are undeserving.

ARLEQUIN [*flying into a rage, wielding his stick*] : Oh, get out, the pack of you . . . go away, off, out, away.

TRIVELIN: But I don't understand.

ARLEQUIN: Go away, I don't like undeserving servants who have no honour.

TRIVELIN: You don't understand . . .

ARLEQUIN: I'll make myself clearer then. [*Striking him*]

TRIVELIN: Stop, stop, what are you doing . . .?

[*Exeunt valets,* ARLEQUIN *chasing them off.* TRIVELIN *hides in the wings.*]

SCENE 10

ARLEQUIN, TRIVELIN

ARLEQUIN [*coming back*]: Fools, morons . . . it's all I can do to dismiss them. It's an odd way of honouring a man, having him followed by a bunch of crooks. It's mocking people. [*to* TRIVELIN] Well, my friend, did I not make myself clear?

TRIVELIN [*keeping his distance*]: Listen to me, you beat me but I forgive you. I believe you to be a reasonable man.

ARLEQUIN: You've noticed?

TRIVELIN [*still from a distance*]: When I said we didn't deserve servants and weren't honourable, I didn't mean it. Not in that sense. It's not honour we lack. But it is only persons of importance, lords and rich gentlemen, who are honoured in this way. If to be honoured all one had to be was honourable, I'd have an army of servants.

ARLEQUIN [*putting aside his stick*]: Now I understand. If you'd explain I wouldn't have beaten you. My arms wouldn't be tired and your shoulders would feel better.

TRIVELIN: You hurt me.

ARLEQUIN: I meant to. Thank goodness, it was just a misunderstanding. You should be glad you were beaten by mistake. I see now that important, rich people are honoured while honourable people aren't.

TRIVELIN: It's the way of the world.

ARLEQUIN [*with disgust*]: In which case there's no point in being honoured, since it doesn't mean you're honourable.

TRIVELIN: It is possible to be both.

ARLEQUIN: For Heaven's sake, leave me alone. If I'm seen by

myself I'll at least be taken for an honest man. I prefer that to being taken for a lord!

TRIVELIN: Our orders are to stay with you.

ARLEQUIN: Then take me to see Silvia.

TRIVELIN: You will have your way. Here she comes! Good-bye, I must withdraw. [*Exit, with valets.*]

SCENE 11

ARLEQUIN

[*Enter* SILVIA *and* FLAMINIA.]

SILVIA [*running into his arms*]: My dear Arlequin, my love ... oh ... I'm with you again, my love ... oh, I'm so happy.

ARLEQUIN [*choking with joy*]: Oh, me too ... [*He takes a deep breath.*] I'm so happy I could die!

SILVIA: Oh, my love! [*Gently.*] How he loves me! What a delight to be loved like this.

FLAMINIA [*looking at the two of them*]: Oh you're enchanting, my dears. It's such a pleasure to see you are so faithful. [*Softly.*] If anyone heard me say that, I'd be lost ... but, in my heart of hearts, I admire and pity you.

SILVIA [*to* FLAMINIA]: Yes, you've a good heart. Oh, Arlequin, I've sighed for you so.

ARLEQUIN [*tenderly, taking her hand*]: Do you still love me?

SILVIA: Do I still love you? Do you have to ask?

FLAMINIA [*naturally, to* ARLEQUIN]: Oh, I can assure you she does. I've seen her distraught, I've seen her cry for you. I was touched, I've been dying to see you together. And now you are together, good-bye, my dears. I'm going because you make me cry. You remind me of a love I had once upon a time ... he died. He looked a little like Arlequin, and I'll never forget him. Good-bye, Silvia. They asked me to spy on you, but I won't betray you. Don't let your love for Arlequin be corrupted. Love Arlequin forever, for he deserves it. And you, Arlequin, whatever happens, you can always look upon me as a friend who would like to help you. I'll do whatever I can for you.

ARLEQUIN [*gently*]: You're a kind woman. Thank you. I'm

your friend as well. I'm sorry your love died. I'm sorry you're upset and I'm sorry we're in trouble.

[*Exit* FLAMINIA.]

SCENE 12

SILVIA, ARLEQUIN

SILVIA [*plaintively*] : Well, my dear love Arlequin?

ARLEQUIN: Well, my soul, my love?

SILVIA: Oh, what trouble we find ourselves in.

ARLEQUIN: If we love each other, it'll help us through.

SILVIA: But what will happen to our love? It worries me.

ARLEQUIN: Yes . . . what will? I say we must be patient, but I have no more courage than you. [*He takes her hand.*] Oh, my love, my treasure, it's three days since I've looked into your beautiful eyes. Please look at me forever, to make up for lost time.

SILVIA [*looks worried*] : Oh, I've so much to tell you. I'm so afraid of losing you. I'm afraid they'll get so jealous and vicious they'll harm you. I'm afraid that you'll be without me for a long time and you'll get used to it.

ARLEQUIN: I won't get used to being unhappy, dear heart!

SILVIA: I don't want you to forget me and I don't want you to have hardships to bear because of me. I don't know how to say what I want, but I love you too much. I'm in such trouble. Everything makes me miserable.

[ARLEQUIN *starts to weep.*]

[*Sadly.*] Don't cry, or I will as well.

ARLEQUIN: How can I stop crying when you insist on being so miserable? If you had any pity you wouldn't be so sad!

SILVIA: Calm down. I promise not to say I'm miserable again.

ARLEQUIN: Yes, but I'll know you are. You must promise not to be miserable.

SILVIA: Yes, my love. And you must promise to love me always.

ARLEQUIN [*stopping to look at her*] : Silvia, I love you and you love me and that's the truth. Never forget it. While I live, it will always be the same. It'll never change. What do you want me to swear on? I'll die in the company of my love for you.

SILVIA: I don't want you to swear, I don't know any oaths. You're honest, you have my love, I have yours. You can't lose my love. Whom should I love instead of you? Is there a more handsome man? Could any girl love you more than I do? Isn't that enough? We just have to stay as we are. Do we need oaths on top of that?

ARLEQUIN: A hundred years from now we'll still love each other.

SILVIA: Yes.

ARLEQUIN: So, we've nothing to fear. Let's be happy.

SILVIA: Perhaps we'll suffer a bit. That's all.

ARLEQUIN: A trifle. It'll make us appreciate our happiness the more.

SILVIA: I don't need to suffer to appreciate it.

ARLEQUIN: We'll just have to forget we're suffering.

SILVIA [*tenderly*]: Oh, my darling, you give me hope.

ARLEQUIN [*tenderly*]: I'm only afraid for you.

SILVIA [*looking at him*]: Oh, what beautiful things you say! There's no one like you in the whole world, but also there's no one who can love you as I do.

ARLEQUIN [*jumping for joy*]: Oh, my love ... your words are like honey.

SCENE 13

ARLEQUIN, SILVIA

[*Enter* FLAMINIA *and* TRIVELIN]

TRIVELIN [*to* SILVIA]: I'm very sorry to interrupt you but your mother is asking for you. She wants to see you at once.

SILVIA: Don't leave me, Arlequin. I've nothing to hide from you.

ARLEQUIN [*taking her arm*]: Then let's go.

FLAMINIA [*confidingly, drawing closer*]: Don't be afraid, my dears. You go to see your mother alone, my dear Silvia. It's more proper that way. You are free to see each other as much as you want, I promise you that, and you know I wouldn't deceive you.

ARLEQUIN: Yes, we know, you're on our side, you are.

SILVIA: All right, I'll come back soon. [*Exit.*]

ARLEQUIN [*stops* FLAMINIA, *who is leaving too*]: While she's gone, Flaminia, will you keep me company to stop me getting bored? You're the only person here whose company pleases me.

FLAMINIA [*confidingly*]: Of course, I like your company too, but I'm afraid people will notice that we're friends.

TRIVELIN: Dinner is ready, Sir Arlequin.

ARLEQUIN [*sadly*]: I'm not hungry.

FLAMINIA [*solicitously*]: I want you to eat. You need it.

ARLEQUIN [*gently*]: You think so?

FLAMINIA: Yes.

ARLEQUIN: I don't know. [*To* TRIVELIN.] Is the soup good?

TRIVELIN: Delicious.

ARLEQUIN: Hm, we must wait for Silvia. She likes soup.

FLAMINIA: She'll dine with her mother, I think. Please yourself, but if I were you I'd leave them together. Isn't that better? You'll see her after dinner.

ARLEQUIN: Very well ... but there's no edge to my appetite yet.

TRIVELIN: The wine is being chilled, the roast is ready.

ARLEQUIN: I'm so sad ... is the roast good?

TRIVELIN: Venison. Exquisite.

ARLEQUIN: Oh! The troubles I have to bear! Well, then, let's go and eat. Cold meat's no good.

FLAMINIA: Don't forget to drink my health.

ARLEQUIN: Come and drink to mine and to our meeting.

FLAMINIA: With all my heart. I've half an hour to spare you.

ARLEQUIN: Good, I'm glad.

[*Exeunt* FLAMINIA, ARLEQUIN, TRIVELIN.]

ACT II

SCENE 1

FLAMINIA, SILVIA

SILVIA: Yes, I believe you. You seem to wish me well. You know you are the only person here I can stand – the others are all my enemies. But where is Arlequin?

FLAMINIA: He's coming. He's still eating.

SILVIA: This is an appalling place to be! I've never seen so many polite women, so many courteous men. They have such fine manners, always bowing and flattering and giving such tokens of friendship that you'd think they were the best people on earth, full of heart and conscience. But not at all. Not one of those people hasn't come to me and said knowingly: 'Trust me, I advise you to abandon Arlequin and marry the Prince.' And they give me this advice naturally, without one jot of shame, as if they were egging me on to some good deed. I reply: 'But I've given my word to Arlequin. What about the duty one has to be faithful, to be honest, to be of good faith?' They don't listen. They have no idea what those words mean. I might as well be speaking Greek; they laugh to my face and tell me I'm being a child. A big girl has to be reasonable. Isn't that pretty? To be worthless, to deceive one's friend, to break one's word to him, to be a liar and a cheat – these seem to be the duties of the noble persons who live in this hell-hole. What kind of creatures are they? Where do they spring from? What stuff are they made of?

FLAMINIA: Of the stuff most people are made of. It shouldn't surprise you. They think you would be happy married to the Prince.

SILVIA: But don't I have to be faithful, and isn't it my duty to stay with Arlequin? Could I be happy, not doing my duty? And, anyway, isn't this faithfulness my whole charm? But they have the impertinence to come and tell me, 'There, do something bad which will only do you harm ... you'll only lose your happiness and your reputation ... but ...' And if I don't want to, they object.

FLAMINIA: What can you do? Their minds work that way. They would like the Prince to be happy.

SILVIA: And why can't this Prince take a girl who wants to give herself to him? What kind of a whim is it to want a girl who doesn't want you? What pleasure can there be in it? And all these concerts and masques and entertainments he has put on for me ... it's ridiculous, tasteless even. And all these banquets that seem like wedding breakfasts! Not to mention all these jewels he sends me. It must cost a fortune. He must be ruining himself. What is he getting out of it? He could give me a whole jewellery store and it wouldn't please me as much as a pin-cushion Arlequin gave me.

FLAMINIA: I know. I know what it is to love. I had the same feeling when I was in love. I remember the pin-cushion well.

SILVIA: Look. If I had to give up Arlequin, I would give him up for a royal guards officer who saw me five or six times and who's as handsome as a man can be. There's little chance that the Prince will be so pleasing. I would have liked to love this officer and I feel more pity for him than for the Prince.

FLAMINIA [*with a hidden smile*]: Of course. I assure you that you'll feel as sorry for the Prince when you finally meet him.

SILVIA: Let the Prince forget me and send me away, let him see other girls. There are some girls here who have lovers too, like me. But they manage to love everyone else as well. I've seen that it doesn't hurt them, but for me it's impossible.

FLAMINIA: Have we no one here who compares with you, who is as good as you?

SILVIA [*modestly*]: There are prettier girls than me. And those that are half as pretty as me make more use of it. And then there are some ugly ones who lard their faces up so you can't tell the difference.

FLAMINIA: Yours doesn't need larding. And that's lovely.

SILVIA: I know. But I'm nothing, I'm dull and staid compared to them ... They laugh and prance. Their eyes caress everyone. They look bold and they have a free, uninhibited beauty. That must be more attractive than a shamefaced girl who doesn't dare look at people and who blushes to be found beautiful.

FLAMINIA: That's just what delights the Prince. You have a simple, graceful beauty that is natural. And, if you would take my advice, don't praise these ladies, for they don't praise you.

SILVIA: What do they say about me?

FLAMINIA: Impertinences! They make fun of you, they tease the Prince and ask him, 'How's your rustic flame?' Yesterday one of the most jealous ones said, 'Have you ever seen a more vulgar face? A more clumsy figure?' One was imitating the way you look and another one the way you speak. And even the men pretended not to find you attractive. I tell you, I was mad!

SILVIA [*angered*]: Fine men! To belie their thoughts to flatter such fools.

FLAMINIA: It's well-bred here.

SILVIA: I loathe them. But if I'm so unattractive why should the Prince love me and not them?

FLAMINIA: Oh, they're quite sure he won't love you long. It's a whim, they say, and he'll be the first to laugh at it quite soon.

SILVIA [*piqued, and after eyeing* FLAMINIA]: Well, they're lucky I love Arlequin so much, I'd like to make them eat their words.

FLAMINIA: They deserve to be punished. I told them, 'You do your best to have Silvia sent away and to make the Prince love you, but, if she wanted to, she could make him ignore you all.'

SILVIA: Oh, quite, I could. I could choose to show them.

FLAMINIA: Company, my dear.

SILVIA: It's the royal guards officer I was telling you about. Isn't he a handsome man?

SCENE 2

SILVIA, FLAMINIA

[*Enter* PRINCE, *disguised as an officer of the palace, and* LISETTE, *disguised as another court lady. The* PRINCE, *when he sees* SILVIA, *bows submissively.*]

SILVIA: You, Sir? You knew I was here, then?

PRINCE: Yes, I knew. But you told me you never wanted to see me again. So I dared not come without this lady who wanted me to escort her and who obtained from the Prince permission to come and pay you homage.

[LISETTE *scrutinizes* SILVIA *silently and exchanges glances with* FLAMINIA.]

SILVIA: I am glad to see you again, but you find me in a sad mood. I thank the lady for her homage. I don't deserve it. But if she desires to pay me her respects, let her. I will give her mine, as best I can. She must forgive me if I am clumsy.

LISETTE: I will forgive you willingly. One should never ask the impossible, after all.

SILVIA [*angry, she curtsies; aside*]: Never ask the impossible! Charming!

LISETTE: How old are you, my child?

SILVIA [*piqued*]: I have forgotten, Mama.

FLAMINIA [*to* SILVIA]: Well done.

[*The* PRINCE *appears to be annoyed.*]

LISETTE: She's getting angry, I think.

PRINCE: What is the meaning of this, Madam? You come to pay your respects to Silvia and you insult her.

LISETTE: I didn't mean to make her angry. I wanted to see this little girl everyone loves so. I wanted to see what it was in her that inspired such passion. They say she is naïve. Naïvety is such a pleasant rustic accomplishment. So entertaining. Be so good, Madam, as to show us some of your naïvety. Let's see your country wit.

SILVIA: It's not worth the trouble. It will not be as sharp as yours.

LISETTE [*laughing*]: There's naïvety for you.

PRINCE [*to* LISETTE]: Go away, Madam.

SILVIA: Yes, I'm getting annoyed. If she doesn't go, I'll really get angry.

PRINCE [*to* LISETTE]: You will regret this.

LISETTE [*disdainfully, as she withdraws*]: Farewell ... It is revenge enough that he should choose a creature like her. [Exit.]

SCENE 3

FLAMINIA, SILVIA, PRINCE

FLAMINIA: A most impertinent creature!

SILVIA: I am outraged! I'm beginning to think they kidnapped me to make fun of me, each in his way. But isn't it clear that I'm worth all those women? I wouldn't change to be like them.

FLAMINIA: Well, her insults are just jealous compliments.

PRINCE: Dear Silvia, that woman deceived the Prince and myself. It makes me despair, I promise you. You know how much I respect you, you know how I feel. I came to have the pleasure of seeing you once more, to look on your dear face once more and to recognize you as mistress of my heart. But I must be careful not to betray myself. Flaminia's listening and I bore you.

FLAMINIA [*naturally*]: There's no harm in that. I know that to set eyes on her is to be captivated.

SILVIA: I wish for my part that he did not love me, for I am sorry not to be able to love him back. If only he were like other men whom one can treat as one likes. But he's too pleasant to be ill-treated. He's always been like that.

PRINCE: How kind you are! What can I do to deserve what you've just said but to love you always?

SILVIA: Well, you may love me! I will be happy as long as you promise to suffer patiently. I can do no better, honestly. Arlequin came first. That's all that hinders you. If I could have guessed that you would come later, I promise you, in good faith, that I would have waited. But you're unhappy and I am not happy either.

PRINCE: Flaminia, you judge: can one ever stop loving her? She is so compassionate, kind, generous. Oh, I confess, if another woman loved me it would mean less to me than Silvia's pity.

SILVIA: Flaminia, you judge, you've heard him. I confess I don't know how to act with a man who always thanks you and who takes kindly whatever you say to him.

FLAMINIA: Frankly, he's right. You are beautiful. If I were a man, I'd feel the same.

SILVIA: Oh don't say that! You'll only make him more tender. You don't have to tell him I'm beautiful; he thinks that enough.

[*To the* PRINCE.] Try to love me quietly and revenge me on that woman.

PRINCE: I will at once. For my part, however you treat me, I am yours. I will at least have the pleasure of loving you forever.

SILVIA: I didn't doubt you. I know you.

FLAMINIA: Go, Sir, hurry to tell the Prince of that woman's infamy. Everyone here must learn to respect Silvia.

PRINCE: You will soon have news. [*Exit.*]

SCENE 4

SILVIA, FLAMINIA

FLAMINIA: I'll go and get Arlequin, who seems to be detained at dinner a little too long, perhaps. Meanwhile you try on that dress they made you. I can't wait to see you in it.

SILVIA: The cloth is fine. It'll suit me. But I don't want all these fineries if the Prince wants me in exchange. We'll never conclude that bargain.

FLAMINIA: He isn't so crude. When he gives you up, you can take all this. Really, you don't know him.

SILVIA: I believe you. But I wouldn't like him to say afterwards: 'Why did you accept my presents?'

FLAMINIA: He'll say: 'Why did you not take more?'

SILVIA: Then I'll take as much as he wants to keep him quiet.

FLAMINIA: Go. I'll take care of everything.

[*Exit* SILVIA.]

SCENE 5

FLAMINIA

[ARLEQUIN, *laughing loudly, comes in with* TRIVELIN.]

FLAMINIA [*aside*]: Things begin to take shape. Here is Arlequin. To tell the strange truth, if the little man came to fall in love with me, I don't think I'd mind. I might even enjoy it.

ARLEQUIN [*laughing*]: Good afternoon, my dear friend.

FLAMINIA: Tell me why you are laughing so that I may laugh too.

ARLEQUIN: My butler Trivelin – I don't pay him, though – took me through all the halls and rooms of this palace where people trot about as if they were streets and gossip like in our market, but the master of the house doesn't seem to mind. They visit him but they never greet him and they watch him eat without his even saying, 'Have a drink.' I was having a great time when I saw a rogue lift up the back of a lady's dress. Well, I thought he was making advances to her and I told him straight: 'Stop that, you scoundrel, that's no way to behave.' She heard me and turned round to say, 'Don't you want him to carry my train?' 'Why should you have it carried?' I said. The rogue started to laugh and the lady started to as well. Then, Trivelin and everyone did, so I laughed, too, to keep them company. What, come to think of it, can you tell me, was I laughing at?

FLAMINIA: At a trifle. You don't know that what the flunkey did is a custom among ladies.

ARLEQUIN: Is it another mark of honour?

FLAMINIA: Oh, certainly!

ARLEQUIN: Well, I was right to laugh. It's a ridiculous way to pay one's respects. And cheap too.

FLAMINIA: I like to see you in high spirits. Did you eat well?

ARLEQUIN: Oh yes! What a magnificent cook! Such roasts! Such sauces! I can't resist his cooking. I drank to Silvia's health and to yours so much that if you're ill I'm not to blame.

FLAMINIA: What? You remembered me?

ARLEQUIN: When I make friends with someone I never forget it, especially not at table. Is Silvia still with her mother?

TRIVELIN: Ah, will you be thinking of Silvia forever, Sir Arlequin?

ARLEQUIN: Shut up when I speak.

FLAMINIA: You are wrong, Trivelin.

TRIVELIN: What? Me, wrong?

FLAMINIA: Why should he not speak of his love?

TRIVELIN: You seem to concern yourself greatly for the Prince's interests.

FLAMINIA [*feigns to be panic-stricken*]: Arlequin! This man will get me into trouble because of you.

ARLEQUIN [*angrily*]: No, my dear. [*To* TRIVELIN] Listen, I'm your master, since you told me so. I didn't know of it.

Scoundrel, if you turn into a sneak, a teller of bad tales, and you cause the slightest trouble to this dear girl, you'll lose both your ears. [*Grabbing his ears*] I guarantee them in my pocket.

TRIVELIN: I don't care – I want to do my duty.

ARLEQUIN: Both ears. Do you hear well – for now? Go away.

TRIVELIN: Yes, yes. You'll pay for this, Flaminia. [*Exit.*]

[ARLEQUIN *wheels about to rush upon him, but* FLAMINIA *stops him.*]

SCENE 6

ARLEQUIN, FLAMINIA

ARLEQUIN [*coming back*]: This is terrible. You're the only person here who speaks any sense and he comes to niggle in our conversation. My dear Flaminia, let's talk of Silvia now. When I'm not with her, you're the only person I care to be with.

FLAMINIA [*simply*]: I'm grateful. There's nothing I wouldn't do to make both of you happy. And you're so fine, Arlequin, that when you're hurt I suffer as much as you do.

ARLEQUIN: Aren't you sweet? Every time you pity me, it soothes me. And I'm much less upset to be sad.

FLAMINIA: Who wouldn't feel pity for you? Who wouldn't care for you? You underestimate yourself.

ARLEQUIN: Perhaps you're right, but I've never estimated myself closely.

FLAMINIA: If only I had some power ... if you could read my heart.

ARLEQUIN: Oh dear, I can't read but you'll explain it to me. Hell, I wish I could stop being upset, if only to stop upsetting you. But we'll manage.

FLAMINIA [*in a sad voice*]: No, I'll never witness your happiness, I'm afraid, Trivelin will report me. I'll be separated from you. And who knows where they'll take me. Arlequin, I'm speaking to you for the last time, perhaps, and there is no joy left in my world.

ARLEQUIN [*sadly*]: For the last time! I really don't have any luck. I only have one poor love and they've taken her away. And now they'll take you away. Where will I find the strength to bear it all? Do they think I've got a heart of iron? Do they mean to kill me? Are they so cruel?

FLAMINIA: In any case I hope you never forget your friend Flaminia who wanted nothing more than your happiness.

ARLEQUIN: You win my heart. Tell me what to do, my dear. What do you think we should do? I can never think when I'm unhappy. I must love Silvia. I mustn't let you go. I want neither my love nor my friendship to suffer. I'm so confused.

FLAMINIA: And I'm so unhappy. Since I lost my lover I've been happy only with you. I breathe with you. You're so like him that ... sometimes ... I think I'm speaking to him. I've not met anyone in the world as sweet as him – except you!

ARLEQUIN: There, there. I am sorry that I love Silvia. I would be happy to replace your lost lover. Was he handsome?

FLAMINIA: Didn't I tell you he was your image?

ARLEQUIN: And you loved him a lot?

FLAMINIA: Look at yourself, Arlequin. You'll see how much you deserve to be loved and you'll see how much I loved him!

ARLEQUIN: I've never known anyone as nice as you. Your friendship knows no bounds. I never thought myself as handsome as you say. But since you loved someone who was my image, I suppose the original must be worth something, too.

FLAMINIA: You would have delighted me even more but I wouldn't have thought myself pretty enough for you.

ARLEQUIN [*passionately*]: Oh heavens, I find you lovely to have that thought.

FLAMINIA: You trouble me and I must leave you. I find it too hard to tear myself away from you. But where will it lead us? Good-bye, I'll come back to you, if they let me. I just don't know where I am.

ARLEQUIN: I feel the same.

FLAMINIA: I take too much pleasure in seeing you.

ARLEQUIN: I won't refuse you that pleasure. I'll look at you and you can look at me.

FLAMINIA [*leaving*]: I daren't. Farewell. [Exit.]

ARLEQUIN [*watching* FLAMINIA *leave*]: This place doesn't deserve to breed a girl as good as her. If I lost Silvia by some misfortune ... I think, in my despair, I'd take her home with me.

SCENE 7

ARLEQUIN

[*Enter* TRIVELIN *with behind him a* LORD.]

TRIVELIN: Sir Arlequin, is it safe to reappear? Am I not risking my neck? You use your wooden sword mighty well.

ARLEQUIN: I will be kind if you are good.

TRIVELIN: A gentleman wants to speak to you. [*Withdraws.*]

[*The* LORD *approaches and makes bows, which* ARLEQUIN *returns.*]

ARLEQUIN [*aside*]: I know him from somewhere.

LORD: I come to ask you a favour. I hope I don't inconvenience you, Sir Arlequin.

ARLEQUIN: No, Sir, you neither please nor disturb me. [*Seeing the* LORD *put on his hat*] Only tell me, do I have to put my hat on?

LORD: Whether you do or not, you will still honour me.

ARLEQUIN [*putting it on*]: I believe you since you say it. What does your Lordiness desire of me? But please don't overwhelm me with compliments because I don't know how to return them.

LORD: Not compliments, my dear Sir, but tokens of my esteem.

ARLEQUIN: Humph! I know you, Sir. I saw you at the hunt, where you were playing the trumpet. I took my hat off to you but you didn't respond. You owed me that salute at least.

LORD: What, didn't I greet you?

ARLEQUIN: Not at all.

LORD: I failed to notice the glow of your honour.

ARLEQUIN: Oh yes, but you had no favour to ask of me then, that's why I didn't get greeted.

LORD: I don't remember.

ARLEQUIN: You didn't lose anything by it then! What is it you want?

LORD: I rely on your heart of gold. I had the misfortune to speak flippantly of you before the Prince.

ARLEQUIN: All you have to do is to 'not remember' that incident too.

LORD: Yes, but the Prince is angry with me.

ARLEQUIN: He dislikes slanderers?

LORD: As you see.

ARLEQUIN: I approve of that. He's a decent chap. If he didn't want to hang on to my mistress I'd be satisfied with him. And what did he tell you? That you were a cheeky fool?

LORD: Yes.

ARLEQUIN: That's very reasonable. What are you complaining about?

LORD: That's not all. 'Arlequin,' he said, 'is an honest lad. I want him to be honoured since I respect him. I wish that all of you had his frankness and his lack of affectation. I endanger his love and I am distressed that my love should force me to.'

ARLEQUIN [*moved*]: Really? By God, I'm his servant. I respect him for that. I thought I was more angry with him than I really am.

LORD: Then he dismissed me. My friends tried to appease him in my favour.

ARLEQUIN: If those friends of yours left with you it'd be no bad thing. Tell me who your friends are and I'll tell you who you are.

LORD: The Prince grew angry with them, too.

ARLEQUIN: May God bless this good man! He's rid his palace of a rotten bunch of people.

LORD: And we can only reappear at court if you plead for us.

ARLEQUIN: Really? Well, Sir, get your tickets! I wish you a good journey.

LORD: What? You refuse? But if you won't forgive me I'll be ruined. If I'm not allowed to see the Prince, what am I to do at court? I will have to return to my estates and live in exile.

ARLEQUIN: What? Is to be exiled just to be made to go home to eat off your own land? Isn't it worse?

LORD: No, it's just that.

ARLEQUIN: And you'll live peacefully and happily? You'll have four square meals a day as usual?

LORD: Of course. What's so strange about that?

ARLEQUIN: You're not deceiving me? You're sure that when one slanders one is exiled?

LORD: It happens quite often.

ARLEQUIN [*jumping for joy*]: Right! I'm going to slander the first man I see. And tell Silvia and Flaminia to do the same.

LORD: What for?

ARLEQUIN: Because I want to be exiled. From the way they punish you here, I think it's more worthwhile to be punished than rewarded.

LORD: Yes, perhaps, but please spare me such punishment. In any case what I said of you was nothing . . .

ARLEQUIN: What did you say?

LORD: It was a trifle, I tell you.

ARLEQUIN: Well? Come on!

LORD: I said you seemed a man without malice, honest, a man of good faith.

ARLEQUIN [*laughing*]: Yes, frankly, I look like a simpleton. So what? You look like a man of wit and I look like a simpleton. Well? Must one therefore always go by what we seem like? Did you say nothing else?

LORD: No, I only added that the moment you speak to anyone you make them laugh.

ARLEQUIN: They make me laugh when I speak to them. Tit for tat. Is that all?

LORD: Yes.

ARLEQUIN: It's ridiculous! You don't deserve the good luck to be exiled.

LORD: But I am, alas. Prevent it, please. A man like me can only live at court. I am esteemed and able to defend myself against my enemies only if I have access to the Prince. I have to win his favour and that of his advisers. They have to be cultivated.

ARLEQUIN: I'd rather cultivate a field. That produces something or other at least. I'm sure that people's friendship here is not easy to win and not easy to keep.

LORD: You're right in the end. They have unpleasant whims but you cannot resent it since they also have power. So you have to smile at them, flatter them, bribe them, because through them you can revenge yourself on others.

ARLEQUIN: What a deal! You get hit on one side to have the privilege of hitting out on the other. An extraordinary vanity! You all do so much creeping here that one wouldn't think you were so mighty.

LORD: We've been brought up to it. Listen, it would be so easy for you to win me the Prince's favour again. You know Flaminia?

ARLEQUIN: I am on intimate terms with her.

LORD: The Prince cares a great deal for her. She's the daughter of one of his officers. I hoped to make her fortune by marrying her to a rich ward of mine who lives in the country. Tell the Prince. My plan will restore me to his favour.

ARLEQUIN: But it won't restore you to mine. I don't like my friends to get married. Don't think of anything that involves your rich ward.

LORD: But I thought . . .

ARLEQUIN: Don't think any more.

LORD: I abandon my plan.

ARLEQUIN: Don't forget to. And I promise to speak to the Prince for you if we leave your rich ward out of it.

LORD: I will be most obliged to you. I await the result of your promises. Farewell, Sir Arlequin . . . [*Exit.*]

ARLEQUIN: I am your servant . . . Heavens, it seems I am well thought of . . . they do what I want. Not a word about the ward to Flaminia.

SCENE 8

ARLEQUIN

[*Enter* FLAMINIA.]

FLAMINIA [*arriving*]: My dear, I bring you Silvia. She's just coming.

ARLEQUIN: You should have warned me before, my friend, we could have chatted while waiting.

[SILVIA *arrives.*]

SCENE 9

SILVIA, ARLEQUIN, FLAMINIA

SILVIA: Arlequin, I've just tried on the most exquisite dress. You'd have thought me really pretty if you'd seen me. Ask

Flaminia. If I wore such clothes I'd soon show up the women here. They wouldn't say I was ungainly. The dressmakers here are so clever!

ARLEQUIN: Not as clever as you're beautiful, my love.

SILVIA: If I'm beautiful, you're just as honest.

FLAMINIA: At least, are you happier now? Do I have that pleasure at least?

SILVIA: Since they don't bother us any more, we might as well be here. It doesn't matter where we are. We love each other wherever we might be.

ARLEQUIN: They certainly don't bother us. They send lords to beg my forgiveness for having made fun of me.

SILVIA [*happily*]: I'm waiting for a lady to come and apologize to me for not having found me beautiful.

FLAMINIA: If either one of you is annoyed in future, you only have to come and tell me.

ARLEQUIN: Flaminia loves us both as brother and sister. [*To* FLAMINIA] And we love you in the same way.

SILVIA: Arlequin, guess who I met here! The palace officer who came to see me at home, that fine gentleman ... I would like you to be friends. He's got a good heart, too.

ARLEQUIN [*carelessly*]: Yes, of course, I agree.

SILVIA: After all, why shouldn't he love me? What harm is there in that? The people who love us are better company than those who don't care for us. Isn't it true?

FLAMINIA: No doubt.

ARLEQUIN [*gaily*]: And with Flaminia who loves us, we'll make a good foursome.

FLAMINIA: I won't forget that mark of friendship, Arlequin.

ARLEQUIN: Since we're together now ... let's go and eat. That's fun.

SILVIA: Go ahead, Arlequin. Since we can see each other now whenever we want, we don't have to cling to each other all the time. Don't restrain your appetite.

[ARLEQUIN *motions to* FLAMINIA *to follow him.*]

FLAMINIA: Well, I'll go with you since here is someone who will keep Silvia company.

[*Exeunt* FLAMINIA *and* ARLEQUIN.]

SCENE 10

SILVIA

[LISETTE *enters with several women as witnesses. She makes elaborate curtsies.*]

SILVIA [*touchily*]: There's no need for you to curtsey so much, Madam. I cannot return them gracefully, you say.

LISETTE [*subdued*]: They find you only too worthy here.

SILVIA: It will pass. I make no effort to please, as you see. I very much regret being so pretty and that you are not beautiful enough.

LISETTE: What a position to be in!

SILVIA: I, a little village girl, make you sigh. You must have nothing better to do. Where have you left your sharp tongue and claws, Madam? Have you no words when you must say something good?

LISETTE: I can't bring myself to speak.

SILVIA: Then don't break your silence. You can snivel all day long without ruining my face. Fine or not, my face will stay as it is. What do you want from me? Have you not insulted me enough? Would you like to add some more?

LISETTE: Spare me, Madam. My quarrel with you has put all my family in danger and difficulty. The Prince has ordered me to come and apologize. I ask you to accept my apology without mocking me.

SILVIA: There! I won't make fun of you. I know that fine gentlemen and ladies aren't given to being humble and it would be vicious to mock you, but you've made me feel spiteful. I'm sorry that you should find yourself embarrassed and I forgive you willingly. Tell me, why did you insult me?

LISETTE: I thought that the Prince had some affection for me and I did not think myself unworthy of it. But, alas, men do not always love charm or manners.

SILVIA [*angrily*]: No, they love plainness and dullness because they fall in love with me. Jealousy does warp the mind, doesn't it?

LISETTE: Well, yes, I am jealous, true. But since you don't love the Prince, help me regain that affection I thought he had for me. I certainly did not displease him, and, if you let me, I'm certain I could cure him of his desperate love for you.

SILVIA [*piqued*]: Believe me, you won't cure him. You are not up to it.

LISETTE: I think it quite possible. After all, I am not so ugly nor so ungraceful.

SILVIA: Come come, let's talk of something else. Your many virtues bore me.

LISETTE: A nice reply. In a few days, however, I assure you that I will show you how much power I have.

SILVIA [*sharply*]: Miracles do happen. I will speak to the Prince then. He has not yet dared address me because I am too angry. But I will tell him to pluck up courage just to see what happens.

LISETTE: Good-bye, each one of us will do her best – or worst. I have done what was expected of me. I have paid you my respects. I would ask you now to forget all that has gone between us.

SILVIA [*brusquely*]: Delighted. Get out! I don't even know you exist!

[*Exit* LISETTE.]

SCENE 11

SILVIA

[*Enter* FLAMINIA.]

FLAMINIA: What is the matter, Silvia? You seem angry?

SILVIA: I am furious. That woman who was impertinent to me came to beg my pardon. And without seeming to do anything she was so vicious that she made me even more angry. She said the Prince loved me because I was ugly and that she was more beautiful and more graceful than me. She said that she would make the Prince's love for me pass away, she would see to that and I would see ... and blah, blah. She made so many accusations against my looks – am I not right to be stung?

FLAMINIA [*hotly and interested*]: I swear that if you do not put all these wretched people to shame, you must never show your face again.

SILVIA: It's not that I don't have the will. But Arlequin hinders me.

FLAMINIA: Oh, I see. There is another passion that seems misplaced, it seems disproportionate.

SILVIA: Oh, I always have ill-luck with meetings.

FLAMINIA: But ... do you think Arlequin will be happy to see you leave court, ashamed and in disgrace?

SILVIA: You mean he would love me less?

FLAMINIA: There is reason to fear that.

SILVIA: That reminds me. Don't you find he has been a little casual since we've been here? He left as soon as he could to eat. A fine excuse.

FLAMINIA: I did notice that, but I hardly felt it right to say. You won't betray me but, in all confidence, woman to woman, do you love him that much?

SILVIA [*indifferently*]: Yes of course I love him, I have to.

FLAMINIA: Shall I be frank with you? You seem ill-matched to me. You have taste, intelligence, manners, distinction. He is crude and gross. Such disparities don't go together and I fail to see how you came to love him. I'd even say you demean yourself.

SILVIA: Put yourself in my place. He was the most eligible young man in my county. He lived in my village. He was my neighbour. He's bright enough and I'm good-humoured. He made me laugh sometimes, he followed me everywhere. I grew used to seeing him and, out of habit, I suppose, I came to love him. But I saw from the first that he had a tendency to eat and drink much too greedily.

FLAMINIA: Hardly the virtues for a lover of the lovely and lovable Silvia. But what have you decided?

SILVIA: I don't know yet. There's a proper whirl in my brain. I say yes – I say no – yes – no – yes – no – I don't know. I'm so confused. Arlequin has been more than casual here and thinks only of food. Then if I am sent away all these fine ladies will make everyone believe I was told: 'You weren't pretty enough; go away.' And then there's the guards officer I saw again.

FLAMINIA: What?

SILVIA: I tell you this secretly ... I don't know how he has affected me since I saw him last but he has always seemed so sweet, he has always used such tenderness towards me, he has always told me of his love so humbly and so politely that he has really touched me. I pity him, and this pity confuses me.

FLAMINIA: You love him?

SILVIA: I don't think so, since I must love Arlequin.

FLAMINIA: This gentleman is indeed worthy.

SILVIA: I know. I can feel that.

FLAMINIA: If you married him instead of the Prince, you would not be revenged on those ladies, but I would forgive you. Truly.

SILVIA: If Arlequin were to marry someone else, I could tell him, 'You left me, I'll leave you and we're quits,' but it's not possible. Who here would want to marry Arlequin? He's so gross and crude.

FLAMINIA: Between you and me, I've always liked the country and wanted to spend my life there. Arlequin is vulgar and, of course, I don't love him, but I don't hate him either. The way I feel at present, I could take him off your hands – if only to please you.

SILVIA: But what will please me? I want this and I want that. I really don't know what I want.

FLAMINIA: You will see the Prince today. Here is the gentleman you like so much. Farewell, we will meet again soon. [*Exit.*]

SCENE 12

SILVIA

[*Enter* PRINCE.]

SILVIA: You again, Sir? Have you come to tell me yet again that you love me, and make me all the more unhappy?

PRINCE: I came to see whether the lady who insulted you had come to ask your pardon properly. For my part, dear Silvia, when you grow tired of my love, when I displease you, you have only to command me to be silent and to leave you. I shall obey, I shall go wherever you wish, and I shall suffer without complaint, ready to obey you in all things.

SILVIA: There! Did I not say as much? How do you think I shall be able to send you away? You will be silent, if I wish, you will go away, if I wish; you will not dare complain, you will obey me in all things. That is the way to get me to command you!

PRINCE: But what more can I do than make you mistress of my fate?

SILVIA: What use is that? Shall I be the cause of your unhappiness? Have I the courage? If I say to you: 'Go away,' you will think that I hate you. If I ask you to be silent, you will think that I do not care for you. Neither would be true and they would cause you pain, and then how can I be content?

PRINCE: What do you want to become of me, beautiful Silvia?

SILVIA: What do I want? I am waiting to find out, for I know that even less than you. There is Arlequin who loves me, there is the Prince who demands my heart, and here you are, you who deserve it. I am surrounded by women who offend me and on whom I would like to be revenged, and I am the one who will suffer if I do not marry the Prince. Arlequin troubles me and you, too, trouble me, for you love me too much. I wish I had never known you, and my brain is in a whirl.

PRINCE: Your words touch my heart, Silvia. You are too much moved at my sorrow. My love, great though it is, is not worth the unhappiness you suffer because you cannot love me.

SILVIA: I could love you very easily; it would not be difficult, if I wished to.

PRINCE: Allow me then to be unhappy, and do not stop me regretting forever the loss of your love.

SILVIA [*impatiently*]: I warn you, I cannot bear to see you look upon me so tenderly. It's almost as if you do it on purpose. Is this any way to behave? I'm sure I would have much less trouble loving you than being the way I am. If it were up to me, I could give all this up.

PRINCE: For that reason I shall trouble you no longer; you want me to leave you, and I have not the right to resist the wishes of one who is so dear to me. Good-bye, Silvia.

SILVIA [*wildly*]: 'Good-bye, Silvia!' Now I shall grow angry; where are you going? Stay, it is my wish, and I understand it perhaps better than you do.

PRINCE: I thought I was doing as you wished.

SILVIA: What a mess! What is to be done with Arlequin? If at least you were the Prince.

PRINCE [*moved*]: And if I were?

SILVIA: That would be different, for then I would tell Arlequin that you had to have your will, and that would be my excuse; but only you could make me want to use such an excuse.

PRINCE [*aside*]: How adorable she is! It is time for me to tell her who I am.

SILVIA: What is the matter? Do I make you angry? It is not for the title that I would have you be the Prince, but solely for your own sake. If you were the Prince, Arlequin would not know that I gave you my hand in love; that is my reason. But no, it is better after all that you are not the Prince, for I would be too tempted then. If you were the Prince, I could hardly commit treason. That would be the end.

PRINCE [*aside*]: Let us wait a little before telling her the truth ... [*To her*] Silvia, only keep in your heart the kindness you show me now. The Prince has prepared an entertainment for you. Allow me to accompany you, and to enjoy a few more moments at your side. After the performance you will see the Prince, and I have been instructed to tell you that you will be free to refuse his hand, if your heart does not speak to you on his behalf.

SILVIA: Oh! My heart won't speak a word; it is as if I were already taking leave of the Court: but when I am at home you will come and see me; who knows what may happen? Perhaps I shall be yours. But let us not stay here – for fear Arlequin should surprise us.

ACT III

SCENE 1

PRINCE, FLAMINIA

FLAMINIA: Yes, my lord, you were wise not to reveal who you really were just then, despite all the tender words Silvia spoke to you. This delay spoils nothing and it will give her time to convince herself of her inclination for you. Thank heavens you have almost reached the point you wanted to reach.

PRINCE: Flaminia, she is so worthy of love.

FLAMINIA: Infinitely so.

PRINCE: I have never known any woman like her in all society. When love forces one's mistress to admit clearly, 'I love you,' it gives one, certainly, great pleasure. Well, Flaminia, that pleasure is paltry and boring compared to the pleasure Silvia's words gave me, even though she did not actually say, 'I love you.'

FLAMINIA: My lord, dare I ask you to repeat some of what she did say?

PRINCE: It's impossible. I am delighted; I am entranced. I can't begin to repeat it in any other way.

FLAMINIA: Such a remarkable record of the conversation lets me presume much.

PRINCE: 'If you knew, sir,' she said, 'how distressed I am not to be able to love you because that makes you unhappy. But I must stay faithful to Arlequin.' I saw the moment coming when she would say to me, 'Don't love me, please, because you would make me love you too.'

FLAMINIA: Good! That is better than a confession.

PRINCE: No, I tell you once more, the only true love is Silvia's. When other women love they still keep a refined air. They have had a particular kind of education and they cling to certain manners. All that serves to make them unnatural. With Silvia it is her heart, pure and simple, that speaks. She shows me her feelings as they come. Because she is naïve it is all art, and because she is so modest it is all comely. You must admit that all that is charming. Only her scruples about loving me without Arlequin's consent prevent her loving me now. So please hurry, Flaminia. Will you soon have conquered Arlequin? You know that I neither can, nor wish to, use violence against him. What does he say?

FLAMINIA: To tell you the truth, my lord, I think he is completely in love with me but he doesn't know it yet. He still calls me his dear *friend* and he thrives on the innocence of that word. But he takes our love for granted.

PRINCE: Excellent!

FLAMINIA: When I next talk to him, I will teach him the true nature of his feelings for me. I will use another device to make him recognize this incognito love of his. And, as we agreed, you will speak gently to him. Together, these two steps will end our worries, and my labours, which I will complete as victor – and vanquished.

PRINCE: Vanquished?

FLAMINIA: It's a trifle that doesn't deserve your attention. It's just that I have taken a fancy to Arlequin so as not to be bored during our intrigue. But we must withdraw and rejoin Silvia. Arlequin mustn't see you yet, and I can spot him coming.

[*They withdraw.*]

SCENE 2

TRIVELIN

[ARLEQUIN *enters, gloomily.*]

TRIVELIN [*after a pause*]: Well, what am I to do with the pen and paper you had me bring?

ARLEQUIN: Patience, my broomstick.

TRIVELIN: I'll have as much as you need.

ARLEQUIN: Tell me. Who feeds me here?

TRIVELIN: The Prince.

ARLEQUIN: The devil! His food's so good it gives me scruples.

TRIVELIN: Why?

ARLEQUIN: I'm afraid of finding out you have to pay in this hotel.

[TRIVELIN *laughs.*]

ARLEQUIN: What are you laughing about, you great oaf?

TRIVELIN: Your idea. It's so amusing. Don't fret, Sir Arlequin, eat and drink your fill in good conscience.

ARLEQUIN: By jove, I'm eating in good faith, so it'd be very rude to bring me a bill at the end. But I believe you. Tell me, now, what is the name of the fellow who deals with the Prince's affairs?

TRIVELIN: You mean his Secretary of State?

ARLEQUIN: Yes, I plan to write to him to inform the Prince that I am bored and to ask when he will be through with us. For my father is all alone.

TRIVELIN: And?

ARLEQUIN: If they want to keep me here, they'll have to send a carriage to get him.

TRIVELIN: You only have to speak and the carriage will be dispatched.

ARLEQUIN: Then, we must be married, Silvia and I, and someone has got to give me a key to the palace. Because it's my habit to trot about everywhere and to roam the fields. Then, we shall live here with our friend Flaminia who doesn't want to leave us because of her affection for us. And if the Prince still wants to feast us, I'm always happy to eat more.

TRIVELIN: But, Sir Arlequin, you don't have to involve Flaminia in all that.

ARLEQUIN: I want to.

TRIVELIN [*looks displeased*]: Hum.

ARLEQUIN [*mimicking*]: Hum! Wretched servant! Get your pen out and scribble out my letter.

TRIVELIN [*pen poised*]: Dictate.

ARLEQUIN: 'Sir.'

TRIVELIN: Stop. You must say, 'Your Excellency.'

ARLEQUIN: Put both – so he can choose.

TRIVELIN: Very well.

ARLEQUIN: 'You will know that I am called Arlequin.'

TRIVELIN: Easy does it! You should say: 'Your Highness will know.'

ARLEQUIN: 'Your Highness will know.' Is he a giant, this secretary?

TRIVELIN: No, but it doesn't matter.

ARLEQUIN: What a lot of nonsense. Whoever heard of addressing a person according to his height.

TRIVELIN [*writing*]: I will say as you wish. 'You will know that I am called Arlequin.' And then?

ARLEQUIN: 'That I have a mistress called Silvia, bourgeoise of my village and an honourable girl.'

TRIVELIN [*writing*]: Patience!

ARLEQUIN: '... and once you receive this, you will know that I have also a good friend made recently who doesn't know how to do without us and we don't without her...'

TRIVELIN [*stopping, pained*]: Flaminia doesn't know what to do without you? Ah, the pen drops from my hands.

ARLEQUIN: What is the meaning of this impertinence?

TRIVELIN: For two years, Sir Arlequin, I have pined in secret for her love.

ARLEQUIN [*drawing his stick*]: That's a pity, my friend. But while you're waiting to inform her of your secret, allow me to thank you for her!

TRIVELIN: I don't want to be thanked by being hit! I can do without such thanks! Anyway, what does it matter to you if I love her? You are only her friend, and friendship doesn't make for jealousy.

ARLEQUIN: You are wrong, my friendship is just like my love. Here's proof. [*He beats* TRIVELIN.]

TRIVELIN [*fleeing*]: Oh! The devil take your friendship!

SCENE 3

ARLEQUIN

[*Enter* FLAMINIA.]

FLAMINIA: What is it? What's the matter, Arlequin?

ARLEQUIN: Good day, my friend. That pest told me he has loved you for two years.

FLAMINIA: That's quite possible.

ARLEQUIN: And what do you say, my friend, to that?

FLAMINIA: That's too bad for him.

ARLEQUIN: Truly?

FLAMINIA: Without doubt. But would you be angry if someone did love me?

ARLEQUIN: Alas, you're your own mistress. But if someone loved you you might love him back. That would spoil the friendship you have for me and it would make it less. And I don't want to lose any of it.

FLAMINIA [*tenderly*]: Arlequin, you know, you don't consider my feelings much.

ARLEQUIN: Me? What have I done to hurt them?

FLAMINIA: If you keep on talking to me in this vein, I will soon be unsure of what my feelings for you really are. To tell you the truth, I dare not question myself on that point. I'm afraid of finding more than I should find.

ARLEQUIN: Well, don't question yourself, Flaminia. Things will be what they can be. Besides, believe me and don't take a lover. I have a mistress and I must keep her. If I didn't have one, I wouldn't look for one. With you, what need would I have of one? She'd bore me.

FLAMINIA: She'd bore you! How can I stay your friend after what you have just said?

ARLEQUIN: What else would you be?

FLAMINIA: Don't ask. I don't want to know. What I do know is that I love no one more than you in the whole world. You can't say as much. Silvia comes first, as is right.

ARLEQUIN: Hush, you go together, in fact. You both come first.

FLAMINIA: I wil send her to you. Will you be happy if I find Silvia for you?

ARLEQUIN: As you please. But don't send just her, you must both come.

FLAMINIA: I can't. The Prince has summoned me and I must see what he wants. Good-bye, Arlequin, I will be back soon.

[*She exits, smiling at the* LORD *who enters.*]

SCENE 4

ARLEQUIN

[*The* LORD *of Act II enters, with letters of nobility for* ARLEQUIN.]

ARLEQUIN [*seeing him*]: Ah, the gentleman! Sir Slander (I don't know your other name), I haven't said anything about you to the Prince for a good reason. I haven't seen him yet.

LORD: I thank you for your good will, Sir Arlequin. But I have come once more into the Prince's favour. I assured him that you would speak on my behalf and that restored my reputation. I hope you'll keep your word.

ARLEQUIN: I may seem a simpleton, but I'm honourable as well.

LORD: Please forget that incident! And I hope the gift I bring you from the Prince will make you forget the past. Of all possible gifts this is the greatest.

ARLEQUIN: Is it Silvia?

LORD: No, the gift is in my pocket. They are letters patent of nobility that the Prince bestows on you, for you are a relation of Silvia. Well, a kind of relation at any rate.

ARLEQUIN: Not at all. Take them away. I'd be dishonest to accept.

LORD: Accept them anyway. What does it matter why? The Prince will be happy if you accept. Would you refuse what is the greatest ambition of good-hearted men?

ARLEQUIN: I've a good heart and I've heard of ambition. But I've never seen it and I may have some without knowing it.

LORD: If you don't have any now, these will give you some.

ARLEQUIN: What is it, then?

LORD [*aside*]: What a question! [*To him*] Ambition is the noble pride one has to rise higher.

ARLEQUIN: A pride that's noble. Do you lot here give pretty names like that to every idiocy?

LORD: You don't understand. This pride only means a desire for glory.

ARLEQUIN: Good Lord, its meaning isn't any better than it is. It's black beard or beard black.

LORD: Take them, I tell you. Won't it please you to be a noble man?

ARLEQUIN: I won't be pleased or displeased. It'll depend on my mood.

LORD: You'll find it an advantage. Your neighbours will respect and fear you more.

ARLEQUIN: My opinion on that is that it'll stop them loving me nicely. When I respect people and when I fear them, I don't love them that much. I don't know how to do all those things at once.

LORD: You astonish me.

ARLEQUIN: That's the way I am. Anyway, you see, I'm the best creature in the world and I don't do anyone any harm. And when I want to, I haven't got the power. Well, if I had the power, if I were noble, Hell, I wouldn't bet I'd always be decent. Sometimes, I'd be like our local lord who doesn't spare us beatings because no one dares beat him back.

LORD: And if someone were to beat you, would you not be glad to be able to hit back?

ARLEQUIN: Yes, on that score, those are debts I like to repay at once!

LORD: Since men are evil sometimes, put yourself in a position where you can do evil – only so that no one dares do any evil to you. So, take your letters of nobility.

ARLEQUIN [*taking the letters*]: God, you're right. I'm stupid. There. Now I'm a noble. I keep the parchment. I'm afraid of no one now, apart from the rats who might gnaw my nobility up. I'll take good care of it. I thank you, Sir, and the Prince. He is very kind after all.

LORD: I'm glad to see you happy, Sir. Good-bye.

ARLEQUIN: I am your servant, Sir. [*Calls him back*] Sir, Sir.

LORD: What do you want?

ARLEQUIN: It doesn't oblige me to anything, my nobility? There are no strings, no duties?

LORD: Your duty is to be honourable.

ARLEQUIN [*very seriously*]: Were you exempted from that duty when you spoke ill of me?

LORD: You must forget that. A noble must be generous.

ARLEQUIN: Generous and honourable. Saints! They're fine duties. I find them nobler than my letters of nobility. And when one fails in them is one no longer noble?

LORD: Certainly not.

ARLEQUIN: Oh, then there are nobles who pay taxes.

LORD: I don't know how many.

ARLEQUIN: Is that all? No other duties.

LORD: No. But you, who, it seems, will be a favourite of the Prince, will have one extra duty: that of earning this favour, by pleasing the Prince, by respecting him, by submitting to his wishes and by obeying him always. Otherwise all you have to do is to be virtuous, to love honour more than your life and you'll be all right.

ARLEQUIN: Wait a minute. I don't like these last duties so much. First, explain to me – what's this honour I must love more than life? What honour?

LORD: You will approve of it. It means you must avenge an insult and die rather than suffer it.

ARLEQUIN: So all you told me was rubbish! You told me I had to be generous and forgive people. If I have to avenge myself I have to attack them. So how do I kill everyone and let them live?

LORD: You will be good and generous when no one insults you.

ARLEQUIN: I understand. I mustn't be better than others. And if I give good for evil and turn the other cheek, I'm not an honourable man. Mother of God! Evil isn't very rare and your recommendations aren't very original. Look, if I'm insulted, I return the insult as long as I'm stronger. Is that the message of your merchandise? Is that all you have to say?

LORD: To return an insult for an insult is insufficient. It can only be washed away by blood – your enemy's or your own.

ARLEQUIN: Then it can stay dirty. Blood isn't water, you know. Here! Have your packet of nobility back. My honour's too reasonable to be noble. Good day.

[*He gives the letters back.*]

LORD: You can't think of it.

ARLEQUIN: I can and I do.

LORD: Come on, keep them. You'll settle things with the Prince. No one will examine your honour too minutely.

ARLEQUIN [*taking them back*]: It'll have to be written in a contract ... I don't have to be killed by my enemy as revenge for an insult.

LORD: Yes, yes, they'll agree to that. Farewell: I am your humble servant.

ARLEQUIN: And I am yours.

[*Exit* LORD.]

SCENE 5

ARLEQUIN

[*Enter* PRINCE.]

ARLEQUIN [*seeing him*]: Who the devil is coming to see me now? Ah, the man whose fault it is they've taken Silvia from me! Here you are, Sir Babbler, who goes squeaking everywhere that other men's mistresses are beautiful. With the result that mine has been stolen from me.

PRINCE: No insults, Arlequin.

ARLEQUIN: Are you a noble then, you?

PRINCE: Certainly.

ARLEQUIN: Well, you're lucky, by God. If you weren't, I'd tell you in good faith what you deserve. But your honour might do its duty and then I'd have to kill you for you to be revenged.

PRINCE: Calm yourself, please, Arlequin. The Prince ordered me to speak to you.

ARLEQUIN: Well speak, you're free to. But I haven't been ordered to listen, I haven't.

PRINCE: You should take a gentler tone. Since it seems that you must, know me. I am your Prince. It is the Prince who speaks to you, not an officer of the palace as both you and Silvia have believed till now.

ARLEQUIN: Is this true?

PRINCE: You must believe me.

ARLEQUIN [*humbly*]: Forgive me, your Highness, I was a fool to be rude to you.

PRINCE: I forgive you willingly.

ARLEQUIN [*sadly*]: As you bear me no grudge, don't let me bear one against you. I'm not fit to be angry with a prince. I'm too small for that. If you hurt me, I shall weep with all my heart. And that will be all. That must make your might compassionate. You wouldn't want to rule the country just for your own pleasure.

PRINCE: You think you have reason to complain of me, then?

ARLEQUIN: What do you want, your Highness? I have one girl who loves me. You have a houseful of girls but, nevertheless, you want mine. Imagine that I am poor and my whole fortune is just a few coppers. You who are rich, with cellars of gold, attack my poverty and rob me of my few coppers. Isn't that sad?

PRINCE [*aside*]: He is right and his complaints touch me.

ARLEQUIN: I know that you are a good prince. Everyone in the country says so. I shall be the only one who shan't have the pleasure of saying so.

PRINCE: I deprive you of Silvia. That is true. But ask of me whatever else you wish. I offer you all the riches you could hope for but leave me just the only person I love.

ARLEQUIN: Let's not discuss that bargain, you'd gain too much out of it. Tell me, Sire, in conscience, if another man had taken her from me, would you not oblige him to return her to me? Well, no one but you has taken her! Isn't this a fine opportunity to show that justice applies to everyone?

PRINCE [*aside*]: What can I say to him?

ARLEQUIN: Say this, your Highness. 'Should I deny this little fellow his happiness because I have the power to do so? Should I not protect him just because I am his master? Should he leave without justice being done? Will I not regret it? Who will perform my duties as prince if I do not? So, I order myself to give Silvia back to him.'

PRINCE: Will you never change tack? See how I'm acting towards you. I could send you away and keep Silvia here without listening to you. Nevertheless, in spite of my love for her, and in spite of your obstinacy and your lack of respect for me, I concern myself for you. I try to assuage your pain with favours. I even go so far as to beg you to yield me Silvia of your own free will. Everyone exhorts you to do that, everyone reproaches you and everyone gives you constant examples of their desire to please me. You are the only one to rebel. You say I am your prince. Well, give me proof of that; show me some obedience.

ARLEQUIN [*sadly*] : Ah, your Highness, don't trust those people who always agree with you against me. They're deceiving you. And you take it for good money, their advice. There's no point in your being a good and honest man then, it doesn't give you any profit. Without those people, you wouldn't seek to harass me, you wouldn't say I lacked respect because I claim my rights. Yes, you are my prince and I like you very much. But I'm your subject and as such you owe me something as well!

PRINCE: You make me despair.

ARLEQUIN: I'm to be pitied.

PRINCE: Must I then renounce Silvia? How can I ever make her love me if you don't help me? Arlequin, I have hurt you but you are causing me even more cruel pain now.

ARLEQUIN: Console yourself, Sire! Why don't you travel a little? Your pain will pass on the roads.

PRINCE: No, my child. I hoped your heart would yield me something and I would have owed you more than I ever have to anyone. But you have done me all the harm that is possible to do me. Never mind, I had decided to honour you and your harshness will not prevent you enjoying my favours.

ARLEQUIN: Oh, how hard life is!

PRINCE: It is true that I have wronged you. I reproach myself for the way I treated you. It was unjust: but you have been more than well revenged.

ARLEQUIN: I must leave. You are too angry at having been wrong. I am afraid I might say you were right.

PRINCE: Now, it is just that you should be happy. You wanted justice. Be happy, now, at my expense.

ARLEQUIN: You have so much charity for me. Should I not have some for you?

PRINCE [*sadly*] : Don't be concerned for me.

ARLEQUIN: It's not easy. He looks so sad.

PRINCE [*patting his hand*] : I am grateful for your compassion. Farewell, Arlequin. I esteem you in spite of your refusal.

ARLEQUIN [*lets the* PRINCE *take a few steps away*] : Your Highness.

PRINCE: What do you want of me? That I should grant some favour?

ARLEQUIN: No! I just don't know if I should give you what you ask.

PRINCE: I must admit you have a generous heart.

ARLEQUIN: You too. That's what's taken my courage away. Alas, how weak good people are!

PRINCE: I admire your feelings.

ARLEQUIN: I should think so. But I promise you nothing. There's too much confusion in my soul. But, just in case, if I gave you Silvia, would I be your favourite?

PRINCE: Who else would be?

ARLEQUIN: It's just that I've been told you're in the habit of being flattered. Well, I'm in the habit of telling the truth, and a good habit like mine doesn't go with a bad one. Your friendship would never be strong enough to put up with mine.

PRINCE: We shall quarrel if you don't always tell me what you think. There's only one more thing to say. Arlequin, remember that I love you. That is all I ask you to remember.

ARLEQUIN: Could Flaminia be my mistress?

PRINCE: Don't speak to me of Flaminia. You could never have hurt me if it hadn't been for her.

ARLEQUIN [*to the* PRINCE *as he withdraws*]: Not at all, she's the best girl in the world. You shouldn't wish her any harm.

SCENE 6

ARLEQUIN, *alone*

ARLEQUIN: It seems that my wretch of a valet slandered my friend. I must go find her, by God. But what will I do now? Leave Silvia? Is that possible? How? No, no, certainly not. I was a little bit dishonest with the Prince because another person's pain always distresses me. But my pain will distress him so he won't say a word.

SCENE 7

ARLEQUIN

[*Enter* FLAMINIA, *looking sad.*]

ARLEQUIN: Flaminia, I was coming to look for you.

FLAMINIA [*sighing*] : Farewell, Arlequin.

ARLEQUIN: What do you mean? Farewell?

FLAMINIA: Trivelin has betrayed us. The Prince has learnt of our meetings and what is between us. He has just ordered me to leave here and never to see you again. But I could not stop myself coming to see you one last time. Then I shall flee to wherever I can avoid his anger.

ARLEQUIN [*surprised and disconcerted*] : Oh, I'm in a fine pickle now!

FLAMINIA: And I'm in despair. I'm to be separated from you for ever, separated from all I held most dear in the world. Time presses and I must leave you. But, before I go, I must unburden my heart.

ARLEQUIN [*breathing hard*] : Alas, my friend, what's the matter with your dear heart?

FLAMINIA: It was not friendship I felt for you, Arlequin. I deceived myself.

ARLEQUIN [*breathless*] : Was it love?

FLAMINIA: Very tender love. Farewell.

ARLEQUIN [*stopping her*] : Wait ... I may also have deceived myself.

FLAMINIA: What! You too were deceived? You love me and we are not to see each other again? Arlequin, don't speak another word. I'm going. [*She takes a couple of steps.*]

ARLEQUIN: Stop.

FLAMINIA: What for? What can we do?

ARLEQUIN: Let us be reasonable.

FLAMINIA: What should I say to you?

ARLEQUIN: My friendship has gone as far as yours. I love you. There, it's been decided and I don't understand it but there it is. Phew!

FLAMINIA: What an adventure!

ARLEQUIN: Luckily, I'm not married.

FLAMINIA: That's true.

ARLEQUIN: Silvia will marry the Prince and he'll be happy.
FLAMINIA: I have no doubt.
ARLEQUIN: Then, because our hearts were deceived, and we love each other by accident, we will be patient and make the necessary arrangements for the future.
FLAMINIA [*sweetly*]: I understand: you mean we'll get married.
ARLEQUIN: Yes. Is it my fault? Why didn't you warn me that you'd trap me and become my mistress?
FLAMINIA: Did you warn me you'd become my lover?
ARLEQUIN: Heavens, did I guess it?
FLAMINIA: You are lovable enough to have guessed it.
ARLEQUIN: We have no reason to reproach ourselves. If it's just a question of being lovable, then it's more your fault than mine.
FLAMINIA: Marry me! I consent. But there's no time to lose: I'm afraid that any minute someone will come to order me away.
ARLEQUIN [*sighing*]: I'll go and speak to the Prince! Don't tell Silvia that I love you. She would think I was in the wrong and you know that I am innocent. I will pretend that nothing has happened and that I am leaving her so that she can make her fortune.
FLAMINIA: Excellent – I was going to suggest just that.
ARLEQUIN: Wait, give me your hand to kiss. Who would have thought I should take so much pleasure in it? It confuses me. [*Exit.*]

SCENE 8

FLAMINIA

FLAMINIA [*aside*]: The Prince is quite right. These little rustics make love most exquisitely. One cannot resist them. Here is the other one:

[*Enter* SILVIA.]

What are you dreaming of, my dear Silvia?

SILVIA: I'm dreaming of myself and I just don't understand myself.
FLAMINIA: What do you find so incomprehensible in yourself?

SILVIA: I wanted to be revenged on those women. You knew that? Well, that passed.

FLAMINIA: You're not that vindictive.

SILVIA: I loved Arlequin, did I not?

FLAMINIA: It seemed so to me.

SILVIA: Well, I think I love him no more.

FLAMINIA: That's not such a catastrophe.

SILVIA: And if it were, what could I do about it? When I loved him it was a love that came to me. And now that love has gone away. I'm no more responsible for its departure than I was for its arrival. I don't think it's my fault.

FLAMINIA [*aside*]: It deserves a smile. Love for love. [To SILVIA] I agree with you more or less.

SILVIA [*hotly*]: What do you mean, more or less? You must agree entirely with me because that's how things have turned out.

FLAMINIA: Why are you so angry?

SILVIA: For good cause. I seek your advice in good faith and you torture me with 'more or less'.

FLAMINIA: I was only teasing you, don't you see? You are only to be praised for your decision. But who is it you love now? The royal guards officer?

SILVIA: Who else? But I still cannot consent to love him. But, finally, I shall have to. One cannot always say 'no' to a man who always begs for 'yes'! I cannot bear to see him always sad, always pitying himself, and I cannot bear to have to console him for the pain I cause him. It becomes tedious. Better not to cause him such pain.

FLAMINIA: You will charm him. He'll die of joy.

SILVIA: He'd die of sadness otherwise, and that's still worse.

FLAMINIA: There's no comparison.

SILVIA: I am waiting for him. We spent two hours together and he will come back to be with me when the Prince speaks to me. However, sometimes I'm afraid Arlequin will suffer too much. What do you think? Only, please don't make me think of my duty.

FLAMINIA: You have no need to worry about Arlequin. He will be easily consoled.

SILVIA [*looking a bit worried*]: Easily! Am I worth so little then? Heavens! Am I so easy to forget? Has he another mistress here?

FLAMINIA: No, no, no, he could never forget you. I would be mad to say that. You will be fortunate if he doesn't despair.

SILVIA: You shouldn't tell me such things – I will have doubts again with your despair.

FLAMINIA: And if I were to tell you that he loves you no more?

SILVIA: If you were to tell me that, you'd best keep quiet.

FLAMINIA: Well, then, if you must, he loves you still and that annoys you. What do you want?

SILVIA: You're laughing! I'd like to see you in my place.

FLAMINIA: Your lover is looking for you. Believe me, conclude with him – and you don't have to worry. [*Exit.*]

SCENE 9

SILVIA

[*Enter* PRINCE *as a royal guardsman.*]

PRINCE: What? My dear Silvia, you don't look at me? You become sad each time I come to you. I am always sad to think I annoy you.

SILVIA: Annoy me? I was speaking of you just now.

PRINCE: You spoke of me? And what did you say, lovely Silvia?

SILVIA: Oh, I said many things. I said you did not know yet what I thought.

PRINCE: I know you are determined to deny me your love. And to know that is to know your thoughts.

SILVIA: You're not as clever as you think, so you need not boast so much. But, tell me, you are an honourable man and I'm sure you will tell me the truth. You know I'm promised to Arlequin. And now imagine that I would care to love you. But suppose I indulged my wish ... Would I be good or wicked? Advise me in good faith.

PRINCE: One is not master of one's heart. If you want to love me, you have the right to. That is my opinion.

SILVIA: Do you speak as my friend?

PRINCE: Yes, Silvia, I speak sincerely.

SILVIA: I agree with you. I have decided to love you, and we are both right, I think. And so, if I want to, I will love you and no one can grumble at it.

PRINCE: I gain nothing, for you do not want to.

SILVIA: How do you know? You have no business to guess. I owe you nothing. And what of this Prince? Since I must see him, when is he going to come?

PRINCE: Only too soon for me. Perhaps when you know him better you will love me no more.

SILVIA: You must be brave. You must not start trembling now. I think you're resolved never to be happy, not once.

PRINCE: I confess I am afraid.

SILVIA: What sort of a man! I have to give him courage. Don't fret, I promise. I will never love the Prince. I'm ready to swear by . . .

PRINCE: No, Silvia, no. No oaths. I beg you.

SILVIA: You won't have me swear. I like that. It shows good breeding.

PRINCE: Should I let you swear against myself?

SILVIA: Against you? Is it you who are the Prince?

PRINCE: Yes, Silvia. Till now I have tried to hide my true rank from you so that I would owe your love only to my love. I did not wish to lose the pleasure of that. But now that you know me, you are free to take my hand and my heart or to refuse them both. Speak, Silvia.

SILVIA: Oh, my dear Prince, I was going to make a fine oath. If you sought the pleasure of being loved by me, you have found what you sought. You know I speak the truth and that it delights me.

PRINCE: Our marriage, then, is certain.

SCENE 10

ARLEQUIN, FLAMINIA, PRINCE, SILVIA

ARLEQUIN: I heard it all, Silvia.

SILVIA: Then I won't have to repeat any of it to you, Arlequin. Console yourself as best you can. The Prince will speak to you more, I'm too emotional. Look, you must get used to it. It's true that there's no more point in reasoning with me. What would you say to me? That I'm leaving you. What would I say? That I know that. Let us pretend you have spoken and I have replied and there's an end of it.

PRINCE: Flaminia, I place Arlequin in your charge. I esteem him and will shower him with rewards. You, Arlequin, accept Flaminia from me to be your wife and be always assured of your Prince's blessing. And my beautiful Silvia, will you allow us to start the celebrations which have been prepared so that some of my subjects whose queen you are about to become can know my joy?

ARLEQUIN: Now, I can laugh at the trick which our friendship has played on us. Patience. Soon, we may turn the tables.

THE GAME OF LOVE AND CHANCE

(Le Jeu de l'amour et du hasard)

Dorante
Silvia
Arlequin
Lisette
Mario, Silvia's *brother*
Orgon, Silvia's *father*
Servants

Paris, 1730

ACT I

SCENE 1

SILVIA, LISETTE

SILVIA: But, tell me once again! What right had you to interfere? Why did you answer for my feelings?

LISETTE: Because I thought your feelings, in this case, would be like those of everyone else. Your father asked me if you were glad he was arranging your marriage. Did it please you? Well, I answered 'yes', it goes without saying. But you are perhaps the only woman alive for whom to say that 'yes' is untrue. To say 'no' is unnatural.

SILVIA: 'No' is unnatural! You are very simple, Lisette. Marriage has great attractions for you, then?

LISETTE: Well, that's another 'yes'!

SILVIA: Oh, keep quiet! Go and victimize someone else with your stupidities. Remember that it is not for you to judge my heart. It is not like yours.

LISETTE: My heart is like everyone else's. Why should yours contrive to be so original?

SILVIA: I tell you, if she dared, she would call me perverse and eccentric.

LISETTE: If I were your equal, we should see.

SILVIA: You are doing your best to make me angry, Lisette.

LISETTE: I don't mean to. But, tell me, what real harm did I do by telling M. Orgon you were glad he was arranging your marriage?

SILVIA: First, what you said was not true. I am not bored with being single.

LISETTE: That's also quite original.

SILVIA: And then my father need not think he is pleasing me so much with this marriage. It makes him act with too much confidence, which may, after all, come to nothing.

LISETTE: What? You might not marry the man he's chosen for you?

SILVIA: Who knows? He may not suit me. And that worries me.

LISETTE: They say that your future husband is one of the most eligible young men alive, that he is charming, attractive, handsome. No man, they say, has more wit, no man has a better character. What more do you want? Can you imagine a happier marriage, a more delicious union?

SILVIA: Delicious! You're mad with your phrases.

LISETTE: Honestly, madam, you're fortunate that a lover with all these qualities is willing to be married formally at all. There are few girls, if he were to woo them, who wouldn't be in danger of getting married without ceremony, church or law. He's handsome and charming – there's fire to kindle love. He's witty and good company – what better companion could you have? Everything about him sounds good. He combines all pleasant and useful qualities.

SILVIA: Yes, as you depict him. They say that he is like that. They say – it is only rumour. I may think otherwise. They say that he is handsome. It is almost a pity.

LISETTE: A pity! A pity! There's an extraordinary idea.

SILVIA: A very sensible one, Lisette. I have noticed that handsome men are often vain.

LISETTE: Oh, he is wrong to be vain but right to be handsome.

SILVIA: It's also said that he has a fine body. But never mind that.

LISETTE: Oh yes, one can forgive him that.

SILVIA: I can do without charm and good looks. In a husband, they are superfluous.

LISETTE: Heavens! If I ever marry, I'll need those superfluities.

SILVIA: You don't know what you're saying. In marriage, it is better to have a reasonable than a charming man. In short, I only want him to have a good temper, and that's more difficult to find than you think. Everyone praises this man, but who has lived with him? Don't men often assume a certain role, especially of they have brains? Have I not seen men who seemed to be the nicest in the world – with their friends? They are all kindness, reason, charm. Their faces seem to guarantee their good qualities. 'Mr So-and-so . . . looks every inch a gentleman . . . he looks so reasonable.' ... People said that of Ergaste every day. 'And so he is,' everyone replied. I have said so myself: 'You can see it in his face.' Well, you can believe in this sweet, gentle, trustworthy face, but it disappears in private. A quarter of an hour later, in his own home, Ergaste has a brooding, brutal face which is the terror of his whole house. Ergaste is married. His wife, his children and his servants only see this second face while we, in public, are treated to the sweet face we know so well. It's a mask he puts on when he leaves home.

LISETTE: Two faces! What an eccentric!

SILVIA: Well, aren't we pleased to see Leandre? At home he is silent. He never laughs, he never scolds. He is a cold, solitary, inaccessible creature. His wife doesn't know him since he will have nothing to do with her. She is married to a statue who locks himself in his study. He comes out to meals and he destroys all around him with his boredom, misery and coldness. Doesn't that make an amusing husband?

LISETTE: Your description gives me the shivers. What about Tersandre?

SILVIA: Oh, yes, Tersandre. The other day he had just quarrelled with his wife. I arrive. I am announced. I see a man come towards me with open arms, relaxed and serene. You would have thought he had just left the most flippant conversation. His mouth and his eyes were still smiling. What a hypocrite! That's what men are like. Who would believe his wife is to be pitied? I found her quite downcast, her face white and tense. She had just been crying. I found her as I shall be, perhaps. Anyhow, I run the risk of being her copy. She was a portrait of my future. I pitied her, Lisette. What if you were to come to pity me! It would be terrible. Just think. Think what a husband might be.

LISETTE: A husband is still a husband. You shouldn't have finished on that word. It reconciles me to all the rest.

SCENE 2

ORGON, SILVIA, LISETTE

ORGON: Good morning, my child. Will the news I have please you? Your intended is coming today. His father informs me of the fact in this letter. What? You have nothing to say? You look sad? Lisette looks down. What does this mean? Tell me, Lisette, what is the matter?

LISETTE: Oh, Sir, it's all a matter of a face which makes one shudder, then another face that kills all joy, a frozen soul who keeps himself aloof in his study, then there is the portrait of a lady who is quite downcast, her face white and tense and her eyes puffy because she's just been crying. That, Sir, is what we have been considering with such attention.

ORGON: What is all this nonsense? A portrait? A soul? Is it a riddle? Explain yourself... I don't understand a word.

SILVIA: I was only telling Lisette how wretched a woman is when she is ill-treated by her husband. I mentioned Tersandre's wife, whom I found quite downcast the other day because her husband had just yelled at her. I was reflecting on the subject. That is all.

LISETTE: Yes, we were speaking of a changeable face. We were saying that a husband wears a mask for the world and a frown for his wife.

ORGON: From which, dear child, I infer that the prospect of marriage frightens you. Especially since you do not know Dorante.

LISETTE: First, it seems that he is handsome and that is almost a pity.

ORGON: A pity? Are you mad with your pity?

LISETTE: I am only repeating my lessons, Sir. This is madam's doctrine. I study at her feet.

ORGON: Come, come, there is no need for all this. My dear child, you know how much I love you. Dorante comes to marry you. On my last visit to the provinces, I arranged this match with his father who is an old companion and friend of mine. But we agreed that there should be a condition – that you and he should please each other. We also agreed that you should have complete freedom to decide. I forbid your mere obedience or respect for my choice. If Dorante does not suit you, you have only to say. He will go. If you do not suit him, he will do the same.

LISETTE: It will be operatic. We shall either have a tender duet: 'I love you.' 'I love you.' Quick – a priest. Or: 'I don't love you.' 'I don't love you.' Quick – to horse.

ORGON: I have never seen Dorante. He was away when I was at his father's. But everyone spoke so well of him that I will be very surprised if you do not make a good match.

SILVIA: You are very kind. You forbid me mere obedience. I shall obey you.

ORGON: I command you to.

SILVIA: But, if I dared, I would tell you of an idea I have had just now. Will you grant me a favour that would set my mind completely at rest?

ORGON: Speak – if I can, I will do it.

SILVIA: You can do it easily. But I am afraid that it would be to abuse your kindness.

ORGON: Well, abuse it. In this world we must be a little too good to be good enough.

LISETTE: Only the best of men would say that.

ORGON: Explain your idea, my child.

SILVIA: Dorante is coming today. If I could see him and observe him a little without his knowing me. Lisette is no fool. For a little while, she could take my place and I could take hers.

ORGON [*aside*]: Amusing idea. [*To her*] Let me think a little, my dear ... [*Aside*] If I let her do what she wants, something quite amazing should happen. It will be very interesting, especially as she won't expect it. [*To her*] Very well, my dear, you may disguise yourself. Lisette, are you sure that you will be able to play your part?

LISETTE: I, Sir? You know who I am. Try to make love to me, Sir, or to lack respect to this haughty face, try, Sir, if you dare. There is a sample of the refinement I shall meet you with. What do you think? Do you recognize Lisette?

ORGON: Never! I am myself actually deceived. But there is no time to lose. Go and dress as befits your roles. Dorante might surprise us. Hurry and tell the whole house of our little scheme!

SILVIA: I only need an apron.

LISETTE: I shall go to my toilette. Lisette, come and do my

hair, you must get used to your duties. And pay attention to your duties, girl, you are too slack.

SILVIA: I'll satisfy you, duchess. Come on.

SCENE 3

MARIO, ORGON, SILVIA

MARIO: My darling sister, congratulations. I gather we are to see your lover.

SILVIA: Yes, dear brother. But I have no time now to explain. I have serious matters to attend to. Father will explain. Good-bye.

[*Exeunt* SILVIA *and* LISETTE.]

SCENE 4

ORGON, MARIO

ORGON: Do not detain her, Mario. Come, and I will tell you what is happening.

MARIO: What news, Sir?

ORGON: I will begin by warning you to be discreet. You must not repeat what I am going to tell you.

MARIO: I shall obey your orders.

ORGON: We shall see Dorante today but we shall see him in disguise.

MARIO: In disguise? Are you giving a masked ball in his honour?

ORGON: Listen to this part of his father's letter. Hum . . . 'But I have no idea what you will think of a fancy that has taken my son. He himself agrees that it is strange. But the reasons for it are understandable and even delicate. He has asked me to allow him to first arrive at your home disguised as his valet who, for his part, will take on the role of his master.'

MARIO: That should be amusing.

ORGON: Listen to the rest: 'My son knows how serious is the course he has embarked upon. He hopes, he says, during this brief period in disguise, to be able to observe his intended and to get to know her better. He will find it easier then to decide what to do in view of the free choice we agreed to give them. I consented, bearing in mind all you told me of your charming daughter, and take here the precaution of informing you of this plan although he did ask me to keep it secret. You will act as you see fit vis-à-vis your daughter . . .' So much for his father. But that, my dear son, is not all. Your sister, anxious on her part about Dorante's real character, and ignorant of his secret, has asked me permission to play the same game. She also wants to be able to observe Dorante just as Dorante wants to observe her. What do you say to that? Have you ever heard of anything more remarkable? At the moment, the mistress and the maid are changing places. What do you advise, Mario? Should I tell your sister?

MARIO: Well, Sir, since matters have taken this course I should leave them be. I would respect their mutual whim. They will have to meet and speak often in their disguises. Let us see if their hearts tell them what the other is really worth. Perhaps Dorante will take a fancy to my sister, even though she is a maid, and that would be delightful for her.

ORGON: We shall see how she gets out of that predicament.

MARIO: It cannot fail to be very amusing. I must be there when they first meet – to annoy them both.

SCENE 5

SILVIA, ORGON, MARIO

SILVIA: Here I am, Sir. Do I look like an incompetent maid? Don't you think I have style? You seem to know what is happening, Mario. What do you think of me?

MARIO: Frankly, the valet is as good as captured. But you may also lure Dorante away from his mistress.

SILVIA: Frankly, brother, I should not mind pleasing him in the part I play. I would not be sorry to make him mad with love and to make him fret because of our differences in rank. If I am attractive enough to achieve that, I shall not be displeased with my charms. I will respect them. And it will help me to know

Dorante! As for his valet, I'm not afraid of his advances. He will not dare approach me. There will be something in my manner that demands respect rather than love from that rascal.

MARIO: Tut, sister, that rascal will be your equal.

ORGON: And will undoubtedly fall in love with you.

SILVIA: I shall make use of that honour, then. Valets are naturally indiscreet, love makes men talk, and so I shall make him tell me the history of his master.

[*Enter valet.*]

VALET: Sir, there is a servant at the door who asks to speak with you. There is a porter with him carrying a bag.

ORGON: Bring him in.

[*Exit valet.*]

It must be Dorante's valet. His master must have been delayed by business. Where is Lisette?

SILVIA: Lisette is dressing. She has decided, in front of her mirror, that we are reckless to yield her Dorante. She will be ready soon.

ORGON: Quiet . . . someone is coming.

SCENE 6

ORGON, SILVIA, MARIO

[*Enter* DORANTE, *dressed as a valet.*]

DORANTE: I am looking for M. Orgon. Is it to him I have the honour to bow?

ORGON: Yes, my good fellow, to his very self.

DORANTE: Sir, you have doubtless received news of us. I am in M. Dorante's service. He is coming shortly and has sent me ahead to assure you of his respects till he can pay them in person.

ORGON: You have acquitted yourself well, young man. Lisette, what do you say of this young man?

SILVIA: I say that he is welcome. He is promising.

DORANTE: You are very kind. I do my best.

MARIO: He is certainly handsome. Lisette, you had better guard your heart.

SILVIA: My heart! What is that to do with him?

DORANTE: Please do not be angry, Miss. What the gentleman says does not fool me.

SILVIA: Good. Your modesty pleases me. You should persevere in it.

MARIO: Oh yes, but I don't think he should call you 'Miss'. There should be few formalities between servants. The lower classes should not be so sensitive on matters of style. Christian names will do. Her name is Lisette and you, my boy, what is your name?

DORANTE: Bourguignon, Sir, at your service.

SILVIA: Well, Bourguignon let it be, then.

DORANTE: Well, Lisette let it be, then. I will still be your servant.

MARIO: Tut-tut, my man, a servant's servant.

ORGON: Ha! Ha! Ha!

SILVIA [*low to* MARIO]: Stop teasing me, brother.

DORANTE: I await your orders, Lisette, as to how formally to address you.

SILVIA: Call me what you please, Bourguignon. There, now the ice is broken just to please these gentlemen.

DORANTE: Thank you, Lisette. As you see, I don't waste any time in returning the honour you've done me.

ORGON: Soon they will be cooing not only Christian names but little words of love.

MARIO: Oh, not so fast, please. Little words of love are quite another thing. You may not know that I mean to win Lisette's heart. She does not love me yet but I do not want Bourguignon as a rival.

SILVIA: Oh, you take that attitude, do you? Well, I want him to love me.

DORANTE: You are wrong to say 'want'. You need not give orders to be obeyed.

MARIO: Come, Bourguignon, you filched that gallantry somewhere.

DORANTE: You are right, Sir. I took it from her eyes.

MARIO: Keep quiet, that's worse yet. I forbid you so much wit.

SILVIA: It isn't at your expense. If he found it in my eyes he has only to take it from there.

ORGON: My boy, you will lose your suit. Let us go tell my

daughter that Dorante is coming. Lisette, will you show this boy his master's rooms. Good-bye, Bourguignon.

DORANTE: You do me too much honour, Sir.

SCENE 7

SILVIA, DORANTE

SILVIA [*aside*]: They are laughing at me. Never mind. I will make use of everything. This young man is no fool and I do not pity the maid who will have him. I can see he is going to make love to me. Let him, as long as he tells me about his master.

DORANTE [*aside*]: This girl amazes me. There is not a woman in the world who would not be proud of such a face. I must know her better. [*To her*] Since we are on such friendly terms and have put formalities aside, tell me, Lisette, is your mistress worthy of you? She must be bold to dare to have a maid like you.

SILVIA: Bourguignon, that question tells me that you have come with the intention of cooing sweet words at me, as is the custom. Am I not right?

DORANTE: I came with no such intention, I assure you. I may be a valet but I have had few entanglements with chambermaids. I have no great liking for their company or attitudes. But with you it is quite different. You subdue me, I am almost timid. I would not dare be familiar with you. I have a constant desire to take off my hat, and when I call you by your first name it sounds to me as if I am swearing. I have an inclination, a whim, to treat you with such respect that it would make you laugh. What kind of maid are you with your princess's air?

SILVIA: What you say you feel on seeing me is precisely what all valets have felt.

DORANTE: I would not be surprised if all masters felt the same, too.

SILVIA: It is a pretty compliment, I grant you. But, I repeat, I am not used to receiving advances from men whose wardrobe is like yours.

DORANTE: That means you do not like my clothes.

SILVIA: No, Bourguignon. Let us forget about love and be good friends.

DORANTE: Only that? Your little treaty consists of two impossible clauses.

SILVIA [*aside*]: What a man for a valet! [*To him*] Nevertheless, my treaty will have to be kept. It has been predicted that I should marry none but a man of quality. I have since then vowed not to give the others a chance.

DORANTE: What a coincidence! I have made the same vow as far as women go. And I have vowed to love none seriously but a lady of quality.

SILVIA: Then please don't stray from your plan.

DORANTE: I may not be going so far astray. You seem very distinguished. People can sometimes be of quality without knowing it.

SILVIA: I'd thank you for the compliment if it weren't at my mother's expense.

DORANTE: Well, revenge yourself on mine – if you think me good enough for that.

SILVIA [*aside*]: He would deserve it. [*To him*] But there's no question of that. Let's call a halt to all this banter. A man of quality has been predicted as my husband and I will not take less.

DORANTE: Heavens, if I were one, the prophecy would be a threat. I might make it come true. I have no faith in astrology but I have a great deal in your face.

SILVIA [*aside*]: He is inexhaustible. [*To him*] Will you please desist? What is the prophecy to you since it excludes you?

DORANTE: It did not say I should not love you.

SILVIA: But it did say you would gain nothing by such love, and I confirm it.

DORANTE: You do well, Lisette. Such pride suits you wonderfully. Though it hinders me, I am glad to see it in you. From the moment I saw you I hoped you might have it, as if you did not have enough charms. And if I lose by it, it is some consolation to me that you should gain.

SILVIA [*aside*]: He really does surprise me, against my will. [*To him*] Tell me, who are you, that speak to me thus?

DORANTE: The son of good people who were not rich.

SILVIA: Look, I wish with all my heart that you were in a better position than you are and I wish that I could help you to one. Fortune has used you ill.

DORANTE: Love has used me worse. I would rather be able to ask you for your love than to have all the riches on earth.

SILVIA [*aside*]: Thank heaven we are back in a formal conversation. [*To him*] Bourguignon, I cannot be angry with you for what you have just said. But, I beg of you, let us change the subject. Let us speak of our masters. You can stop yourself talking love to me, I suppose?

DORANTE: You can stop making me feel love, I suppose?

SILVIA: You will start annoying me. I shall become impatient. Once again, my friend, let us leave your love behind us.

DORANTE: Then, you leave your face behind.

SILVIA [*aside*]: In the end I will think he's only teasing me. [*To him*] Well, Bourguignon, will you not conclude and leave it at that. Do I have to go? [*Aside*] I should have done so already.

DORANTE: Wait, Lisette, I too wanted to speak to you of something else but I have forgotten what it was.

SILVIA: I also had something to say to you but you have made me lose the thread of my thoughts.

DORANTE: I remember asking you if your mistress was worthy of you.

SILVIA: You are coming back to the point you started from. Good-bye.

DORANTE: I promise you, Lisette, I only want to speak of my master.

SILVIA: Fine, I wanted to speak of him as well. I hope you will tell me in confidence what kind of man he is. That you are his servant speaks well of him. He must be distinguished for you to be his servant.

DORANTE: Will you let me thank you for what you just said?

SILVIA: Will you be good enough to ignore my recklessness in saying it?

DORANTE: Must your replies always tantalize me? Do as you wish, I shall not resist your will. I am sad indeed to be detained by the loveliest woman alive.

SILVIA: And I would like to know how it is that I am still here. It is very curious that I should have the kindness to listen to you all this while.

DORANTE: You are right, our experience is unique.

SILVIA [*aside*]: In spite of all that he has said I have not gone. I am not going, I am still here and I am replying to him. This is more than ridiculous. [*To* DORANTE] Good-bye.

DORANTE: Let's finish what we wanted to say.

SILVIA: Good-bye, I say. I will indulge you no more. When your master comes I will try, for the sake of my mistress, to get to know him myself – if he is worth the trouble. Meanwhile, the rooms through there are yours.

DORANTE: Here is my master.

SCENE 8

DORANTE, SILVIA

[*Enter* ARLEQUIN.]

ARLEQUIN: There you are, Bourguignon! Were you and my other baggage well-received?

DORANTE: They could not receive us badly, Sir.

ARLEQUIN: A servant out there told me to come in. He said he would tell my father-in-law, who was with my wife, I've arrived.

SILVIA: No doubt, you mean M. Orgon and his daughter?

ARLEQUIN: That's right. My father-in-law and my wife, as good as. I've come to get married and they're waiting for me to marry her. It's all been agreed. We just need the ceremony and that's a mere trifle.

SILVIA: It's a trifle well worth thinking about.

ARLEQUIN: But once one's thought about it, one can forget it.

SILVIA [*low to* DORANTE]: It seems to me that one is a person of quality rather cheaply in your parts.

ARLEQUIN: What are you saying to my man, my dear?

SILVIA: Oh nothing, just that we should fetch M. Orgon.

ARLEQUIN: And why not call him my father-in-law, like I do?

SILVIA: Because he is not your father-in-law yet.

DORANTE: She is right, Sir. The wedding has yet to happen.

ARLEQUIN: Here I am to make it happen.

DORANTE: Wait until it has happened...

ARLEQUIN: Heavens, those are a lot of shenanigans... what is the difference if I call him father-in-law today or tomorrow?

SILVIA: The difference, Sir, is the same as that between being married and not being married. Wouldn't you say? No, you probably wouldn't. You're right, Sir, we are wrong and I will rush to fetch your father-in-law.

ARLEQUIN: And my wife, too, please. But before you go, little maid, tell me something... you are the little maid here?

SILVIA: As you say... I am the little maid.

ARLEQUIN: Good... I'm so glad. Now, do you think I'll please them here? How do I strike you?

SILVIA: You strike me as... quite extraordinary, Sir.

ARLEQUIN: Oh excellent! Extraordinary! I hope you'll go on thinking like that.

SILVIA: You're obviously so modest, Sir, to be content with that. But I must go, since no one seems to have told your father-in-law you are here.

ARLEQUIN: Go tell him I await him with affection.

SILVIA [*aside*]: How strange fate is. Neither of those two men is in his proper place. [*Exit.*]

SCENE 9

DORANTE, ARLEQUIN

ARLEQUIN: Well, Sir, I did get off to a flying start. I've already impressed the maid.

DORANTE: You are a fool.

ARLEQUIN: A fool? Wasn't my entrance genteel?

DORANTE: You promised me to abandon your silly and trivial ways of speech. I spent long enough teaching you. I told you to be serious and grave. I must have been mad to entrust myself to you.

ARLEQUIN: I'll get better, Sir, I promise. Since it is not enough to be serious, I will be melancholic. If I have to, I will produce tears.

DORANTE: Oh, I don't know where I am any more. This is the strangest adventure. I'm confused. What should I do?

ARLEQUIN: Don't you like the girl? What's wrong with her?

DORANTE: Shut up. Here is M. Orgon.

SCENE 10

DORANTE, ARLEQUIN

[*Enter* ORGON.]

ORGON: My dear Sir, I ask a thousand pardons for keeping you waiting so long. But I have only just learned you were here.

ARLEQUIN: Oh, Sir, a thousand pardons is far too many. When you've made just one mistake you need just one pardon. And, moreover, all my pardons are at your service.

ORGON: I will try not to need them.

ARLEQUIN: You are the master, Sir, and I the servant.

ORGON: I am, I assure you, charmed and delighted to see you. I was waiting for you with impatience.

ARLEQUIN: I would have come at once with Bourguignon. But when one finishes a journey one is not very savoury and I wanted to present myself in a more savoury aspect.

ORGON: You have succeeded admirably. My daughter is getting dressed. She has been a little ill of late. Until she comes, would you care for some refreshment?

ARLEQUIN: Oh, I've never refused a drink with anyone.

ORGON: Bourguignon, my friend, take good care of yourself.

ARLEQUIN: He's a choosy rascal, only drinks the best wine.

ORGON: And there is plenty of it to drink.

[*Exeunt* ORGON *and* ARLEQUIN.]

ACT II

SCENE 1

ORGON, LISETTE

ORGON: Well, what do you want, Lisette?

LISETTE: I must speak to you for a moment.

ORGON: And on what subject?

LISETTE: I must tell you how things stand because it is important that they should be clear to you. I do not want you to have cause to complain of me, Sir.

ORGON: This must be very serious, then.

LISETTE: Yes, very serious. You consented to Miss Silvia's disguise. At first, I also thought it of no consequence, but I was wrong.

ORGON: And to what consequences has it led?

LISETTE: Sir, I hesitate to praise myself; but, in spite of all the conventions of modesty, I must tell you that if you do not take matters in hand soon, your would-be son-in-law will no longer have a heart to give to your daughter. The moment has come, Sir, for her to reveal herself. Time is short. One day more and I won't answer for the consequences.

ORGON: What! Why should he not want my daughter when he finds her out? Have you no faith in her charms?

LISETTE: No, Sir. But you have too little faith in mine. I must warn you, Sir, that my charms are beginning to make their mark and I would advise you not to let them.

ORGON: My congratulations, Lisette. Well done! [*He laughs*] Ha! Ha!

LISETTE: Well, I never! You're laughing at me. I see you think it a joke, Sir, and are making fun of me. I am sorry because yours won't be the last laugh, Sir.

ORGON: You need not be so flustered, Lisette. Do as you will.

LISETTE: I repeat once more: Dorante's affections are quick to grow. Look, at the moment he likes me a great deal. By this evening he will love me. Tomorrow he will adore me. I do not deserve it, he has bad taste, you may say what you please, but that will not prevent it. Don't you see? Tomorrow, Sir, I guarantee myself adored.

ORGON: Well, and what of it? If he loves you so much, let him marry you.

LISETTE: What! You would not prevent it?

ORGON: No, on my honour as a man of honour, if you can get him to the altar.

LISETTE: I warn you, Sir, take care. Up to now I have done nothing to add to my charms, I have left them to fend for themselves. I have been scrupulous in dealing with his affections. But should I engage myself further, I shall overwhelm him, Sir. He will be defenceless!

ORGON: Overwhelm him, dazzle him, burn him, marry him. You have my permission, if you can do it.

LISETTE: If that's the case, my fortune's made.

ORGON: Quite so. But tell me, have you talked with my daughter? What does she think of her intended?

LISETTE: We have found hardly a moment to talk together because her intended lays constant siege to me. Judging from a distance, I do not think she is happy. She seems sad and preoccupied. I expect her to ask me to rebuff him for her.

ORGON: And I forbid you to do that. I am trying to avoid explanations with her for now, but I have my reasons for letting the disguise continue. I want her to have more time to consider her intended. But, tell me, what about the valet? How does he behave himself? Has he not taken it on himself to love my daughter?

LISETTE: He is a strange fellow. I have noticed that he puts on important airs with her because he is handsome. He looks at her and sighs.

ORGON: It must make her furious.

LISETTE: But . . . she blushes.

ORGON: Really! You must be wrong. A valet's sighs would not embarrass her so much.

LISETTE: Sir, she blushes.

ORGON: Yes – with indignation.

LISETTE: If you say so, Sir.

ORGON: When you next see her, you must say you suspect that the valet has prejudiced her against his master. If that makes her angry, don't let it worry you. That is my affair. But ... here is Dorante and looking for you, it seems.

SCENE 2

ORGON, LISETTE

[*Enter* ARLEQUIN.]

ARLEQUIN: Ah, I have found you at last, gorgeous lady. I have been asking for you all over the house. Your servant, dear father-in-law, or nearly father-in-law.

ORGON: Your servant. Good-bye, my children, I leave you alone, together. It is good that you should love each other a little before you are married.

ARLEQUIN: I'll manage to achieve both love and marriage with her at one go, Sir.

ORGON: Don't be impatient, though. [*Exit.*]

SCENE 3

ARLEQUIN, LISETTE

ARLEQUIN: Oh, madam, he says that I should be patient. It is easy for him to speak, he is old.

LISETTE: I find it hard to believe that it is so difficult for you to be patient. It is because you are gallant that you pretend to be impatient. But you have only just arrived! Your love could not be very strong for, at the very most it is a new-born love.

ARLEQUIN: You are wrong, prodigious lady. A love inflamed by you does not stay long in the cradle. Your first look gave birth to my love; your second gave it strength and your third brought it to manhood. Let us try to set our love up properly as soon as we can. You must care for it, since you are its mother.

LISETTE: Do you think that it has been ill-treated? Has it been so abandoned?

ARLEQUIN: Until it is provided for, give it your beautiful white hand – to play with a little.

LISETTE: Here it is, little nuisance, since there can be no peace till you have toys.

ARLEQUIN [*kissing her hand*]: Dear plaything of my soul! This makes me as happy as does a rare wine. It is a pity to have only a sip.

LISETTE: Stop, come, come, you are too greedy.

ARLEQUIN: I only want a little sustenance till I come alive.

LISETTE: Shouldn't you be reasonable?

ARLEQUIN: Reasonable? Oh, alas, I have lost my reason. Your lovely eyes are the rascals that took it away.

LISETTE: Oh, Sir! But is it possible for you to love me so much? I cannot convince myself of it.

ARLEQUIN: I don't care what is or is not possible. I love you desperately, and you will see in your mirror that I am right.

LISETTE: Oh, Sir, my mirror will only make me believe it less.

ARLEQUIN: Oh, my adorable little darling! Your humility is only hypocrisy.

LISETTE: Someone is coming. Your valet.

SCENE 4

ARLEQUIN, LISETTE

[*Enter* DORANTE.]

DORANTE: Sir, may I speak to you a moment?

ARLEQUIN: No! Cursed be these menials who will not leave us in peace.

LISETTE: See what he wants, Sir.

DORANTE: Sir, just one word!

ARLEQUIN: And, Madam, if he speaks two words, the third will be his dismissal. Well?

DORANTE [*low to* ARLEQUIN]: Come here, you rascal.

ARLEQUIN [*low to* DORANTE]: That's no word, it's an insult. [*To* LISETTE] Excuse me, my queen.

LISETTE: Oh, please go ahead.

DORANTE [*low*]: Stop all this strutting, at once. You need not exaggerate. You must seem serious and melancholy, even discontented. Do you understand?

ARLEQUIN: Yes, my friend. You need not concern yourself. You may go now. That will be all.

[*Exit* DORANTE.]

SCENE 5

ARLEQUIN, LISETTE

ARLEQUIN: Ah, Madam, but for him I was going to say such marvellous things to you and now I shall find only ordinary ones, apart from my love which is extraordinary. And, speaking of my love, when will yours keep mine company?

LISETTE: One must hope that it will come.

ARLEQUIN: And do you think it is coming soon?

LISETTE: That is a delicate question – do you know that you are making me uncomfortable?

ARLEQUIN: What do you want? I am burning so I shout 'FIRE'.

LISETTE: If I could explain myself sooner...

ARLEQUIN: I think that you may explain yourself now.

LISETTE: The modesty of my sex forbids it.

ARLEQUIN: The fashion in modesty at present is not to be so modest. Many other things are permitted...

LISETTE: But what do you want of me?

ARLEQUIN: Tell me that you love me just a little. See, I love you, all you need to do now is play the echo. Echo me, Princess.

LISETTE: You are insatiable. Well, Sir, I love you.

ARLEQUIN: Ah, Madam, I die. My happiness is such I am quite giddy. It will overwhelm my poor wits. You love me, that is wonderful.

LISETTE: For my part, I could be surprised by the pace of your passion. Perhaps, when you know me better, you will love me less.

ARLEQUIN: Ah, Madam, when we get to that point, I will lose a great deal and there will be an awkward account to settle.

LISETTE: You believe me to have more qualities than I have.
ARLEQUIN: And you, Madam, do not know all my qualities yet. I should speak to you only on my knees.
LISETTE: Remember that we are not the masters of our fate.
ARLEQUIN: That lies in the hands of our mothers and fathers.
LISETTE: For my part, my heart would have chosen you whatever your station.
ARLEQUIN: It will have a good chance to choose me all over again then.
LISETTE: May I flatter myself that your feelings for me are the same?
ARLEQUIN: Alas, Madam, had you been a country girl, a rustic wench, and I had first seen you wearing a mucky apron or tending the cows, you would still have been my princess.
LISETTE: May such noble sentiments last!
ARLEQUIN: To confirm them on both sides, let us swear to love each other always despite all the misunderstandings you will suffer on my account.
LISETTE: I have more to gain by that oath than you, and I swear it with all my heart.
ARLEQUIN [*kneeling*]: Your goodness overwhelms me and I kneel before it.
LISETTE: Please, please, rise, Sir, I could not allow you to stay in that posture. It would be ridiculous. Rise, Sir, someone else is coming.

SCENE 6

ARLEQUIN, LISETTE

[*Enter* SILVIA.]
LISETTE: What do you want, Lisette?
SILVIA: I must speak to you, Madam.
ARLEQUIN: Is that really so? Well, my dear, come back in a quarter of an hour. Go away! Where I come from, chambermaids only come in when they are called.
SILVIA: But, Sir, I must speak to Madam.
ARLEQUIN: Huh, look at the stubborn wench. Queen of my

life, send her away. Go away, my girl. We have been told to love each other before we are married, and you are obstructing the course of our duty.

LISETTE: Could you not come back in a minute, Lisette?

SILVIA: But, Madam...

ARLEQUIN: That 'but' serves only to make my blood boil.

SILVIA [*aside*]: Oh, the nasty creature. [*Aloud*] Madam, I assure you that it is very pressing.

LISETTE: In which case, Sir, be good enough to let me deal with it.

ARLEQUIN: Since it is the devil's wish and hers as well... patience. I will stroll awhile while she unburdens her nonsense. What fools our servants are! [*Exit.*]

SCENE 7

SILVIA, LISETTE

SILVIA: I must admit that I find it delightful of you not to send him away at once. You were happy no doubt to subject me to the insults of that brute.

LISETTE: Goodness, Madam, I cannot play two parts at once. I must appear to be either the mistress or the maid, I must obey or be obeyed.

SILVIA: Very well. But now that he has gone, listen to me as your mistress. You do see that a man like that does not suit me.

LISETTE: You have not had the time to study him very closely.

SILVIA: Are you mad with your studying? Do I need to see him twice to see how unsuitable he is? In a word, I want none of him. It seems that my father does not approve of my revulsion, since he avoids me and says nothing. So as things stand, I rely on you to extricate me delicately. You will discreetly let the young man understand that you have no wish to marry him.

LISETTE: I do not know how I could.

SILVIA: You do not know how? What prevents you knowing?

LISETTE: M. Orgon forbad me to.

SILVIA: He forbad you to? But that is quite unlike my father.

LISETTE: He positively forbad me to.

SILVIA: Well, I order you to convey to him my disgust for

Dorante and to assure him that nothing will change it. When he knows that, I cannot believe that he will let matters go any further.

LISETTE: But, Madam, what do you find so unpleasant, so repulsive in your intended?

SILVIA: I told you I don't like him, and I don't like your attitude, either.

LISETTE: Give yourself the chance to see what kind of man he is. That is all your father asks.

SILVIA: I hate him enough as it is, I do not need more time to hate him more.

LISETTE: His valet, who puts on such important airs, wouldn't have spoilt your feelings for his master?

SILVIA: Fool! What has his valet to do with it?

LISETTE: I have no confidence in him because he is sophistical and ...

SILVIA: *Do* finish your descriptions. We have nothing better to do than listen to them. I take good care not to let the valet speak much to me, and the little that he has said has all been sensible.

LISETTE: I think the man has been telling you wicked tales to dazzle you with his polished wit.

SILVIA: My disguise forces me to listen to fine things, doesn't it? What is the matter with you? Where did you get this mad notion of blaming the valet for my feelings against his master? He isn't responsible for them. In the end you will force me to defend him. There is no question of causing trouble for him with his master, and I warn you not to make him out to be a knave so that you can make me out to be a fool because I listen to his stories.

LISETTE: Oh, Madam, if you defend him in such a tone and if you go so far as to grow passionate, I have nothing more to say, of course.

SILVIA: Passionate? If I defend him in what tone? What about the tone that you yourself accused him in? What do you mean? What is going on in your mind?

LISETTE: Madam, I have never seen you in such a state as you are now, and I do not understand your vicious mood. Why, if the valet has said nothing, fine! You need not frenzy yourself to defend him. I believe you, that is that. I would not dream of contradicting your good opinion of him, Madam.

SILVIA: Oh, what a warped mind! The way she turns things round ... Oh, it makes me so angry ... I think I shall cry.

LISETTE: But at what, Madam? What innuendoes did you find in what I said?

SILVIA: What innuendoes! What innuendoes! I, I defend him, I have a good opinion of him ... It shows how little respect you have for me. Heavens, good opinion of him! What must I say to that? What do you mean by it? Good opinion? Who are you speaking to? Is anybody safe from this kind of persecution? What a situation to find myself in!

LISETTE: I know nothing of all this, Madam, but I know that it will take me a long time to recover from my surprise at seeing you so distraught.

SILVIA: Distraught? She has a way of speaking that puts me beside myself ... Go away, I find you intolerable ... Go away, I will find other means ...

[*Exit* LISETTE.]

SCENE 8

SILVIA, *alone*

SILVIA: I still tremble because of what I heard her say. In their thoughts our servants treat us with nothing but impudence. Oh, how they degrade us! I do not know how I shall ever recover, and I dare not think of what she said! It frightens me still. A valet! A valet! What a strange turn of events! I must put out of my mind the idea with which that wretch blackened it. Here is Bourguignon. Here is the object for which I rush into frenzies. But it is not his fault, poor boy, and I should not take it out on him.

SCENE 9

SILVIA

[*Enter* DORANTE.]

DORANTE: Lisette, however distant you may feel, I am forced to speak to you. I think I have cause to complain of you.

SILVIA: Let us not be so familiar with each other, I beg of you. No more christian names, Bourguignon, please.

DORANTE: If you like, Lisette.

SILVIA: But you're doing nothing about it, Bourguignon.

DORANTE: No more are you, Lisette!

SILVIA: It slipped out that time.

DORANTE: Well, let's not change anything now, let us speak together as we have before. We have so little time left to speak together, it hardly seems worth it.

SILVIA: Is your master going away, then? Well, that won't be a great loss.

DORANTE: My departure won't be, either – just to complete your thought?

SILVIA: Thank you, but I'll complete my thoughts for myself. I wasn't even thinking of you.

DORANTE: And I think only of you.

SILVIA: Listen, Bourguignon, for the last time. Whether you go, whether you stay, whether you come back, all these movements must not affect me – nor do they, in fact. I wish you neither well nor ill. I neither hate you, nor love you, nor will ever love you unless my wits turn. These are my resolutions! My reason allows me no others and I should not even let myself tell you about them.

DORANTE: You cannot imagine how unhappy it makes me. You will destroy my peace of mind for the rest of my life.

SILVIA: What delusions has he filled his head with? He grieves me. Come to your senses. You are speaking to me and I am replying. That is a great deal, too much even, you can believe me. And if you were aware, honestly, you would not complain of me. You would find my kindness without precedent. I have been too kind and I would condemn such kindness in another. Yet I do not reproach myself. In the depths of my heart I know that what I'm doing is commendable. I speak to you out of generosity, but it must not go on, for such generosity is not supposed to last and I cannot always convince myself of the innocence of my intentions. So, Bourguignon, come, let us put an end to it. What does it mean? This is foolish. So, please, let us speak no more of it.

DORANTE: Oh, my dear Lisette, how you make me suffer!

SILVIA: Come to the point. When you came in, you said you had reason to complain of me. What was the matter?

DORANTE: Nothing, it was a trifle. I wanted to see you and I think I seized on some pretext.

SILVIA [*aside*]: What can I say to that? If I were to grow angry, it would change nothing.

DORANTE: As she left, your mistress seemed to accuse me of having spoken badly of my master to you.

SILVIA: She is imagining things. And if she accuses you of it again, you may deny it flatly. I will see to the rest.

DORANTE: It is not that that worries me.

SILVIA: If that is all you have to say to me, we have no more business together.

DORANTE: Leave me at least the pleasure of looking at you.

SILVIA: What a good reason you give me for staying! I must amuse the passion of Bourguignon. One day the memory of all this will make me laugh.

DORANTE: You are making fun of me, but you are right. I know neither what I am saying nor what I am asking of you. Farewell!

SILVIA: Farewell! It's for the best ... But, speaking of your farewells, there is one final thing I must know. You said that you were leaving? Is that true?

DORANTE: As far as I'm concerned, I must go away or go mad.

SILVIA: I did not call you back for an answer like that.

DORANTE: And I only made one mistake: that was not to leave the moment I set eyes on you.

SILVIA [*aside*]: I have to forget each instant that I am listening to him.

DORANTE: If you knew, Lisette, the state I find myself in ...

SILVIA: Oh, I promise you, it cannot be more curious than mine ...

DORANTE: What can you complain of? I don't propose to make you susceptible.

SILVIA [*aside*]: One shouldn't count on that.

DORANTE: What could I hope to gain by trying to make you love me? Alas, if I won your heart...

SILVIA: Heaven forbid! When you have won it, you will not know it and I will take good care that I won't know it either. Really, the ideas the man has!

DORANTE: It is true then that you don't hate me, you don't love me and you never will love me.

SILVIA: Without difficulty.

DORANTE: Without difficulty? What in me then is so ... vile?

SILVIA: Nothing. It isn't that that goes against you.

DORANTE: Well, my dear Lisette, tell me a hundred times then that you won't love me.

SILVIA: I've said it enough. Why don't you try to believe it for a change?

DORANTE: I must believe it. Make me feel this dangerous passion is hopeless! Then you can save me from the consequences I dread. You don't hate me, you don't love me and you never will love me. Crush my heart with that certainty. I'm acting in good faith. Help me against myself. It's necessary. I ask you on my knees to do so.

[ORGON *and* MARIO *enter but do not reveal themselves.*]

SILVIA: Ah, there we are! We just needed that display to round off my adventure. Oh, I am unhappy! It's my generosity that has put him there. Get up, Bourguignon, get up, I beg you. Someone might come. I will say what you like. What do you want of me? I don't hate you. Get up. I would love you if I could, you don't displease me. That must satisfy you.

DORANTE: What, Lisette, if I weren't what I am ... if I were rich, if I were of a good station and if I loved you as much as I love you, your heart would feel no revulsion for me?

SILVIA: None, I assure you.

DORANTE: You would not hate me? You would endure me?

SILVIA: Willingly – but get up.

DORANTE: You seem to be speaking seriously and, if you are, then my reason is gone.

SILVIA: I'm saying what you want, and still you won't get up.

SCENE 10

ORGON, MARIO, SILVIA, DORANTE

ORGON [*approaching*]: It is a great pity to interrupt you, my dears, especially after such interesting developments.

SILVIA: Developments, Sir? I simply could not prevent this boy from falling to his knees. I am in no position to force him up, I think.

ORGON: You suit each other perfectly, my children. But I must have a word in private with you, Lisette. You will continue your charming conversation when we have gone. Are we agreed? If you will be so good, Bourguignon . . .

DORANTE: I withdraw, Sir.

ORGON: And try to speak of your master with a bit more respect, my lad, than up to now.

DORANTE: Who, Sir, me, Sir?

MARIO: Yes, Sir, you, Sir. I gather you do not shine in that department, and that you are not utterly consumed by respect for him.

DORANTE: I don't understand you, Sir.

ORGON: Well, you will explain yourself later. Good-bye.

[Exit DORANTE.]

SCENE 11

SILVIA, ORGON, MARIO

ORGON: Tut, my dear Silvia, you are not looking at us. You seem very embarrassed.

SILVIA: Me, father dear? What would have made me embarrassed? I am, thank Heaven, quite my usual self. I am sorry to have to tell you that you are imagining things.

MARIO: And yet, sister dear, there does seem to be something, something the matter.

SILVIA: Something may be the matter in your head, brother dear. But my head is, I'm glad to say, in perfect shape, and I'm only surprised by what you say.

ORGON: That lad who has just left has prejudiced you. He has made you dislike his master so much.

SILVIA: Who has? Dorante's valet?

ORGON: Yes, the gallant Bourguignon.

SILVIA: Gallant? I did not know Bourguignon was so qualified. The gallant Bourguignon does not speak of his master.

ORGON: Quite, I maintain that he has destroyed both his master's reputation and his chances with you, and I wanted to speak to you about that.

SILVIA: It isn't worth your while, father. No one in the wide world made me dislike his master so much as his master himself. It was quite spontaneous.

MARIO: So you may pretend, sister dear. But you hate him too much for it to be spontaneous. Someone has made you so prejudiced.

SILVIA [*fiercely*]: What a subtle, insinuating air you have, brother! Who is this someone who prejudiced me? Do tell me.

MARIO: What a strange mood you are in, sister darling. Quite a frenzy!

SILVIA: I am tired of the part I have to play. And I would have unmasked a long time ago if I were not afraid of displeasing my father.

ORGON: That's just what I came to warn you about: don't you dare displease me. I was indulgent enough to allow you this disguise. Now you must, if you please, be gracious enough not to judge Dorante too quickly. I want you to see if this revulsion that you have been made to feel is justified.

SILVIA: I see that you don't even listen to me any more. I told you that no one made me hate him.

MARIO: Hasn't that loose-tongued fellow who just left spoilt your appetite for his master? Not even a little?

SILVIA [*fiery*]: I find your thoughts even nastier than your words. Spoilt my appetite? Spoilt my appetite for his master? I have to suffer such strange expressions! Lately, I have only been addressed in insults and innuendoes. 'I am embarrassed', 'Something is the matter'. And it is the 'gallant' Bourguignon, a valet, who is supposed to have spoiled my appetite. You may say whatever you please but I don't understand a word of it.

MARIO: You are the one who's strange. What motive do you suspect us of? Why are you so touchy?

SILVIA: Go on, brother dear. What ill fate has willed that each word you say should provoke me today? What suspicions do you suspect me of? Have you had visions?

ORGON: I must defend your brother. You are so distraught I do not recognize you either. It must have been your agitation that made Lisette speak to us as she did. She merely implied that this valet might have spoken to you unfavourably of his master. 'And Madam,' she told us, 'leapt to his defence so passionately that it quite surprised me.' It was her use of the word 'surprised' that annoyed us, but these common people do not know the implications of such a word.

SILVIA: The impertinent hussy! I hate her! I suppose I may have been a little emphatic – out of a sense of justice for the boy.

MARIO: I see no harm in that.

SILVIA: Could there be anything simpler? Just because I am fair and I would like no one to suffer, just because I want to protect a servant from trouble with his master, she says I am in frenzies and passions that surprise her. A second later her warped mind starts to weave fairy tales. You should defend me. You should silence her. You should take my side because of the implications of what she says. Take my side! Do I really need someone to defend and justify me? Can one see anything wrong in what I have done? But what is it that I have done? What am I accused of? Tell me, I beg you. Is it a grave and weighty offence? Are you making fun of me? I am not at all calm.

ORGON: Calm down then.

SILVIA: No, Sir, we have no place for calm. We have passions and surprises to deal with. What do you mean? You accuse a valet and you are all wrong to do so. Lisette is a lunatic. He is innocent. And that is all. But why tell me of it again? I am beside myself.

ORGON: Don't restrain yourself, my dear, I see you would like to upbraid me too. Let us be more reasonable. The valet is suspected. Dorante has only to dismiss him.

SILVIA: What a wretched disguise this is! Warn Lisette not to come near me! I hate her more than I do Dorante.

ORGON: As you wish. But you must be delighted the valet is going away. He loves you and that must surely annoy you.

SILVIA: I have no reason to complain. He takes me for a servant and addresses me as one. But I make quite sure he does not take advantage of me.

MARIO: I do not think that you are as much mistress of the situation as you claim.

ORGON: Did we not find him on his knees in spite of you? Were you not forced to make him get up again, to say that he did not displease you?

SILVIA [*aside*]: I can hardly breathe.

MARIO: And when he asked you if you would like him, you were forced to say most tenderly, 'willingly' – if you had not, he would still be there. [*He kneels.*]

SILVIA: What an admirable conclusion, brother, to your speech! I did not like the original and I don't like the repetition either. Let's be serious. When may we bring to an end this comedy at my expense which you seem to be enjoying so?

ORGON: I only ask you, my girl, not to resolve to refuse him without knowing him well enough first. Be patient, my dear! You will thank me one day, I promise you.

MARIO: You will marry Dorante, and with much enthusiasm. I have seen it in the stars. But, my dear father, I would crave mercy for the valet.

SILVIA: Why mercy? I want him to go.

ORGON: His master will decide his fate. It is time to go, Mario.

MARIO: Farewell, sister dear. No hard feelings?

[*Exeunt* ORGON *and* MARIO.]

SCENE 12

SILVIA, *alone*

SILVIA: How wretched I feel! I am more than distressed. I feel burdened and disturbed. What it is eludes me. I can't explain my feeling, but I wish I had never disguised myself. I am happy with no one, and especially not with myself.

[*Enter* DORANTE.]

DORANTE: Ah, Lisette, I was looking for you.

SILVIA: It isn't worth your while finding me since I am avoiding you.

DORANTE [*prevents her going out*]: Wait, Lisette, I must speak to you for the last time. It is a matter of some importance to your masters.

SILVIA: Then speak to them. Every time I see you you make me sad. Leave me.

DORANTE: I am about to offer to. But listen to me, please. What I am going to say, you will see, puts a very new complexion on things.

SILVIA: Very we.l, then. I am listening, since it seems decreed that my kindness for you is to know no bounds.

DORANTE: Do you promise to keep it secret?

SILVIA: I have never betrayed anyone.

DORANTE: You owe the confidence I am about to make only to the esteem I feel for you.

SILVIA: I believe you. But I would rather you esteemed me without telling me so or I shall smell a pretext.

DORANTE: You are wrong, Lisette. You promised to keep this secret. Let's get to the point. You have seen me greatly troubled. I could not stop myself loving you.

SILVIA: Well, what did I say? Here he goes again. Well, I can stop myself listening to the rest again. [*She starts to go.*]

DORANTE: Stop! It isn't Bourguignon any more who speaks to you.

SILVIA: Well, who are you then?

DORANTE: Ah, Lisette, you will now appreciate how troubled my heart has been!

SILVIA: I am not speaking to your heart but to you.

DORANTE [*going to door*]: Is no one coming?

SILVIA: No.

DORANTE: At this point I must tell you the truth. I am too honourable a man not to put a stop to this turn of events.

SILVIA: Very well.

DORANTE: Let me tell you that the person who is with your mistress is not what he is thought to be.

SILVIA: What is he, then?

DORANTE: A valet.

SILVIA: So?

DORANTE: I am Dorante.

SILVIA [*aside*]: Ah! I understand myself now.

DORANTE: I wanted, in this disguise, to get to know your mistress a little before I married her. Before I left, my father consented, and what should have been an intrigue has turned into a bad dream. I loathe the girl whose husband I should have become and I love the maid who should find in me only a new master. What am I to do now? I blush to say it, but your mistress has so little taste that she is infatuated with my valet, and to such an extent that, if we let her, she will marry him. What should I do?

SILVIA [*aside*]: Let us not reveal yet who we are. [*To* DORANTE] Your position is, to say the least, original. But please, Sir, let me apologize for any lack of respect I may have shown you during our conversations.

DORANTE [*passionately*]: Be silent, Lisette. Your apologies vex me. They serve only to remind me of the distance between us and make it more painful.

SILVIA: Is your inclination for me that serious? Do you love me so much?

DORANTE: Further – to the point of renouncing all my engagements if I am not to be allowed to link my fate to yours. And so the only joy I can still hope to have is to think that you do not hate me.

SILVIA: A heart that has chosen me in spite of my position is surely worthy and should be accepted, and I would willingly give you mine in exchange if I did not fear it would be to your disadvantage.

DORANTE: Have you not enough charms, Lisette? Must you also have the nobility with which you just spoke to me?

SILVIA: Someone is coming. Don't worry about your valet – things will sort themselves out. Be patient. We will meet again and find a solution to all our problems.

DORANTE: I will follow your advice. [*Exit.*]

SILVIA: Well, I must confess I truly needed that man to be Dorante.

SCENE 13

SILVIA

[*Enter* MARIO.]

MARIO: We left you in such distress, sister dear, that I was touched. I have come to set your mind at ease, so listen to me.

SILVIA [*spirited*] : Really, well, I have news for you.

MARIO: Oh yes, what?

SILVIA: He isn't Bourguignon at all. He's Dorante.

MARIO: Which one is?

SILVIA: He is, I tell you. I have only just heard it. He has just left. He told me so himself.

MARIO: Who did?

SILVIA: Why do you never listen to me?

MARIO: I have been listening to you, but I'll be hanged if I understand a word of it.

SILVIA: You're a fool. But never mind, let's find father. He must be told. I shall need you as well. I have a lot of new ideas. You will have to pretend to be in love with me. You have already hinted as much in your flippant way. But, above all things, you must promise to keep it a secret.

MARIO: I certainly will keep it a secret since I don't know what it is.

SILVIA: Come on, come on, there's no time to lose. There's never been anything to equal this.

MARIO: I think, quite frankly, she's gone mad.

ACT III

SCENE 1

DORANTE, ARLEQUIN

ARLEQUIN: No, no no, Sir, please, my most honoured master, I beg you.

DORANTE: Have you not finished?

ARLEQUIN: Have compassion on me, Sir. Respect my good fortune. Don't begrudge me my happiness, which is coming along so nicely. Please don't obstruct it.

DORANTE: I've had enough of this, you rogue. I think you're making fun of me! You deserve a hundred lashes.

ARLEQUIN [*obsequiously*]: Oh yes, Sir, anything you say, Sir. I will not refuse them if I deserve them. And when I've had a hundred, allow me to deserve more. Shall I fetch the lash?

DORANTE: Fool!

ARLEQUIN: Fool? Well, yes, as you say, Sir, I am a fool. But that won't stop me making my fortune.

DORANTE: What a rogue! Who does he think he is?

ARLEQUIN: Rogue? Well, yes, as you say, Sir, I am a rogue. A fool isn't insulted when he's called a rogue. But even a rogue can make a good match.

DORANTE: Is there no limit to your insolence? Do you expect me to deceive a good gentleman and to allow you to marry his daughter under my name? Now, you listen to me. If you ever mention such impertinences to me again I will send you packing – as soon as I have told M. Orgon who you really are. Do you understand?

ARLEQUIN: Now, now, Sir, we are reasonable men. Let us compromise. The young lady adores me. She worships me. Suppose I were to tell her my true estate and her sweet young heart were still greedy to wed me? Would you then allow the violins to play?

DORANTE: As soon as they know who you really are, you may do whatever you want.

ARLEQUIN: Very well! I will warn this young and very generous lady at once of my true estate ... I'm sure that a mere accident of birth will not jar the passion between us. Her love will elevate me whom Fate left behind in the pantry, to a seat at the table. [*Exit.*]

SCENE 2

DORANTE

DORANTE: Everything that happens here, everything that happens to me, is incredible. I would like to see Lisette and know how she has fared with her mistress. She promised to help extricate me from this entanglement. Perhaps I can find her alone ...

[*Enter* MARIO *as* DORANTE *is about to leave.*]

MARIO: Wait, Bourguignon, I have something to tell you.

DORANTE: How may I serve you, Sir?

MARIO: You are speaking of love to Lisette?

DORANTE: She is so worthy of love, it would be hard not to speak to her of it.

MARIO: How does she receive your sweet nothings?

DORANTE: She toys with them, Sir.

MARIO: You are no fool. You wouldn't lie?

DORANTE: No. But how does it affect you? Suppose Lisette were to find a place for me in her heart ...

MARIO: Find a place for you in her heart? Where do you filch your phrases? For a boy of your class you speak quite affectedly.

DORANTE: I don't know how to speak any other way, Sir.

MARIO: It's delicate touches like that which you must be using to seduce Lisette. They smack of a man of quality.

DORANTE: I assure you, Sir, I imitate no one, but I am sure you did not come just to make fun of me and that you have something to say. We were speaking of Lisette, of how attractive I find her and of your interest in the matter.

MARIO: Well, by God, I can already detect a jealous strain in the way you answer. You should make your tone a little more gentle! Well, you were saying what *if*, if Lisette were to find a place for you in her heart – and then?

DORANTE: Why would you have to know?

MARIO: Well, here is why. In spite of the light tone I just took, I would be very sorry if she loved you. And with no other explanation, I forbid you to speak any more of it to her. It isn't, you must understand, that I am afraid she might love you, for she seems to me to have too haughty a heart for that. But I do not wish to have Bourguignon as a rival.

DORANTE: In faith, I believe you. Bourguignon, though he may be just Bourguignon, is not happy to have you as a rival, either.

MARIO: He will have to resign himself.

DORANTE: He will have to. But, Sir, do you love her much?

MARIO: Enough to attach myself seriously to her as soon as I have taken certain steps. Do you understand what that means?

DORANTE: Yes, I think I understand. And, on those conditions, are you loved?

MARIO: What do you think? Am I not worthy of being loved?

DORANTE: Do you expect compliments from your rivals? Am I to sing your praises?

MARIO: I suppose not and I forgive you your reply. But, I am grieved, as I cannot say that she loves me too. You will appreciate that I confess this not to please or inform you but because one must tell the truth.

DORANTE: You astonish me, Sir. Lisette does not know of your intentions.

MARIO: Lisette knows all the good I wish her and it seems to have no effect on her at all. But I hope reason will win me her heart. She is indifferent in spite of all the advantages I can offer her, and that must be your consolation for losing her to me. Your livery is not good enough to tip the scales in your favour and you hardly have the weapons to fight a gentleman.

SCENE 3

DORANTE, MARIO

[*Enter* SILVIA.]

MARIO: Ah, there you are, Lisette.

SILVIA: What is the matter, Sir? You seem annoyed.

MARIO: I was just having a word with Bourguignon.

SILVIA: He looks sad. Have you been complaining of him?

DORANTE: The gentleman was telling me he loved you.

SILVIA: It's not my fault.

DORANTE: And that he forbids me to love you.

SILVIA: So he forbids me to seem lovable to you?

MARIO: I cannot prevent him loving you, Lisette, but I don't want him to tell you of it.

SILVIA: He doesn't tell me he loves me any more. He just repeats it.

MARIO: Well, he won't repeat it in my presence. You may go, Bourguignon.

DORANTE: I await her orders.

MARIO: Really!

SILVIA: He said he is waiting, so be patient.

DORANTE: Have you any affection for the gentleman?

SILVIA: Oh, you mean, do I love him? There is no need to forbid me to love him.

DORANTE: Would you be deceiving me?

MARIO: Really! I cut a fine figure here. [*To* DORANTE] Go away! After all, who am I speaking to?

DORANTE: Only to Bourguignon.

MARIO: Well, let this Bourguignon go!

DORANTE [*aside*]: I suffer!

SILVIA: Since he's getting angry, perhaps you should comply.

DORANTE [*to* SILVIA, *low*]: Perhaps that's just what you want.

MARIO: Really! Enough of this!

DORANTE: You had not told me of this love, Lisette. [*Exit.*]

SCENE 4

ORGON, MARIO, SILVIA

SILVIA: If I didn't love that man, you must admit I'd be very ungrateful.

[MARIO *laughs*.]

ORGON: What are you laughing at, Mario?

MARIO: At the fury in which Dorante left because I forced him to leave our Lisette.

SILVIA: But what did he tell you during your private little talk?

MARIO: I have never seen a man more confused or in a worse mood.

ORGON: I am quite glad he should be caught in his own trap. And, besides, when he knows the truth he will realize there could have been nothing more flattering or gracious than what you have done for him till now, my dear. But enough is enough!

MARIO: Tell me, sister dear, how far have things gone?

SILVIA [*sighs*]: Alas, brother dear, I must confess that I have every reason to be happy.

MARIO [*imitating*]: 'Alas, brother dear.' Do you not sense a certain mellowness in what she says?

ORGON: You don't hope he will go so far as to offer you his hand while you are still disguised?

SILVIA: Yes, my dear father – that's exactly what I hope.

MARIO: My dear father! You little hypocrite! You've stopped shouting and scolding us. You are all sweetness now!

SILVIA: Will you never let me be?

MARIO: I'm taking my revenge, sister dear. A short while ago, you quibbled at my words. Be fair! The time has come for me to quibble at yours. I find your joy quite as entertaining as I found your distress.

ORGON: You won't have reason to complain of me, my dear. I will do whatever you wish.

SILVIA: Oh, Sir, if you knew how much I shall owe to you. Dorante and I, we were fated for each other. He must marry me. If you knew how I will treasure what he has done for me today, how I will never forget the overwhelming love he has shown me. If you only knew how sweet all this will make our marriage. Each time he remembers this charade of ours he will love me, and I will never be able to think of it without loving him. You let me do what I wanted and so have secured our happiness for life. Oh, it will be a unique marriage. People will only have to hear our story to be moved. There has never been a more remarkable stroke of fortune. It's the most...

MARIO: Your heart is a real chatterbox, sister. Such eloquence!

ORGON: I admit that the delights you conjure up are charming – if you achieve them.

SILVIA: They are as good as achieved. Dorante is conquered. I await my prisoner.

MARIO: His chains will be more golden than he expects. But I believe him to be suffering, and I feel sorry for him now.

SILVIA: I am not. The pain his decision costs him makes him more worthy of me. He thinks that if he marries me he will betray his birth and his wealth and that he will grieve his father. These are not light obstacles. I will be delighted to triumph over them. But I must fight for my triumph, I can almost feel the conflict in him. I want a battle between Love and Reason.

MARIO: And death to Reason, I suppose!

ORGON: So you want him to realize all the implications of the folly he thinks he is about to commit. What insatiable vanity!

MARIO: It's only a woman's vanity. There is none greater.

SCENE 5

ORGON, SILVIA, MARIO

[*Enter* LISETTE.]

ORGON: Here is Lisette. I wonder what she wants.

LISETTE: Sir, you told me a short while ago that you delivered Dorante to me, that I could dispose of his heart at my discretion. I took you at your word. I have worked as if for myself. You will see that I have worked well on him. His is a heart that has been truly pickled. What do you wish me to do with it now? Will Madam reclaim it?

ORGON: My child, have you any claims to make upon his heart?

SILVIA: No! I give it to you, Lisette, yielding to you all my claims. To use your delicate phrase, I could never really enjoy a heart I had not pickled myself.

LISETTE: What, you'll let me marry him? You are also willing, Sir?

ORGON: Yes – if he agrees. Why, does he love you?

MARIO: And I also give my consent.

LISETTE: And I too. And I thank you all.

ORGON: Wait a second, I have a small condition to add, so that I cannot be held responsible. You must tell him a little of who you really are.

LISETTE: If I tell him a little, he will know it all.

ORGON: What are you afraid of? Have you not pickled him enough? Is not his heart preserved against such shocks? He does not seem the kind of man to be discouraged by such trifles.

LISETTE: Here he is! If you would be so kind as to withdraw and leave me the field, please. The time has come for my masterstroke.

ORGON: Quite right! Let us withdraw.

SILVIA: With all my heart.

MARIO: Let's go.

[*Exeunt* MARIO *and* ORGON.]

SCENE 6

LISETTE, *preparing herself for* ARLEQUIN

[*Enter* ARLEQUIN.]

ARLEQUIN: At last, my queen, I see you, and I will never leave you again. I found your absence too cruel a burden to bear. And when I'm not with you I always suspect that you're avoiding me.

LISETTE: I must confess that I might have been.

ARLEQUIN [*swooning*]: What, queen of my soul, elixir of my life, have you decided to kill me?

LISETTE [*reviving him*]: No, no, no, your life is much too precious to me.

ARLEQUIN [*reviving fast*]: Oh, how those words give me strength!

LISETTE: You mustn't doubt my love.

ARLEQUIN: Oh, I would like to kiss those lovely words and to pluck them from your lips with mine.

LISETTE [*restraining his embrace*]: Yes, but ... but you were pressing the question of marriage, and my father had not given me leave to reply to you then. Well, I have just spoken to him and he has told me that you are free to ask him for my hand whenever you like.

ARLEQUIN: Before I ask him for your hand, let me ask you. I want to thank your hand for its charity. It is so generous to be willing to take mine, which is truly unworthy.

LISETTE: I will not refuse to lend it to you for a moment, as long as you agree to keep it for ever.

ARLEQUIN: O plump, soft, angelic little hand! I take thee without bargaining. It is not the honour you will do me that upsets me, but that which I will do you in return worries me.

LISETTE: You will give me more honour than I need.

ARLEQUIN: Ah, alas, I know that bit of arithmetic better than you do.

LISETTE: But I look upon you as a gift from Heaven!

ARLEQUIN: It is a gift that won't ruin Heaven. Heaven has been mean to you.

LISETTE: I find the gift magnificent.

ARLEQUIN: Oh! Alas, you do not see it clearly.

LISETTE: You can have no idea how embarrassing I find your modesty.

ARLEQUIN: There is no need to waste good embarrassment. I would be pretty shameless if I were not modest.

LISETTE: Really, Sir, need I tell you that your love honours *me*?

ARLEQUIN: Oh! Oh! I don't know where to go.

LISETTE: Once more, Sir, I know who I am.

ARLEQUIN: Well, I know who I am too, and it's not a great bit of knowledge I have there. Nor will you have neither when you know it too! It's the devil's luck to know me. Alas, you do not expect what you will find at the bottom of this sack.

LISETTE [*aside*]: So much humility is not natural. [*To him*] For what reason are you telling me all this?

ARLEQUIN: Well, here is how the land lies.

LISETTE: What, again? You are beginning to disturb me. Are you not . . .?

ARLEQUIN: Oh, please don't. You are taking my trousers off.

LISETTE: Tell me what is the matter.

ARLEQUIN [*aside*]: We must prepare the ground a little . . . [*To her*] Madam, your love, is it of sound constitution? Will it be able to withstand the shocks I am about to deliver? Is it frightened by the prospect of a bad home? I will house it only modestly.

LISETTE: Please stop this shilly-shallying. In one word, who are you?

ARLEQUIN: I am . . . Have you ever seen counterfeit money? Do you know what a shiny sovereign of bad gold feels like? I am something like that.

LISETTE: Oh, come to the point! What is your name?

ARLEQUIN [*aside*]: My name? Shall I tell her my name is Arlequin? No, it rhymes too much with vermin.

LISETTE: Well?

ARLEQUIN: There is still some difficulty here. Madam, do you despise the rank of soldier?

LISETTE: What do you mean by soldier?

ARLEQUIN: Yes, well, I mean, for instance, a waiting-room soldier?

LISETTE: A waiting-room soldier. Are you now telling me you are not Dorante?

ARLEQUIN: He is my captain.

LISETTE: Louse! Vermin!

ARLEQUIN [*aside*]: I could not avoid the rhyme.

LISETTE: But look at this worm! Maggot!

ARLEQUIN: What a come-down!

LISETTE: For a whole hour I have been begging him for mercy and I have exhausted myself with humilities, and what for? For this beast.

ARLEQUIN: Alas, Madam, if you put love before pride, I will be as good for you as any gentleman.

LISETTE [*laughing*]: But I really find it impossible not to laugh. There. Him and his pride. There is only one thing now to do. There. My pride is most magnanimous and forgives you.

ARLEQUIN: Truly, charitable lady, oh, how my love will repay this generosity.

LISETTE: Let's shake hands: I have been fooled. The gentleman's valet is well worth the lady's maid?

ARLEQUIN: The maid of Madam?

LISETTE: She is my captain, so to speak.

ARLEQUIN: Hypocrite! Impostor!

LISETTE: Take your revenge.

ARLEQUIN: But consider this creature, this worm of the species. For an hour I have been sweating with anxiety because I thought she was a lady.

LISETTE: Let us come to the point. Do you love me?

ARLEQUIN: By God, yes! You may have changed names but you have not changed your face and you know quite well that we promised to love each other in spite of all spelling mistakes.

LISETTE: No great harm has been done. Let's console ourselves. But for now let us behave as if nothing has happened and wear very solemn faces. It seems that your master is still innocent of my mistress's plot. Do not warn him. Let us leave things to themselves. I think I hear him come. I am your servant, sir ...

ARLEQUIN: And I, madam, am your valet. [*Laughs.*]

SCENE 7

DORANTE, ARLEQUIN

DORANTE: I see you have just left Orgon's daughter. Did you tell her who you really were?

ARLEQUIN: By God, I did. Poor child! I found her heart more tender than a lamb's. It did not breathe. When I told her I was called Arlequin and was used to servant's livery, she said: 'Well, my friend, in life everyone must have a name and everyone must have some sort of clothes. Yours may have cost you nothing but they do not prevent your being graceful.'

DORANTE: What is this nonsense?

ARLEQUIN: And, as things stand, I shall ask for her hand.

DORANTE: What? She consents to marry you?

ARLEQUIN: She is very sick with love.

DORANTE: You are exaggerating. She does not know who you really are.

ARLEQUIN: By Bluebeard! I'll wager that if you insist she will marry me in my valet's livery and with a clothesbrush in my hand! I would like you to know, Sir, that when I love, I love. I don't need your finery to woo my girl, all you need do is hand me back my own rags.

DORANTE: You are a rogue. That is impossible. I see that I will have to warn M. Orgon.

ARLEQUIN: Ah! Our dear father! Such a good man. He eats out of our hands. He is the best man alive, a fine chap ... You will come back and tell me what he says?

DORANTE: You must be mad! Have you seen Lisette?

ARLEQUIN: Lisette? No. She may have passed before my eyes but a gentleman takes no notice of a chambermaid. I yield to you all my rights in that direction.

DORANTE: Go away, you are raving.

ARLEQUIN: Of course, your manners are a trifle casual, but that comes from the company you keep these days. Good-bye. When I am wed, we shall live as equals. Your chambermaid is coming. Good-day, my dear. Allow me to praise Bourguignon to you, he is a lad with a few good points. [*Exit.*]

SCENE 8

DORANTE

[*Enter* SILVIA.]

DORANTE [*aside*]: How worthy she is to be loved! Why did Mario have to win her before me?

SILVIA: Where have you been, Sir! Since I left, I have been unable to find you to tell you what I said to M. Orgon.

DORANTE: And yet I did not stray far away, I assure you. What is the matter?

SILVIA [*aside*]: So cold! [*Aloud*] For all that I denounced your valet and singled out his bad faith to prove how worthless he is, for all that I urged M. Orgon to postpone his marriage at least,

I might as well not have spoken, for he did not listen. I warn you that they are even talking of sending for a priest right now. It is time you revealed who you are.

DORANTE: That is my intention. I will leave incognito and I will write a note to M. Orgon that will explain all.

SILVIA [*aside*]: Leave? But that was not in my plan...

DORANTE: Do you not approve my idea?

SILVIA: No... not really.

DORANTE: Yet, I can see nothing better I could do in such a situation unless I were to speak myself and I could never bring myself to do that. Besides, there are other reasons which force me to leave. I have no more to do here.

SILVIA: Since I do not know your reasons, I can neither agree nor disagree with them. And it is not for me to ask you what they are.

DORANTE: Nor hard for you to guess what they might be, Lisette.

SILVIA: For instance, it might be that you are drawn to M. Orgon's daughter.

DORANTE: Is that all you can see?

SILVIA: There are, of course, certain other reasons I could imagine would make you leave. But I am neither mad nor vain enough to believe them.

DORANTE: Nor brave enough to speak of them. Because you would have nothing kind to tell me, Lisette. Good-bye.

SILVIA: Take care. I must tell you – I think you do not understand my meaning.

DORANTE: Excellent! If you explained your meaning, it would do me no good. So keep your meaning secret till I go.

SILVIA: You are going then? Seriously?

DORANTE: You seem anxious lest I change my mind.

SILVIA: How sweet it is of you to understand so well.

DORANTE: That was very candid. Good-bye.

SILVIA [*aside*]: If he leaves, I don't love him any more, I will never marry him. [*She follows him with her eyes*] But he's stopped; he's hesitating, he's looking to see if I am looking; I couldn't call him back, not... I would not know how to. And yet it would be very strange if he did leave after all that I have done. Ah, there, it's all over now. He is going. I did not have as much hold over him as I thought I had. My brother is clumsy. Insensitive people ruin everything. Have I not committed myself too far? What a way to end! But Dorante reappears, he seems to be coming back. I correct myself . . . I still love him. I will pretend to go so that he can stop me. Our reconciliation must cost him something, after all.

DORANTE [*stopping her*]: Stay, I beg you. I have still something to say to you.

SILVIA: To me, Sir?

DORANTE: I would be sorry to go without having convinced you that I am right to do so.

SILVIA: Really, Sir, of what importance is it to justify yourself to me? It is not worth your trouble. I am only a servant and you have made me feel it enough.

DORANTE: Me, Lisette? Is it for you to complain when I am taking my leave without a murmur?

SILVIA: Hum, if I cared to, I could tell you a few things on that score.

DORANTE: Tell me, then. I ask for nothing more than to be wrong. But what am I saying? Mario loves you.

SILVIA: That is true.

DORANTE: And you are not indifferent to his love. I saw that by your obvious desire to be rid of me just now. So you could not love me.

SILVIA: Not indifferent to his love? Who told you so? I could not love you? What do you know of it? You decide too quickly.

DORANTE: Well, Lisette, by all that you hold dearest in the world, reveal the truth to me. I beg it of you.

SILVIA: Reveal all to a man about to leave?

DORANTE: I will not leave.

SILVIA: Leave me alone. If you love me, do not question me. It is only my indifference you are afraid of, and you are only too glad that I should say nothing. What do my feelings matter to you?

DORANTE: What do they matter to me, Lisette? Can you still doubt that I love you?

SILVIA: No, and you repeat it to me so often that I believe you. But why persuade me of it? What am I to do with the thought, Sir? I will speak to you with an open heart. You love me. But your love is not a serious matter for you. What distractions, what difficulties are there not, to help you renounce this love? There is the difference of degree between us, there are all the amusements a man of your rank is used to, and there are other women who will want to charm you. You will find a thousand other obstacles in your way. All these will wear away this love with which you assault me so mercilessly. When you leave this house, you will laugh at it perhaps, and you will be right. But I, Sir, I . . . If, as I fear, I remember this love and if it possessed me, what refuge would I have against its mark? Who will console me for losing you? Who should my heart put in your place? Do you know that if I were to love you, all that is finest and richest in the world would not move me? Consider the state in which you would leave me then. And be generous enough to hide your love from me. I, speaking to you now, I would hesitate to tell you I loved you in your present mood. If I confessed my feelings for you, your reason might be in danger, and so, you see, I must take good care to hide my feelings from you, and I do.

DORANTE: Ah, my dear Lisette, what do I hear? Your words have such passion. They make me feel aglow. I love you, I respect you. There is no degree, no birth, no fortune that does not wither away before your love. I should be ashamed if I let the pride of my position fight against you. My heart and my hand are both yours.

SILVIA: And, truly, you deserve that I accept. I would have to be over-scrupulous to deny the pleasure they both give me! I could no longer hide that.

DORANTE: Do you love me then?

SILVIA: No, no. But if you ask again so much the worse for you.

DORANTE: Your threats no longer frighten me.

SILVIA: And Mario? Have you forgotten him entirely?

DORANTE: No, Lisette. Mario alarms me no more. You do not love him. You can deceive me no more. You are sincere and you are not indifferent to my love. I cannot doubt the passion that has taken possession of me, I am sure of it, and you will never be able to take the certainty of your love away from me.

SILVIA: I will not try to. You may keep that conviction and we shall see what you will do with it.

DORANTE: Will you not consent to be mine?

SILVIA: What? You would marry me in spite of who you are, in spite of your father's wrath, in spite of your fortune?

DORANTE: As soon as my father sets eyes on you, he will forgive me. I have enough fortune for the two of us and I would rather marry a woman who is worthy than one who is well-born. There is no point in arguing because I will not change my mind.

SILVIA: You will not change your mind. Oh, do you know that you delight me, Dorante?

DORANTE: Don't be ashamed of your love any more ... Let it show.

SILVIA: Well, I have come to the end of my game and you ... you will never change.

DORANTE: Never, my dear Lisette.

SILVIA: What love!

SCENE 9

SILVIA, DORANTE

[*Enter* OMNES]

SILVIA: Ah, my dear father, you wanted me to belong to Dorante. Come and watch your daughter obey you with more joy than you ever saw.

DORANTE: What do I hear? You, Sir, are her father?

SILVIA: Yes, Dorante, we both used the same masquerade to become better acquainted. That said, there is no more to say. You love me and I will never be able to doubt it. And for your part, think of my feelings for you. Judge, by the subtlety with which I tried to gain it, how much I wanted your heart.

ORGON: Do you recognize this letter? That is how I learnt of your disguise which she only learnt of through you.

DORANTE: I cannot tell you how happy I am. But what is most enchanting is the proof I have given you of my love.

MARIO: Will Dorante forgive me the passionate temper in which I put Bourguignon?

DORANTE: He does not forgive you, he thanks you for it.

ARLEQUIN [to LISETTE]: Be happy, lady! You have lost your

nobility but you are not to be pitied, for you picked Arlequin up in exchange.

LISETTE: That's some consolation! The only one to profit is you.

ARLEQUIN: I haven't lost anything. Before the revelations started, your dowry was worth more than you, and now you are worth more than your dowry. Come on, my friends.

MORE ABOUT PENGUINS AND PELICANS

Penguinews, which appears every month, contains details of all the new books issued by Penguins as they are published. It is supplemented by our stocklist, which includes around 5,000 titles.

A specimen copy of *Penguinews* will be sent to you free on request. Please write to Dept EP, Penguin Books Ltd, Harmondsworth, Middlesex for your copy.

In the U.S.A.: For a complete list of books available from Penguins in the United States write to Dept CS, Penguin Books, 625 Madison Avenue, New York, New York 10022.

In Canada: For a complete list of books available from Penguins in Canada write to Penguin Books Canada Ltd, 2801 John Street, Markham, Ontario L3R 1B4.

In Australia: For a complete list of books available from Penguins in Australia write to the Marketing Department, Penguin Books Australia Ltd, P.O. Box 257, Ringwood. Victoria 3134.